Praise for the Novels of Elin Hilderbrand

The Love Season

"In a juicy peach of a summer tome, Hilderbrand again alchemizes her three favorite elements—food, love, and Nantucket—with eminently readable results. . . . *Season* is so gratifying."
—*Entertainment Weekly* (Grade: A–)

"Summer fare that's a cut above the usual beach provisions . . . Hilderbrand, who wrote 2002's *Nantucket Nights*, serves up a mouthwatering menu, keeps the Veuve Clicquot flowing, and tops it all with a dollop of mystery that will have even drowsy sunbathers turning pages until the very satisfying end."
—*People* (four stars)

"Hilderbrand's fifth book is a fulfilling tale of familial excavation and self-exploration. . . . It's a refreshing, resonant summertime treat."
—*Publishers Weekly*

"Hilderbrand's sensitive portrayal of a young motherless woman on a journey of self-discovery, and her guilt-ridden godmother's attempt to find the courage to confront the past, is very moving."
—*Booklist*

"A good page-turner."
—*Library Journal*

"As a storyteller, Hilderbrand ranks among the best, and she has ingeniously constructed this foray into the past around a meal. . . . This is a don't-miss novel."
—*The Star-Ledger* (Newark)

The Blue Bistro

"A perfectly enjoyable beach book."
—*Publishers Weekly*

"Hilderbrand keeps things moving briskly in between sumptuous descriptions of food, drink, and tableware, throwing in an in-depth lesson on the restaurant business for good measure. Fun, stylish, and absorbing vacation reading." —*Booklist*

"A wonderful, wonderful love story . . . the kind that you read, then recommend to many, many friends—and so, I recommend it to you. Highly." —James Patterson, bestselling author of *Suzanne's Diary for Nicholas*

"A wonderfully poignant behind-the-scenes journey into the world of high-end restaurants, island life, and the inner workings of the human heart. A great summer story." —Lolly Winston, *New York Times* bestselling author of *Good Grief*

"Hilderbrand adds depth to the novel with her multifaceted char-acters. The restaurant comes alive with believable conflicts between the staff and patrons. But the love story between Adrienne and Thatcher is the jewel of the novel. Together they discover the meaning of devotion and the rarity of real love." —*RT Book Reviews*

"This brand-new book is sure to become a summer favorite." —*ReadersDigest.com* (chosen as their #1 Unforgettable Beach Read)

Nantucket Nights

"Things get more twisted at every turn with enough lies and betrayals to fuel a whole season of soap operas. . . . Readers will be hooked." —*Publishers Weekly*

"What a perfect summer pleasure Elin Hilderbrand provides in *Nantucket Nights*, mixing the complexities of family life and friend-ship with suspense, romance, and moonlit Nantucket nights." —Nancy Thayer, author of *Custody*

"Dips deep into *Peyton Place* country."   —*Kirkus Reviews*

"Ms. Hilderbrand paints a picture of idyllic Nantucket life that slowly starts to unravel as the ugly underbelly is revealed. Hidden secrets, a mysterious disappearance, and the pain of betrayal form the basis for this haunting read."   — *RT Book Reviews*

"The novel is fast paced and suspenseful enough to keep readers interested. A likely candidate for summer-vacation reading."
—*Booklist*

The Beach Club

"Surprisingly touching . . . a work of fiction you're likely to think about long after you've put it down."   —*People*

"A strong, emotional pull . . . readers will remain absorbed until the surprising denouement."   —*Publishers Weekly*

"A feisty novel . . . lively enough to keep a sunbather awake."
—*Kirkus Reviews*

"A charming, easygoing story about the tangled lives and loves of the summer crew and guests at a hotel and beach club."
—*The Boston Globe*

"A steamy tale."   —*Boston Herald*

Also by Elin Hilderbrand

❧

The Island

The Castaways

Barefoot

A Summer Affair

Love Season

The Blue Bistro

Nantucket Nights

The Beach Club

Elin Hilderbrand

Summer People

St. Martin's Griffin ⚜ New York

SUMMER PEOPLE. Copyright © 2003 by Elin Hilderbrand. All
rights reserved. Printed in the United States of America. For
information, address St. Martin's Press, 175 Fifth Avenue,
New York, N.Y. 10010.

www.stmartins.com

Design by Kathryn Parise

The Library of Congress has cataloged the hardcover edition as
follows:

Hilderbrand, Elin.
    Summer people / Elin Hilderbrand.—1st ed.
      p. cm.
    ISBN 978-0-312-28367-9
    1. Vacation homes—Fiction. 2. Summer resorts—Fiction.
3. Single mothers—Fiction. 4. Teenagers—Fiction. 5. Strangers—
Fiction. 6. Widows—Fiction. 7. Twins—Fiction. 8. Nantucket
Island (Mass.)—Fiction. I. Title.
  PS3558.I384355 S86 2003
  813'.6—dc21

                      2003046587

ISBN 978-0-312-62827-7 (trade paperback)

10 9 8 7 6

In loving, loving memory of my father,

Robert H. Hilderbrand, Jr.

(1944–1985)

chapter 1

Driving off the ferry, they looked like any other family coming to spend the summer on Nantucket—or almost. The car was a 1998 Range Rover in flat forest green, its rear section packed to within inches of the roof with Pierre Deux weekend duffels, boxes of kitchen equipment, four shopping bags from Zabar's, and a plastic trash bag of linens. (The summer house, Horizon, had its own linens, of course, but Beth remembered those sheets and towels from her childhood—the towels, for example, were chocolate brown and patterned with leaves. Threadbare. Beth wanted plush towels; she took comfort now wherever she could find it.)

Three out of the four passengers in the car were related, as any one of the people milling around Steamship Wharf could tell. Beth, the mother, was forty-four years old and at the end of pretty with blond hair pulled back in a clip, a light tan already (from running in Central Park in the mornings), and green eyes flecked with yellow, which made one think of a meadow. White linen blouse, wrinkled now. A diamond ring, too big to be over-looked. One of Beth's seventeen-year-old twins, her daughter, Winnie, slumped in the front seat, and the other twin, her son, Garrett, sat in back. That there was no father in the car was hardly unusual—lots of women Beth knew took their kids away for the summer while their husbands toiled on Wall Street or in law firms. So it wasn't Arch's absence that set their family apart from the others on this clear, hot day. Rather it was the dark-skinned boy, also seventeen, who shared the backseat with Gar-rett: Marcus Tyler, living proof of their larger, sadder story.

Beth lifted her ass off the driver's seat. She'd driven the whole way, even though the twins had their learner's permits and might have helped. She'd been awake since five o'clock that morning, and after four hours on the highway and two on the ferry, her mind stalled in inconvenient places, like a car dying in a busy intersection. In her side-view mirror, Beth checked on the two mountain bikes hanging off the back of the car. (It had always been Arch's job to secure them, and this year she did it herself. Miraculously, they were both intact.) When she brought her at-tention forward again—she couldn't *wait* to get off this boat!—her gaze stuck on her diamond ring, perched as it was on top of the steering wheel. This wasn't the ring that Arch gave her twenty years ago when he proposed, but a really extravagant ring that he presented to her last summer. He called it the "We Made It" ring, because they *had* made it, financially, at least. They had enough money that a not-insignificant amount could be wasted on this diamond ring. "Wasted" was Beth's word; she was the frugal one, always worrying that they had two kids headed for college, and what if the car got stolen, what if there were a fire. What if there were some kind of accident.

You worry too much, Arch said.

A rotund man wearing a Day-Glo vest, long pants, and a long-sleeved shirt in industrial blue, even on this sweltering day in June, motioned for Beth to drive off the ramp, following, though not too closely, the car in front of her. Seconds later Beth was not on the ferry anymore—not on the ferry, not on I-95, not in a parking garage on East Eighty-second Street. She was on Nantucket Island. The rotund steamship man waved at her (she could see him mouthing, "Come on, lady, come on," as if she were just another elegant housewife from Chappaqua), but he didn't know what had happened to her. He didn't know that, along with the Pierre Deux bags and the expensive mountain bikes, they'd brought along the urn that held her husband's ashes.

Beth's forehead grew hot, her nose tingled. Here, again, were the tears. It was the new way she evaluated her day: On a good day she cried only twice, in the morning shower and before her Valium kicked in at night. On a bad day, a *stressful* day, it was like this—without warning, in front of the kids, while she was *driving,* in *traffic.* Tears assaulting her like a migraine.

"Mom," Winnie said. She'd slept for most of the drive and the ferry ride, and now she gazed out the window as they cruised past the bike shops, the ice cream parlor, the Sunken Ship on the corner. The whaling museum. The Dreamland Theater. People were everywhere—on the sidewalks, in the stores, riding bikes, eating ice cream cones. As if nothing bad could happen. As if nothing could hurt them. Meanwhile, Beth negotiated the traffic surprisingly well at full sob.

"Mom," Winnie said again, touching her mother's leg. But what else could she say? Winnie pulled the neck of her sweatshirt up over her nose and inhaled. It was her father's old, raggedy

Princeton sweatshirt, which he'd worn often, sometimes to the gym in their building, and it smelled like him. Of all their father's clothes, the sweatshirt had smelled the most like him and so that was what Winnie took. She'd worn it every day since he died, ninety-three days ago. Winnie tried to convince herself that it still smelled like him, but his smell was fading, much the way her father's vivid, everyday presence in her mind was fading. She couldn't remember the whole of him, only bits and pieces: the way he loosened his tie when he walked into the apartment at the end of the day, the way he ate a piece of pizza folded in half, the way he'd fidgeted with a twig when he told her and Garrett the facts of life one warm and very embarrassing autumn afternoon in Strawberry Fields. (Why hadn't her mother done "the talk?" Winnie had asked her mother that question a few weeks after the memorial service—now that Daddy was dead, certain topics could be broached—and Beth said simply, "Your father wanted to do it. He considered it one of the joys of parenting.") A whole life lived and all Winnie would be left with were snippets, a box of snapshots. She breathed in, listening to the atonality of her mother's sobs as if it were bad music. The sweatshirt no longer smelled like her father. Now it smelled like Winnie.

The Rover bounced up Main Street, which was paved with cobblestones. Garrett shifted uneasily in his seat and checked for the hundredth time on the urn, which was a solid, silent presence between him and Marcus. It was embarrassing to have his mom losing it with a stranger in the car. Beth kept Garrett awake at night with her crying and he had a weird sense of role reversal, like she was the kid and he was the parent. The Man of the House, now. And Winnie—well, Winnie was even worse than his mother, wearing that sweatshirt every day since March six-teenth—every day: to school over her uniform, to sleep, even. And Winnie refused to eat. She looked like a Holocaust victim, a person with anorexia. And yet these two loonies were far pref-erable company to the individual sitting next to him. Garrett couldn't believe their bad luck. The last thing Arch had done, practically, before his plane went down, was to invite Marcus Tyler to Nantucket—not for a week, not for a month—but for the entire summer. And since a dead man's words were as good as law, they were stuck with Marcus.

Your father invited him to come along, Beth said. *We can't exactly back out.*

Yeah, Winnie said. *Daddy invited him.*

Garrett tried to talk to his mother about it, using the most powerful words he had at his disposal, the words of their ther-apist, Dr. Schau, whom they all saw together and separately.

We need to heal this summer, Garrett said. *As a family.*

Your father invited him for a reason, Beth said, though Garrett could tell even she wasn't sure what the reason was, and Garrett called her on it.

We need to help those less fortunate, his mother responded lamely.

Why is Marcus less fortunate? Garrett said. *He has a father.*

You know why, his mother said.

Because Marcus was the son of a murderer. Even as the Range Rover jostled up Main Street, Marcus's mother, Constance Ben-nett Tyler, was locked up in Bedford Hills Correctional Facility because she had killed two people. Arch had been Constance's defense attorney, and he'd gotten to know Marcus and like him. That was why Garrett shared the backseat with this huge black kid, this refugee from one of the most talked-about court cases in New York City in years. And because Marcus was the same age as Winnie and Garrett they had to be friends. Because of the tragedies in life that had converged on the four people sitting in this car, they had to join together. Empathize. It was the most twisted, unfair situation Garrett could imagine, and yet it was happening to him this summer.

Garrett glanced sideways at Marcus. Marcus was wearing an expensive-looking white dress shirt with his initials—"MGT"— embroidered on the pocket. It was the kind of shirt one wore to brunch or a college interview, though it was inappropriate for seven hours of car travel. Marcus had been sweating the whole ride and now the shirt looked like it'd been plucked from the bottom of a laundry hamper. Marcus had shown up at their apartment that morning wearing a squeaky new pair of dock shoes, which looked so unlikely on Marcus's feet that Garrett wondered if he'd worn the shoes to mock them somehow, to mock this trip to Nantucket. He'd taken the shoes off before they even hit Connecticut and his enormous bare feet gave off an odor that nearly caused Garrett to gag. Before Garrett could dwell on the other aspects of Marcus's appearance that bothered him—his closely-shaved head, his heavy-lidded eyes that made it seem like he was always half asleep—Garrett realized that Marcus had his elbow on the urn. He was using the urn as an *armrest*. Garrett held no fantasies about the contents of the urn—it was only ashes, another form of matter. There had been a few weak attempts at levity since the urn arrived from the crematorium— one night, Garrett set the urn at their father's place at the dining room table—but Garrett didn't believe the urn in any way contained his father. Only the remains of the body that once belonged to his father. Still, using the urn as an armrest was *not* okay. Garrett glared at Marcus, but refrained from saying anything. They'd made it all the way from New York City without incident and Garrett didn't want to start trouble now, when they were almost at the house. An instant later, as if reading Garrett's mind, Marcus lifted his oxford-clad elbow and Garrett moved the urn into his lap, where it would be safe from further indignities.

Marcus was the only one who thought to offer Beth a tissue. She seemed genuinely grateful, turning her head so that he could see her try to smile. "Thanks, Marcus," she said. She stopped crying long enough to blot her eyes and wipe the runny stuff from her nose. "Here it is your first time on Nantucket and I'm blubbering so hard I can't point things out. I'm sorry."

"S'okay," he said. He'd gotten the gist of the place already: the gray shingled houses, the cobblestone streets, the shops with expensive clothes and brass lanterns and antique rocking horses in the windows. White people everywhere all excited about summer.

Beth stopped crying and put on her sunglasses. Marcus wasn't sure what to make of the woman. He couldn't tell if she was being nice to him because she wanted to, or because she felt she had to—if pressed, he would lean toward the latter. She spoke to him like he was in nursery school. (At McDonald's that morning for breakfast, with a pinched smile, "And, Marcus, what would *you* like? How about some pancakes?" As if he was too simple to navigate his way around the menu.)

Marcus had met the twins twice before. The first time was when Arch brought them along to visit Marcus and his family in

Queens. The twins had stood in the apartment looking around like they were on a field trip about poverty; he could almost hear them thinking, "So this is where it happened." The second time Marcus met them was at Trinity Episcopal Church on East Eighty-eighth Street, at the memorial service for Arch. The twins' father, Arch Newton, had been the gold standard of human beings (Marcus intended to use this phrase in the book he was writing), the only white person in all of America who was willing to help save his mother's life. And for free—an expensive Manhattan lawyer who offered to defend Constance Bennett Tyler against the death penalty, even though everyone knew she was guilty as sin.

I'm going to help your mom, Arch told Marcus. *I'm going to see that she gets the best possible defense.*

Arch was there through the worst of it: the hot hours in the courtroom, the cold visits to Rikers, the reporters, the TV cameras, the disturbing photographs in the *New York Times*, especially the one of Candy's body being carried from the building, all of her covered by a sheet except for her patent leather shoes, the shoes that, ironically, Constance had bought for her. They reprinted this photo a lot; it became the icon for the case. Every time Arch saw the photo, he tore it in half. *They love it because it screams, "Baby killer!"* he said. If it weren't for Arch's powerful, steadying presence—his defense less a legal term and more like a physical shield that he held over Marcus and his family—Marcus never would have made it. But then, on the evening of March fifteenth, flying back from Albany, where Arch had traveled to meet with an attorney he knew who was close to the governor and might be able to speak out on Constance's behalf, Arch's plane crashed into Long Island Sound. Ice on the wings. It was a week before the trial was to start, and bizarrely, Arch's death added an element of humanity that had been missing from the defense's case; the media softened, hailing Arch as a hero for the common man, specifically, for a woman facing death row with no resources to fight it. Another attorney from Arch's firm took the case to trial, which lasted only three days. The jury convicted Constance of one count of first-degree murder and one count of second-degree murder, but the judge spared her the death penalty and nobody protested. It was as if Arch had taken the punishment for her.

Offering Beth a tissue was the least Marcus could do. Because what all four people in the car knew but nobody acknowledged out loud was that if Arch hadn't been defending Constance, he wouldn't have died. And so, Marcus *would* be a slave to these people if that was what they wanted. He'd haul out the garbage cans, he'd sweep sand off the porch, he'd rub oil onto their backs so they didn't burn in the sun. Yes, he would. Before Marcus left New York, his father, Bo, said, *These people didn't have to invite you, son. So be a big help, and make me proud.*

As they drove out of town, the houses grew farther apart. Then Beth signaled left and they turned onto a dirt road. Bumpy. Dirt and sand filled the air, gravel crunched under the tires.

Marcus would offer to wash the car.

He saw the ocean—it was in front of them suddenly, glinting in the sun like a big silver platter. Beth shut off the air-conditioning and put down all four windows.

"We're here," she said. She pulled into a white shell driveway that led to a house—a big, old, gray-shingled house—which sat on a ledge overlooking the water.

"Whoa," Marcus said.

Beth shut off the engine and climbed out of the car, raising her hands to the sky. "It takes my breath away every time. I feel better. Kids, I feel better already."

Marcus stuffed his feet into his very uncomfortable white-person shoes, wondering if he should help unload the car, but before he could make a move, Winnie took his hand and pulled him to the edge of the bluff. "Look, Marcus. What do you think?"

Marcus thought he might be experiencing some kind of re-verse claustrophobia. Because he felt queasy, unsettled, unable to place himself. He was used to the Elmhurst section of Queens, and Main Street, Flushing. He was used to dirty streets and bo-degas that smelled like too many cats and the long line outside the yellow brick public health building on Junction Boulevard. He was used to Shea Stadium and LaGuardia Airport—obnox-ious Mets fans in their blue and orange hats crowding the subway cars, jumbo jets overhead at any given moment. He was used to sitting in the back row of the classrooms at Benjamin N. Cardozo High School so nobody could stare him down. He was used to a dark, low-ceilinged apartment that he shared with his father, his sister LaTisha, and the belongings of his mother—her head scarves, her record albums, her knock-off Prada bag—things that now simply took up space because she would never be back to reclaim them. He was *not* used to this—a Range Rover with leather seats, a white shell driveway, a golden beach, the Atlantic fucking Ocean, not to mention people who were civil to him even though they knew his mother was a murderer.

"It's cool," he said.

Winnie steered him toward the front door. "Come inside," she said.

Beth pulled the key out from under the welcome mat.

"Has that been there all winter?" Marcus asked.

"It has," she said. "And this is the last time we'll use the key until we leave in September."

"You're kidding," Marcus said. "What if somebody steals your stuff?"

Beth laughed. "That's the beauty of this place. Nobody's going to steal our stuff."

When Marcus got inside, he realized there wasn't much worth stealing. He followed Beth through the rooms, nervously thinking of Garrett behind him carrying bags. He should be helping Garrett. But Winnie had taken his hand and now he was sandwiched between Beth and Winnie both asking him, *Didn't he just love it? Didn't he think it was magnificent?*

The house was big. Marcus could say that with confidence. There was a hallway where you walked in with a living room on the right. A flight of stairs on the left. Past the stairs were a kitchen and dining room that had a row of windows and glass doors looking out over the water, and a deck beyond the kitchen with a green plastic table and chairs. The house was big but not fancy. The furniture was white wicker, except for one nasty-looking recliner the color of a dead mouse. The pictures on the walls were faded watercolors of the beach; the curtains were a creepy filmy material. The floorboards creaked and the house had a smell. An old, grandmother smell. Marcus wasn't sure what he'd expected—he guessed he pictured something like a fashion magazine, something more like the Newtons' apartment on Park Avenue which he'd seen for the first time that morning—with real antiques and Oriental carpets and brass candlesticks and sculpture. This house didn't feel like poverty, just like a house owned by white people who'd stopped caring. How had Arch described it? *A funky old summer cottage*—and Marcus had pretended to understand what that meant. Now he knew, it meant this. This was how white people lived when they relaxed at the beach.

Marcus checked out the view from the deck and then wandered back through the first floor. Garrett brought in a second load of stuff and dropped it at Marcus's feet in the living room. Marcus was looking for the TV; he didn't see one anywhere.

"Is there TV?" Marcus asked.

"No," Garrett said. "Sorry, man, you're going to have to do without *Bernie Mac* for the summer."

"Hey," Marcus said, straightening his shoulders in his new white shirt that was so fine it felt like money on his back. *Fuck you* was on the tip of his tongue. What the fuck was that supposed to mean? Was that a racial comment already? Well, why not? Why not put him in his slave's place right away? Before Marcus could prepare a response, Garrett was headed out the door again, aiming for load number three. Marcus followed him out.

"I don't appreciate your tone," Marcus said. He sounded, ridiculously, like a homeroom teacher. Garrett didn't even turn around. "I'm sorry I'm bumming you out. I don't want to ruin your summer with your family." Marcus couldn't believe he was talking like this. What he'd learned in the past nine months was that the easiest response to other people's shit was silence. Let his eyes drop to half mast, pretend like he hadn't heard. Pretend like nothing they said could bother him. Marcus would get his revenge on everyone later, once his book was published.

"Why did you come then?" Garrett said. "I know my mother offered. But you could have said no. You could have spent the summer at home. Closer to . . . your own family. Why did you come with us?"

Marcus felt guilt rising in his throat along with his long-ago-eaten breakfast. He *should* be at home. His father was going through a very stressful time trying to live without Mama. But things at home had gotten so horrible that Marcus needed to escape. At home, the phone was always ringing, the press calling, or people who had somehow gotten their number who wanted to share their feelings about what a monster Constance was. Marcus had lost all his friends, he suffered cold-eyed glares from his neighbors and teachers and people he didn't even know. He couldn't get an aspirin from the medicine chest without seeing all of Constance's half-used make-up, the tubes of lipstick, the skin stuff she loved that made her smell like apricots. He couldn't walk in or out of the apartment without thinking of Angela and Candy's bodies bleeding onto the floorboards. The worst had passed—the weeks after the murders when they were forced to stay in that fleabag motel, the humiliating afternoon in the swim team locker room—but Marcus's life in Queens, his new identity as the *murderer's son*, suffocated him. His mother was gone forever but at the same time she was everywhere, tainting every moment. He wanted out. On the whiter, brighter side, there was Marcus's book deal, Mr. Zachary Celtic, true crime editor at Dome Books, the thirty thousand dollar advance that no one knew a thing about except for Marcus and his English teacher. At home, Marcus would have had to get a job. Here, he had the luxury of a summer without work—long days of quiet hours to write the truth about his mother, whatever that was.

But he couldn't say any of that to Garrett. He reached past Garrett into the car for his own bag—a black leather duffel that had cost him nearly two hundred dollars. He'd bought it to impress these people, but in the Nantucket sun, Marcus saw it was all wrong. It looked like a drug dealer's bag with garish brass buckles and a strong smell of leather.

"I don't know," Marcus said. "But here I am. A nigger boy on your turf."

Garrett glared at him. "That's a low blow. You're calling me a racist, and that's not what this is about."

"What's it about, then?" Marcus said. He felt himself sweating and worried about the expense of dry-cleaning his new shirt. It was at least ninety degrees out.

"It's about us losing our father," Garrett said. "That's what this summer is about. That's what every day has been about since his plane crashed. That's the only thing anything's going to be about ever again, okay?" Garrett got tears in his eyes, but because his hands were full, he wiped his face on his shoulder.

"Okay," Marcus said. He was proud of himself because he understood not only what Garrett was saying, but what he hadn't said. *Our father is dead because of your mama. If he hadn't been defending her, he wouldn't have gone to Albany. If he hadn't gone to Albany, his plane wouldn't have crashed.* Arch was another victim of the day Connie Tyler lost her mind. Marcus wanted to apologize on his mother's behalf, but apologizing wouldn't help. If Garrett hated him, Marcus would have to live with it. It wouldn't be worse than the other stuff Marcus was living with.

Suddenly Winnie appeared, tugging on Marcus's arm in an eager, excited way, like a little kid. All three of them were seventeen, but Winnie seemed younger. Maybe because she was a girl. Or because she was so skinny. She had no body to speak of, certainly not the way some of the girls at Cardozo had bodies—with huge tits like balloons under their sweaters and curvy asses. Winnie was a stick person—right now she was wearing jean shorts that showed two Popsicle-stick legs, and her torso was swimming in her sweatshirt. She had blond hair like her mother and she was cute in a way that elves are cute. But not womanly. Even Marcus's twelve-year-old sister LaTisha had more action going on than Winnie.

"Come on," she said. "I'll show you your bedroom."

"In a minute," Marcus said. He wanted to finish with Garrett, although he could see that the moment had passed. Garrett walked by them with his load of luggage and Marcus slung his bag over his shoulder and reached for another box. He needed to catch up.

"Come on," Winnie said. "Please?"

Marcus managed to stave her off until he and Garrett had unloaded most of the car. In silence, except for the squeaky complaints of Marcus's shoes.

"Come on, Marcus," Winnie said.

Marcus picked up his leather duffel, which looked nothing but ugly compared to the Newtons' luggage, and followed Winnie up the stairs.

❧

"This is your room," Winnie announced. She could feel herself gushing but she didn't know how to stop. Ever since Marcus appeared at their apartment at, like, five that morning, it was as if Winnie were wearing some kind of electric bracelet that sent shocks up her arm to her heart. She'd had a crush on him since the minute she knew of his existence. More than six months ago now, since the morning that Arch took her to EJ's Luncheonette to have breakfast (she and her father both loved the red flannel hash). They were supposed to be talking about grades, school, her prospects for college (he wanted her to apply to Princeton; she wanted to stay in the city—NYU, Barnard), but instead they got on the topic of Constance Tyler's case and once Arch was on that topic, he couldn't stop.

He'd read about the murders in the *New York Times* the day after they were committed. That was a second morning emblazoned in Winnie's memory. Her father so engrossed in the front-page story and the photograph of the dead girl wearing black party shoes, that he held his hand up for quiet when Beth asked him what his schedule looked like that day. He drank the story in, and then hurried with the newspaper into the living room where he plucked his Princeton face book off the shelf and rifled through it, holding up the paper for comparison—because next to the picture of the dead girl in the Mary Janes was a picture of the suspected murderer, Constance Bennett Tyler, a public school teacher.

"Bingo!" Arch shouted. "Constance Bennett, Queens, New York. I went to school with this woman." He held the face book up. "Nineteen-seventy-five freshman class, Princeton University." Then his expression crumbled. "Well, she killed someone."

"That's Dad for you," Garrett said. "He loves all things Princeton. Even the murderers."

"Did you know her, Dad?" Winnie asked.

"Never seen her before in my life," Arch said. He tucked the paper into his briefcase and Winnie forgot all about it.

But not Arch. Although he didn't generally handle criminal cases, he made a few phone calls that day, and discovered that the woman's case had been taken by a P.D.—no real surprise—

and the D.A.'s office had already announced it was seeking the death penalty. They wanted Constance Bennett Tyler to be the first woman to die of lethal injection in the state of New York. Arch decided to go to Rikers where Connie was being held and talk to her. She had been indicted for the murder of her sister-in-law and her sister-in-law's nine-year-old daughter. She explained the whole story to Arch, and he was so intrigued by the circumstances and by Connie herself that he took the case and refused to be paid a penny.

Arch told Winnie all this as he sat across from her in EJ's, moving hash around his plate, but not eating because he was too nervous to eat. *If I save this woman,* he said *my life will have been worthwhile.* Trent Trammelman, the managing partner at Arch's firm, discouraged Arch from taking the case. It would bring too much unwanted publicity—every time the damn case was written up in the papers, the name of their firm would be mentioned. Arch countered that no publicity was unwanted, that the majority of New Yorkers were against the death penalty anyway. He was taking the case and that was final. *Trent knows that when I say final, I mean final,* Arch had said. Winnie understood that her father had power. He was a full partner and a top earner, and yet when he was with her, he was just a dad, motioning to the waitress for more coffee for both of them. Then he said, *Connie has a son, you know. A son your age.*

Does she?

She does, and that's another reason I took her case. She has a son who's on the swim team at Cardozo High School. You'd like him, Winnie. You two have a lot in common.

Winnie wasn't sure what sparked her interest. It was everything, probably, in combination. She liked swimmers. Her last and, truth be told, only boyfriend, Charlie Hess, was on the swim team with her at Danforth. Charlie was all arms and legs, lean, muscular, pale. She liked the way he looked when his goggles were on top of his head and his wet eyelashes stuck together. But she hadn't been serious about Charlie Hess. When swim season ended, they broke up.

Winnie also saw Marcus as her ticket into her father's new, consuming passion. She championed this boy whose circumstances were so dire. When her father got home from work at night, she asked about Marcus as though he were an old, dear friend.

Winnie had loved him before she ever laid eyes on him.

His actual person won her over permanently. Marcus was six feet tall with gorgeous brown skin and hair shaved close to his head. He was a man, not at all like the boys she went to school with. He had dimples when he smiled, although Winnie had only seen him smile once—when Winnie and Garrett went with their father to Marcus's apartment. As they were leaving, Arch made a joke and Marcus smiled, thus the dimples, which had now taken on the fleeting, mystical properties of, say, a rainbow. One of the reasons Winnie was thrilled to learn that Arch had invited Marcus for the summer was that she might, with good luck, get to see his dimples again. And yet every time she was around him she felt stupid and talked too much and couldn't locate her sense of humor.

Not only was Marcus beautiful, but he was kind. He escorted his younger sister to the memorial service and they sat in the row behind Winnie and her family. Winnie heard Marcus crying. When she turned around to peek, she saw Marcus with his arm around his sister, wiping his sister's tears. She decided right then that Marcus was a person to whom goodness came naturally. Unlike Winnie herself, who was selfish and mean-spirited at times, and petty. She tried to be good, but again and again she failed. There was a nagging part of her that suspected these flaws had caused her father's death. That she somehow deserved it.

Marcus dropped his black bag on the floor. That was all he'd brought, just one bag. "The room's fine," he said. "It's good."

"You have your own bathroom," Winnie said. "Well, toilet and sink. The bathroom with the shower's down the hall. And there's a shower outside. Actually, this used to be my room."

"Did it?" Marcus sat on the edge of the double bed and bounced a little, testing the mattress. The room, just like the family and the population of the island, was white. White walls, white furniture, white curtains, white bed. He tried to imagine writing a memoir of darkness and death in this room; it wasn't ideal.

Winnie noticed Marcus's eyes falling closed, like she was boring him to death. He looked way too big for the bed with its white chenille spread. The bed, and the room in general, were too dainty. But all the other bedrooms had two singles, except for the master bedroom which had a queen. Winnie thought she was being generous by giving Marcus her room, but now she wasn't sure. He didn't look happy.

"Aren't you happy?" she asked.

Marcus sat perfectly still, his hands resting on his knees. He wasn't sure yet what kind of responses these people expected of him. *Happy?* There was a word that had lost its meaning. All he could think about was setting his feet free from these damn shoes and putting on his pool flip-flops with a pair of tube socks. "I'm just getting used to it here," he said.

"Yeah, it's different from where you grew up, huh? Different from New York, I mean. That's why Mom likes it. It's quiet. There isn't even a phone in the house. Which is going to be a problem, I guess, if you want to call your family? Your dad? Or . . . do they let you call your mom?"

"They let me," Marcus said. "But I don't call." His voice was dead; he had no desire to talk about his mother. He liked the idea, though, of no telephone, no TV, no papers, no connection to the outside world. He liked the idea of three months isolated at the edge of the water. He needed it. Arch had known he needed it, and that was why Arch invited him here.

The room, Winnie realized, was stifling hot. "Maybe we should open the window," she said. "Maybe you'd like some air, for, you know, breathing purposes." She checked for the dimples but Marcus just stared at her.

"I can do it," he said.

"Right," Winnie said. She could make a pest of herself no longer. Her mother always referred to the things "any self-respecting woman" would or would not do. In this case, any self-respecting woman would leave Marcus alone for half a second so he could get adjusted.

Winnie backed out of the room. "Okay," she said. "I'll see you, I guess? I mean, obviously, we both live here. Want to swim later? I'm on the swim team at Danforth, you know."

"I know," Marcus said. "Your dad told me."

Winnie's mouth fell open. She was filled with an incredible emotion that she couldn't name: her father talked about her to Marcus. Bragged about her, maybe. "Did he?"

"He said I'd like you," Marcus answered, truthfully, because Arch was always telling him that. *My daughter, Winnie, you'd like her.*

"That's what he said to me about you," Winnie said. "Those were his exact words."

Marcus didn't respond except to nod almost imperceptibly.

"Do you?" Winnie asked.

"Do I what?"

She almost said, *Do you like me?* But she felt her self-respect about to fly away forever, so she made herself leave the room. "Oh, nothing," she said. "Never mind."

⚘

Beth did feel better although she'd planned on saying so regardless, for the kids' sake. Was it possible that Arch's spirit resided here, that his soul had slogged through the icy waters of Long Island Sound to wait for them on Miacomet Beach in Nantucket? When Beth looked out over the water she felt a sense of peace, she heard Arch sending her a distinct message, *It's going to be okay, honey. It's all going to be okay.* That was, perhaps, just the healing property of water, of clean air, of open space. Of being, finally, in the place that she loved more than anywhere on earth. Her family's house on Nantucket.

The house, the house. The house was named Horizon by Beth's grandfather, her mother's father, who bought the land and built the house in 1927. Beth had been coming to the island every summer since she was in utero, but her memories started at age five, the summer of 1963, when her grandfather bought a cherry red Volkswagen bug convertible and drove her around the island with the top down, while she ate lollipops in the backseat. She remembered sitting on Horizon's upper deck with her grandmother at night, looking at stars, her grandmother singing, "Mister Moon." Ordering take-out fried shrimp dinners from Sayle's and eating them on the beach at sunset. The summers

lined up in Beth's mind like the scallop shells that she and her
younger brothers collected and left to fade on the windowsill all
winter. Starry nights, shrimp dinners, long days at the beach,
outdoor showers, rides in a convertible with a fresh lollipop,
bonfires, her first cold beer, falling in love, blueberry pie, riding
the waves all the way back to shore, cool white sheets against
sunburned skin—every detail that defined an American summer—
that was what this island meant to Beth.

In honesty, Beth wasn't certain that either of her kids felt the
magic of Nantucket the way she did. Arch never understood it:
he joined them every weekend, and for two weeks at the end of
August, but even then he set up camp at the dining room table
and worked. Even then the FedEx truck rumbled out to their spot
on West Miacomet Road every day but Sunday. No, this was
Beth's place.

If they could just make it through the first day, Beth thought,
things would be all right. If they could just settle into a routine.
But that wasn't going to happen instantly. Beth wanted to dive
right in, she wanted to be in her bathing suit lying on the beach
with a sandwich and a cold Coca-Cola five minutes from now,
listening to the pound and rush of the surf, listening to the twins
and Marcus, poor Marcus, playing Frisbee, laughing, getting
along. But there had to be process first: pulling the cushions for
the furniture from the dank basement and airing them out on the
deck (she could ask Marcus to do that; she needed to start treating him like one of the other kids, and less like a charity case
that Arch had left her to handle). They had to unpack—put the
kitchen supplies away, move their shorts and T-shirts and sandals
from their suitcases into the empty dresser drawers and closets
that smelled like old shelf paper and mothballs. They had to let

the hot and cold water run in all of the spigots to clear the residue out of the pipes. Beth would clean—dust the bookshelves that were crammed with bloated and rippled paperbacks, vacuum the floors, and convince Winnie to beat the braided rugs with the long-handled brush that hung in the outdoor shower.

Before Beth could organize her thoughts—new ones kept materializing like clowns popping out of a car—Garrett collapsed in one of the wooden chairs at the kitchen table. The chair groaned like it was an inch away from breaking.

"Mom," he said.

Mom, Beth thought. The one-word sentence that both Garrett and Winnie used all the time now. It had so many meanings and it was up to Beth to decipher which one was relevant at any given time. *Mom, I'm angry. Mom, I'm bored. Mom, please make the pain go away. Mom, stop harassing me. Mom, please stop crying, you're embarrassing me. Mom, why aren't you Dad?* Beth twisted her diamond ring. The "We Made It" ring. A constant reminder of how sadly ironic the world could be.

"You have to be careful with this furniture," Beth said. "It's old and you're big. You're the man of the house now, don't forget."

"I'm hungry," he said.

"Me, too," she said. The McDonald's in Devon, Connecticut, where they stopped for breakfast, seemed like another lifetime ago. She had to shop for food, cleaning supplies, paper towels. She had to go to the store. That would be first. "There's cheese and stuff in the Zabar's bags. Some bagels. Can you just make do for now? I'll go to the store. You should really unpack. It would make me happy. Has anyone shown Marcus his room?"

"Why are you so worried about Marcus?" Garrett asked.

"Because he's our *guest,*" Beth said.

"He's not my guest," Garrett said.

"He's your father's guest," Beth said. "And we have to respect that." The subject of Marcus made Beth anxious. As if, she thought, as if we didn't have enough to deal with. Now there was Marcus, a casualty of a complicated and excruciating murder case. But Arch adored the kid, and Beth suspected that he used Marcus's merits to justify taking Connie Tyler's case at all. Certainly a woman with such a fine son was worth spending months of unpaid time saving. Arch bragged about the kid—how he won second place in the All-Queens Invitational in the two hundred meter butterfly, how his grades hadn't faltered since the murders and he hadn't missed a day of school except to attend Connie's important court dates. This was all leading up to the big announcement—only a week before the plane crash—that Arch had invited Marcus to Nantucket for the summer. Arch was glowing when he told Beth, so happy was he to be able to give yet more to this poor family. Beth, however, was not happy. First of all, Arch hadn't asked her. Not only had they agreed long ago to confer about all important family decisions, but the house on Nantucket was *her house*. Furthermore, she was the one who spent the summer there while Arch worked; she wasn't exactly thrilled at the idea of a third teenager to keep track of—fine young man or not. But Beth bit her tongue and said nothing, which was how she'd handled the Constance Tyler matter since the beginning. She let Arch fight Connie's fight since it inspired him the way his regular work did not. Then, after Arch died, Beth felt obligated to re-extend the invitation to Marcus for the summer since it definitely fell under the category of "What Arch Would Have Wanted."

The twins knew this as well as she did. *Marcus is here out of respect to your father.* She hoped she didn't have to repeat this phrase too many more times.

"Now, are you okay with lunch?" Beth asked Garrett. "The bagels and stuff?"

"Yes."

"Okay," she said. "I'm off to the store."

⁂

At the Stop & Shop, Beth was so caught up in her thoughts—Arch, the twins, Marcus, would this summer be okay?—that she didn't even see David until he touched her shoulder.

"Beth?"

Her nipples hardened. Because it was chilly; they were standing in the produce section in front of the hydroponic lettuce.

"Oh, God. David." Beth put her hands to her face in such a way that her elbows shielded her chest. She felt like she was going to cry, but no, she was just overwhelmed. Why him? Why now? She'd been in the store, what? thirty seconds, only long enough to chastise herself for not making a list, and here was David Ronan, her first love. Her first love and more. David fucking Ronan.

She peeked through her fingers. Yes, he was still standing there. Staring at her like she was from outer space. Of course—who acted this way upon bumping into an old friend at the store? Who hid like this? Well, he was still as handsome as ever—dark blond hair, a great tan. Wearing a red button-down shirt turned back at the cuffs, khaki shorts, and black flip-flops. Holding a head of lettuce. David Ronan, owner of Island Painting, year-round resident of Nantucket, father of two daughters, husband of Rosie Ronan who was a gourmet cook and threw notorious cocktail parties (Beth and Arch went to one, years ago). He had every right to be here at the Stop & Shop, and yet Beth felt taken by surprise. Affronted, even. Like he planned this somehow, to fuck her up.

"I heard about Arch," David said softly. "I read about it in the *New York Times*. I wanted to call, or write, or something to let you know how incredibly sorry I am for your loss."

"I can't talk about it," Beth said. She still hadn't moved her hands. David reached out, circled her wrist and gently pulled it away from her face.

"It's okay," he said.

She blinked away her tears, was it the second time she'd cried today, or the third?—and then, because it was David Ronan standing before her, she began to worry what she looked like. Her hair, her wrinkled blouse. The bags under her eyes.

"I'm fine," she said finally. "I am fine. Thank you for your condolences. How are you?"

"Surviving," he said.

"That's all we can hope for," Beth said. "I want to ask about Rosie and the girls, but I can't right now, David. I'm too . . . I'm too frazzled. We just got on-island an hour ago. Will you forgive me if I just shop?"

"I forgive you," he said. "We can catch up later. I'll stop by the house sometime."

"Good idea," Beth said. He was being polite, just like every time she happened into him. He wouldn't come by the house; he never did. He was busy in the summer. If she bumped into him again in a few weeks, or a month, he would explain how busy he'd been.

David made haste in dumping his lettuce into a plastic bag and headed for the deli. Then around the corner, out of sight.

Beth took a head of lettuce herself and breathed out a long stream of anxious air. David Ronan. Of all people.

Beth lingered in the produce section trying to transfer her angst into concentration on the mundane task at hand: Did she want strawberries? Yes. Grapes and bananas? Yes. What else? What kind of fruit would Marcus eat? The same as everybody else, she assumed. He was, after all, just a person. No different because he was black, because he was poor, because he was sad. David Ronan, too, was just a person. Why then did he seem like so much more? Beth was afraid to leave the produce section. She bought red and yellow peppers and some button mushrooms. It was too early in the season yet for really good zucchini or corn. She was afraid that David Ronan would be standing at the cheese case or in front of the cereal. She couldn't bear to see him again. She would have to stay by the produce until she was certain he'd left the store.

The produce section, however, was freezing. Beth had to move on. Besides, she was an adult. That was one of Dr. Schau's favorite refrains: *You're an adult, Beth. You have years of experience in how to cope. Use that experience.* Okay, Beth thought. She saw David every summer, sometimes several times a summer, and that one year they'd even socialized at the cocktail party. (Arch was the one who'd wanted to go. Beth pleaded to stay home until Arch insinuated that her reluctance meant that she still felt something for David. So they went to the party and Beth drank too much.)

She'd never been this alarmed to see David Ronan before, so why now? Because Arch was gone? Yes, that was it. She was no longer happily married. Her fairy tale had come to an end, and so she felt vulnerable, somehow, to David Ronan and the memories of pain and love that came with him.

As she moved carefully into the next aisle, her insides filled with an awful, heavy guilt. She remembered Arch, years earlier, in the hour before they left for the Ronan cocktail party. Arch teased her because she stood in the closet in her bra and panties with a glass of white wine debating what to wear. She put on a sundress, then declared it too matronly and went with silk pants and a skimpy halter. Arch whistled in such a way that let her know the outfit was too sexy. She poured herself another glass of wine and changed her top.

You're making a big deal out of this, Beth, Arch said.

No, I'm not.

The guy's crazy about you. He always has been. He'll think you look beautiful whatever you wear.

Shut up, she said. *Why aren't you jealous?*

Why should I be jealous? I got you in the end, didn't I? I'm happy to go. I want to gloat.

That was Arch through and through. Never jealous, only proud. That was the perfect way in which he loved her. At the party, Beth drank too much, laughed too loudly in conversation with Rosie Ronan, and stumbled on her way out, catching the heel of her sandal between the flagstones of the walk. The ride home was the closest she had ever come to telling Arch the truth about David, but blessedly, she'd kept her mouth shut. Back at Horizon, Arch put her to bed with two aspirin and a glass of ice water, kissed her forehead and deemed the night an enormous success.

Long ago, Beth had decided that every man, woman, and child had the right to one secret. One piece of private history, and hers was David Ronan.

But what did she care about David Ronan now? The way she reacted probably made him think she was still in love with him.

She should find him and try to act like a normal person. Set things straight.

Beth abandoned her cart and hurried through the store until she spotted the red of David's shirt in the dairy section. She stopped. He was buying—What? Milk, half-and-half, two packages of Philadelphia cream cheese. She moved in front of him.

"Oh," he said. "Hi."

"I'm sorry I acted strangely back there," she said. "I don't know what's wrong with me."

"You've been through a lot," David said. "I was just thinking how awful it must be for you. And the kids."

"And Arch's mother, and Arch's partners, and his clients, one of whom narrowly escaped death row. It amazes me. He was just one person but he left behind such a big hole."

"He was a good man," David said. "I feel lucky to have met him."

"That's nice of you to say."

"I mean it, Beth."

She looked at him and realized that she'd been avoiding his eyes this whole time. He smiled. His face was as familiar to her as the faces of her own brothers. She'd devoted so many hours to studying it when she was younger.

"Okay, listen, let's not make excuses. Will you bring your family for dinner on Friday?"

He frowned. "Friday?"

"Are you busy? It would be great if Winnie and Garrett could meet your girls and we have another boy their age staying with us this summer. It'll be fun. We'll cook out?"

"Thanks for the offer, Beth, but I . . ."

"You won't come?"

"Well, you haven't let me explain."

"Okay, explain."

He put his hand over his mouth and wiped at his lips. "I'll explain on Friday, I guess. It's too much to go into here. What time would you like us?"

"How about seven?"

"Fine. We'll see you then. Friday at seven."

"You remember the house?"

"You're kidding, right?" David asked.

"Right," Beth said. How could he forget Horizon, the house her father threw him out of so many years ago? David left her with a little dance step, a wave and a half-turn in which he gathered up a dozen eggs and disappeared around a display of meringue cookies. Beth took a minute to regroup. The Ronan family was coming for dinner. Perfect. Right? Beth hoped she hadn't made things worse by trying to make them better.

She found her cart and resumed shopping. She went back to produce and selected eight russet potatoes and three pounds of asparagus. An additional head of lettuce. Rib-eye steaks, butter, sour cream. Some Ben & Jerry's. She wasn't a gourmet cook like Rosie Ronan, but that was okay. She wouldn't go to any great lengths; she would wear jeans and flip-flops. Having old friends for a cookout was no big deal. It was just one of the things you did in the summertime.

❧

As soon as his mother got home, Garrett realized something had happened at the store. Or maybe it was just the effect of Nantucket on his mother's brain. He heard the car swing into the driveway and then the car horn and his mother proclaiming, "Kids, I'm home!"

Garrett was the only one around. Marcus and Winnie were swimming together and Garrett watched them from the deck, the two of them trying to do the butterfly against the tough surf. Garrett wouldn't admit to any racist feelings except for when it came to Marcus and his sister. Winnie fawned all over the guy, which wasn't surprising considering how mentally unstable she'd become, but Garrett was damned if he were going to stand by and let Marcus fuck his sister. He was the man of the house, now. He'd kill Marcus before allowing that to happen.

Garrett walked through the house and out the front door to help his mother with the groceries. She looked different. She looked manic, overexcited, like a kid who'd eaten too much Halloween candy.

"Thanks, sweetie. Thanks a million. You've been such a big help today. Really, I mean it. You've been an angel."

"Mom?"

Beth sailed into the kitchen and flung open all of the cabinet doors. "I forget, every year, where we put things. I guess it doesn't matter. We can make it up as we go along!"

It occurred to Garrett that his mother had been drinking. Or maybe she'd popped the pills that Dr. Schau gave her (their mother was the only one to get pills). Garrett unloaded the bags and handed groceries to his mother. She was moving around the kitchen like she'd been shot out of a pinball machine. Bouncing around with all this extra energy.

Garrett is very sensitive to other people's moods, Mrs. Marshall had written on his end-of-the-year student evaluation. *He is tuned in to their needs, desires, and intentions.* It was true, he thought. He could read other people in a matter of seconds. Some people might call it intuition, but that word sounded too feminine. Garrett preferred the word "perceptive." Like a detective. Or a writer. Or like Dr. Schau, who could tell what you were thinking before you even opened your mouth. Right now, watching his mother, Garrett knew something had happened at the store. He pulled out the steaks.

"Why so many steaks?" Garrett said.

"Steaks?" his mother cried out. She knit her brow as though she didn't know what he was referring to, as though it was easy to forget what must have been a hundred dollars worth of steaks in one of the bags. Just repeating that word, "steaks," was as good as lying.

"Why so many?" Garrett asked.

"Well, because," his mother said. "There are four of us and we're having four dinner guests on Friday."

Garrett dropped his ass into a kitchen chair. It squealed, but thankfully did not break. *"Dinner* guests?"

"Before you get all worked up, let me tell you who it is," his mother said. "It's my friend David from growing up, his wife, and their two *teenage daughters.* You know, girls, girls, girls. I thought you'd thank me. It seems like all your friends here are either at camp or their parents moved to the Hamptons."

Garrett closed his eyes. More teenagers he was supposed to connect with. He couldn't believe his mother. She barely kept it together in front of her family; what made her think she might make it through an evening with other people? The topic of Garrett's father would inevitably come up. His mother would drink too much wine and start to cry. Maybe Winnie, too. The guests would sit dumbfounded and uncomfortable, the *teenage daughters* wishing they were anywhere but trapped in this house.

"No one's moved to the Hamptons," Garrett said irritably.

"The Alishes," Beth said. "Carson Alish's parents moved to the Hamptons."

"That is so beside the point," Garrett said.

"What point?"

"We're supposed to be healing as a *family*," Garrett said. "It's bad enough you invited Marcus, and now we're having some strange people over?"

"Just for dinner," she said. "Besides, they're not strange. David and I have known each other since we were sixteen years old. For six or seven summers, he was the best friend I had."

The way his mother said the word "friend" tipped Garrett off immediately.

"So this is an old boyfriend, then?"

"He's a friend. From a hundred years ago, Garrett. And he's coming with his wife and kids."

"Dad's only been dead for three months," Garrett said.

Beth fell into the chair next to him. "I know you're having a hard time, sweetie. We all are. But I worry about you especially because you're putting up such a strong front. You're being tough for all of us. I'm sorry I keep telling you you're the man of the house. That isn't fair. I want you to know it's okay to grieve— to cry, to scream, to be angry. But don't misdirect your anger at me."

"Except I *am* angry at you," he said. "You invited your old boyfriend here for dinner. You invited Marcus here for the whole summer. We're never going to have time alone, just our family."

"We'll make time," she said, patting his hand. "We'll take bike rides, we'll walk on the beach, and we'll find the right time and place to scatter Daddy's ashes. Just you, me, and Winnie. I promise."

Beth returned to the groceries and Garrett watched for a minute. Then he heard Winnie blabbering and he turned to see her and Marcus trudging up the steps from the beach. Winnie's blond ponytail was dripping wet; she wore the sweatshirt over her bikini. Unbelievable. But she had taken it off before she went into the water. Garrett wondered if she felt lighter, freer, without it. It was an interesting concept: grief as something she could take off every once in a while, like when she wanted to enjoy the first swim of the summer. Garrett was almost envious of his sister and the way she'd appropriated their father's sweatshirt and made it her own symbol: *I'm sad.* Garrett's sadness churned inside of him like food that was impossible to digest.

Marcus wore a pair of cut-off jeans as his swimsuit. He looked like a kid who should be getting wet under a fire hydrant.

"Are you two hungry?" Beth asked. "I went shopping."

"I'm not hungry," Winnie said.

Garrett gauged Beth's response to this, which was no response at all. She was definitely distracted. Winnie never ate anymore, and this was a manifestation of her grief that Garrett didn't envy. Food made Winnie sick. If she was eating and accidentally thought about their father, she threw up. Every day at Danforth she bought lunch in the cafeteria and then walked it right out the front door and down half a block to where three homeless men in turbans camped out under some scaffolding. Every day Winnie gave them her lunch then walked back to school with the empty tray.

"Do you want anything, Marcus?" Beth asked. "A sandwich or something? We have smoked turkey here, and some cheese. Or I could fry you an egg."

"Turkey's fine," Marcus said.

"I'll make his sandwich," Winnie said.

"I'll make it," Beth said. "You kids dry off."

Garrett watched his mother make Marcus's sandwich. It was as if she were entered in a sandwich-making contest. She'd bought three loaves of Something Natural herb bread, unsliced, so she brandished her serrated knife and cut two thick slices. Then mayonnaise, mustard, three leaves of lettuce that she washed and dried first, two pieces of Swiss Lorraine, and finally the smoked turkey that she draped over the cheese one slice at a time. She put the top on the sandwich, cut it in half diagonally. Arranged it on a plate with two handfuls of Cape Cod potato chips.

"Marcus, what would you like to drink?" she called out.

Garrett had seen enough. He'd made do with an untoasted bagel with cream cheese that had traveled with them in the warm car all the way from New York. But that wasn't what got him mad. It was something else. Winnie and his mother fighting over who got to make Marcus's sandwich, for starters. Garrett found the urn on the mantel in the living room and he carried it upstairs to his room. They'd been here all of three hours, and already he could tell this summer was going to suck.

☙

Garrett's room was on the side of the house that faced the ocean. The room had been built for Garrett's great-great-uncle Burton, his great-grandfather's brother. Burton had been a world traveler and insisted on a room where he could see the horizon. The room had two single beds with a nightstand between them. The lamp on the nightstand had a fringed shade. On the wall was a map of the world from 1932—no Israel, Garrett noticed, and the

names and boundaries of the nations in Africa were different.
The map was marked with multicolored pushpins, showing all
the places across the planet where Uncle Burton had laid his
head for the night. Singapore, Guatemala, Marrakech. Katmandu,
the Fiji Islands, Santiago, Cape Town. Underneath the bed that
Garrett didn't use was Uncle Burton's traveling trunk. Garrett and
his father had sifted through it once, examining the masks, the
kris knife from Malaysia, a ladle made out of a coconut, the
postcards and cocktail napkins from fancy hotels in Europe.

Garrett placed the urn on top of the dresser. He wanted to
convince his mother to let him take a year off before he went
to college. He wanted to go to Perth, Australia. Garrett stepped
out onto his one-person balcony, dreaming about a flat in Cot-
tlesloe Beach, long drives into the Outback, sightings of emus
and crocodiles and kangaroos, which he'd heard were as plentiful
as rabbits. Arch had spent a year in Perth between college and
law school, and he told Garrett all about the Fremantle Doctor,
which was the name of a breeze that came off the water in
January, and about the sheilas, a term for gorgeous Australian
women with *Baywatch* bodies.

Garrett wanted to live a life exactly like his father's—Australia, college, law school. A career as a Manhattan attorney, a wife
and two kids, including a son of his own. He could then pick
up where his father's life tragically ended. Arch's plane crash was,
quite simply, the worst disaster imaginable. The plane was a
Cessna Skylark. It had been gassed up at the Albany airport, and
checked by mechanics. The flight pattern was cleared by the
FAA, by the tower in Albany, by the tower in LaGuardia. The
pilot had over two thousand hours of flight time. But he was only
twenty-five years old, and the plane had propellers, like the toy
planes Garrett used to play with as a kid.

When they recovered the body, and the black box, two days after the crash, Garrett had wanted to see both. He wanted to see his father's body; he wanted to listen to the flight recorder. But no one was willing to let him do either. The managing partner at his father's firm, Trent Trammelman, identified the body. Garrett summoned the courage to ask Trent, *What did he look like? Please tell me.*

He looked fine, Trent said. *Peaceful.* That word, "peaceful," clued Garrett right in: Trent was lying. And so Garrett was left to imagine his father's body. Blue, bloated, broken. Garrett's father, his dad, whom he knew so well and had seen happy and healthy and handily in control of every situation that arose since Garrett had been born, was altered forever in a matter of seconds. Killed. Boom, just like that.

The cause of the crash was ruled as ice on the wings. There had been a driving freezing rain and it was dark—the worst possible flying conditions. There was a mechanical failure—something called a "boot" on one of the wings was supposed to expand and crack off the ice, but it malfunctioned, and one wing grew heavier than the other. The pilot changed altitudes several times, but nothing worked. The pilot couldn't recover. The plane went into a spin and crashed. The thing that Garrett hated to think of even more than the condition of his father's body after the crash was those seconds or minute when the plane spun toward earth. What could those seconds possibly have been like for his father? Did his father scream? Did his father think about Garrett, Winnie, their mother? He must have. The only reaction Garrett wanted to imagine from his father was anger. His father would have been yelling at the pilot to regain control. *I have kids!* he would have said. *I have a beautiful wife!* Garrett chose to believe his father was too angry to be scared, too furious to cry out in fear for his life. But those images slid into Garrett's brain despite his best efforts to push them away: his father crying, stricken with terror.

Better to watch your parent die of cancer, Garrett thought. Like Katie Corrigan's mother who got breast cancer and died a year later. Then, at least, you could prepare yourself. You could say good-bye. But Garrett's father had been ripped from their lives suddenly, leaving behind a hole that was ragged and bloody, smoking.

Garrett stayed in his room until the sun sank into the water. His walls turned a shade of dark pink; the urn was a silhouette against the wall. There was a knock at the door.

"Who is it?" Only one answer would be acceptable.

"Mom. Can I come in?"

"Okay," he said.

She stood in the doorway. "We miss you downstairs. I'm about to start dinner. What are you doing up here?"

"Sleeping," he said. "Thinking."

"What are you thinking about?" she asked. She glanced at the urn.

I'm a seventeen-year old boy. I need my father. As if there were anything else to think about. "Nothing," he said.

chapter 2

Three days later, Marcus felt like the main character in that Disney movie where the little boy is adopted by wild animals and lives among them in the jungle. Here it was, two o'clock in the afternoon, and he was lying on a beach. There was no one else for miles, except Winnie, who lay in a chaise next to him wearing purple bikini bottoms and her Princeton sweatshirt. She seemed intent on getting a tan—all shiny with baby oil— but she refused to take off the sweatshirt. Except for when she swam, which she and Marcus did whenever they got too warm. This, Marcus thought, was what people meant by "the good life." Sitting on a deserted beach in the hot sun—no bugs, no trash, no other people kicking sand onto his blanket or blaring Top 40 stations on the boom box like at Jones Beach—and he could swim in the cool water whenever he wanted. Plus, he had a handmaiden. Winnie made lunch for both of them—smoked turkey sandwiches and tall glasses of Coca-Cola that she spiked with Malibu rum. At first, when Marcus tasted the rum in his drink, he balked. Because he did *not* want to have his summer over before it even began for getting caught drinking. He said so to Winnie and she promised him that they would just have this one cocktail—he loved how she called it a "cocktail"—and that her mother was out doing a two-hour jog and would never know. The Malibu rum had been sitting in the liquor cabinet for a couple of years; she and Garrett dipped into it all the time, even with her father around, she said, and they had never gotten caught.

The mention of Garrett made Marcus uneasy. Garrett was lying up on the deck, presumably because he never swam and didn't like to get all sandy, but Marcus suspected it was because he wanted to keep his distance. And up on the deck he could watch everything Marcus and Winnie were doing. Like Big Brother. Like God.

Marcus squinted at Winnie. "If you're so concerned about getting tan, you should take your sweatshirt off."

"You just want a better look at my body," Winnie said.

Marcus found that funny enough to laugh, but he didn't want to piss her off. "Why do you always wear it?"

"It was Daddy's."

Immediately, Marcus's reality kicked back in. Despite the hot day, he felt the chill of humiliation as he recalled the worst personal shame of his life. At the beginning of swim season, he'd come out of the showers to find the locker room abandoned, to find his locker jimmied open, to find all of his clothes missing, even his wet bathing suit. He stood in his towel, shivering, not because he was cold, but because he'd thought the guys on the swim team, at least, would cut him some slack about his mother. But no: they, too, wanted to expose him. Marcus sat for a long while on the wooden bench by his empty locker, too mortified to wander the school's hallways for help, too ashamed to contact his father, before he thought to call Arch, collect, at his office. Arch came all the way out to Queens with a gym bag and Marcus got dressed in Arch's sweats. The very same Princeton sweatshirt that Winnie was wearing. If Arch had asked a single question, Marcus probably would have broken down. But Arch just offered him the gym bag and said, *Put these on and let's get you home.*

Winnie, it seemed, was trying to get his attention. "Marcus?" she said.

"Huh?"

"Now can I ask you something?"

"What?" he said, warily.

"Why do you lie out in the sun when you're already black?" She giggled.

Marcus tried to relax. If she was going to wear the damn sweatshirt all summer, there was nothing he could do about it except let it be a reminder of how far he'd come. How he didn't let other people get to him anymore. How he'd shown the jackasses on the swim team something by placing second in every single meet all season. Placing second *on purpose* so his name wouldn't make it into any headlines. "Black people get tans, too, you know. Look." He lowered the waistband of his shorts a fraction of an inch so that Winnie could see his tan line. "In winter I get kind of ashy. Besides, I like the feel of the sun on my skin."

"Me, too," Winnie said. She pushed up her sleeves and rolled up the bottom of her sweatshirt so that her stomach showed. "You're right," she said. "That's better." She picked up the bottle of baby oil and squirted some on her stomach and rubbed it in with slow, downward strokes that made Marcus think she was trying to be all sexy for him. The poor child, as his mother used to say.

Winnie had a crush on him. Anyone could see it. The past two nights she'd enticed Marcus into playing board games after dinner. Marcus asked if there were anything to do in town, and Beth offered to drive them in for an ice cream or the movies, but there were only two movie theaters showing one movie apiece that all of them had already seen, and Winnie turned down the ice cream without a reason. Not going into town left them with what Marcus's mother used to call Nothing to Do but Stand on Your Head and Spit in Your Shoe Syndrome. So Winnie pulled a stack of board games out of a closet. The boxes of the games were disintegrating and some games were missing pieces and dice, and the bank in Monopoly only had three one-dollar bills but Winnie cut some more out of blank typing paper. They made do. Marcus and Winnie spent two long evenings building pretend real estate fortunes and getting out of jail free.

It was as different from his life in Queens as anything could be. Winnie kept apologizing because *There's practically nothing to do here at night, not until I get my license, anyway.* She had some notion that Marcus went out every night at home, clubbing, or hanging out on the streets. But in fact, at home, Marcus stayed off the streets. He couldn't afford to get into any trouble, and the best way to stay out of it was to stay home. Last summer, he'd worked all day on the maintenance crew at Queens College—mowing lawns, trimming hedges, recindering the running track—and by the time he got home, his ass was kicked. He ate dinner with his family and then either watched TV or went over to Vanessa Lydecker's apartment and drank a beer with Vanessa's brother and fooled around with Vanessa in her bedroom.

Before the murders, Marcus's family was nothing special. His father worked at the printing press for the *New York Times* as a supervisor, and his mother, with one year of Ivy League education and three years of city college, was a reading specialist who split her time between I.S. 224 and P.S. 136. She tutored kids on weekends for extra money, which she tucked into Marcus's college account. And then, on October seventh, Constance murdered her sister-in-law Angela Bennett and Angela's nine-year-old daughter, Candy Cohut. Constance stabbed Angela to death, and in the process fatally wounded Candy. Even now, when Marcus thought about the murders, it seemed so incredible it was as if it had happened to somebody else.

"I'm going to eat my sandwich," Marcus said. He'd drained his cocktail and the ocean began to take on a wavy shimmer. He needed food.

"Okay," Winnie said. "Enjoy."

"Aren't you going to eat?" he asked.

"I'll wait until later."

In just three days, Marcus had learned what this meant: Winnie would let her sandwich sit for another hour or two, then throw it away, claiming the mayonnaise had gone bad.

"You know why you're so skinny, don't you?"

Winnie didn't respond.

"Because you don't eat. If my father had to sit here and watch you waste a sandwich with turkey on it that costs, like, ten dollars a pound, he'd throw a French fit on your ass." Marcus took a lusty bite of his sandwich. Even the food here tasted better. These sandwiches he'd been eating, for example. The bread was homemade, the smoked turkey was real turkey, not some white meat paste that was processed to taste like turkey, the lettuce was crisp, the tomato ripe. Beth used gourmet mustard. It was so superior to any sandwich that could be purchased in Marcus's neighborhood or in his school cafeteria, that it was as if he'd been eating cardboard and ashes all these years and only now had stumbled upon actual food. "I mean, really," Marcus said. "Why don't you eat? Do you have some kind of problem? There was a girl at my school who had anorexia. She walked around looking like she had AIDS or something."

"I don't have anorexia," Winnie said. "And I don't have AIDS."

"But you look like a skeleton. I haven't seen you eat the whole time you've been here."

"I eat when I'm hungry," she said.

Marcus finished the first half of his sandwich, then wished he'd saved some of his cocktail to wash it down with. He eyed Winnie's cocktail. She'd give it to him if he asked her for it. Then he remembered that Beth had slipped two bottles of Evian into their beach bag. That woman was improving in his eyes. Marcus drank one of the bottles down to the bottom. He felt much, much better.

"There are people in Queens, you know, and the rest of New York City, who don't eat because they can't afford to."

"I'm well aware of that, thanks," Winnie said. "I do my part to feed the homeless."

"Do you?"

She sat bolt upright. "For your information, I gave my lunch to homeless people every day this spring."

"Good for you," Marcus said. He believed her. Although he'd only known Winnie for three days, he could tell that was exactly the kind of thing she would do. She loved charity cases. Him, for example. "But you should take care of yourself while you're at it."

Winnie stood up and her sweatshirt dropped to her waist. She put on her sunglasses, snapped up her towel and headed up the stairs without a word. Marcus had pissed off his handmaiden by telling her the truth. She looked like a skeleton. If she didn't start eating soon, she was going to make herself sick.

Well, fine then. Marcus concentrated on his sandwich. Actually, it tasted better now that he was alone. He noticed that Winnie had left her sandwich behind, and since there was no hope that she'd ever eat it, and since the rum made him extra hungry, he finished that one, too, and drank the second bottle of Evian, and while he was at it, polished off the remains of Winnie's cocktail. Then he lay back on his blanket and listened to the sound of the ocean. It was almost pleasant enough for him to forget about his worries. His mother. The photo of Candy, all covered up except for her shiny black shoes. The unwritten book. The tactile memory of five crisp hundred dollar bills that his editor, Zachary Celtic, handed him on the day they sealed the book deal with a handshake. Zachary gave him the cash with the understanding that at the end of the summer Marcus would have fifty pages to show him, and an outline for the remainder of the book. Marcus spent the money in less than a week, buying items for his trip to Nantucket that he'd hoped would convince the Newtons that he wasn't a charity case after all: the all-wrong leather bag, the uncomfortable dock shoes, the portable CD player. The best thing Marcus bought was his white shirt. He'd taken the subway into Manhattan to buy it—at Paul Stuart, where a young German woman waited on him as though he might pull a gun on her at any moment. He charmed her, though, and by the end of the transaction, she suggested the monogram and threw it in for free.

Now that the money was gone (there had been some idiot-spending, too: two or three meals at Roy Rogers, a ten-dollar scratch ticket, a bouquet of red roses for his sister LaTisha as an apology for leaving her alone with their father all summer), Marcus felt an urgent pressure to write. But yesterday afternoon when he'd closed the door of his white bedroom and sat on the bed to write, he couldn't think of how to start. Zachary Celtic had spewed forth all sorts of garbagy ideas when he pitched the book, but Marcus pushed those phrases from his mind, leaving a blank slate. And so instead of writing, he'd spent ninety minutes doing a line drawing of what he saw out his window—low lying brush, a rutted dirt road, the pond in the distance.

Zachary Celtic was a friend of Nick Last Name Unknown. Nick was the boyfriend of Marcus's English teacher, Ms. Marchese. Nick showed up at school a lot wearing gold rings and suits paired with shiny ties, and since no kid at Benjamin N. Cardozo High School was truly stupid, it was agreed upon that Nick was in the mob. For this reason, everyone behaved in Ms. Marchese's class and everyone, even the absolute lowlifes and basketball players, turned in the assignments. Marcus liked English class anyway, and he liked Ms. Marchese, because she was the only teacher whose attitude toward Marcus didn't change after the murders, and plus, she was always telling him he was a gifted writer. So his guard wasn't up like it should have been, maybe, when Nick stopped by at the end of class one day with a better-looking guy in a better-looking suit and Ms. Marchese said that the second guy was a book editor from Manhattan and he was there to talk to Marcus.

Since October seventh, Marcus had fielded hundreds of phone calls from reporters, producers, publicists—from New York One, the *New York Post*, the *Daily News*, *The Geraldo Rivera*

Show. Everyone wanted the inside scoop on his mother. She was a black inner-city woman who had made it as far as the Ivy League—how did she end up a baby killer? In response to all publicity, Marcus's father had issued these directives. *Politely decline, then hang up!* If photographers come to the door, tell them through the chain that they will never get a picture inside the apartment. But something about the phrase "book editor in Manhattan" got past Marcus's radar. He thought, stupidly, that this guy was interested in him for a reason other than that he was a *murderer's son.* He thought the editor had shown up at their high school in Queens wearing a thousand-dollar suit (which, when Marcus asked, Zachary told him he'd gotten at Paul Stuart) because Marcus was a *gifted writer.*

Nick and Zachary Celtic invited Marcus to lunch. Although it was two-thirty and Marcus had already eaten lunch in the cafeteria at noon, he agreed to go along. They went to a diner down the street from the school, and after Nick made it clear that Zachary was picking up the check, Marcus went crazy ordering a roast beef club, fries with gravy, chocolate milkshake, lemon chiffon pie. Zachary asked Marcus all kinds of questions about how he liked school (*fine*), why he liked English class (*liked to read*), who his favorite writers were (*Salinger, Faulkner, John Edgar Wideman*). It was as Marcus was slipping into a food coma induced by this second lunch that Zachary announced that he was the true crime editor at Dome Books and that he wanted to offer Marcus thirty thousand dollars to write a first-person account of life with his mother, before and after the murders.

Marcus dropped his fork. He worried he might be sick—not because he was disgusted at this man for suggesting such a thing or disgusted at himself for falling for it—but because he'd eaten too much and the whole idea of a *first-person account* and *thirty thousand dollars* overwhelmed him.

"There are a lot of people who will pay to read your story," Zachary said. "I'm thinking of a real insider's view. Your mother as, like, an educated woman, a teacher and everything, and Princeton in her background, and then one day she just . . . you know . . . snaps." Zachary snapped his fingers with such force that both Marcus and Nick flinched. "Goes totally haywire on members of her own family. I'm thinking . . . you know . . . the blood-splattered sheet and how that made you feel. The dead bodies in your own apartment. The little girl in the shoes. God, everybody's going to want to read this. And there was sex involved, too, right? I mean, in your mother's testimony . . ."

Marcus belched, loudly, then worried once again that he might be sick. Zachary moved his hand like he was clearing smoke and said, "The mere *mention* of death row is going to have the citizens of this great city flocking to Barnes & Noble to buy your book. What it felt like to have your own mother, a pretty woman, too, facing the strap-down on the gurney, the long needle . . ."

It was Nick who finally stopped him. "You get to tell the story in your own words, kid. I'll bet that's something you've been itching to do."

Marcus wondered if Ms. Marchese told Nick about Marcus's isolation, his status as the class pariah. How he switched seats from the front row, where he could stretch out his legs, to the back row, where nobody could see him, throw shit at him, or mouth dirty words at the back of his head.

Marcus asked for time to think about it. Zachary held up his palms in agreement, saying, "Take as much time as you want. My offer stands." He slid a business card across the table towards

Marcus and an American Express Platinum card toward the check.

There was no one to ask for advice. Marcus couldn't ask his father because his father would say no, absolutely no. And Arch was dead, he'd been dead for five weeks by that point, and all of the protection and hope that Arch provided had vanished. As awful as Zachary Celtic was, Marcus sensed this book deal was a way out. It was thirty thousand dollars which, Zachary promised, he wouldn't have to pay back even if the book tanked. Thirty thousand dollars would buy a lot more college than Marcus could afford without writing a book. He'd seen the bank statement of the account his mother stashed her tutoring money in, Marcus's "college" fund. The balance was $1,204.82.

Finally, Nick's comment stuck with him. *You get to tell the story in your own words, kid.* That appealed to Marcus, even though he didn't know *how* he felt. It was possible that he still loved his mother, but that love was buried under a huge, crushing anger. Marcus was furious. Constance had murdered their way of life that, although not luxurious, had at least been tolerable. If he was coerced into write terrible things about her, she probably deserved it.

The following morning, Marcus called Zachary Celtic from a pay phone outside the school cafeteria and agreed to write the book. That day after English class, Zachary appeared with Nick, and Zachary handed Marcus an envelope containing the five hundred dollars.

"An advance on the advance," Zachary said. "You get me the first fifty pages and a complete synopsis by the end of the summer. I show it to my people. If they like it, the big money rolls your way."

Marcus accepted the envelope. Ms. Marchese looked away,

just like other teachers did when they saw a drug deal.

Now, Marcus lay on the beach, filled with turkey sandwich, buzzed on pilfered rum, and toasty in the sun—a better set of circumstances than he ever could have imagined for himself— except he should be up in his room *writing*. And now there was this problem of Winnie being mad at him. He should go up to the house and apologize before Garrett and Winnie formed a coalition and kicked Marcus off the island, like on that dumb-ass TV show. Or, worse, Winnie might tell Beth that Marcus was drinking. Frame him, then turn him in. That was the kind of thing that happened to black people all over America, getting blamed and busted for things that weren't their fault. Marcus could write a whole book on that topic alone. He could write a book about a lot of things, once he found his groove. He decided to nap, take a swim, and think about everything else in a little while.

Beth left the house for a run at noon. This was her new way of torturing her body, by running ten miles in the heat of the day. She put on a white hat, tucked a bottle of Evian into her fanny pack, and kicked off down the dusty road. Tonight was her din-ner party and she'd spent the morning cleaning every nook and cranny of the house with a giant sponge from the car wash and a bucket of bleach and water. Garrett had looked at her stonily and she read his mind—she was going to a lot of trouble for her old boyfriend.

"The house needed to be cleaned anyway," she said, sounding more defensive than she intended. "It's been sitting here all win-ter collecting dust and mouse droppings."

Garrett shook his head and retreated to the deck. When had he gotten so *judgmental?* Well, she knew when. And he wasn't judgmental so much as protective. He was the man of the house, now, and thus it was his job to protect his women. Fine. She would let it go.

Since Arch died, running had become Beth's only pleasure. The motion placated her anxieties, the symbolism of it quenched her secret desire to run away. At home in New York, she ran four, five, six times around the Reservoir, or tackled the long, hilly route around Central Park. Both were cathartic, but nothing in the world was like running on Nantucket in the summertime. Beth ran past Miacomet Pond, which today was the deepest blue, bordered by tall dune grass that sheltered a clump of wild iris and red-winged blackbirds. It was beautiful here, and even in the heat, the air was fresh and clean. For the hour or two that she was gone, she didn't have to be a mother. She didn't have to be the problem-solver or the ultimate authority. Beth had discussed this sense of relief with Dr. Schau. It was wrong and unnatural, wasn't it, for a mother to want to escape her kids? And especially Beth. Beth loved her children to distraction. When they were born, she felt she was the luckiest person on the planet—she'd hit the birthing jackpot—a boy and a girl. Two perfect healthy babies, one of each. The entire first year of the kids' lives she and Arch would take a second every so often and marvel. How had they gotten so lucky? Why had they of all people been so blessed?

Beth adored the trappings of motherhood: the pacifiers, the wooden blocks, the Cheerios underfoot, the darling outfits (always matching boy/girl outfits until the twins went off to kindergarten.) She loved *Sesame Street* and playgrounds and *Pat the Bunny* and even nursing the kids when they had earaches and the chicken pox. Other mothers complained, secretly, that kids took up so much time, that they left the house a mess—fingerprints on the TV screen, and yes, Cheerios underfoot—that they sucked the intelligence out of everyday life. These complaints baffled Beth. She didn't have a job outside of the home, maybe that was it, but she never expected Winnie and Garrett to appreciate Chagall or Bizet at age three. She didn't care that they took all her time—what, she wondered, could she possibly be doing that would be more worthwhile?

As the kids grew, life got more interesting. There were friends and multiplication tables and soccer. Trips to the dentist, to the Bronx Zoo, to Wollman Rink for ice skating every Christmas Eve. Then high school—advance placement classes, soccer team (Garrett), swim team (Winnie), phone calls, proms, learner's permits.

Beth loved it all. Yes, she did.

But when Arch died, one of the many, many things that changed was the way she felt about her children. It wasn't that she loved them less—if anything, she loved them more. Especially since they were dangerously close to leaving home; a year from now, they'd be headed for college. What Beth felt was just an occasional sense of relief—when they walked out the door in the morning to go to school, for example. Dr. Schau assured her it was perfectly normal: Beth was alone now, her job was doubly hard. She'd lost not only her husband but her coparent, and so all the duties she once shared with Arch now fell to her alone. It was perfectly normal to feel relief at escaping the pressure, if only for a little while.

Beth ran all the way to Madaket, the hamlet at the western

tip of the island. She stopped at the drawbridge that looked out over Madaket Harbor and drank her bottle of water, slowly, cautiously, to avoid getting cramps. There were sailboats and red-and-white buoys bouncing gently in the breeze. Beth was dripping with sweat. She worried that she'd come too far and wouldn't make it home.

But the way home was into the wind and that cooled Beth off somewhat, and the water helped, and she allowed herself to think about the dinner that night. David Ronan was going to set foot in her house for the first time since August 31, 1979, when Beth's father threw him out. That morning was such ancient history, such a drop in the ocean by now, and yet it caused Beth's chest to contract with guilt. The best thing was to have this dinner and put the past behind them.

Beth made it all the way back to where the road turned to dirt before she had to stop and walk. She judged it to be almost two o'clock and she was parched. The Evian bottle had a quarter inch of water left, enough to get the dusty film out of her mouth. She'd run eleven or twelve miles. She felt light, clean, and completely spent.

A car rumbled up behind her, a horn beeped. She stepped into the tall grass to let the car pass, but when she turned around, she saw it wasn't a car and it wasn't passing. It was David Ronan in his Island Painting van idling there in the road, window down.

"Hi," he said.

"Hi." Beth wiped her forehead. Well, here was the worst possible luck. She was slick with sweat and coated with dirt and certainly she stank to high heaven. Not to mention her hair. "Are you . . . working out here? You have a job out here?" Her teeth were gritty.

"No, actually, I was headed to your house. I need to talk to you."

"Oh, really? Why?" Though Beth feared she knew: Rosie didn't want to come to dinner. And who could blame her? Especially with Arch gone. It would be a sadly uneven equation; Beth had considered this numerous times since leaving the Stop & Shop on Tuesday.

"I didn't think it was fair to show up tonight without telling you something first," David said. "There's something I have to explain."

Beth looked nervously in both directions. No one was coming. She remembered from their conversation at the store that there was something David wanted to explain, but she hadn't even let herself venture a guess. And now here was David tracking her down because clearly whatever it was couldn't wait.

David motioned for her to come closer, which was not something she was particularly anxious to do. But she obeyed and stood only inches from his open window. She glanced into his van: it was messy with clipboards and newspapers and a couple of wadded-up bags from Henry's. He was listening to NPR. Then Beth caught sight of something on the dashboard—a yellow stick-'em on which a single word was written "Beth." Her name was stuck to his dashboard right where he could see it. Her name.

"Rosie's not coming to dinner," David said.

As Beth suspected. A host of indignations rose in her chest: Rosie was being childish, jealous, unreasonable. But she said, simply, "Oh?"

David turned down the radio and squinted out the windshield. His sunglasses hung around his neck on a Croakie. He wore a blue chambray shirt and navy blue shorts, the same black flip-flops. Beth was amazed at how clean he looked even though he was in the painting business. He was the owner, of course; Beth was pretty sure he didn't go near any actual paint.

"Rosie left," he said.

"What?"

"Rosie left. She left me and the girls."

Beth pushed the lock button of David's door down, then pulled it back up again. She heard an approaching engine and saw a car coming toward them.

"Oh, shit," she said.

The other car slowed to a stop, waiting for Beth to move, but she could do nothing more than grind the soles of her Nikes into the dirt and will the road to swallow her up. She should never have asked David for dinner. She should have let him go on his merry way and forgotten all about him. She should have kept him safely in her past where he belonged—yet now, here he was, most definitely occupying her present. Right now—and tonight, without a wife.

"Shit," Beth said again. The driver of the other car hit his horn then shrugged at Beth as if to say, *What, exactly, would you like me to do?*

"Will you get in?" David said. "Please? So we can talk?"

"Get into your van?" She tried to swallow but the inside of her mouth was like crumbling plaster. "Don't you have work?"

"Work can wait. Hop in."

Beth saw she had no choice. She ran around and climbed in the passenger side. She discovered a bottle of water hidden underneath *The Inquirer & Mirror.* This was a very small positive.

"Mind if I have a swig?" she asked. "I'm dying of thirst."

"Help yourself." David said. "Sorry I don't have anything stronger." He started to drive. "Shall we go to your house?"

"No," Beth said. "No, no. Let's . . . well, let's drive around or park somewhere." She was sorry as soon as she said "park somewhere," because it brought back memories of when she and David had parked at the beach right up the road and made love in the sand. "Let's drive around."

He stepped on the gas and Beth appreciated the cool wind through her window. She finished the entire bottle of water, trying not to panic. Trying not to think of Garrett. Trying not to bombard David with questions, the most obvious being, *Why didn't you just tell me at the store?*

"So," David said.

"So," Beth said. "So Rosie left. Are you going to tell me what happened?"

"She moved to the Cape after Christmas. She said the island was suffocating her. It was too small, too limited, and suddenly after eighteen years of living here, not at all what she wanted. And she said I was emotionally cruel."

"Emotionally cruel?"

"That's what she said."

"What about the girls?"

"Rosie didn't want to take the girls. She said they were happy in school and that she could be an equally effective mother from the Cape. If not more so." David spoke the words like a robot, like he'd committed them to memory then spoken them on a hundred separate occasions. "She rented a house in Wellfleet, which is to say, *I* rented a house, and she started a catering company, which is to say, *I* started the catering company, and I fly the girls over whenever their hearts desire. The three of them have a fine time, shopping and going to movies and spending my money in any other way they can find."

"A catering company," Beth said. "That makes sense. So the girls are all right with this, then?"

"They appear to be. Piper just turned seventeen, and she's developed a very independent, very empowered personality. She's thrilled that her mother has broken free of male domination."

"Oh," Beth said. "What about the younger one?"

"Peyton still loves me the best, thank God," David said. "But she wouldn't admit it in front of her mother or her sister. She's not brave enough. She's not brave at all."

"How old is Peyton?"

"Thirteen."

"I can't believe you and Rosie split," Beth said. "I just can't believe it." This was dangerous news. Beth stared at the stick 'em on the dashboard, wishing for clarity. David Ronan had split from his wife, and now he was driving around Nantucket with Beth's name on his dashboard. "How are you doing?" she asked. "Are you . . . are you angry?"

"Shit, yeah, I'm angry," David said. "And heartbroken and discouraged and deeply incredulous. I loved Rosie. She saved my life."

This comment, Beth knew, was aimed at her. What David really meant was: *Rosie saved me from you.* Beth heard the old pain, the old intensity in David's voice and she knew where the conversation was headed if she didn't stop it—blame for Rosie that was really blame for Beth. The first woman who'd left him.

"We'll have to cancel dinner," Beth said, cringing at how hardhearted, not to mention *rude*, that sounded. But the whole point had been to invite the Ronan *family*. To prove to the kids and Beth herself, and Arch, wherever he was, that this was just a normal friendship.

"I already told the girls. They're excited to come. But I guess you don't want us now? I hope you don't think I'm on the prowl."

"No, I never—"

"My girls," he said. "They think this is a date, even though I *assured* them it's not. I mean, I told them about your husband. But I haven't been out, anywhere, well, in six months, so they're hopeful." He smiled. "They want me to move on. I explained to them that I'm not ready to move on, and that even if I were, *you* weren't ready to move on." He glanced at her. "I'm embarrassed telling you all this. I came to find you because I knew it was unfair to spring it on you tonight. So we won't come."

The world's most awkward situation. What should she *do*? If she disinvited David, what did *that* say? That she didn't trust herself? That it wasn't okay for two old friends to have dinner together? "Forgive me," Beth said. "It's just that this took me by surprise. You could have told me at the store."

David tucked his chin guiltily. "You seemed upset at the store," he said. "About Arch, I mean. I didn't want to burden you with my problems."

"It wouldn't have been a burden," Beth said. "It would have been useful information."

"I guess subconsciously I wanted to come to dinner, and so that's why I didn't tell you," David said. "Since Rosie left, the whole island has treated me like an untouchable."

"You're not an untouchable."

David held out his hand. "Prove it."

Beth stared at his hand, the knobby knuckles, the golden

hairs, the clean, clipped nails. How many years had passed since she'd noticed David's hands?

She squeezed David's pinky. "I'm sorry Rosie left."

"Thanks. It makes me feel better to hear that opinion expressed, even by a summer person."

Beth smirked. She'd only spent ten minutes in David's presence and already they'd resumed their old roles. Year-rounder versus summer person. How old would they have to be before they rose above. "I hereby cancel my cancellation," she said. "Please come to dinner. I'd like to meet your girls and it'll be good for Winnie and Garrett. Just come at seven and we'll have a good time." *A good time.* It sounded so refreshing that Beth almost believed it was possible. "But don't bring me flowers or anything."

"No purple cosmos?" he said.

That hit too close to home. Beth shut her eyes, remembering the flowers wilting in her hand because she held them so tightly. They left golden dust on her skin.

"I'm sorry, Beth," he said.

"You don't know what I'm like these days," she said. "Boiled turnips can make me cry." She wiped her eyes. "Just take me home. I need to shower. Take a nap. And I don't want the kids worrying about where I am."

They drove to her house in silence, and then Beth leapt from the van. She needed David to drive away before anyone saw him. "I'll expect you at seven," she said.

"You're sure about this?" he said.

"I'm sure."

He waved. "Looking forward to it."

As Beth headed inside, she noticed the mail basket was full.

Already, some of her mail had been forwarded from New York. There were two bills, a credit card solicitation addressed to Archer Newton, and a letter for Marcus. The return address was 247 Harris Road, Bedford Hills, New York. It was a letter from Constance Tyler.

Garrett watched his mother closely from the minute she walked in the door from her run. The first thing she did was to look in the hallway mirror—the one that she and Uncle Danny and Uncle Scott had decorated with scallop shells in their youth—and groan.

"I look like a dirt sandwich," she said.

Although she hadn't acknowledged him, Garrett assumed the comment was for his benefit, and that he was expected to refute it.

"What do you care what you look like?" he said.

She turned, apparently surprised to see him there, sitting at the kitchen table, eating a lunch that he'd made himself. It might seem a small detail, but Garrett was keeping track of the fact that three days into the summer, neither his mother nor Winnie had offered to make him lunch, although they both fell over themselves to prepare food for Marcus.

"Garrett," she said. "It's two-thirty."

"So?"

"So, don't you think it's a little late to be eating such a big lunch? We're having dinner at seven."

As if he were likely to forget "the dinner," which, judging by the way his mother cleaned this morning, was a bigger event than she originally promised.

"I'll manage," he said.

As his mother walked toward him, he saw that she was holding some envelopes. She waved one in the air. "Where's Marcus?"

"I have no idea," Garrett said, though he had every idea. Marcus was on the beach. Alone. Winnie had come running up about forty-five minutes earlier in a state. It seemed Marcus had given Winnie some flak about not eating. *As if my digestive tract is his concern,* Winnie said in this bitchy, conspiratorial way, nudging Garrett to agree with her. Although Garrett wanted nothing more than to gang up on Marcus, it wasn't going to be for that reason. In this instance, Marcus was right: Winnie needed to eat. Garrett said as much to Winnie and she stomped up the stairs, her empty stomach clenched in fury against him.

"Well, can you find him for me, please?" Beth said. "There's a letter for him."

"I think he's on the beach," Garrett said. "He can read it when he comes up."

"It's a letter from Constance," Beth said. "It can't wait."

There was faulty logic there somewhere, but clearly this letter had put ants in his mother's pants and so Garrett walked out onto the deck and was about to yell down to the beach when he saw Marcus marching up the rickety stairs, loaded down like a pack mule with all the beach stuff—towels, beach bag, and Winnie's chaise lounge. Once Marcus reached the deck, he dropped the stuff and rubbed his eyes.

"Whoa," he said. "I fell asleep down there."

Garrett studied him. He heard the clink of glasses in the beach bag and realized that Marcus and Winnie had been drinking. The Malibu, probably. How easy it would be to bust this kid, Garrett thought. He shook his head. "Mom has a letter for you. From Constance."

Not even the faintest glimmer of interest crossed Marcus's

face. "Okay, man, thanks." He headed for the outdoor shower and Garrett watched him step in and close the door. Then he heard the water. Garrett returned to the kitchen where his mother was drinking straight from the big bottle of purple Gatorade.

"Marcus is in the shower," Garrett said.

Beth paused in her drinking. "Did you tell him about the letter?"

"Of course. I guess it can wait after all."

"Hmmpf," Beth said. Garrett noticed her staring at the envelope, and he moved closer to inspect it. A regular number ten business envelope addressed in blue ink. The return address said, "247 Harris Road, Bedford Hills, New York," as if this were a domestic street address and not the address of the largest women's correctional facility in the state. The penmanship was neat, pretty even, and European, like the handwriting of Garrett's French teacher, Mr. Alevain. Of course, Constance Tyler was no dummy. She'd gone to Princeton, and that was how Garrett's father got involved in all this in the first place.

Although the envelope was unremarkable in every way, it had power, and Garrett found himself wondering what the letter might say. On the one hand, there was so much to explain, but on the other, how could mere language convey the range of emotions Constance Tyler might be experiencing when she knew she would never be free again? She would never lie on a beach, ride a bike, dip her foot in the ocean. Garrett picked up the envelope and held it to the window trying to make out a word or two, and naturally, as soon as he gave in to this temptation, Marcus stepped into the kitchen, one beach towel wrapped around his waist, one wrapped around his head like a turban.

Except for these two towels, Marcus was naked—dark and muscular and imposing, like some two-hundred-year-old tree.

He nodded. "That my letter?"

Beth spoke up. She, too, had an impulse to scrutinize the letter, though it was none of hers or Garrett's business. "It's from Constance."

Marcus snatched the letter from Garrett's fingers. "All right, then," he said, and he disappeared upstairs.

⚘

At five o'clock, Garrett was slumped in the only comfortable chair in the house, reading. The chair was a bona fide La-Z-Boy recliner upholstered with worn fawn-colored velour; Garrett's grandfather had brought it home one summer from the dump, and although all the women complained that it was an eyesore and smelled like mildew, they kept it around because it was so comfortable. Garrett was reading *Franny and Zooey*, the first book on his required summer reading list. He'd reached the part where Zooey was soaking in the bathtub reading a letter wishing that his mother would leave him alone. Garrett paused for a minute, identifying with Zooey's frustration with Bessie Glass, except Garrett was frustrated by too little attention from his mother, or the wrong kind of attention. Something about his mother was really bugging him, although Garrett couldn't put it into words. If Garrett were the one taking a two-hour bath, for example, Beth would knock on the door and explain that since Garrett was the man of the house now, it was his responsibility to offer the same hot bath to Marcus. Garrett honestly couldn't believe that Marcus was here this summer. After all, if it weren't for Marcus's mother, Arch would still be alive. Garrett mentioned this glaring fact at one of their family therapy sessions, but Dr. Schau told him that was a small person's point of view. Constance Tyler didn't kill Arch, she said; he died by accident. It was nobody's fault.

Garrett rested the open book on his chest and closed his eyes. It was embarrassing that he'd even found time to start his required reading. He needed to get a life.

Suddenly, he heard his mother. "This is *going* to be a low-key affair." She said this as if trying to convince someone—herself, he supposed, or anyone else who might be listening. The ghost of his father, maybe. Garrett opened his eyes to see Beth come down the stairs wearing jeans, a pale pink T-shirt, and a pair of flip-flops. Her hair was still wet, and as she grew closer to him he caught the scent of her lotion. "I am *not* going to a lot of trouble."

"Okay," Garrett mumbled. "Whatever you say."

"Oh, *Garrett*," she said. She stopped at the hall mirror and inspected her face closely, much the way Garrett himself did when he was worried about acne. "Will you please just participate here? Will you play along?"

He dog-eared the page of his book and climbed out of the recliner. "Sure," he said. "What can I do?"

Beth turned to him with narrowed eyes, suspicious of his sudden willingness. "Well," she said. "You can help me in the kitchen."

It was on the tip of Garrett's tongue to ask *Where's Winnie? Where's Marcus? Why can't they help?* But he kept quiet and followed his mother.

Garrett had helped with his parents' dinner parties for years, and he knew from looking at the raw ingredients that tonight was a big deal disguised to look like no big deal. His mother pulled a bag of jumbo shrimp out of the fridge—all peeled and deveined and steamed to a lurid pink. At least fifty dollars worth of shrimp, which his mother shook out of the bag onto a hand painted platter that one of Garrett's cousins had made on a rainy day. She took a bottle of cocktail sauce out of the fridge, then grinned at Garrett sheepishly and said, "I think I'll doctor this a little." She proceeded to mix in mayonnaise, horseradish, lemon juice, and a generous splash from the vodka bottle she kept in the freezer. "We have chives, I think," she said. "For a garnish."

"What do you want me to do?" Garrett asked. "You need help, right? When did you go to the fish store?"

"This morning before you got up," she admitted. "Why don't you set the table."

"Okay," he said. "How many of us are there again?"

Beth paused. "Eight, right? Isn't that right? Set the table for eight people. The dining room table."

"Do we have eight of everything?" he asked.

"If not, make do," Beth said. "This is no big deal. The world won't end if someone is short a steak knife."

"Obviously not," Garrett said. He checked a few drawers and found five disintegrating straw place mats and three green plastic place mats that were meant to resemble large cabbage roses. He laid these out on the dining room table, pleased by how awful they looked. As he headed back to the kitchen to find napkins, he bumped into Beth. She eyed the table over his shoulder.

"No, Garrett, sorry," she said. "Those are hideous. I brought the place mats from home, the blue ones, and the napkins. They're in one of the plastic bags in the pantry."

"But you said—"

"Thanks, sweetie." She collected the place mats quickly, like a poker player who didn't want anyone to see her losing hand. "These are going right into the trash."

For the next hour, Garrett watched Beth break all her promises. The blue linen place mats and matching floral napkins went on the table along with the "good," meaning unchipped, china, three balloon wineglasses for the adults, and a bouquet of daisies and bachelor buttons that Beth had somehow found time to purchase at Bartlett Farm. Beth asked him to wash the silverware before he put it on the table, even though it was already clean. As Garrett stood at the sink, he catalogued all the effort that went into the dinner. The thick steaks seasoned with salt and pepper, the baking potatoes scrubbed and nestled in foil, the asparagus trimmed and drizzled with the special olive oil from Zabar's. The butter brought to room temperature, the sour cream garnished with chives, and while his mother was at it, a little crumbled bacon.

It was the smell of bacon, maybe, that lured Marcus down from his room.

"What's going on in here?" he asked.

"Don't you remember, Marcus?" Beth said. "We're having dinner guests."

"Who?"

"Old friends of mine," Beth said. "And their kids. Two girls. A little younger than you."

"Okay," Marcus said. "Can I help?"

"Where's Winnie?" Beth said. "It's five minutes to seven. They'll be here soon."

"Her door was closed," Marcus said. "She must be napping."

Beth let out a very long stream of air and Garrett knew this meant she was trying to hold back her tears. He wanted to yell at her. It was a terrible idea to throw this dinner party, what was she trying to prove, anyway? What made her think she could act like a happy, normal person? But as angry as Garrett was with Beth, he felt sorry for her, too. Her pain was as real as his own and Winnie's; it was immense and unwieldy and it had a deeper element—she had lost the man she was in love with. Dr. Schau had gone over this with Garrett many times: losing a spouse was different, and yes, worse, than losing a parent.

"I'll go get her," Garrett conceded.

"Thank you," Beth said. "Marcus, would you like a Coke?"

Garrett marched upstairs and tapped lightly on Winnie's door.

"Go away," she said.

"Winnifred!" Garrett said in his most playful falsetto. "Winnifred, open the door this instant!"

"Fuck off, Garrett," she said.

Garrett cracked open the door. It was a much-disdained fact that none of the doors in Horizon had a working lock. Winnie was curled up on her narrow bed wearing her sweatshirt and a pair of jean shorts.

"You have to come downstairs," he said. He paused, then decided to try one of their father's favorite jokes. "We're having people for dinner."

Winnie sat up. She'd been crying, of course, but she gave him a tiny smile. "I hope they taste good," she said.

For the first time in a long time, Garrett felt a connection with his sister. No matter what happened with their mother, the two of them could keep their father's spirit alive. "I'm serious. Mom wants you to come down."

"Not a chance," Winnie said. "I'm not hungry and I don't want to meet anyone new."

"Me either," Garrett admitted.

"Teenage girls. Yuck. Marcus will probably fall in love with one of them."

This was something Garrett hadn't considered. He figured the daughters would be awkward and gangly, with braces and zits. But maybe Marcus would have the hots for one of them and then Garrett could stop worrying about Marcus and Winnie.

"Okay," he said. "I'll tell Mom you don't feel well."

"Thanks," Winnie said, snuggling back down into her pillow. "You're my best friend, you know that?"

"Yeah," Garrett said. This little bit of affirmation from his sister made him happier than it should have. He really needed to get a life.

❧

The doorbell rang as Garrett was coming down the stairs. Beth shouted, "Garrett, would you let our guests in, please?" He cursed to himself and considered running back upstairs to hide with Winnie in her room. His newly discovered sense of optimism dissolved. He dreaded opening the door.

But open it he did, to find a man and two girls.

"You must be Garrett," the man said. He thrust a bottle in a brown paper bag into Garrett's hands, then stepped aside and ushered the girls in. "I'm David Ronan, and these are my daughters, Piper and Peyton."

"Hi," Garrett heard himself say. His mind was grappling with two equally alarming facts. The first was that the mother, the wife, Mrs. Whomever, didn't seem to be present—Garrett glanced out toward their car, a silver Dodge Dakota pickup, but no, she wasn't lagging behind carrying a pie or anything. This was it: just the man and two girls. Garrett had been duped. This was a date for his mother, after all. But before he could deal with that thought, he needed to contend with the other pressing fact, which was that one of the girls, the older, taller one, was a complete knockout. As in, one of the hottest chicks Garrett had ever seen. "Hi," he said, right into the girl's face. "I'm Garrett Newton."

"Piper," she said. She had long light brown hair and green eyes and what looked to be an incredible body. She wore a tank top and tight white shorts and sandals with cork heels. She had two silver hoops in her right ear, and a diamond stud in her nose. She was a goddess. Beth appeared in the hallway and gushed, "Welcome to Horizon, let's go out on the deck, we'll watch the sun set, can I get you all something to drink?" Garrett nearly hugged his mother, despite the fact that she'd been lying to him about the purpose of this dinner for days.

Thank you, he thought, thank you for inviting this beautiful person to our house. He loved the way Piper moved down the hall, flipping back her hair, shaking Beth's hand, saying "Thanks for inviting us, Beth. It was about time Daddy got out of the house."

"I'm glad you could come," Beth said. She felt Garrett's judgmental gaze boring into her back and she tried to keep her voice light and steady. "It's no big deal tonight. Just a casual cookout."

Garrett remained in the hallway holding the bottle of wine while everyone else moved out to the deck. He needed a minute alone. He watched Marcus shake hands with Piper, then the other girl, who was also pretty, but younger. He watched Marcus and David shake hands. Then he watched Beth and David shake hands and kiss on the sides of their mouths. These greetings took a few minutes, then everyone seemed to appreciate the view, and

Garrett heard Beth taking drink orders. The shrimp was on the table outside and Piper was the first to help herself.

"I'm absolutely *famished*," Garrett heard her say, and he thought how that word, "famished," would have sounded phony if anyone else had said it, but when Piper said it, it sounded retro and cool. Famished.

Beth stepped into the kitchen and Garrett moved toward her holding out the bottle of wine.

"They brought this," he said.

"David just told me he lets Piper have a glass of wine at dinner parties," Beth said. "Would *you* like a glass of wine?"

"Yeah," Garrett said.

Beth took the bottle from him and brought another bottle out of the fridge. The Ronans had only been here two minutes and already she'd resorted to bribery. Arch had never approved of the twins drinking—not even watered-down wine at a fancy dinner. "We won't overdo it though, okay?"

"Okay."

Then, suddenly, Beth sensed something wrong. She checked her jeans pockets as though she'd misplaced her wallet. "Where's your sister?"

"Upstairs. She's sick."

"Sick?"

"Yeah."

They both paused for a minute, thinking the same thing: Winnie was sick, very sick, but not in a way that should keep her from this dinner party. Garrett could tell by the liberal way his mother poured the wine that she was going to let it go. She handed Garrett two glasses to carry out. "Let's go socialize," she said.

The world was treating him fairly again. That was what Garrett thought as he sat on the end of a chaise lounge at Piper Ronan's feet, drinking wine, watching the sun set from the deck of his family's summer home. The party had split up into three conversations: David chatted with Marcus, Beth talked to the younger daughter, Peyton, and that left Garrett to hang out with Piper, who immediately started asking him what it was like to live in Manhattan. It must be cool, she said, to actually *live* in the same city with the Empire State Building and Greenwich Village. The Metropolitan Museum of Art and the Guggenheim *and* Soho. Garrett felt like a rock star. The wine went right to his head.

"Yeah, it's okay," he said. "I mean, I was born there so I don't know what's it's like to live anywhere else. Except here, I guess, in the summer."

"Do you take cabs all the time?" Piper asked. "Do you take a cab to school?"

"I walk to school," Garrett said. "Danforth's on the Upper East Side, where I live."

"Upper East Side," Piper said. "God, I just *love* the way that sounds! I can't wait until I graduate from college. I'm moving to Manhattan. What about clubbing? Do you go clubbing?"

"Sometimes," Garrett said. "But that scene gets old pretty quick. There are long lines and the people are fake, and you come home smelling like smoke."

"Oh," she said. She sounded crestfallen. "Really?"

He took a long moment to drink some wine. "Yeah. But some great bands play in the city. At Roseland and Irving Plaza. I saw Dave Matthews last year, and Fishbone."

Piper lay back in the chaise and waved her wineglass in the direction of her father. "Save your money, Daddy!" she said. "I'm headed for the Big Apple!"

David groaned. Garrett looked at Piper's ankles and let his eyes glide up her legs, over her tight shorts, the six inches of exposed midriff to her breasts, which he knew better than to stare at for too long, to her face. She was smiling at him.

"Want to go for a walk on the beach later?" she asked.

"Yeah," he said. The wine made him feel like he was levitating. "Definitely, yeah."

"There it goes!" Beth cried out. She leaned over the railing and pointed at the sun, which was just about to sink into the ocean. Beth led them in a round of applause. "Garrett, will you light the grill?" she asked. "It's getting time to eat."

Beth controlled the dinner conversation like it was a big, unwieldy bus that she had to keep on safe roads: What was it like to live on Nantucket year-round? How did Peyton like school? Where was Piper applying to college? Every time Piper opened her mouth, Garrett stopped chewing and listened.

"I'm only applying to three schools," she said. "BU is my safety, BC is my probable, and Harvard is my reach."

"Boston schools," Beth said.

"I'm a city person. I wanted to apply in Manhattan, but Dad said no."

Garrett looked at David Ronan. He was busy digging every last bit of potato out of the skin. He took a sip of wine and cleared his throat. "I have to keep the girls close otherwise they'll never come see me and I'll be left alone."

"Where's your wife?"

Everyone at the table stopped eating, or maybe it just seemed that way to Garrett who sat in utter confusion. The words had been right there in his brain, in his mouth, but he never would have had the guts to speak them aloud. No, it was Marcus who'd asked. Marcus who had already finished every bite of food on his plate and who was reaching for more salad had asked the question. *Where's your wife?*

Quietly, David said, "She's on the Cape."

Marcus loaded his plate with salad. "The Cape?"

"Cape Cod," Beth said.

"We're separated," David said.

"My mom is a caterer now." This came from Peyton, the younger girl, who, Garrett noticed, had a piece of meat stuck in the front of her braces. It was the first thing Peyton had said at dinner other than "please" and "thank you." "She makes little quiches."

"She makes a lot more than just quiches, Peyton," Piper said. "She's chosen to pursue her life's dream, and that's one of the beauties of living in this country. Freedom to change your life if you don't like the way it's going."

"Freedom to leave your husband and children if that's what your heart desires," David said. Garrett watched him empty the contents of the wine bottle into his glass and then carry the empty bottle into the kitchen. "Shall we open the bottle I brought?" he asked Beth.

Beth was cutting her steak into tiny pieces and moving them around her plate, a trick she'd learned from Winnie, to make it look like she'd been eating. She turned her head in David's direction; her cheeks were hot. "It's on the counter."

"Maybe you shouldn't drink any more, Dad," Piper said.

"Maybe you should keep your opinions to yourself, young lady," David said.

"God, you're being so confrontational, I can't believe you." Piper touched the diamond stud in her nose with her pinky finger. "You're angry at Mom and it's causing you to drink too much. Or maybe," she said, "maybe you're drinking too much because you're nervous about seeing Beth."

Garrett's stomach flipped. He put down his knife and fork with a clang. "May I be excused?"

Piper's eyebrows shot up. "Did my saying that *upset* you?"

David came back into the dining room, pulling the cork from his bottle of wine. "This is a Bordeaux," David said to Beth as he filled her empty glass. "I hope you like it." He threw a killer look at Piper. "You, my dear, aren't making many friends at this table."

Peyton, too, dropped her utensils abruptly and held her face in her hands. "She does this all the time."

"I do *what* all the time?" Piper demanded.

"Make trouble for Daddy."

"I wasn't making any trouble," Piper said. "I was merely defending our mother and her choices. She's running her own *business*, for God's sake."

Suddenly, Marcus spoke up. "It's my fault," he said. "I shouldn't have asked."

"It's not your fault, Marcus," Beth said, and this made Garrett angrier than anything else that had been said all evening. Of course his mother would jump to Marcus's aid, and *of course* nothing was Marcus's fault, even when it was.

Beth tried to change the subject. The bus was swerving. "We have ice cream for dessert," she said. "Ben & Jerry's."

"I've lost my appetite," Piper said.

"You're being rude," David said. "I expected more from you."

Piper flipped her hair in response. "I'm only playing the role you cast me in," she said. "The difficult child? I hear you say so all the time."

"That's enough, Piper," David said and Garrett could tell he meant business. Garrett's own father never raised his voice; when Arch got angry he became cool and polite in a way that let you know you'd disappointed him, and then you'd be willing to cut off your left hand to make him talk and joke with you again.

Piper stood. "Garrett and I are going for a walk on the beach," she said, and with that, she stormed through the kitchen and out onto the deck.

Garrett remained in his chair, returning the stares of the other people at the table: Peyton, Marcus, David, his mother.

"Go ahead," Beth said.

He almost stayed put just to spite her—he didn't need his mother's permission to walk on the beach—but his desire to be outside with Piper overwhelmed him. He went.

She was smoking a cigarette and he wondered where she'd gotten it until he noticed a jean jacket lying across a chair and he figured there must be cigarettes and a lighter in the pocket. She was sucking on the cigarette in an angry way, like the young, jilted, male lover in an old movie, and Garrett understood it was high drama for his benefit.

"I can't stand it when people smoke," he said.

"Why should I care what you think?"

"You shouldn't care," he said.

"I don't."

"Fine. Do you really want to go for a walk or were you just using me as an excuse to leave the house?"

"I'll walk."

"If you're walking with me, please put out the cigarette."

She stabbed it on the sole of her sandal and flicked it down into the dune grass. "There."

"Yeah, except you littered."

"So call the police."

"You *are* difficult," Garrett said.

"As advertised," she said.

At home, in New York, Garrett had success with girls, mostly because they weren't important to him. Soccer was important, his grades were important, and his friends were important—and by putting these things first, Garrett found he could have any girlfriend he wanted. Girls loved to sit on the sidelines at Van Cortland Park watching him play striker, they loved it when he left beer parties early because he had a math quiz the next day. Morgan, Priscilla, Brooke—they all went out with him whenever he asked and allowed him to touch their bodies in various ways. He'd lost his virginity the previous Christmas to a girl named Anna, who was a freshman at Columbia. He met her at Lowe Library while he was doing special research for a paper on Blaise Pascal; she showed Garrett how to access the university computer system, then later invited him back to her room and once they started making out, Garrett discovered he couldn't stop and she didn't force him to. His father had given him condoms for his sixteenth birthday and made Garrett promise to always use them. "I don't want anything to happen to you or anyone you're close to," he said.

Garrett didn't see Anna again—she went home to Pough-keepsie for Christmas break and never resurfaced.

Garrett didn't tell his father that he lost his virginity; he was too embarrassed.

He got an A on the Pascal paper.

❧

As Garrett led Piper down the steep staircase to the beach, he felt his attitude about girls changing. Maybe because this girl was so beautiful and spoke to her father with exactly the same rage that Garrett felt for his mother. He wanted this girl. That was what he thought as they took their shoes off and stepped on the cold sand.

There was no moon, but there were millions of stars. Garrett craned his neck to get a good look.

"I never see stars like this," he said. "In New York, the sky is pink at night."

Piper pulled her jean jacket close to her body. "I can't wait to go away to college. I can't wait to get off this rock."

"You were hard on your dad," Garrett said.

"He drives me nuts."

"Which way do you want to walk?" Garrett asked.

She pointed to the left. The beach was dark—only a couple of houses along the bluff had lights on—and the ocean pounded to their right. Garrett felt pleasantly buzzed from the wine, pleasantly buzzed from the way Piper had managed to set them free from the dinner party. He felt bold and confident—he took Piper's hand, and she let him. They walked, but the only part of his body that Garrett could feel was his hand. He was so consumed by it that he couldn't think of a single thing to say.

"Do you have a girlfriend?" Piper asked him.

"Not right now," he said. "What about you?"

"I have lots of girlfriends." She giggled.

He tightened his grip on her fingers. "Boyfriend?"

"Sort of."

"Oh."

"I'm breaking up with him tomorrow."

"How come?" Garrett said.

"Because I met you," she said.

Garrett sent a message to his father, whom he sometimes thought of as a satellite dish in the sky, always there to receive information. *Are you listening to this?*

"He's just a stupid football player, anyway," Piper said. "He's never been anywhere."

Garrett imagined the hulking, unsophisticated brute who was currently Piper's boyfriend. Garrett knew the type—the kind of guy who would pound Garrett into the sand like a horseshoe stake if he knew Garrett was holding Piper's hand right now.

"If you could go anywhere in the world," he asked. "where would you go?"

"I already said, New York City."

Garrett had been hoping for a more imaginative answer. "I want to go to Australia. I've wanted to go there ever since I was, like, six years old. I'm going to ask my mom to let me travel after I graduate from high school. I might not go to college right away."

"Really?" she said.

Garrett could tell she thought that was crazy. "I'm different," he said. "My father used to tell me I thought outside the box."

She coughed a hacky, smoker's cough. "Your dad died, right?"

The question took Garrett by surprise and he seized up with

panic. He hadn't encountered very many kids his age who wanted to talk about what happened to his father. Everyone knew, of course. Practically the entire student body of Danforth attended the memorial service. But no one wanted to talk to Garrett about the loss, not even his good friends. The other kids were afraid to talk about it and that made Garrett afraid. He felt that losing his father, that being *fatherless*, was something to be ashamed of.

"Right. My dad died."

"In a plane crash?"

"Yep."

Piper raised her face to the night sky, giving Garrett a view of her beautiful throat. "I can't imagine how awful that would be. Even though I get angry at my dad, I want him alive. If anything ever happened to him or my mom, I'd go crazy."

"Yeah," Garrett said. "My sister's pretty much gone crazy. That's why she wasn't at dinner. We have to keep her locked in her room."

Piper stopped. "Oh, God," she said. "You're kidding."

"Yeah," he said. "I am."

She swatted his arm and walked on. "How has it changed you? Losing a parent, I mean."

It was an insightful question, and one he'd never been asked. How to explain? It was as if his seventeenth year were a bridge that had broken in half. His old life, his life before his father died, was on one side of the bridge, and now he found himself standing on the other side, with no choice but to move forward. What else could he say? He felt jaded now, hardened. The things that other kids worried about—grades, for example, or clothes, or the score of a soccer game—seemed inconsequential. In some sense, losing his father allowed Garrett to see what was important. This moment, right now, was important. Garrett stopped and slipped his hands inside of Piper's jean jacket so that he was touching the bare skin under her rib cage. Her skin was warm; she was radiating heat. Garrett had no clue where he was finding the courage to touch Piper.

"I'm a difficult child, too," he said. "That's how my dad dying changed me."

"So we're two difficult children," Piper said. She locked her hands behind Garrett's back and pressed her hips against his. "However, I notice you haven't pierced your nose."

"Not yet," he said. "But maybe I will."

"You have such a pretty nose," she said. "Don't ruin it."

"*You* have a pretty nose," Garrett said. He leaned forward and kissed the tip of her nose, then lifted her chin and kissed her lips. She tasted smoky, but smoky like charcoal, not cigarettes. He kissed her again, parting her lips with his tongue. She kissed him back for a second or two, enough time for Garrett to marvel at his good fortune, but then she pushed him gently away.

"I'm difficult, as in, not easy," she said.

"Oh," Garrett said. He was dying, *dying*, to kiss her, but he liked it that she had boundaries. And he had all summer to knock them down, so he gave up without asking for more. He took her hand and led her down the beach.

⁂

At ten o'clock, Beth found herself sitting alone at the table with David. The candles were burnt down to nubs, and two quarts of Ben & Jerry's Phish Food had been decimated—Marcus finished one quart single-handedly before he excused himself and headed upstairs. Garrett and Piper were still on their walk—they'd been gone for over an hour, a fact which embarrassed Beth—and Peyton had wandered into the living room, plucked a paperback off the shelf and fell asleep reading in the recliner. Her soft snoring was audible in the dining room where Beth and David nursed the last two glasses of wine.

"Was dinner a success?" Beth asked. Her words came out slurred. It had been a long time since she drank this much. Across the table, David had taken on a mystical aura. Was that really David Ronan in this house after so many years?

"Huge success," David said. "If only because we managed to get rid of all the kids."

"Winnie never even showed her face," Beth said.

"I'd like to meet her sometime," David said. "Is she beautiful like her mother?"

"She's beautiful like Winnie," Beth said. "But she's very sad. I don't know what to do to help her."

"She needs time," David said. He lowered his voice. "What's the deal with Marcus? I asked him if he was a friend of the kids' from school, and he said no."

Beth dropped her head into her hands. "It's a long story. I don't want to get into it."

David stood up. "Come on. Let's go out onto the deck."

"I don't think we should."

"Why not?"

"Because," Beth said. Her voice was louder than she meant it to be, and she noticed a snag in Peyton's breathing, but then the gentle snoring resumed. "Because," Beth said again, "I'm drunk and I can't help the things I'm thinking."

"Such as?"

"Such as, what are you *doing* here?"

"Aside from drinking myself silly?"

"Why did I bump into you at the grocery store my first day here? Why did I ask you to dinner? Why did you have my name stuck to your dashboard?"

David extended his hand. "Let's go out to the deck. Your grandfather built that deck for nights like this one."

Beth rose but she didn't take David's hand. Instead she carried her wineglass forward carefully, solemnly, like a chalice. Out onto the deck they went.

The beach was dark below them. "Should we be worried about the kids?" Beth asked.

"Garrett seemed trustworthy."

"Is Piper trustworthy?"

"With everyone but me."

"She's a lot angrier about you and Rosie splitting up than you realize."

"She's not angry about us splitting. She's angry at me, alone, because I won't give Rosie my blessing."

Beth lay back in the chaise lounge and David pulled a chair up next to her. Beth closed her eyes. Six summers she'd spent with this man—from ages sixteen to twenty-one. That last summer was the most magical summer of her life, until it ended. Ended with Beth's father throwing David out of this house, and Beth watching the whole scene from up in her room, like a princess locked in a tower. She was twenty-one, an adult, with only a year left at Sarah Lawrence; she could have defied her father. That was what David wrote later in the letters that arrived at her college post office box. *You could have defied your father. You could have honored our commitment.*

Beth thought fleetingly of the purple cosmos.

"I never told my kids about us," she said. She took a deep breath. "And I never told Arch."

"You never told Arch?" David asked.

"No," she said, the guilt souring the back of her throat. On top of everything else, the guilt. "I decided to keep that part of my past private. What about your girls?"

"I'm not sure how much they know. Rosie might have said something. She was always jealous of you, because you were first."

"Arch wasn't jealous of anyone," Beth said. "He wouldn't have been jealous of you, even if I had told him the truth. Arch was a man who was perfectly confident in who he was and content with all he'd been given. He never looked sideways, only forward." Just speaking this way about Arch revived Beth. She sat up. "I'm glad you came tonight, David Ronan," she said. "It was good to see you. And to meet your girls. They're beautiful."

"Why does it feel like I'm getting thrown out?" David said. He leaned closer to her and lowered his voice. "The reason why your name was on my dashboard was because I wanted it there."

It was chilly out, but Beth flushed. Heat bloomed in her chest. He wanted her name there.

"Where I could see it." He let his hand fall onto her thigh, as lightly as a leaf.

"This is not okay," she said, lifting his hand. "I'm not yours to touch."

"But you were."

"Yes, I was. Twenty-five years ago. In the interim, though, I married Arch and had two children and lived a very happy and fulfilled life that came to an end three months ago."

"I understand," he said. "You're not ready."

"I may never be ready."

"Well, if and when you are . . ."

"David . . ."

"You don't have to say anything else. I'm sorry I'm being forward. Is it okay if we see each other again?"

"See each other, how?"

"Can I take you to breakfast in the morning?"

"No."

"Lunch?"

"No."

"How about the sunset, then, in Madaket?"

"I can watch the sun set from here."

"Fine," he said. "Be that way."

"You can call me," Beth said.

He seemed placated by that, but only for a second. "This house has no phone," he said.

"That's right."

"Do you have a cell phone?" he asked.

"In New York," Beth said. "I didn't bring it. I didn't anticipate having suitors."

"So how will I call you?"

"I guess you won't. But we'll bump into each other. It's a small island, David. Right now, though, you must go."

"Well, I'm not leaving without my daughter."

"No, I guess you're not," Beth said. She felt guilty because she was the mother of the boy. If it were Winnie out there, she'd feel panicked. But before she could wonder too long about where Garrett had taken Piper, she heard voices, and a minute later, the kids ascended the stairs holding hands. Beth smiled. When Beth and David were seventeen, they'd been dating for a year already. They'd had sex already. They'd said "I love you" already and meant it with all their hearts.

And now here were Garrett and Piper, their children: Beth and David a generation removed. It touched Beth in a way she couldn't name.

"We're going to see each other tomorrow night," Garrett announced.

"Fine," Beth said, as if he'd been asking permission.

"Can you drop me off here tomorrow night around seven, Dad?" Piper asked her father. "If you say no, I'll ride my bike. I don't care if it's dark."

"I'd prefer you not hand me any ultimatums," David said. "But, yes, I'd be happy to bring you here tomorrow." He winked at Beth. Victory for him. Then he woke Peyton and directed his girls out to the car.

Beth and Garrett stood at the screen door until the Ronans pulled away.

"Piper seems nice," Beth said. "She's very pretty."

"You told me his wife was coming," Garrett said.

Beth closed the front door and turned off the porch light. The house was quiet. That was perhaps the most noticeable difference between Nantucket and New York. The absence of noise. "I thought she was coming. I didn't realize they had split up." A little background noise—some cars honking, people yelling or singing or hailing cabs—might disguise the lie in her voice. Here, the lie was naked, exposed. Garrett would hear it.

"Piper told me her dad considered this to be a date."

"David might have considered this a date," Beth said. "But I didn't."

Garrett looked at her in a way that let her know he could see right through her. She hoped and prayed that Piper didn't know about her and David. Every man, woman, and child was entitled to a secret and Beth had hers; she didn't want to fear its disclosure if Garrett and Piper started dating. She grew angry at the unfairness of it—it was *her* past, her secret, her history, years before she met Arch and had these children. It was not mandatory for her to share it—not even with Arch. Her husband and kids did not automatically own everything that happened in her life.

Beth sighed. This summer was going to be even harder than she'd initially thought. And she could blame nobody but herself. *She'd* invited David for dinner. Disinvited him, then invited him again.

"What are you and Piper doing tomorrow?" she asked.

"Don't know yet."

"But you had a good time tonight?"

Garrett's stare softened into a smile. He looked at the floor. "Yeah."

Beth hugged her son, who was rigid and unyielding in her arms. This was what it felt like to hold an angry teenager.

"Okay," she said. "Sweet dreams."

Winnie woke up in the middle of the night, hungrier than she'd ever been in her life. A voice in her head screamed out for food. She waited until her eyes adjusted to the dark and then she padded downstairs to the kitchen. Her mother, of course, had cleaned everything up. (Winnie's father used to say, "Mom can't sleep at night if there's an unwashed dish in the house.") All of the leftovers were in the fridge, covered with plastic wrap. Sliced steak, two baked potatoes, some sour cream. Winnie fixed herself a plate, poured a glass of milk and sat down at the kitchen table. The trick was to keep from thinking about her father. Thinking about her father made eating impossible. Even thinking that one stupid thing: her father lingering in the kitchen after a dinner party while Beth cleaned up. Wearing his blue pajamas and his tortoiseshell glasses because he would have taken out his contacts, the top of his head grazing the copper pots that hung from the ceiling. Drinking ice water from the Yankees mug he'd gotten as a kid that he kept by his bed every night. Saying, "Mom can't sleep at night if there's an unwashed dish in the house." That was Winnie's father in one of his simple, human moments, a moment she never would have given a second thought, except now he was dead and every memory seemed unspeakably precious. It made Winnie upset enough that she stared at her plate of food. Yes, it looked delicious, yes, she was hungry, but no, she couldn't eat.

Then she heard a whisper. "A-ha! Caught you."

It was Marcus. Wearing boxer shorts and a gray Benjamin N. Cardozo swim team T-shirt. Holding an envelope in one hand and his CD player in the other. He opened the fridge and brought out the platter of leftover steak. Popped open a Coke, found utensils, and sat next to her. Winnie felt so happy that she managed to poke open the top of her potato and stuff it full of sour cream. It wasn't eating, exactly, but it was close.

Marcus started in on the steak, eating right off the platter. He noticed her staring at him. "I didn't get myself another plate because I plan to finish all this."

"You eat a lot," she said.

"I'm hungry a lot."

"Me, too," she said.

"You don't eat in front of other people?" he said. "Is that it? Because if I'm keeping you from eating, I'll go into the other room. You need to eat, Winnie."

"I have a problem," she said. She wished she'd just been able to say those words that afternoon at the beach instead of getting angry at him. Sustaining anger at Marcus was not something that made her happy. She loved Marcus! "I have an eating problem." She expected him to say, *Yeah, no shit,* but he didn't. He just chewed his steak, waiting for her to say more.

"What's that envelope?" she asked.

"A letter from my mother."

"Really?"

"Yep."

She paused, hoping he would offer more information. He downed half the Coke, then he belched.

"Excuse me."

Winnie stared at her cold, cream-filled potato. She reached for the salt and pepper. "What does it say?"

"I have no idea," Marcus said.

"You haven't read it?" Winnie asked.

"Nope."

"How come?"

Marcus chewed his steak and drank some more Coke. Winnie trembled internally. She wanted to have a real conversation with Marcus. If they couldn't talk here, in the dark kitchen in the middle of the night, intimacy would be hopeless.

Finally Marcus said, "I don't read my mother's letters."

"Why not?" Winnie asked.

"Because I don't want to," Marcus said.

"But you brought it down here with you," Winnie said.

"To throw it away." He pointed the tines of his fork at her. "Are you going to eat or what?"

Winnie picked up her knife and fork, cut a piece of steak and deposited it into her mouth. Chewed. Swallowed.

It was delicious.

"Good job," Marcus said.

She ate another piece of steak, then some potato, which was good even cold, and she felt her body thanking her. She drank some milk; the screaming in her head quieted.

"Why don't you want to read her letters?" she asked.

Marcus put down his utensils and sank back into his chair, which squeaked. "Girls just have to know everything."

"Your mother's in jail for the rest of her life," Winnie said. "I'd think you'd want to read her letters and maybe write some back."

"My mother's in jail for the rest of her life because she killed two people, one of whom was only nine years old. You know the story."

"I know what I read in the papers," Winnie said, though this was a lie. Arch had asked both Winnie and Garrett not to read the papers, and out of respect for him, they didn't. All Winnie knew about the case were the most basic facts. She'd seen the photographs, naturally, the one they showed again and again of the little girl in black Mary Janes covered with a bloody sheet. Winnie had also caught a clip on TV of Constance Tyler, hands cuffed behind her back, being led from the courthouse in Queens. Winnie was surprised by how pretty she was. No one expected a murderer to be pretty. "My dad said that Constance didn't deserve the death penalty. He said killing the little girl was an accident."

"You don't know what you're talking about."

"Tell me then," Winnie said. She stared at her plate, then to prove to Marcus that she could do it, she devoured her potato until the empty brown skin sagged like an old shoe.

Marcus dragged the last slice of steak through the juices and popped it into his mouth. When he'd left the dinner table earlier that evening, he'd gone up to his room, pulled out his legal pad and tried to write, but nothing happened. He groaned at the memory of the five hundred squandered dollars and the items he now owned in their place. The spent money was a shackle on his creative spirit. Now the writing felt like a job at McDonald's—he had to do it to earn money! He closed his eyes and conjured the face of Ms. Marchese, her full Italian lips painted dark purple. *You're a gifted writer, Marcus.* He'd even considered opening his mother's letter, thinking it might give him a place to start other than with *the blood-splattered sheet, dead bodies in your own apartment.* There was far more to the story than Zachary Celtic knew. But just looking at his mother's handwriting on the envelope pissed Marcus off. *How could you? You killed them!* Before he went to bed, he wrote one line at the top of his tablet: "My mother is a murderer."

Now here he was being egged on to write the next sentence. Only this time by Winnie, and she wasn't paying him thirty thousand dollars. The murders: How? When? Why? He felt his eyes drooping closed in defense, even though the reason he came downstairs was because he couldn't sleep. Maybe if he started slowly, it would come to him. "My mother killed her sister-in-law, Angela Bennett, and Angela's daughter Candy. My uncle Leon has basically killed himself, but you could hold Mama responsible for that one, too."

"Why did she kill them?" Winnie said. "Do you know why?"

"Well, the newspapers made it sound like she woke up one

morning and decided to kidnap and kill people, but it wasn't like that."

This much Winnie knew. Her father *hated* the newspapers. He even went so far as to suspend their delivery of the *New York Times;* Winnie hadn't seen a single edition the whole time leading up to the trial—until the day her father's obituary came out. Arch used to rant, *They're making her out to be a monster! The most esteemed paper in the country and they aren't reporting the facts!* Thankfully, Danforth was a liberal school. Most teachers and kids thought Arch was doing the right thing. *The death penalty is abominable, inhumane,* everyone said out loud. Still, Winnie sensed a lack of understanding because murder was also abominable and inhumane and Constance Tyler was guilty of murder. She could almost hear everyone's unspoken thoughts: *How did Arch Newton get involved in this mess?*

"What was it like?" Winnie asked. She wanted details so badly, but she was embarrassed to pry. She turned her attention to finishing what was left on her plate.

Because Winnie wasn't looking right at him, demanding an explanation, Marcus felt okay to speak. "First you need to know who Angela Bennett is. Angela Bennett was married to my uncle Leon, my mother's older brother."

Winnie nodded, head down. She had only two bites of steak remaining.

"Uncle Leon and Angela were married for twenty years."

"I didn't know that," Winnie said. She was mortified to find this surprised her. But why? Lots of black people were married for that long and longer. She needed to get in touch with reality. As Arch used to say, *The world includes more than Park Avenue and Nantucket.*

"They met in the seventies. At a party somewhere. Angela

was white, Italian, and her parents had some money. Not a lot of money . . . not like you people . . . but some money. Except Angela's father disowned her when he found out she was marrying Leon."

"Because he was black?" Winnie asked. "That is so backwater."

Marcus waited until Winnie finished her last two bites and then he cleared their dishes. Doing something with his hands made talking easier.

"It was the seventies," he said. "Everyone was supposed to be in tune with civil rights, but nobody was."

"So what happened next? The father disowned her . . ."

"And she moved into my grandmother's apartment with Leon. My mother was a senior in high school."

"Our age," Winnie said.

"Yeah. And she told me about the weird stuff that happened when they all lived together. Like one time my mother woke up in the middle of the night and Angela was sitting on the end of her bed staring at her."

"What do you mean, 'staring at her'?"

"She was just staring at her. It really freaked my mother out. She thought from the beginning that Angela was bad news. But then, a while later, my mother found out that Angela was into drugs and the reason she was in my mother's room was because she had lifted money and jewelry and stuff from my mother's dresser. Angela and Leon basically robbed my grandmother of everything she had and spent it on smack. Somehow Angela accessed my grandmother's savings account and emptied it. My mother's college money. That was why she only stayed a year at Princeton. Angela spent Mama's college money on drugs for her and Uncle Leon."

"Your mother must have been angry," Winnie said.

"That was only the beginning," Marcus said. Oh, was it ever. He washed the plates and left them to dry in the rack, then he turned off the light over the sink and came back to the table and sat next to Winnie. The kitchen was dark now and they could hear the sound of the waves through the open window. Marcus lowered his voice.

"Angela was like a disease in the house, my mother said. She basically caused my grandmother to die of a heart attack, and once my grandmother was dead, Angela and Uncle Leon kicked Mama out of the apartment. But she said she was glad to go. She married my father a little while later and then I was born."

"It must have been the proudest day of your mother's life," Winnie said.

Marcus smiled sadly. "Except my mother never wanted to be young and married with a child. She wanted a career, you know, something better." This was easy for Marcus to understand but difficult to swallow. What his mother had dreamed of her whole life was something other than Bo Tyler, Marcus, and LaTisha. Constance was the smartest person Marcus knew—she had a near-perfect score on her SATs, a fact she'd reminded Marcus of since he was in the ninth grade. She used words like "egregious" and "polemic." She did the puzzle in the back of the *Times* magazine. Once Marcus was old enough to understand how smart she was, he began to wonder what she was doing still living in Queens. In his earliest memories, Constance's favorite topic of conversation was what her life *could* have been like. Her year at Princeton had taken on a romantic shimmer that Marcus was pretty sure hadn't existed at the time—the tailgate parties, the eating clubs, the fireplaces in the living suites that they kept lit

as they studied for finals. One of Constance's English professors
reading aloud from a paper Constance had written on James Bald-
win. Constance had sung madrigals in Latin and Italian and
French. She ran the one-hundred-meter hurdles for the track
team in the spring.

From his father, Marcus also knew a few of the less glamorous
details. His mother had a work-study job in the dining hall that
required her to wear high rubber boots and long rubber gloves
and spend fifteen hours a week scraping trays and loading an
industrial dishwasher with a crew of university-employed food
service workers, all of whom were black women from Trenton.
Marcus learned that Constance had initially been assigned to a
living suite with a girl from Hattiesburg, Mississippi, who pitched
such a fit about having a *Negro* roommate that Constance was
moved, for her own good, the dean of students said, to a living
suite with twin girls from Pakistan. But to hear Constance tell it,
if it hadn't been for Angela and Leon, her life would have been
a cake walk. It would have meant a real career as a college professor; it would have meant a brownstone apartment in Manhattan filled with books and leather furniture. It would have meant
a husband, possibly even a white husband, who sat on boards
and took her to the symphony.

Instead, Constance's whole slumping, resentful demeanor suggested she had gotten stuck with Bo, Marcus, LaTisha, a job
working for the New York Board of Education, and an apartment
in the same neighborhood she grew up in.

Marcus noticed Winnie staring at him, waiting for more.

"Angela and Leon got hooked on smack," he said. He cringed
at how typically urban, how typically *black* this sounded. "Then
Angela disappeared for a while. She ran off with another man

for two years, and my mother managed to get Leon into rehab. But Angela turned up again with this baby girl, Candy. My uncle went right back to her."

"Why?" Winnie asked. "If she had a baby with another man. Wasn't your uncle angry about that?"

"Some people like what's bad for them," Marcus said, parroting his mother's words on the topic. "Leon was under this woman's spell. She asked him to do all this crazy stuff. Do drugs, steal money from his friends." Marcus paused for air. He didn't want to tell the story anymore. It was too gruesome. But this was the point Zachary Celtic had tried to make during their lunch: the grislier the content of the book, the more people would flock to buy it. Marcus eyed Winnie; he thought of the five hundred dollar bills slipping through his fingers like water.

"When Candy got older, and I'm talking, like, eight and nine years old, Angela used to pimp her out. Let men come to their apartment and have sex with her daughter for money. Because neither she nor Leon worked that was, like, their source of income."

"I think I'm going to be sick," Winnie said. Her stomach was churning in an unpleasant way and she concentrated on her breathing. Her science teacher, Mr. Halperin, told their class once that nearly all pain could be managed by deep breathing.

"I should stop," Marcus said. He knew, though, that even if he stopped talking, he wouldn't be able to stop the images: how Angela used to dress Candy up like a woman, in nylon stockings and high heels. Marcus and LaTisha joked about it—the way Candy teetered around in the heels, the nylons bunching around her skinny, eight-year-old ankles. They had no idea what was going on, that Angela was offering Candy up to the low-life men

who hung around their apartment building. Marcus had no idea
that this was why Constance bought Candy the pair of black
patent leather shoes and thick white cotton tights—so that she
would look like a little girl and not a prostitute.

"I'll be okay," Winnie said. "Go ahead."

"When my mother found out what Angela was doing—when
she found out how *bad* it all was—she demanded that Angela let
Candy live at our house. She told Angela if she didn't let Candy
come to our house to live, she'd call the police. But it was tricky,
see, because *then* Angela told my mother that Leon had been
having sex with Candy, too, and so he'd be the first person to
go to jail."

Winnie felt herself shaking on the inside. Marcus took her
hand, and this surprised her. His hand was huge and warm,
which made Winnie realize how small and cold and brittle her
own hand was. She stared at their interlocking hands. He stared,
too, confused by his own gesture. He'd taken Winnie's hand
instinctively, like he was reaching out to steady himself.

"My mother decided she didn't care about Leon and she didn't
think Angela would turn him in anyway since he did all the dirty
work scoring their drugs. Angela never left the house; she just
laid in bed all day, got high and ate Hostess cakes." Marcus
emptied the last few drops from his Coke can into his mouth,
then with his free hand he pried off the tab and dropped it into
the can. "My mother was a teacher so she planned it." There it
was, the premeditation. "On October seventh Candy had a half
day of school because of in-service. My mother waited for Candy
on the street at noon and brought her home. Like, to live with
us." *Intent to abduct,* the D.A. said. "Mama gave her some lunch
and told her, you know, that Angela and Leon were sick and

needed time to get better so Candy was going to move in with us. Candy nodded and said she understood but she was crying. Mama gave her a glass of milk and let her watch cartoons on PBS." Marcus rattled the Coke can, a sound effect—his jittery nerves, his dried-out brain rattling in his skull. "Angela wasn't as clueless as my mother thought. When Candy didn't make it home from school she knew where to look. She came over to take Candy back."

Here was where the story got convoluted—for the judge, for the jury, and for Marcus. Why did Constance let the woman in? In his mind, Marcus reconfigured the end of the story so that Mama just bolted the door shut and waited for someone else to get home—Bo, Marcus, even LaTisha. Or waited for one of the neighbors to call the police. There might have been an ugly scene, but no one would have been killed.

꙳

Marcus was in the room the first time Arch met with Connie at Riker's. Bo and LaTisha had walked out—Marcus could tell his father was nervous about having a private attorney show up because how would they ever pay for it? Connie asked Marcus to stay. The public defender was a milky-skinned woman named Fiona Dobbs who got bright pink spots on her cheeks when she spoke to Constance. She was twenty-seven years old, eighteen months out of Pace Law School, and although there was no way her defense would be effective, Constance felt comfortable around her. Arch was another story—a tall, successful-looking man with such a cheerful demeanor that Marcus wondered if he realized the reason they were here was *murder*. Arch introduced himself, shook hands with both Connie and Marcus, smiling right into their eyes. To Connie, he said, "We were freshmen together at Princeton. 1975, right?"

"Right," Connie answered warily, as if it were some kind of trap. "Did I know you?"

"No," Arch said. "But that's why I'm here. I looked you up in the facebook. I thought maybe I could help you."

"I can't afford your help," Connie said.

Arch sat down and pulled a yellow pad out of his briefcase. "Free of charge," he said. "Let me ask you a couple of questions."

A couple of questions turned into her whole life history up until the murders. Marcus fell asleep, his head resting against the cinder block wall behind his chair, his arms crossed in front of him. When Arch started asking about October seventh, Marcus opened his eyes. Arch's voice was much more serious.

You were holding the knife when you opened the door?

I was trying to scare her.

That doesn't answer my question.

Yes, I was holding the knife. She was there to take the child, and I wasn't about to let that happen. I hated the woman. I'd always hated her.

That's not something you're ever going to tell a jury. What happened, exactly, when you opened the door? What did you say? What kind of movements did you make?

I can't remember.

You're going to have to remember. They want to execute you, Connie.

My life was over a long time ago.

That's not true. What about your family?

Connie glanced in Marcus's direction, her eyes like a couple of closed doors. Marcus stood up to leave. His father and sister had the right idea. He didn't want to listen to this. *Poor child. It's not his fault. My life was over before he was even born.*

Arch nodded at Marcus, as if giving him permission to go. He leaned forward, elbows on his knees. *Can you tell me what happened with Candy?*

Connie started to cry. *She's dead. God, she's dead.*

※

In Constance's official testimony, there was a fight, a struggle, just like in the movies—a duel between herself, Candy's savior, and Angela, who wanted her nine-year-old daughter to have sex with grown men for money. But in this day and age, you can't lie about something like that. The forensic expert found no evidence of a struggle. Connie opened the door. Angela stepped in and Connie stabbed her.

※

"Whatever," Marcus said now to Winnie, shaking the vision out of his head. "Mama stabbed her to death."

Winnie swallowed sour saliva. "What about Candy?"

What *about* Candy? Marcus might someday forgive Mama for killing Angela—the woman was strung out every time Marcus saw her, with her dark hair wild and frizzy, her skin pasty, track marks like the red eyes of rats running up the inside of both arms. But the worst thing about Angela was her foul mouth, the trashy language she threw around even the youngest children. Words that the worst kid at Benjamin N. Cardozo High School wouldn't dream of using. Angela, in Marcus's opinion, could barely be considered human. But Marcus would never forgive his mother for killing Candy, nor understand how the sweet little girl his mother had tried to look out for—the tights, the patent leather shoes!—and had taken into her home to *save* ended up dead. Stabbed, just once, in the neck. Constance claimed all along that it was a "tragic mistake," that Candy got in the middle of things, that when she saw her mother at the door she ran to her then started shrieking and kicking and lashing out at Constance. "Like she didn't know I was trying to save her," Constance had testified. "Like she didn't understand the sacrifice I was making. I was trying to save the girl's life and she starts fighting me and calling me a bitch." The next thing Constance knew, Candy was bleeding from a dark spot at the base of her neck. Constance called 911 then pressed a bath towel over Candy's wound, but Candy bled right through it.

"Candy got mixed up in it," Marcus said. "Mama cut her, maybe accidentally, maybe on purpose. She bled to death." Marcus squeezed Winnie's hand. "My uncle Leon shot himself when he found out. He blew half his head off, but he lived. He's retarded now. In a state hospital." Head permanently tilted to one side, tongue hanging out like a thirsty dog. Marcus had been forced to visit him once, but would never go back.

Winnie leaned against Marcus's shoulder and closed her eyes. It was the most horrible story she had ever heard, worse than a movie or TV. And it was true. It happened in the life of this person right here. Winnie was impressed by Marcus in a way she knew she'd never be impressed by anybody again. Because he'd survived. Because he'd just had the courage to tell her the truth, instead of making excuses. She was impressed by him because he had the courage to spend the summer with three people he barely knew when he had this nightmare to contend with.

"It's going to be okay," Winnie said.

"No, it won't," Marcus said. "My mother is a murderer, Winnie. She killed a *third grader*. Do you hear what I'm telling you?"

"Yes," Winnie said.

"She's a bad person. Everyone thinks so."

"I don't believe that," Winnie said. "My father would not have died defending a bad person. He didn't think Connie was bad."

"No, he didn't," Marcus said. In fact, Arch's confidence in Constance was the only thing that kept Marcus from drowning. Arch, for whatever reason, was able to see the good in Connie. He was able to make Marcus recall the admirable things about his mother—her beautiful singing voice (she was always a soloist with the church choir) and the way, when she tutored kids at the kitchen table, she would give them as much milk as they wanted, many times sending Marcus or LaTisha to the store for more. "But he was the only person in New York City who thought she deserved to live. Everyone else called her a monster. And they think I'm a monster because I'm her son. At my school . . . whatever, its like I have this permanent stink following me around." He ran a hand over his hair. It needed to be trimmed already—it felt like a pilled-up vinyl rug. "If Arch hadn't taken my mother's case, he would still be alive. Have you ever considered that? Of course you have. Your brother knows it well enough."

Winnie sat with this awhile. True, Garrett blamed Constance Tyler for their father's death. But what Garrett didn't understand was how strongly Arch felt about the case. If Arch had known he was going to die saving Constance Bennett Tyler, he probably would have done it anyway. *If I save this woman,* he told Winnie at EJ's, *my life will have been worthwhile.* And he'd saved her.

"It was an accident that killed my father," Winnie said. "Pilot error."

"I guess we'll all believe what we want," Marcus said.

"I guess we will." Winnie sighed. She waited to see if there was anything else Marcus wanted to say, but she could tell by the way his eyelids flagged that he was shutting down. Their conversation was over. Winnie wanted to talk to Marcus all night long for the rest of the summer. "Want to go up?" she asked.

"Sure."

They ascended the stairs and when they reached Winnie's room, she took Marcus's hand and realized he was holding his mother's letter. "I don't want to go to bed now," she said. "I'm scared."

"Me, too," he said. "I'm scared all the time." He stood close to her in the dark. Winnie thought he might kiss her. She lifted her face and closed her eyes, but then she heard him whisper, "Good night, Winnie," and by the time she opened her eyes, he had disappeared down the hallway to his room.

chapter 3

I can't believe I'm not going to see you for three whole days," Garrett said. He was at the airport terminal sitting on a bench with Piper until her plane was called. She was flying to Hyannis to visit her mom. Beth was parked outside, waiting in the car.

"Ssshh, don't even say it." Piper kissed him slowly with tongue. She tasted like the blueberry pie they'd shared at Hutch's for lunch. Whenever Garrett kissed Piper, he felt like he was falling. A rush went to his head. He shifted on the bench and looked around the terminal: lots of people and dogs and guys carrying toolboxes who stole glances at Piper. Because she was gorgeous, sexy, a knockout. Looking especially hot today in a pink string halter and a little jean skirt. When she bent over earlier at the Nantucket Air counter to hoist her bag onto the scale, he caught a glimpse of her white panties.

"For God's sake," he said, blushing. "Bend at the knees."

Now Garrett held her around the waist, trying to memorize

how her skin felt against his fingertips. He couldn't wait for three days to pass. By the time Piper got back, he was going to have his driver's license. He'd convinced his mother that getting a Massachusetts license was the right thing to do. He could use the Nantucket address, and he might end up going to college in Boston anyway. He and Piper had already talked about applying to the same schools.

"That way," Piper had said, "we'll only have to be apart for one school year."

The thought of nine months away from Piper was too much to bear. The thought of the next three days without her was nearly as bad, since the last two weeks she and Garrett had been inseparable. But she had to leave, she said. This was the longest she'd gone without seeing her mother since Rosie moved off-island in December, and Rosie called to complain, saying a new boyfriend was no excuse for staying away. Piper didn't tell her mother Garrett's name, and she wasn't going to any time soon. David had asked her not to.

"He doesn't want Mom to know that Beth's around," Piper said. "Don't ask me why. Those were strict orders, punishable by a very long grounding, he said."

"I think you should go ahead and tell your mom about me," Garrett said. "If she gets angry at your dad maybe he'll stop chasing after my mom." One bad side effect to Garrett and Piper dating, and Garrett not having his license, was that every time they saw each other, David stopped in to talk to Beth. Or if Beth were the one driving, David came out into the driveway. One night he'd gone so far as to climb into the front seat and ride with them into town. He popped a cassette tape into the stereo without even *asking*, and he sang to Beth. Old-fashioned stuff, like Elton John. It made Garrett want to puke.

"I promised Daddy I wouldn't," Piper said.

"Since when do you keep promises to your dad?"

"Since now," Piper said. "I'd die if I got grounded and couldn't see you. Besides, I'm not ready to tell Mom your name yet. First you have to prove yourself."

He kissed her and bit her lip. "I intend to." As soon as Garrett got his license, they were going to drive out to the beach and have sex. They'd decided this together, last night, when they'd made out on the beach and Garrett's shorts were down to his knees and Piper's tank top was pushed up. She made him stop. She said she wanted to wait until they had a car.

She was a virgin, she said.

A voice came over the loudspeaker: "Anyone holding a green boarding card please proceed to the gate." Piper's plane. She stood to go, her purse hitched over her shoulder. She blinked rapidly.

"I'll have Daddy bring me over the second I get back," she said. "Tuesday at four. Or four-thirty. Okay? Promise you'll be home waiting for me?"

"Promise," he said. He kissed her again until he knew if he didn't stop, he'd never let her go. "Be good."

She skipped out onto the tarmac, waving to him the whole way.

Outside, it was hot. Beth sat at the wheel of the Range Rover reading the *New Yorker*. She smiled when Garrett opened the door.

"Piper got off okay?" she asked.

"I guess," he said. "Can I drive home? I have to practice for my test."

"Sure," his mother said. They passed each other in front of the car, switching seats. Garrett got himself buckled in behind the wheel and started the engine. Shifted into drive and eased out of the parking space.

"You're going to miss her," Beth said. "But you're probably ready for some time alone. You kids have spent every waking second together. That's not usually your style."

"My style's changing," Garrett said. He and Piper had been together so much that he felt weird now, without her. He checked the air for her plane, wishing she could see him driving. As he turned onto the main road, he thought about the past two weeks. He and Piper sat out on the deck in the afternoons drinking Malibu and Coke, they swam, they walked the beach at night and made out in the sand. They rode their bikes to Sconset one day and had lunch at Claudette's. They walked to Bartlett Farm to get Beth the first zucchini of the summer. They went to two movies. They played Monopoly with Winnie and Marcus—with Piper there even that was fun.

There had been only one bad night, the beginnings of an argument. Piper took Garrett to a bonfire on Cisco Beach where kids from her high school were having a keg. They walked there from Garrett's house—a long walk in the dark—and Garrett stepped in a shallow hole and twisted his ankle. Piper stopped to inspect his injury. *A little tender,* she said, *but nothing you can't handle, right? You don't want to turn back?*

No, he said, *it's fine.*

He limped along, enjoying the way Piper held him closer, cooing in his ear, rubbing his lower back. Then they saw the distant flash of the fire and the silhouette of bodies. Piper hurried him along. Her friend Jenna was going to be at the party and her friend Kyle. Garrett was uncomfortable as he hobbled toward the group. The fire was in a pit; it was smoky and a couple of people fed it newspapers and paper bags.

"All the guys at my high school have a car," Piper had told him earlier. Garrett saw the vehicles lined up on the beach: Jeep Wranglers, a rusty old Bronco, and one brand new canary yellow Land Rover Defender series with all the bars.

"We're here," Piper announced to the party in general. There were high-pitched screams and girls came running up to her, kissing her, touching her hair. Just the way the girls at Danforth acted when they saw each other outside of the classroom—freaking out like they'd been separated by continents and decades.

Everyone was looking at Garrett; he could tell even in the dark. So many orange glowing faces. Garrett nodded in the direction of the male population who were either feeding the fire or standing around the keg. He took a deep breath. His science teacher had once told the class that nearly all pain could be managed by deep breathing. His ankle swelled.

"I need a drink," he said.

A kid with a shaved head wearing a fisherman's sweater held up a plastic cup. "Beck's."

"Nice," Garrett said. Piper was completely encircled by friends, and so Garrett made his way over to the keg, found the sleeve of cups lying in the sand and poured two beers. He drank his down right away. His ankle really hurt and he could tell already he was going to have a sucky time at this party. He tried to remind himself that these kids weren't as smart or sophisticated as the kids at Danforth. They drove their Wranglers on the beach, but Garrett was pretty sure they'd get lost taking the cross-town bus.

Piper tugged on his arm. "My friends think you're cute," she whispered. "Jenna actually said '*gorgeous*.' "

Garrett couldn't hide his smile. "Am I going to meet them?"

"Later," she said. "Right now I want you to meet my friend Kyle. He's definitely here. That's his Rover."

"Okay," Garrett said. "Let me fill up." He topped off his beer. It was warm, but it did lighten his mood. "I'm not sure how long I want to stay."

"We just got here."

"What time is your dad picking you up?"

"Not until eleven," she said. "Come on, there's Kyle."

They found Kyle on the far side of the Rover, lying in the sand, smoking a cigarette. A girl sat on either side of him. Kyle wore jeans and a gray tank top. He, too, had a shaved head.

"You guys all use the same barber?" Garrett said.

"Football team," Kyle said. "Who the fuck are you?"

Garrett stepped forward on his good leg. "Garrett Newton. I'm a friend of Piper's. Nice to meet you."

"Garrett's a summer person," Piper said. "From Manhattan, New York City."

Kyle regarded Garrett and blew smoke out his nose. " 'Manhattan, New York City,' " he mimicked in a high voice.

Garrett swallowed half his beer. He looked up into the sky and heard, despite his wishes, words from his father. *These are her friends. This is her life. She wants to show it to you. Yes, it's difficult, life is difficult. If you want easy, date a girl from Danforth. Date Tracy Hayes whom you've known since Montessori.*

"I like your car," Garrett said.

Kyle nodded, then he touched Piper's leg. "Ronan," he said. "Where've you been lately?"

"With Garrett," she said.

"You were supposed to meet us at Ego's on Tuesday."

Piper swatted Kyle's hand away, like it was a fly on her food. "I was busy Tuesday. With Garrett."

Garrett laughed nervously. "You actually know someone named Ego?"

"Nickname," Piper said. "My old boyfriend. They call him that because he's so full of himself."

One of Kyle's girls stood up to get Kyle another beer and Kyle pulled Piper down into her place. Then he passed her his cigarette and she took a drag. Garrett shifted his weight. He couldn't believe she was smoking. He was about to say something when Kyle slid his arm around Piper's waist and pressed his face against her stomach to make a farting sound. The girl on the far side of Kyle, who looked completely stoned, burst out in giggles, and Piper pushed Kyle's head away. "Gross," she said. "You need to grow up."

"I thought you loved my boyish charm," Kyle said.

"I'm out of beer," Garrett said.

He limped back to the keg and filled his cup, taking the tap from Kyle's minion, then decided he was angry. Piper was smoking, she was letting this asshole Kyle touch her, she wasn't introducing him to her girlfriends which was the reason he came. She didn't seem to care that his ankle hurt. Hurt so much that he dreaded walking home, except that home meant an ice pack.

He left the party without her, trying not to think about how uneasy he'd felt around Kyle or about the ex-boyfriend named Ego, or about how pissed Piper would be when she realized he was gone. He concentrated only on making the dark stretch of beach before him disappear.

She caught up with him an hour later. He was very slowly climbing the stairs to his house. Wishing he'd kicked sand in Kyle's face, thinking he might be better off with Tracy Hayes or Brooke Casserhill or some girl whose idea of a good time did not include smoking Marlboros and fawning over someone who looked like Mr. Clean's delinquent son.

But then he heard her calling his name and when he turned around he saw that she was close to tears.

"Thank God I found you," she said. "I can't believe you just *left*."

"My ankle hurts," he said. "I need to ice it."

"You should have told me."

"It looked like you were having fun."

"Fun?" she said. "With those bozos? I can see them whenever I want. My time with you is precious." She linked her arm through his and helped him up to the deck where Beth and David were playing cards. Garrett realized that David hadn't gone home and come back; he'd been here all along.

"How was the party?" Beth asked.

"Fine," Garrett said.

"Terrible," Piper said. "I need to get out of this place."

Now that Piper was gone, the memory of the party was even more painful to Garrett. Later, Piper had accused him of not liking her friends and Garrett pointed out that he hadn't even met her friends, only Kyle. Kyle was her friend, she said, and Garrett admitted that Kyle seemed like a jerk. *Yeah*, Piper said, *Kyle is a jerk*. They'd left it at that, but somehow Garrett understood that he'd failed in her eyes. The people at that party were her real life, and he hadn't fit in. He was a "summer person." Now, in the car, a turn was coming up and Garrett signaled. He hit the brake kind of hard and the car bucked a little. His turn was tight. If there had been another car at the intersection, he would have smashed it. He sighed.

"What's wrong?" Beth asked. "You're doing fine."

"Nothing," he said. He never talked to his mother about girls, although truth be told, he felt differently this time. Maybe because his mother was connected to Piper through David. Maybe because Beth seemed different now that she was unmarried. Garrett couldn't believe he was thinking such things. He checked his rearview mirror. The road was deserted, ahead and behind. He gave the Rover some gas. It surged forward.

"How did you and Dad meet?" Garrett asked.

"You know the story," Beth said.

"I know the Disney version," Garrett said. "Tell me the real story."

Beth leaned her head back and closed her eyes. "I had just graduated from Sarah Lawrence. I was twenty-two. We met in July. I spent that summer in New York—it was the only summer of my whole life when I wasn't here on Nantucket. Your father was in law school at NYU and he says he was studying on the subway platform when he got distracted by a pair of legs coming down the stairway."

Garrett said, "And he vowed to himself, 'I am going to marry the woman attached to those beautiful legs.'"

"See," Beth said. "You already know."

"But what was it *like?*" Garrett said. "When you first started dating? Did you know you were in love with him?"

"No," Beth said. "I'd sworn off men at that point in my life. I wanted to make some money so I could pay my rent. But your father was persistent. Once a week he took me on what he called 'Date Package A,' which was a fancy restaurant and drinks at a club. Sometimes dancing. Then once a week we went on 'Date Package B,' which was the movies, and beers afterwards. Some nights we walked in Central Park or the Village or Chinatown. We went to the Frick or the MOMA on Sunday afternoons. We ate at the Turkish restaurants on Eightieth Street. Your father knew the city inside and out. I always teased him that he had the subway maps tattooed on the inside of his eyelids."

"He knew every stop on every train," Garrett said.

"He lived with Gram and Grandad on Sutton Place, so he had no rent to pay. They gave him plenty of money to take me out. They wanted him to get married."

"What about you? Did you want to get married?"

"No."

"Why did you, then?"

"Well, because. We dated for almost two years and then it was time."

A stop sign up ahead. Garrett touched his foot to the brake gently. "You married Dad because it was *time?*" he said. "What about being madly in love?"

Beth pointed out the windshield, indicating that it was safe to proceed. "Why are you asking me this?"

"Because I want to know."

"You and Piper just met, sweetheart. It's infatuation. Puppy love."

Garrett clenched his teeth. "Don't tell me what it is."

Beth bit her lower lip. "Okay, sorry. You're right. Yes, I married your father because he was smart and funny and I knew he'd take care of me. I'll tell you something now that I've never told anyone else. I didn't fall in love with your father until after we were married, and even then I can't pinpoint a moment. It was a process—the process of shedding the cells of Beth Eyler and growing the cells of Beth Newton. I very slowly became a woman who was deeply in love with your father. That is the real story."

Garrett turned onto their dirt road and his heart crumbled at the thought of three days in their house without Piper. He reviewed his mother's story. It was funny to think of his mother as a single woman who at one time could have decided to resist his father's advances. Who, in fact, had married his father without loving him.

"So you gambled on him, then?" Garrett said.

"I trusted myself," Beth said. "I had a gut feeling that marrying Arch was the right thing to do."

"If you'd married someone else, you wouldn't be a widow," Garrett said. He pulled into the driveway and shut off the car, hoping his mother wouldn't cry. He wasn't sure why he'd just said that.

"True enough," Beth said. "But I don't regret being married to your father for one second. If I'd known he was going to die at the age of forty-five, I would have married him anyway."

"Really?" Garrett said.

"Really," Beth said. "Because that's what unconditional love is all about. The 'no-matter-what's.' "

Garrett walked into the house. It was quiet; Winnie and Marcus were probably at the beach. He would join them; he felt too lonely to hang out in his room by himself, although he needed to finish *Franny and Zooey*. He wondered, would he love Piper no matter what? Not yet, but Garrett felt the possibility growing. As he changed into his swim trunks, he eyed the urn of ashes on his dresser.

"I never thought I'd say this," he said. "But you were a lucky man."

⚘

With Piper gone, Beth figured she would finally get a break from David. She had seen him every day since the dinner party. When he came to pick Garrett up, he showed up early and knocked on the screen door, and just seeing his silhouette on the other side of the front door brought back a host of memories—David knocking on that door when he was still a teenager. His very presence in her life now was so astonishing that Beth couldn't help herself from inviting him in for a beer. They talked about everyday things—his work on huge summer homes owned by twenty-eight-year-old millionaires, traffic, taxes, the new recycling laws. Every so often, he called Beth by her old nickname, "Bethie," pronounced in a drawn-out New York accent, and as their conversations deepened, he unearthed a memory or two from their summers together: watching the meteor shower from First Point on Coatue, the time they went blackberry picking at Lily Pond and David got stung by a bee, fell into the prickly bushes and ended up the next day not only with awful scratches, but a bad case of poison ivy.

"I can honestly, say, Bethie, I haven't eaten a blackberry since then."

For the first time since Arch died, she found herself able to laugh.

Although she relished the companionship, she was still steeped in the morass of her sorrow. She still half expected to be picking up Arch at the airport on Friday afternoons. She still took a Valium in order to sleep. One night, when Garrett and Piper went to a party, David enticed her into a game of cards on the deck, and she made a point of telling David about her marriage to Arch.

"It wasn't perfect by any means," Beth said. "But it was good."

She and Arch had laughed together. They enjoyed the kids. They took a vacation each winter by themselves, to exciting places—Tahiti, the Seychelles, Venezuela. Of course, it went deeper than that. Beth and Arch had understood each other on every level. They occupied each other's psychic lives. They were each other, to the extent that this was possible in a marriage. Yes, Arch worked long hours in his office downtown; yes, Beth administered every detail of their domestic life. No, they didn't have a lot in common in the way people understood that phrase. Rather, they were opposite sides of the same coin. They complemented each other, completed each other. They'd created a life that glowed.

"I just can't get over him and move on," Beth said. "He was my husband for twenty years."

David appeared to be listening but it was as if he didn't understand her language, or chose to ignore the meaning of her words. Beth grew close to screaming out, *Yes. I loved you but that was years ago and now I need you to leave me alone!*

Yes, I loved you, she thought.

Beth was grateful when Piper went away. She needed time to regroup. To strengthen her resolve.

Horizon had no telephone on principle. Living without a phone was the ultimate nod to a Nantucket summer, which in the mind of Beth's grandfather, was reserved for long hours of undisturbed reading or beach time, leisurely meals. Interaction should be conducted as in the old days: in person. Or by mail. It was outdated, yes, but Beth respected it. She never considered putting in a phone line.

Once Piper flew to the Cape and Beth had a respite from David, she hunted down a phone booth in town. She wanted to call Kara Schau, her therapist. First to set up an appointment, and then, the next day, to talk. It was more than inconvenient to talk to her therapist in the booth outside of Visitor Services; it was embarrassing. She turned her body so that she faced the building. She would keep her voice low.

Kara Schau came on the line sounding chipper and enthusiastic, and Beth pictured her wearing a beige linen blouse and black skirt, her dark curly hair escaping its bun. Kara was a dream—the kindest, most perceptive woman Beth knew. In the months since Arch died, she'd become a friend, which Beth viewed as a problem. She wanted Kara to like her; she wanted Kara to praise her. She didn't want to delve into the messy emotional situation at hand, but Beth needed to talk to someone, and Kara was a professional.

"How's Nantucket?" Kara asked. "I'm terrifically envious, you know."

"It's fine," Beth said. "Therapeutic."

"As long as it's not putting me out of business," Kara said. "And since you called, I gather it's not. How's everything going?"

"Fine," Beth said. "The kids seem to be coping okay. Marcus is adjusting. He and Winnie spend a lot of time together."

"Good," Kara said. "They both need peer support. Garrett, too, but he's not as forthcoming. I would have been surprised to hear that Garrett and Marcus were close. That bond, if it forms at all, is going to take some time."

"They're not close," Beth said. "At first I worried that they would, you know, *fight*, but that problem has been headed off, for the time being, anyway."

"How?"

"Garrett found a girlfriend."

"Already?" Kara said. "Someone he knew before?"

"Someone he just met," Beth said. "Her name is Piper Ronan. Her father and I are old friends."

"Is it serious?" Kara asked. "Are there sexual issues?"

"Oh, God," Beth said. She took a breath and turned to inspect the street scene. Thankfully, it was a gorgeous day and town was deserted. Everyone was at the beach. "I haven't given the nature of their relationship that much thought. They've only been dating a couple of weeks."

"Fair enough," Kara said. "So it sounds like the kids have found peer support. Winnie and Marcus with each other and Garrett with the new girlfriend. That's excellent. They need it. But what about you? How are *you* doing, Beth?"

"I'm confused," Beth said. Her nose tingled. She couldn't believe the way crying had become such a natural instinct for her, like blinking or yawning. "I miss Arch."

"Yes, you do," Kara said.

Tears fell and Beth pulled a tissue out of her purse. "I really, really miss him."

"It's perfectly natural," Kara said.

"But this thing has happened," Beth said. "This man I mentioned? Piper's father? He's sort of . . . well, he's put himself in my life."

Silence. Beth knew this meant she was to explain further, but she was ashamed to say more. Arch had only been gone for three and a half months and here she was on the phone to her therapist talking about another man. Kara would think she was a terrible person, a cheap, insincere person. But Kara didn't know David Ronan.

"Listen, there are some things I can share with you about this man, and some things I can't. He was my first love. We were together for six summers, from age sixteen to twenty-one. We were . . . very serious. Very. And then we split up and I haven't really seen him since. Oh, once, maybe twice a summer. Arch and I went to his house for a party a million years ago. Then, my first day here, I bumped into him at the grocery store and later I found out he'd separated from his wife, and next thing I know, my son is dating his daughter and he's started pursuing me."

"Pursuing you?" Kara's tone of voice was neutral.

"Well, it's not as if he sends flowers every day," Beth said. In fact, Beth half expected David to produce a big handful of purple cosmos from behind his back every time she saw him, but thank God he hadn't gone that far. "He's just always around. Wanting to talk, wanting to have a beer together. That kind of thing."

"Any physical contact?" Kara asked.

"Minimal," Beth said. This was true, thank God. David hadn't touched her in any significant way. But the way he looked at her—the way his eyes ran up and down her body—made Beth feel like she was standing there naked. He made her feel self-conscious about her appearance. She had actually bought a hair dryer and mascara at the pharmacy last week. How to explain *that?*

"And yet you feel confused?" Kara said.

"Part of me feels drawn to this man," Beth admitted. Okay, there, she'd said it. Part of her was *flattered* by David's attention; if it suddenly stopped, she might miss it. But the guilt—God, the guilt was enough to weigh her to the ocean floor. "But it hasn't been long enough. My grief for Arch is so raw, so consuming—it's exhausting. And I feel disloyal because being with David makes me less unhappy."

"Frequently, one sees a couple who is married for a long time, and then, let's say, the wife dies, and the husband remarries right away. It causes confusion and anger in the people close to him because of the very issue of loyalty. One way to explain this behavior is that he believes in marriage. The second marriage as a tribute, of sorts, to the first. Now, I'm not saying this example applies in your case. But it might. You were married to Arch for a long time. This man fills needs that have been unattended since Arch died."

"Maybe," Beth said. Naturally, she and Arch had talked over the years about what would happen if the other one died. Beth had said she would not want Arch to remarry, mostly because she didn't want another woman raising her children. It was a selfish response, but honest. It made her sick to think of Arch married to someone else. When Beth asked Arch if he would want her to remarry, he said, *Oh, Beth, I would want you to be happy. As happy as you could be without me.*

"What do the kids think?" Kara asked.

"They have no idea," Beth said.

"It's interesting, isn't it, that your relationship with this man . . . what's his name again?"

"David," Beth said, her voice practically a whisper. "David Ronan."

"That your relationship with David is directly tied to Garrett's relationship with his new girlfriend. You can expect some conflicting emotions regarding that."

"I do," Beth said. She waited a beat. "So what do you think? It's wrong, isn't it? I have to stop this before it goes any further." She laughed at her own absurdity. "It's wrong to give him any hope."

"It sounds like you want me to tell you it's wrong," Kara said. "And I'm not going to do that."

There was more to it than just David's advances. There was the whole problem of David himself, their shared past. Beth remembered the ride home from the Ronan cocktail party. She could have told Arch then, she could have come clean. But she clung to her privacy. *Every man, woman, and child is entitled to one secret.* Even from her therapist. Kara Schau was the wrong person to talk to about this. Beth was looking for absolution where there was none. Arch was dead. There was nothing Beth could do now except live with her decision. "I can remember when David was the only person who mattered to me," she said. "His voice was the only voice I wanted to hear."

"Couldn't you pursue a friendship with this man?" Kara asked. "You need more friends, Beth. I've been telling you that for months."

"We're 'just friends' right now," Beth said. "The reason I called is because I sense that David wants the relationship to head in another direction."

"Do *you* want the relationship to turn into a romance?" Kara said.

"I can't believe you're asking me that."

"But that's the question here. That's why you called me. You want me to ask you because you're afraid to ask yourself. Do you want a romantic relationship with this man?"

"Arch just died."

"That's right," Kara said. "I'm not going to tell you what to do, Beth. But I will tell you this one thing. It is very difficult, if not impossible, to relinquish and attach at the same time. Do you understand what I'm saying?"

Did Beth understand? The words brought up a series of perplexing images. She pictured herself relinquishing Arch, like he was a security blanket she was clinging to. Relinquishing Arch like he was a heavy suitcase she could put down. Relinquishing Arch like he was the string of a balloon she could just let go. She thought of her kids: Garrett with the urn of ashes on his dresser, Winnie in the raggedy Princeton sweatshirt. But was it that simple? When the ashes were scattered and the sweatshirt doffed, would the pain go away? Would Arch be gone, finally? And what about the word *attach*? Would she attach to David like a barnacle on his boat? Like they were two subway cars hooked together? Relinquish and attach; what Kara was talking about was the flow of energy in opposite directions. Beth twisted her diamond ring, then realized she was keeping Kara waiting.

"I'm not sure," Beth said.

"You have mourning yet to do," Kara said. "Grief to process. You've been through a lot, Beth."

"I know. I think about it all the time."

"Well, don't do too much thinking," Kara said. "Remember what I told you before you left: less thinking and more doing. Hug your kids. Walk the beach. Pick flowers. Appreciate the moment."

"Pick flowers," Beth repeated. Those damn purple cosmos! "Thanks, Kara."

"Call me whenever you need me," Kara said. "The kids, too."

"Okay," Beth said. " 'Bye."

She hung up and hurried across Federal Street to her car. She felt vaguely criminal, like she'd smoked marijuana or trespassed on private property, and she had to remind herself that what she'd done was perfectly legal. She'd just made a phone call.

At noon, Beth left the house for a run. It was hot outside, which suited her just fine. She wanted to sweat, she wanted to punish herself. She couldn't believe she'd had the guts to tell Kara Schau about David. She thought again about Kara's words: *It is very difficult, if not impossible, to relinquish and attach at the same time.* Like trying to drink wine while standing on her head. Like trying to raise a flag in a hurricane. The next time she saw David, she would repeat Kara's line. And what would David say? That they had beaten odds before. They kept their love alive over six long winters. Every year at the end of August when Beth left Nantucket, she cried all the way back to her family's house in New Jersey. Her mother was kind, offering new clothes for school, reciting the names of Beth's friends whom she would see again after three months away. *We'll have a party!* Beth's father said. *You'll forget about that boy before you know it.* But Beth never forgot. She and David wrote letters, they talked on the telephone at Christmas, and once they were at college—he at UMass/Amherst and she at Sarah Lawrence—they visited each other.

Nothing was like the summertime, though. The warm days at the beach, driving David's Jeep to Coatue, getting munched by mosquitoes when they sailed his Sunfish on Coskata Pond. Spending rainy days reading magazines at the Athenuem, skinny-dipping at the Sankaty Beach Club late at night. Dancing at the Chicken Box, back when it still had a dirt floor. Once a summer splurging on dinner at the Galley at Cliffside Beach where everyone applauded when the sun went down. Standing on Horizon's deck looking at the stars while Beth's brothers whistled out their bedroom windows. Driving to the beach at night to kiss, grope, and finally make love in the sand.

They had loved each other so completely. The last summer they were together, David rented a cottage on Bear Street, and everything grew more serious. They practically lived together. Beth invented a fictional friend from Sarah Lawrence—Olivia Marsh—whose parents owned a summer house. Several times a week, Beth told her parents she was spending the night at Olivia's house, and because there was no phone at Horizon, and no phone at Olivia's parents' cottage, her mother never checked on her. Beth and David cooked meals, they lit a fire if it was chilly, they made love in the bed and fell asleep intertwined.

Beth didn't want to think any further. She couldn't. She was running down Hummock Pond Road towards Cisco Beach and she decided to take a left onto Ahab Drive, the road where David lived. This was a very stupid move, Beth knew. This was counterproductive. She wanted to stay away from David! But David wouldn't be home. He was at work, and he ate lunch on the job. The last place she would be likely to see David was here on Ahab Drive. Peyton had camp until four; Piper was away.

Beth had been to the house the one time for the cocktail party, and then several times these past two weeks, but only as far as the driveway. As she ran past the house, she waved. *Hello, David's house.* She glimpsed the manicured front lawn and the flagstone walk where she'd caught the heel of her sandal as she was leaving the cocktail party.

Beth jogged to the end of the street. The roads in this development all wound back into each other somehow, but Beth wasn't sure exactly how, and so she returned past David's house. It was a nice property, she thought. An actual house rather than a summer cottage like Horizon. It had heat, insulation, a garage.

Without thinking, Beth ran into the gravel driveway. It was as if her feet weren't connected to her brain. All Beth could do was narrate to Kara Schau in her mind.

I went inside David's house when he wasn't home. The door was open. I knew it would be. I wanted to look around.

The house was neat. The kitchen was painted bright blue and there was a package of hamburger defrosting on the counter. There were photographs on the refrigerator—of the girls and David mostly, but some of Rosie. I wasn't surprised because Rosie is still the girls' mother, she's still part of their life as a family. It bugged me a little that Rosie was so beautiful in the pictures—the long hair and the long legs like Piper. And the stomach and ass like she never gave birth to one child, much less two. I spent a fair amount of time studying the pictures of Rosie. Then I went upstairs to David's bedroom. His bed was made. He had a copy of the New Yorker on the nightstand. That caught my eye because I was reading the same issue, and then I wondered if he'd bought it because he knew I had read it.

I went into his bathroom, and this was when I began to wonder if I was losing my mind. What was I doing snooping around David's house? I found a framed picture of Rosie and David on their wedding day. The picture was sitting on top of a small bureau and a reflection of the picture was in the bathroom mirror, which was how I noticed it. David looked so young. He was my David, but he had his arm wrapped around Rosie's tiny waist. They both looked very tan and very happy. The picture made me strangely jealous. I was in Manhattan the summer they got married, the summer after David and I split, and I felt as if Rosie had somehow snatched away what was mine—though of course that wasn't the case. Without thinking twice, I flipped the picture down.

Then I heard a noise downstairs and I nearly leapt out the window. A man yelled out, "UPS!" So I jogged down the stairs and there was the nice UPS boy holding out a manila envelope. He said, "Mrs. Ronan?" And I nodded. He showed me where to sign. Elizabeth Ronan.

Beth left shortly thereafter and ran home thinking, *Forgive me, Arch. I am sicker than I thought.*

🌿

That night, she bought lobsters for dinner. She lugged the big cooking pot up from the basement, she melted a pound of butter, quartered lemons, and shucked some early corn.

"We're going to do it right," she said to Marcus and Winnie when they came up the stairs from the beach. "Lobster dinner."

Marcus eyed the dark creatures suspiciously as they lumbered across the counter. "They're still alive."

Winnie's forehead crinkled. "She's going to boil them alive. They scream. I've heard them."

"They do not scream," Beth said. "This is a treat. A luxury. Where's your brother?"

"Upstairs in his room, moping," Winnie said. "He spent the afternoon writing Piper a letter. I told him that by the time he mailed it, she'd be home. He said it's for her to read when she gets back."

"You shouldn't give your brother a hard time," Beth said. "It's nice that he found a friend."

"He said you're taking him to get his license tomorrow," Winnie said. "True?"

"True," Beth said. "Does that bother you? Do you want to take your driver's test, too? You haven't practiced much."

"I'm not ready yet," Winnie said. "I'd fail."

"Dinner's in thirty minutes," Beth said. As she set the table with the lobster crackers and plastic bibs and butter warmers, she thought about how, at heart, she didn't want Garrett to get his driver's license. Once the word "accident" popped into her brain, it was impossible to stop worrying. Another horrible accident. But the good news was that when Garrett got his license, Beth wouldn't have to see David as often. In fact, she might not see him at all.

I'm sicker than I thought.

Beth dropped the lobsters into the boiling water, then left the kitchen, in case they did scream.

There was something festive about the way the table looked with a scarlet lobster sitting on each plate, but Beth seemed to be the only one who was excited about it. Garrett slouched miserably in his chair, and Winnie picked her lobster up by the claw and plopped it into the bowl meant for empty shells.

"I'm not eating that."

Marcus was inspecting his plastic bib. "Weird," he said. "This is a bib like a baby wears."

Garrett and Winnie hadn't even deigned to acknowledge their bibs. "It's to keep the melted butter off your shirt," Beth said.

Marcus frowned, but tied the bib behind his neck anyway. "If you say so."

Beth secured her own bib in solidarity, then she lifted her glass of white wine. "Cheers, everyone! Happy summer."

"What do I do with this thing?" Marcus asked, wielding his lobster cracker.

Garrett rolled his eyes and huffed a little.

"Sorry," Marcus said. "We don't eat a lot of boiled lobster in Queens."

Beth showed Marcus how to crack open the claws, and she

separated the meat of the tail from the shell. This, she knew, was the kind of scene Arch had in mind when he invited Marcus to Nantucket. "You're going to love this," she said. "When you get the meat free, you dip it in the melted butter."

Garrett cracked his lobster. Winnie helped herself to a roll, which she tore into pieces. Once Marcus tasted the lobster, his face brightened. "This is great!" he said. "This is delicious." He picked up the extra lobster. "I'll eat Winnie's if she doesn't want it."

"Go ahead," Winnie said.

Beth sipped her wine. She felt empty, scooped out. As a kid, lobster night was magical. It was symbolic of a good, rich life. Her parents always drank too much wine on lobster night; they sang the old songs. *Falling in love again . . . I can't help it.* Now here she sat, alone, with her recalcitrant twins and this boy whose life was anything but good and rich. Beth felt tears coming, but no, she wouldn't ruin it. She was going to work with what she had. Garrett and Marcus were both eating. Winnie had torn up her roll and was now tentatively considering an ear of corn. Beth picked the snowy flesh out of her lobster claw, dunked it in butter and let the taste fill her mouth. She was doing the best she could.

"Piper comes home tomorrow?" she asked Garrett.

"Friday."

"It's nice to have you around for a change. We haven't sat down to dinner like this in a while."

"We should go out more," Winnie said. "When Daddy was here, we used to go out more."

"What do you care if we go out or stay in?" Garrett asked. "You never eat."

"Shut up, man," Marcus said. "I've seen Winnie eat plenty."

"Thank you," Winnie said.

"Maybe we should go out," Beth said. "Maybe all of us should go out when Piper gets back."

"Who cares about Piper?" Winnie said.

"I'll take Piper out alone, thanks," Garrett said. "And if you want to go out with David alone, then just go. Don't use me as an excuse to see him."

"Who said anything about wanting to go out with David?" Beth asked. She ripped off one of the lobster's legs and sucked the juice out of it. "Are you ready for your driver's test tomorrow?"

"You're changing the subject, Mom," Winnie said.

"What subject is that?"

"The subject of David," Winnie said. "I think we should talk about it."

"There's nothing to talk about."

"He likes you."

"He's an old friend. I've known David since I was sixteen years old."

"If you want to date him, I think it's okay," Winnie said. "You don't have to keep blowing him off because of us."

Garrett gagged on his food, sending a shower of corn kernels across the table.

"Spare me," Winnie said to Garrett. "It's okay for you to be happy with Piper, but it's not okay for Mom to be happy?"

Garrett reddened. "These are personal matters," he said. "Family matters."

"Oh, what?" Winnie said. "Now you're going to blast me for bringing this up in front of Marcus? You suck. You really suck."

"I love you, too," Garrett said.

"I'll leave," Marcus said. "I can eat outside."

"You'll do no such thing," Beth said. "This summer, you're part of the family. You're going to have to tolerate our squabbles."

"I like David," Marcus said. "He seems straight up and down. But he's not Arch. Arch was one in a million."

Everyone at the table was silent at those words. Beth put a finger under her nose. *Don't cry,* she told herself.

"Thank you for saying that, Marcus," she said. "That means a lot."

Marcus shrugged and dug meat out of a lobster claw. "It's true," he said. "Arch will never be replaced. He died trying to save my mother."

"Arch's death had nothing to do with your mother," Beth said. "It was an accident."

"He wouldn't have been on that plane if it weren't for my mother," Marcus said.

"That's true," Garrett said. He looked defiantly around the table. "I mean, no one can really deny that."

Winnie glared at Garrett, then rolled the ear of corn away from her on the plate. "Let's get back to the subject at hand. We won't think you're trying to replace Daddy if you want to date David, Mom."

"I will not be dating David," Beth said. Her voice sounded unusually firm. She wanted to set the record straight, for the kids and for herself. "We're just friends. But thank you for your permission. It's nice to know you realize I'm a person, too. I get lonely, too. In fact, sometimes it's very lonely being the mom."

"But you have us," Winnie said.

Beth tried to smile. "Of course," she said. "I have you."

⁂

Beth sat on the wicker sofa drinking wine long after the kids went to bed, thinking about how unfair it was that David Ronan should reappear to haunt her *this* summer, which was already so painful. She couldn't believe she had gone to his house. She had signed her name as "Elizabeth *Ronan*." Beth cringed, thinking that in a million years she would never have the guts to admit that one to Kara Schau, much less anyone else.

She didn't want to waste her time thinking about David Ronan. She should be thinking of Arch, remembering him. Remembering what was the freshest in her mind—their last day together. It was early March, not a romantic time of the year in anyone's book, but Arch had called mid-morning from the office.

"Lunch at Le Refuge?" he said. "I can get out of here in ten minutes and meet you at quarter to one if traffic's not too bad."

"Sure," she said. "What's the occasion?"

"I have to go to Albany in the morning," Arch said.

"For how long?"

"Just the day," Arch said. "But for a good reason. Alex Benson has agreed to meet with me about Connie."

Alex Benson was an old law school friend of Arch's. He was close to the governor, politically and personally, and Beth knew Arch had been trying for months to set up this meeting. "Anything promising?" she asked.

"Oh, who knows," Arch said. "To be honest, honey, the most

promising thing in my life right now is our lunch date. I'll see you in a little while."

Beth could remember thinking, as she hung up the phone, that she wished Constance Tyler's trial would start and finish, if only because the gravity of it sapped Arch of his usual sunny disposition. Since Arch had started working on the case, he'd become preoccupied, and less tolerant of frivolity. He'd snapped at Winnie the week before for complaining about her SAT prep course.

"Thank God you don't have any real problems," Arch said. "You could be sitting on Riker's Island facing lethal injection or life in prison."

He was impossible now, too, at cocktail parties. He took legal research to the gym and read on the StairMaster.

Taking on the case and taking it on for free made Arch feel righteous. He earned lots of money defending corporate Manhattan against charges of fraud, false advertising, sexual harassment, and general bad faith, but with the Constance Tyler case he felt he was helping someone who needed help. He knew she was guilty, but he was so opposed to the death penalty that to be able to fight it and win just once would make his career worthwhile. His partners at the law firm frowned on all the time the case was eating up, and the enormous expense, but this didn't phase Arch in the slightest. He brought in twice as much business as any other partner—he'd earned the right to take this case, a point he made quietly at the monthly partners' meeting. Constance Tyler was his top priority, period. At times, Beth actually felt *jealous* of Connie, so thoroughly did she consume Arch's thoughts.

At lunch, Arch was in a surprisingly good mood. He arrived before Beth and was waiting at their favorite table with a bouquet of flame-colored roses.

"Look at you," Beth said. "Look what you've done."

"Orange roses," he said, presenting them to her. "They seemed right somehow for a dreary day in March." He kissed her. "I love dating my wife."

"This is a great surprise," Beth said. "I was just at home thinking about how I might clean out the china cabinet."

"Let the china cabinet go uncleaned!" he said. He called the waiter over and ordered a bottle of Sancerre. "I'm not going back to the office today."

"You're not?"

"No, I'm not. Once the trial starts next week I'm going to be slammed. So today I'm going to have a long, leisurely, wine-soaked lunch with my wife and then I'm going to walk her home in the rain and spend the afternoon in bed with her."

What Beth remembered now was how fortunate she felt that afternoon. They drank not one, but two bottles of wine, they ate goat cheese and wild mushrooms and garlic-studded lamb and lemon tart. They talked about all of the things they never had time to talk about at home—trips they wanted to take once the kids went to college, the books they were reading, current events. After Arch paid the bill, Beth floated to the door inhaling the scent of her roses. She was certainly the luckiest woman on earth.

They walked home in the cold drizzle, giggling and falling against each other. Arch pulled Beth past their apartment building, up to Madison Avenue.

"I want to buy shoes," he said.

They went into Giovanni Bellini's, which was hushed and smelled of expensive leather. The sumptuous pairs of hand-crafted loafers were lined up on the shelves. The first pair Arch reached for were an outlandish electric blue.

"To go with my seersucker suit," he said. To the salesman, whose mouth was a grim line, he said, "Ten and a half, *por favor.* Oops, wait a minute, that's Spanish. Beth, how do you say 'please' in Italian?"

She sat on the plush bench in the middle of the room. "*Prego,* I think."

"Like the spaghetti sauce?"

They started giggling and the salesman disappeared and returned with a box. Arch tried the shoes on. He looked adorably clownish—his dark suit and the blue shoes.

"The thing is," Arch said, "some people actually buy these. Europeans."

Beth urged him to be quiet.

"You know," Arch said to the salesman, "these are a little flamboyant for me. May I see the black tasseled loafers in a ten and a half?"

Arch bought two pairs of shoes and three pairs of dress socks. This improved the salesman's humor. When they left the store, he bid them farewell with an authentic sounding "*Ciao!*"

Beth and Arch returned to the apartment and showered together, something they hadn't done in years. They made love on the bathroom floor, then wrapped themselves in towels and fell into bed.

It was dark when Beth woke up. Arch lay next to her, snoring. She was confused for a minute, thinking it was the middle of the night, but then she remembered the lunch. It was still afternoon.

Five minutes to five. Winnie had swimming until six, and what was today? Monday. Garrett had floor hockey on Monday. He'd also be home around six. Beth snuggled up to Arch. She loved to watch him sleep. He slept so devotedly, like he was giving sleep everything he had.

She switched on the TV and caught the last half hour of *Love Story* on TNT. Oliver buys plane tickets to Paris, but no, it's too late. Jennifer has leukemia. She dies, Oliver sits alone in the snowy park. Beth was sniffling when Arch finally opened his eyes.

"Jennifer's dead," she said. She turned off the TV and sank back into the pillows. "I love that movie but I always hope that it will end differently. Of course it never does. We should get up. The kids'll be home soon. They'll need to eat."

"Jade Palace?" Arch said. "Pu-pu platter for four?"

"After that lunch, I thought I'd skip dinner," Beth said. "But I could go for a pu-pu platter."

⁂

Now, at Horizon, Beth poured herself the last of the wine. She remembered that dinner, the four of them at Jade Palace eating potstickers and spare ribs and crab rangoons. She remembered Arch and her sitting in the backseat of the cab with Winnie on the way home—Arch in the middle with his arms around both of them, saying, "I love my girls." She remembered getting home and listening to the phone messages—one message from Arch's secretary, Polly, with his travel arrangements for the next day, and one message from Caroline Margolis inviting them to a dinner party on Saturday.

"Tell her we'll come if she makes her key lime pie," Arch said.

The day ended with Beth calling Caroline to accept, the kids going to their rooms to do homework, and Arch disappearing into his office to prepare for his trip to Albany. Later, Beth and Arch climbed into bed and read for a while.

"This was the perfect day," Beth said. "Thank you."

Arch kissed her. "If I could, Beth, I'd spend every day with you just like I did today."

He was gone in the morning before she woke up, but when she rolled over she found one of the flame-colored roses on his pillow.

The painful part about remembering all the details from her last day with Arch was that these same details were cruelly present two days later—she didn't find out Arch's plane had crashed until very early on the morning of March 16th. Beth was wakened by the phone at quarter to six in the morning, and when she noticed Arch wasn't in bed, she yelled to him to answer it. She didn't realize he wasn't home. He'd called the night before to say his flight was delayed because of weather and he'd be home late, and Beth assumed he came to bed then got up early to work in his study. When the phone didn't get answered and the machine picked up, Beth groaned and reached for the phone through the fog of her sleep. That groan, that action of reaching, was the last innocent moment before learning the awful truth. At times, she wished she could freeze time and stay there, half asleep, in the not-knowing.

It was Trent Trammelman on the phone, the managing partner of Arch's firm. The authorities had called him first because it was the law firm's plane.

Beth screamed like she was falling into a hole she knew she would never escape from. And then, the absolute worst thing she'd ever had to do in her life: tell Winnie and Garrett, who were in their rooms getting ready for school, that their father was dead. Winnie was in her bra and panties, shrieking with embarrassment when Beth opened her bedroom door. Beth didn't remember speaking any words, but she must have conveyed the news in some way because Winnie crumpled to the ground like she'd been hit by a bullet, and Beth sank to her knees and covered Winnie's body with her own, the two of them moaning. Garrett found them there and he, too, started wailing, which really pushed Beth over the edge: her strong teenage son crying like a baby.

Before she knew it, the apartment was filled with people. People from the law firm, friends, Arch's mother, kids from Danforth. In Beth's mind, this happened instantly. The apartment was filled with people and the smell of coffee and cell phones ringing and talk of the black box, and there was Beth still in her nightgown, like one of those bad dreams where she was throwing a party but had forgotten to get dressed. The buzzer from downstairs rang again and again—the florist with sickly-sweet arrangements, her neighbor with a ham, Caroline Margolis with a key lime pie. Was she imagining this? It was all happening so fast, so soon, these condolences, that Beth grew confused. She was waiting for Arch to walk through the door to the apartment and send everyone else home. By evening, hysteria set in. Arch was never coming home. She would never see him again.

One of the people who came that first day was Dr. Schau, who was Trent's wife's therapist. She showed up after office hours and gave Beth a shot and finally everything slowed down. Beth was able to see the horrible things in the apartment that no one else could see: the eleven orange roses, the boxes with two brand new pairs of men's shoes, the leftover moo shu pork in the refrigerator.

The vision, when she closed her eyes, of Oliver sitting alone in the snowy park.

❧

By midnight, Beth had finished the wine but she was still wide awake. She would be forced to take a Valium, but first she stood up and went to the screen door. It frightened her to remember how raw her grief had been. Now, after four months, she had coping mechanisms in place. The thing that helped the most was that she was here on Nantucket. Not only was Nantucket quieter than New York, it was darker. All she could see were the stars and a couple of tiny lights from her neighbors' houses in the distance. Then, a pair of headlights approached. Kids headed to the beach. Drunk, probably. Beth shuddered: when she woke up, she would have to take Garrett to get his license. As the car drew closer to Beth's house, it slowed down. Beth switched on the porch light. David's truck. She blinked twice, certain she was hallucinating. Too much wine. But no—it was David, driving by her house in the middle of the night. Beth's first instinct was indignation, until she realized it was no worse than her walking through his house that afternoon. She opened the door as quietly as she could and tiptoed down the shell driveway in her bare feet. She climbed into the truck.

David was in a T-shirt and shorts. His hair was mussed. Without a word, he drove toward the water. When all that was in front of them was ocean and night sky, he stopped. He undid his seatbelt and slumped against his door. "I couldn't sleep."

"Me, either."

"I missed you so much. I managed twenty years without you, but the last three days almost killed me."

Beth had no idea how to respond to this. Part of her felt the same way—she had gone to his *house!* But, as ever, there was her guilt and longing for Arch. She remembered back to March sixteenth. At night, after all the people went home, she and Winnie and Garrett slept in the same bed. They did that for two weeks.

"David, we have to stop this."

"I feel like a teenager," he said. "I used to do this all the time after you left for the summer. I'd drive by your house and imagine you standing inside the screen door, just like you were doing a few seconds ago. It used to make me feel better to look at your house because I knew you'd always come back to it."

Beth put her hands over her eyes; he was so handsome she was afraid to look at him. The smart thing, she realized, would have been to stay safely inside her house. "We can't recreate those days, David. Too much has happened in our lives."

David rubbed his stubbly chin. "We were in love."

"Yes, we were."

"Were, Bethie?"

"Were," she said.

"I'm in love with you now," David said. "When I split with Rosie . . . when I read about Arch in the paper . . . when I saw you at the store . . . actually, no. Forget all that. I never stopped loving you. I had to *live* here, Beth. I had to live each day with all of our memories. It made getting over you impossible."

"You managed fine without me," Beth said. "You married Rosie the next year. You had kids."

"It was never quite right," David said. "Rosie finally realized it and left."

"You're not blaming me for your separation?" Beth said. "That's absurd."

"It's only your fault in the larger sense," David said. "In the sense that during all those years with Rosie, a part of my heart was missing."

"Don't tell me that, David," Beth said. "Your problems with Rosie are between the two of you. They have nothing to do with me." She remembered the wedding picture she found in David's bathroom. Something about how it was placed so that there were actually two pictures in the bathroom—the picture itself and its reflection—made Beth understand that the picture was important to David. What it represented was important. After all, Rosie was still alive; her marriage to David was still viable. Maybe he'd go back to her. That would be for the best.

"The past two weeks have been the happiest weeks I've had in ages," David said. "Just knowing I would see you, even for a few minutes." He leaned over the console that separated the two seats and took her chin. He held her face and hooked her eyes, making her look at him. Making her see him. What did he want from her? Maybe he wanted her to admit the truth—that she felt the same way, that she, too, looked forward, a little bit, to seeing him, that he made her feel less sad, that he provided hope, a glimpse into what might someday lie beyond all this heavy grief. But a second later, Beth understood that what David wanted was beyond words. His face grew closer; he kept his fingers on her chin. He was going to kiss her.

He was kissing her; they were kissing.

Beth forgot herself for a second. She was tired, she'd had a

lot of wine, and surely just one second wasn't going to hurt
anyone, one second of David's lips, which tasted like the best
young love imaginable, which tasted like summer, which tasted
like home. One second then one second more. David's tongue
touched her bottom lip lightly, and that was enough. Beth
opened her eyes.

"Whoa," she said, pulling away. "Whoa. Wait."

David stared at her. Her cover was blown, her lie exposed.
She wasn't a woman in mourning after all. She had kissed him
back. A hideous blackness gathered behind her eyes and she
gazed out the window at the water. She had kissed him back.

"There," he whispered.

There? As in, *take that?* Beth wasn't sure what he meant by
"there," but it didn't make her feel any better. "Okay," she said,
fresh out of words herself.

"You can pretend that never happened," David said. "I, of
course, won't be able to."

Beth's mind raced around in search of something to say.
A kiss! What a perfect ending for today—she had walked
through David's empty house, she had signed her name Eliza-
beth Ronan, *and for my final trick, ladies and gentlemen* . . . the kiss.
Only months after the death of her husband, she had kissed
David Ronan.

"I'm taking Garrett to get his license tomorrow," she said.
"Once he can drive, the kids won't need us to chauffeur them
around."

"So we'll go out alone," David said.

"We will not," Beth said. "I know I'm sending mixed messages—and not only to you, but to myself. But I just lost my
husband, and unlike you, a piece of my heart *wasn't* missing. I
loved Arch Newton with my whole heart. I loved him with my
mind and soul and spirit."

David straightened his arms to the steering wheel. "Because you left me with your heart intact," he said. "*You* left *me.* I was the one who got his heart broken. I was the one who had to face your father at the front door of that house back there and listen to him tell me that you never wanted to see me again and that I'd be hearing from his lawyer."

"I won't talk about that," Beth said. "And I don't want you to talk about it either."

"You do remember what happened, don't you?"

"*Of course* I remember what happened," Beth said. "But guess what? Splitting with you wasn't the worst thing that ever happened to me. The worst thing was—"

"Losing your husband," David said. "I know, I know."

"You do *not* know," Beth said. "I'm offended that you pretend to know."

"I know about losing the person I loved most in the world," David said. "That's what it was for me when you left."

Beth was quiet. She deserved this and worse, even twenty-five years after the fact. But she felt she needed to address the kiss; she had to let him know that there would be no more kisses and certainly no dating.

"I'm going to ask you to give up," Beth said. "I'm going to ask you to leave me alone."

"I will not give up," David said. "Because some day you'll recover. And when you do, I'm going to be here. I'm going to be waiting for you."

Beth bumped her head against the passenger window. She felt sixteen, as emotionally inept as her children. "I'm tired," Beth said. "Will you please take me home?"

They drove back to Horizon in silence. David let her out at the end of the driveway, but as she walked past his window, he grabbed her arm.

"You never once said you were sorry," he said. "You broke a solemn vow without explaining why. I figured it out eventually—you were too young, you were scared—but you didn't even apologize."

When she looked at him, she saw the past in his eyes. She recognized the look of loss on his face as he stood at the front door of Horizon confronting her father. It was too painful to remember. Beth turned away.

"Good night, David," she said.

chapter 4

He'd been on Nantucket for three weeks but it felt like three months. Or three years. His reality had changed. He was now a person who ate steak and lobsters, he was a person who lounged on the beach and took outdoor showers. He was a person who read Robert Ludlum novels and played Monopoly, amassing paper fortunes.

Now that Garrett was dating Piper, Marcus spent a lot of time alone with Winnie. Since the night he found her eating in the kitchen, they'd grown closer. Marcus saw that Winnie was like Arch—beneath her little-girl, noneating, self-pitying facade lay a decent heart. She listened, she asked questions, and she moved through her days utterly devoted to him, Marcus, a black kid from Queens with a now awful-looking Afro. Not because she felt sorry for him, but because she thought he was special. Marcus could tell she was genuine in this.

After nine months of losing people in his life, he had found a friend.

They spent practically every day at the beach together. Swimming in the waves—almost always the butterfly, which was Marcus's stroke. He was teaching Winnie how to improve her form; he wanted her to be a kick-ass flyer in time for her senior year. When the tide was right, they swam out past the breaking waves where Marcus could still stand on the sandy bottom and he held Winnie—one hand under her stomach, one hand on the back of her thighs—and showed her how to strengthen her kick. He only touched her when they were in the water, and he had to admit, he was starting to like the way she felt weightless in his arms. He liked to watch her body do the stroke, her ass bucking through the water. He liked how she tried so hard to do exactly what he said, *keep your head down, lengthen your reach.*

One day when they were drying off, she said, "So what do you think? Are Garrett and Piper having sex?"

Marcus fell face-first onto his striped beach towel. This wasn't a conversation he wanted to have. Especially since he knew the answer was yes; he'd seen a Trojan wrapper in the bathroom trash when he emptied the can three days before. "What do you care?" he said.

"He's my twin brother."

"I'd think that would make you not want to know."

"Of course I want to know. I mean, I guess it's no big deal if he has sex before I do. He *is* a boy."

"Whatever that means."

Winnie rested back in her chaise. "I just worry about getting left behind."

"It's not a race," Marcus said.

Winnie rolled her sweatshirt up under her bikini top. "Piper is so pretty. Don't you think she's pretty?"

"She's pretty," Marcus said. "But not as pretty as you."

Winnie whipped her head around. "Really?"

"Relax," he said.

"You just implied that I'm prettier than Piper. You think that? Really, Marcus?"

"The correct response was 'thank you.' I never say stuff unless I mean it, but I'm not going to repeat it a hundred times so you can feel all wonderful about yourself."

"How about repeating it once?"

"You're prettier than Piper," Marcus said. Winnie beamed and lay back in her chaise, smiling at the sun. Yes, she was prettier. Piper was good-looking, but she knew it. She wore outfits that put her commodities on display for the world to see. Winnie was pretty in a quiet, natural way, like Beth. Half the time, she looked terrible—hair wet, eyes red and puffy from crying, and always wearing that god-awful, misshapen sweatshirt—and yet her humanity made her beautiful.

As July approached, Marcus found himself with two new worries. The first was that twenty-one days had passed and he'd gotten nowhere with his writing. His legal pad was blank but for the one sentence: *My mother is a murderer.* The five hundred dollars, gone forever, took on *Alice in Wonderland*–like proportions in his mind. He now had three unopened letters from his mother, which he'd stuffed into his left dock shoe. His dock shoes were in the back corner of his closet where he didn't have to think about them. He would only open his mother's letters if he got really desperate. Marcus tried to banish the memory of Zachary Celtic (*your own mother, pretty woman, too, facing the strap-down on the gurney, the long needle . . .*) and concentrated instead on Nick's sole comment, "You get to tell the story in your own words, kid." It was beginning to seem that Marcus had no words. Not on this topic, anyway.

Marcus's other worry was that he was attracted to Winnie. Maybe because she had brought up sex, or because Garrett was having sex, sex became an invisible third party hanging around whenever Winnie and Marcus were together. And sex was out of the question. If it ever happened, Garrett would kill him and Beth would send him home immediately.

Marcus was supposed to call his father every two weeks, but since Horizon had no phone, Marcus only called when he got the chance. At the beginning of July, he called from a phone booth in town. Too anxious to sit, Marcus stood in the booth and stared at the street, all the white people in their fancy clothes shopping for scented candles and needlepoint pillows. The first question his father asked was, "Why haven't you answered your mother's letters?"

"How do you know I haven't answered them?"

"I know," Bo Tyler said, "because your sister and I visited her last week and she told me she's written to you three times and hasn't heard back."

"I don't feel like writing," Marcus said. Man, was that the truth!

Bo made one of his *hmmphing* noises. Then he said, "Your mother needs our support."

Here was the thing Marcus couldn't get his mind around. Constance had committed murder—she was responsible for two deaths, three if you included Uncle Leon, four if you included Arch—and now she needed their support? The Newtons all went to see some kind of therapist to help them deal with their loss, and that sounded like what Marcus needed—someone to help him with his loss. He had lost his mother. She woke up on the morning of October seventh, and without warning, changed their lives forever.

On that day, Marcus was sitting in trigonometry class trying to file away what he would have to remember about sine, cosine, tangent, and cotangent for the next quiz, when the intercom buzzed and the secretary asked for Marcus to be sent to the office. The kids in his class all *ooob*ed and *ub-ob*ed, because a student generally got sent to the office for bad things, although Marcus was one of the least likely people in the class to be in trouble. Marcus himself thought uneasily of how, the month before, his friend Eriq had been called to the office because Eriq's girlfriend had given birth to twin girls. And that was it for Eriq and Benjamin N. Cardozo High School. He dropped out the following week and Marcus hadn't seen him since.

Whatever Marcus was preparing himself for as he loped down the hall to the main office, it certainly wasn't the sight of his father, Bo, in brown pants, yellow shirt, brown sweater vest, his face twisted into an unrecognizable, sobbing mess. What could Marcus think but that his mother or sister had died? Without a word, Bo led Marcus out of the school and into a waiting police car. Marcus's sister, LaTisha, was sitting in the back screaming and crying like her limbs had been severed, and so, Marcus concluded, *My mother is dead.*

And really, Marcus thought now, wasn't that the truth of the matter? With her incredible act of violence, Constance had ended her life. She had ripped herself from the family. Marcus and LaTisha no longer had a mother, Bo no longer had a wife. And yet here was Bo on the other end of the phone telling Marcus that they needed to support his mother. Marcus loved his father—Bo was a sturdy, hard-working man who went to church and put food on the table. But Bo had moments of ignorance and weakness and it took effort for Marcus not to feel sorry for his father. Bo worked at the printing press of the *New York Times* and so he had been one of the first people to read the incriminating articles, to see the ghoulish photographs. Right there in the newspaper that he himself printed! Marcus asked Bo why he didn't quit on the spot, and Bo said, "I've had the job for seventeen years, son. It's not something I would just walk out on." The same was true for their apartment. The blood damage in the apartment was so bad that Marcus, Bo and LaTisha spent the subsequent twenty days in the Sunday Sermon Motel while disaster specialists cleaned up. Marcus and LaTisha had to share a room; the hotel had roaches and intermittent hot water, and it took Marcus an extra 40 minutes to get to school. The whole time, Marcus begged his father to consider moving. He couldn't stomach the idea of living on the place where "it" happened.

"Where would we go?" Bo said. "Our apartment is rent-controlled. We'll stick it out, and eventually people will forget. They'll move on to the next thing. I've seen enough news pass before my eyes to know this to be true."

Bo had remained loyal to Connie through it all, but Marcus felt differently. He was going to write this book, take the money, and leave his old life behind.

"Okay," Marcus said to his father, just to say something. "I'll give it some thought."

"See that you do," Bo said. "Are you having fun up there?"

"Yep."

"Helping out?"

"Yes, Pop."

"All right, then. We miss you, son."

"I miss you, too, Pop," Marcus said, feeling like he'd eaten nothing but guilt for breakfast.

"We'll talk to you. Please write to your mother."

" 'Bye," Marcus said. He hated to admit it, but he was relieved to hang up the phone.

⁂

That night, Marcus woke up when Garrett came home from his date with Piper. Marcus checked his clock: one-fifteen. He waited until Garrett used the bathroom, brushed his teeth, and returned to his room, then he went to the door and peered down the hallway. Dark. The door to Winnie's room was a few yards away. It was hung crooked and didn't close properly and something about that door, slightly ajar, was irresistible. But Marcus knew what would happen if he went into her room. Just the way Mama knew what would happen when she opened the door to see Angela. Marcus tried to steady his breathing; he should go back to sleep. But his throat ached with the need to talk to someone and Winnie was the best friend he had now.

The house made some eerie creaking noises beneath his feet. He stood at Winnie's door and held onto the frame on either side, steadying himself. He was afraid that if he knocked, the door might swing open and she would be frightened and yell. So he knocked on the frame. The wood was dense and the sound of knocking was hard to hear, even to Marcus's own ears. Three tough knocks, indistinguishable from the house's other settling noises. Marcus was terrified that Garrett or Beth would come out into the hallway. He figured Garrett had stayed up late many nights trying to catch Marcus in this very act: going after his sister. And then Marcus remembered the horrible scene from *Native Son* where Bigger Thomas goes in to the rich white girl's room—she asks him to—and he's so afraid of getting caught that he kills her. Marcus shook his head. When they'd read the book in Ms. Marchese's English class, Marcus never imagined he'd be involved with a white girl. But here he was, scaring himself. He would go back to bed.

Right then the door opened and Marcus saw a very narrow slice of Winnie. One eye, a sliver of gray sweatshirt, one toenail painted pink.

"I'm sorry to bother you," Marcus whispered. Already, he felt like a fool. He hadn't considered what he would say if Winnie actually answered the door, and now that she had, he sounded like a Jehovah's Witness. "Do you mind if we talk?"

She opened the door a little wider. He could see most of her mouth. "You want to come in?"

He noticed she was wearing only the sweatshirt and some underwear. He looked beyond her to her rumpled bed. He was making a huge mistake. He should wait and talk to her in the morning, on the beach. But he couldn't make himself move away. He was sucked into Winnie's gravitational pull.

Winnie took his hand. She had prayed to God every night since they got here that this would happen, and now she was so elated she practically pushed Marcus into her bed. She'd made out with Charlie Hess in the humid, chlorine-smelling corridors outside the pool, but that was the extent of her sex life. She was ready for more.

Kissing her, really kissing her, lying down on the bed, Marcus almost cried. Winnie fit in his arms perfectly, like a child would have. She was so small, so slender. He wanted to go slowly. He wanted to kiss her until sleep carried them both off. But Winnie was going crazy. Her hands were all over him, and she was warm. He was overwhelmed by having her so close, and he willed his body to relax. He had a sense that sex would change things, possibly even ruin them, and yet he was so turned on, he was rigid, pulsing, and utterly confused. He should have stayed in his own bed, in his own room! He pulled away from her and tried to get his bearings—they were falling off the bed. Talking—what was the right posture for talking? He sat against the headboard and gathered the covers into his lap to hide himself from her.

Winnie sat up next to him. She knew she'd gotten him worked up and it made her proud. "So," she said, teasing him. "What do you want to talk about?"

He tasted different words: "my mother," "Mama," "Constance." But he couldn't bring himself to speak. There were so many things he wanted to tell her. About the sweatshirt for starters—how his own teammates had left him without a stitch of clothing and how Arch had come all the way to Queens with the sweatshirt, and how that afternoon proved to Marcus that Arch was one person in the world that he could trust. Everyone else had abandoned him—his friends, his teachers, his cowardly father. His mother. Marcus also wanted to explain to Winnie how dealing with all that made him stronger. How he knew he could have won every race of the swim season, but he held himself to second each time, so that Marcus's swim coach seemed to forget that Marcus was the murderer's son and presented him with the most consistent swimmer trophy at the end-of-the-season banquet. He wanted to tell Winnie about how he was going to write a book and with the money, put himself through college. Marcus was afraid that just saying the words, "book deal," would sound like bragging and quite possibly the magic attached to those words would vanish.

Marcus felt badly because he came here with noble intentions—of talking—but now he found his body in stiff revolt. His body wanted to be kissing Winnie and rubbing her right up against him.

"I like you," he said, finally. Because this seemed like a truth that had to be acknowledged.

"I like you, too," she said, snaking a hand under the covers.

He banged his head lightly against the wooden headboard of her bed and moved her hand away. He remembered when Arch invited him to Nantucket. It was only a few days before his trip to Albany, it was early March—cold, wet, and miserable. Arch called Marcus at home, ostensibly to see how Marcus had fared in the All-Queens Invitational (second place) but really just to check in, take Marcus's temperature, as it were.

Only ten days before the trial. How are you hanging in?

My life sucks, Marcus said. *I can't wait for this thing to be over.*

Arch was quiet for a minute, then he cleared his throat and said, *What are your plans for this summer?*

This summer?

You like to swim, right? Do you like the beach?

Yeah, Marcus said. *I guess so, yeah.*

How about you join my family and me on Nantucket this summer? We stay in a funky old summer cottage that my wife inherited. It's right on the ocean.

I don't know, Marcus said. At the time, it seemed like Arch was offering too much and Marcus had the sinking feeling that Arch knew something Marcus didn't. Like they were going to lose the trial and Constance was going to die.

I want you to consider it, Arch said. *Seriously. It would be good for you to get away. It would be good for my family, too.*

Marcus had doubted that, even at the time. The Newtons needed him around like they needed bugs in their beds.

"I shouldn't be here this summer," Marcus said now, to Winnie.

"What?" Winnie said. "You don't know what you're talking about. I love it that you're here."

"Garrett hates me," Marcus said. "He looks at me funny."

"He looks at everybody funny," Winnie said.

This was true. As many times as Arch had said, *My daughter, Winnie, you'll like her,* he'd never said anything similar about Garrett.

"There was something else I wanted to tell you," Marcus said. "Something you should know."

"What is it?" Winnie said.

"I miss him, too."

"Who?"

"Your father," Marcus said. "Arch . . ." He didn't know how to continue. What to say about Arch that Winnie didn't already know or that hadn't already been said by somebody else? In the *New York Times* a city councilman was quoted as saying "New York has lost not only a good attorney, but a good citizen, a hero for the common man." A hero, Marcus thought, for one family on the verge of imploding. "Your dad. Arch. I miss him just like the rest of you do."

Winnie covered her eyes with her hand. "Will you please stay here with me tonight?"

"I can't," Marcus said, though sex, that tangible presence, seemed to be standing next to the bed, egging Marcus on. "What if we get caught?"

"We won't get caught," Winnie said.

"Not tonight," Marcus said.

"Tomorrow night?"

"Another night," he said. Talking, too, would have to wait for another night. Real talking—telling Winnie all the secrets that were crowded into his heart. He couldn't go into any of it while he was in Winnie's bed with Winnie half naked and all over him. With enormous effort, he moved away from Winnie and put his feet on the cool wood floor. When he stood up, the floorboards squeaked. He pushed sex out of the way and tiptoed into the hall, closing Winnie's door behind him. Arch was dead, Constance was alive. It was wrong and yet with all his anger and confusion, Marcus also felt gratitude, an enormous gratitude because he was *here*. Suddenly the summer seemed short and precious; he wanted it to last forever.

In the Elmhurst section of Queens, the Fourth of July was a huge, multicultural block party. Whole streets were closed off and the half-barrel bar-b-q pits appeared for jerk chicken and pork shoulder—the Laotian women passed around hand-rolled lumpia. Kids set off bottle rockets and adults drank beer on the front stoops. The music was loud; there was a fist fight or two. Constance had always disdained the chaos—year after year she stayed inside with the air-conditioning cranked, drinking from a cold bottle of white wine while she prepared coleslaw for a hundred people. At dinnertime, she sent Marcus down to the street with the coleslaw mounded in her one good wooden salad bowl with more or less the same sentence: "Make sure nobody walks off with that bowl, child!" No one would confuse Connie for a patriot.

This year things were going to be different. Beth had gotten up at six in the morning to beat the rush to the grocery store, where she bought red, white, and blue napkins, plates, cups, miniature flags, and bags and bags of food. When Marcus woke up and went downstairs, he helped Beth put the groceries away.

"Are you, like, a member of the D.A.R. or something?" he asked.

"No," Beth said. "But we're taking a picnic to Jetties Beach tonight. We do it every year. And this year's special because you're here. And Piper and Peyton are coming."

"And David?" Marcus asked.

"No, not David." Beth didn't explain why, and Marcus knew enough to keep his foot out of that mud puddle.

Every day on Nantucket was summer, but the Fourth of July was especially summer. Beth made blueberry pancakes for breakfast and then Marcus and Winnie rode their bikes into town to watch the small parade up Main Street, the water fight between the Fire Department and the elementary school kids, and the pie-eating contest. Marcus and Winnie held hands—which started as Winnie grabbing Marcus's hand so that he wouldn't get lost in the crowd, and ended up as just plain holding hands. They went into some shops, looking for a suitable souvenir to send home to Marcus's sister. Marcus found nothing suitable, although he wasn't really concentrating. He was too aware of Winnie's hand in his, how good it felt, and yet he was concerned about what they must look like, a black boy and a white girl. Marcus felt as if he had a flashing red light on his head, announcing, INTERRACIAL COUPLE! But nobody even glanced at them sideways until they rounded the corner onto Federal Street and bumped smack into Garrett and Piper.

Marcus dropped Winnie's hand immediately but she made things worse by putting her arm around his waist and squeezing him. He moved away. He'd told her that one of the conditions of their being together was that they had to conceal it from Beth and Garrett. Winnie didn't understand why he felt this way; she didn't like hiding things from her mom and brother, but she agreed. She had said, *Okay, I promise,* and yet now here she was, in Garrett's face, hugging Marcus.

Garrett frowned. Marcus couldn't believe they'd run into him. He had still been asleep when Marcus and Winnie left the house on their bikes.

"What's up?" Marcus said.

"Nothing," Garrett said.

"We're shopping for LaTisha," Winnie said. Winnie pronounced the name like it belonged to a white person: "Leticia." "We watched the pie-eating contest. This skinny girl won. She ate a whole pie in, like, thirty seconds."

"You should have entered, Winnie," Garrett said. "You could use a whole pie."

"Okay, we're going," Winnie said, taking Marcus's unwilling hand. "Hi, good-bye."

"I'll see you tonight," Piper said. "I think my dad might join us even though he's technically not invited."

Winnie pulled Marcus down the street, like he was a stubborn dog. "See ya!"

Marcus said, "I thought we agreed to keep this a secret."

"We all live in the same house," Winnie said. "It's been a secret for two days. You think they don't know something's changed between us?"

"They didn't know until now."

"Who cares what Garrett thinks anyway. He's turned into such a jerk since Daddy died."

"He'll try to kill me."

"He doesn't care about you and me. All he cares about is having sex with Piper." Winnie stopped in front of another souvenir shop. "What about pot holders? Do you think LaTisha would like some pot holders?"

When they got home, the Range Rover was in the driveway; Garrett had beaten them back. Marcus wanted to go up to his room and give writing a try, but Beth had made a special Fourth of July lunch. Grilled hotdogs, pasta salad, homemade lemonade. Marcus ate three hotdogs sitting next to Winnie at the picnic table. Garrett sat across from them, scowling. Even Beth seemed impatient. She snapped at Winnie for cutting her hotdog into pieces.

"I went to a lot of trouble to make this lunch, young lady," Beth said. "You *will* eat it."

This was so unlike Beth that everyone at the table stopped eating, except for Winnie, who actually put a piece of hotdog into her mouth.

When, after lunch, Winnie asked him if he wanted to swim, Marcus said no. He was going upstairs to his room. He wanted to let things cool off, then make Winnie come to her senses.

She knocked on his door later that afternoon. It was four-thirty; he had fallen asleep over his still-blank legal pad, which he shoved into the drawer of his nightstand.

"Come in," he said.

Her hair was wet—from a shower, not the ocean. She wore

the sweatshirt and a white tennis skirt with blue and red piping.

"A skirt," he said. "That looks nice."

She shrugged. "Fourth of July. Mom gets a big kick out of it."

"I noticed."

"No one cares about us being together, Marcus," she said. "Trust me, I know."

"Garrett cares. And your mother cares. She yelled at you at lunch. She's never done that before."

"She's upset about something else. She's upset about David."

"What about him?"

"He's coming with us tonight and I guess she doesn't want him to."

"Oh."

Winnie closed the door and climbed on top of him. She lay her head on his chest and he could feel his heart pounding into her ear.

"Mom and Garrett don't have time to worry about us," Winnie said. "They have their own lives to worry about. So let's just be ourselves, okay?"

Marcus looked around the room, which over the past four weeks had become as familiar to him as his own room: the wainscoted walls, the ceiling fan that didn't work, his bed with the white cover. He wasn't sure who he was anymore. He'd changed so much, he'd lost track. Last year everyone in his neighborhood stayed on the street until the fireworks over Shea Stadium ended. When Marcus and LaTisha went upstairs they found Constance asleep in front of the television; she liked to watch the Boston Pops. This year he applauded as little kids with streamers on their bikes rode up a cobblestone street in a procession. He had grilled hotdogs and homemade lemonade for lunch. And now he had a white girl lying across his body.

Sex grinned at Marcus from its post by the door. "You have to go," Marcus said. "You're driving me crazy."

Winnie pressed her hips against his. "In a good way or a bad way?"

Marcus lifted her off of him. "Good way," he said, knowing how this would thrill her. "Now *go*."

Later, Marcus helped Beth pack the picnic into coolers: fried chicken, potato salad, cucumbers in vinaigrette, deviled eggs, oatmeal cookies, iced tea, beer. She had a special red, white, and blue tablecloth, and all of the matching plates and napkins.

"This looks great," Marcus said. And then, before he could stop himself, he said, "My mom always made coleslaw. With horseradish in it. It was a big hit."

Beth stopped what she was doing and stared at him, and Marcus got the awful feeling that followed whenever Constance was mentioned. Marcus wished Winnie would come down and rescue him—but she was napping, and Garrett had taken the car to pick up Piper and Peyton. Marcus tucked a sleeve of plastic cups into the picnic basket.

"Oh, Marcus, I'm sorry," Beth said. She got an unsteady vibe in her voice, like she might start to cry. "I didn't even *think* what this would feel like for you. With your mother in jail, you probably don't want to celebrate Independence Day."

"Uh . . ." Marcus was caught off-guard. "No, don't worry about it. It's fine."

"It's *not* fine," Beth said. "It was insensitive of me. But we do this whole rigmarole every year, and I just thought that if I kept things normal they might start to *feel* normal."

"I'm excited about a picnic," Marcus said. "I've never been on an actual picnic, with a picnic basket and everything."

Beth sank into one of the kitchen chairs, thinking that this was another thing Arch would have loved: taking Marcus on his first picnic. "You're sure you don't mind? Maybe we should just forget it."

"I want to go," he said.

Beth threw her hands into the air. "I don't want to see David!" she said. "I should never have invited the girls, but I thought a big group of kids would be fun. Plus, David goes to the same party every year, at this huge house on the Cliff. But no! This year as soon as he hears the girls are coming with us, he decides to forget the party. He's only coming along because he knows I don't want him to."

Marcus began to wonder if what Winnie said were true. Maybe Beth and Garrett were too consumed with their own lives to give their little romance a second thought. But before Marcus could pursue this reasoning further, he heard Beth whisper something under her breath.

"I'm sorry?" Marcus said. "I didn't hear you."

"I said, I'm keeping a big secret from my children."

She was crying now. Marcus handed her a red, white, and blue napkin. He sat quietly, wondering if she was going to tell him the secret. He felt extremely interested, but also ashamed at this interest. If she told him the secret, he might have to keep it from Winnie.

Beth crumpled her napkin and tossed it lamely in the direction of the trash can. Marcus had an urge to pick it up and throw it away, but he was rooted to his chair.

"It's about David."

Marcus let his eyelids droop, his standard defense when he heard something he didn't like. "Please," he said. He stalled, unsure of what to say. He liked Beth; he could see the woman was in pain, the kind of pain you felt when you had something to admit and couldn't wait to get it off your chest. The kind of pain Mama had been in right after the murders. She had called the police and turned herself in. "Please don't tell me."

Beth looked crestfallen, and he felt bad. Beth was the reason he was here. She'd given him the great gift of this summer, with picnics and fireworks and everything.

"I wouldn't be able to keep it from Winnie," he explained.

Beth smiled. "You like Winnie."

Marcus squeezed his eyes shut. "Yeah."

"Just promise me that you'll be there for her this summer when she needs you."

"I'm here for her," Marcus said.

"She's so fragile, and your friendship is important to her."

Marcus felt embarrassed and proud, and relieved, because it sounded like she was going to let him off the hook. He opened his eyes.

Beth lifted herself out of her chair and stood by him. She put her hand on his shoulder and left it there a second. Marcus's throat ached. For the first time all summer, he missed his own mother, the way she used to be, when she put her hands on either side of his face if she couldn't find the words to express herself.

Marcus heard a car pull into the driveway. Beth walked out into the hall.

"There they are," she said. "Marcus, will you go up and wake Winnie? We have to get ready to leave."

The screen door opened and Garrett walked in, followed by Piper, Peyton, and David. David was carrying a six-pack of Heineken.

"I hope someone made deviled eggs," he said jovially.

As Marcus headed up the stairs he tried to imagine what the secret might be, and he figured it had to do with sex. An affair, maybe. Marcus was irritated; he could tell he'd be thinking about this all the time now, although he was interested to know that sex was plaguing people other than him. He knocked on Winnie's door.

"Come on," he said. "We're going."

Her hair was mussed and she was rubbing her eyes. "I'm grouchy," she said.

Marcus felt a rush of emotion. She was so childlike, so funny and adorable that he flashed her his dimples. That worked. Her face brightened and she hugged him.

⁂

Walking down the cliff toward Jetties Beach, Beth noticed that Peyton was the only one without something to carry. In front, leading the way, were Garrett and Piper holding hands, each lugging a thermos in the other hand. Behind them were Winnie and Marcus holding either side of the big cooler. Beth had the picnic basket and two blankets and David was loaded down with folding chairs. Peyton slunk along at David's side, empty-handed.

"Why don't you catch up to your sister?" David asked her.

"I don't want to. She's with Garrett."

"Well, go anyway. I need you to scout out a good spot for us."

"I'm hungry," Peyton said.

"Exactly why we need you up front. We can't eat until we've found a place to sit."

In her mind, Beth willed Peyton to stay right where she was, next to her father, but Peyton succumbed to her hunger. She ran ahead, if you could call stumbling forward in clunky sandals running, leaving Beth and David to bring up the rear alone, if you could call walking with four thousand strangers alone.

"You don't want me here," David said.

"I thought you had the Swifts' party."

"I wanted to be with my girls," David said.

"Maybe," Beth said. "Or maybe you wanted to be with me."

"You have a high opinion of yourself."

"The kiss was an accident, David."

"An accident?"

That was the wrong word. An accident was breaking a glass in the kitchen sink, a fender bender; an accident was what had happened to Arch. The kiss was something more intentional— it was a mistake.

"It didn't mean anything," she said, cringing at how cruel that sounded. But didn't he see? It *couldn't* mean anything. "I was kind of drunk."

"Drunk," David said flatly. "That's original. You kissed me because you were drunk."

Beth pressed her lips together. She liked the way Winnie and Marcus were carrying the cooler. They made it seem effortless. Piper and Garrett, on the other hand, appeared lopsided, and a second later they stopped in their tracks. Piper had to set down her thermos and rest.

"I need you to respect my wishes," Beth said. "I'm not interested in a relationship with anyone right now."

"You sound ridiculous."

"Why is it so ridiculous?" Beth said. Winnie turned around with raised eyebrows. Beth smiled at her reassuringly, then lowered her voice. "I need time and space to grieve for my husband."

"I understand that, Beth."

"You don't understand. If you understood, you wouldn't be here. You would be giving me space."

"Don't you ever ask yourself why it's *me* you don't want around? I'll tell you why. Because you still have feelings for me and you're afraid of those feelings."

"I don't have feelings for you."

"You love me."

Beth looked to see if he was being funny. But his eyes gave off a searing heat. He was serious; he was challenging her to deny that preposterous statement.

"I loved you twenty-five years ago," she said. "Trust me when I say things have changed."

"It didn't seem that way the other night," he said.

Beth didn't have to respond because seconds later, Peyton found a spot on the beach large enough to accommodate all of them, and then there was the welcome distraction of setting up camp: spreading out the blankets, unfolding the chairs, taking out the food and pouring drinks. David opened a beer and hovered at the far edge of the blanket while Beth took charge of doling out fried chicken, spooning mounds of potato salad onto paper plates, and trying to keep pieces of plastic wrap from flying into the water. This time last year it was the same menu, but there was only four of them: Beth, Arch, and the twins. Arch loved drumsticks. He ate them all—a total of seven—then joked about the poor one-legged chicken that was limping around somewhere. Stupid, maybe, but the kids thought he was the funniest man on the planet, and so did Beth. She put a drumstick on Garrett's plate, hoping he would remember, but he was too absorbed with rubbing Piper's arms. She was chilly, it seemed. Well, yeah, Beth thought, that's what you got when you wore a halter top to the beach at night. When Garrett finally did notice the drumstick, he ate it in three bites without comment. Beth almost said, *Hey, Garrett, remember when Dad . . .* but she knew she wouldn't be able to pull off the happy nostalgia she intended.

As she ate her dinner, she thought about how one day Garrett and Winnie would get married and have families of their own, and Beth would be left to remember all of the funny jokes alone. She watched as David wandered away to talk to some people he knew, waving his beer around in defiance of the open container law. Maybe she should listen to him, otherwise she might end up old and alone, still clinging to her grief.

It grew dark. Beth collected the paper plates and the wadded napkins and passed around oatmeal cookies. David appeared back at the blanket with a box of sparklers and he gave one to everybody, including Beth, and lit them with a Bic he borrowed from Piper. He watched Beth's face as he held the lighter to the tip of her sparkler and when the sparkler came to life, bright stars dancing and hissing, he said, "There you go, my dear. Now you can write your name."

Garrett and Piper wrote their names in a heart, as did Winnie and Marcus. Beth turned her back to the group and wrote her name in the dark air over Nantucket Sound. *Beth.* She hoped that Arch would see it, from wherever he was watching her.

Beth collected everyone's spent sparklers and the rest of the trash and settled back in her chair in time for the first burst of fireworks. Red, gold, purple. David sat in the chair next to hers and opened another beer. Beth loved fireworks, the whistle and crackle in the air, the smell of cordite, the *oohs* and *aahs*. When the sky was all lit up, she watched the silhouettes of her kids— both of them obviously paired up now. Marcus was leaning back on his hands and Winnie sat close to him, resting her head on his shoulder. Piper lay on her back and Garrett lounged on his side right behind her. They were kissing. Beth studied them for a minute, enough time to dispel any illusions about their innocence. They were having sex. Beth glanced at David to see if he saw what she saw: the tongues when they kissed, the way Garrett's fingers tugged insistently on Piper's belt loops. Beth didn't know how to feel about the situation. She and Arch had always vowed to be honest with the twins about sex and the responsibility that came with it. Arch gave Garrett condoms, and, Beth assumed, informed him how and when they should be used. Beth herself had lost her virginity at sixteen with the man sitting next to her, but somehow she had seemed older then, at sixteen, than Garrett did now, at seventeen. She would have to say something to Garrett about the sex this week—and to Winnie, too, if this thing with Marcus developed. It would embarrass all three of them—really, Arch had been much better at dealing with the kids' emerging sexuality—yet what could she do? Let her kids go wild in the sack without a few words of caution?

Blue spirals shot through the air, enhanced by a bunch of silver flashes that sounded like very loud popcorn. David applauded for that one. Beth was bothered by everything David had said earlier. Okay, maybe she did have feelings for him, but any fool could see that the feelings made her so uncomfortable that all she wanted to do was push them away.

The finale started and the sky was a messy artists' palette of color, one bright burst inside another. The great thing about the finale was that just when Beth thought the sky was saturated, just when she thought it must be the end, they shot off more. It kept going and going. Beth leaned her head back against the webbing of her chair. She tried to conjure Kara Schau's words: *Don't think. Smell the flowers.* Don't worry about packing up and fighting the crowds all the way back to the car. Don't worry about David Ronan in the chair next to yours. Just enjoy.

Beth couldn't help herself from doing a visual sweep of their area, mentally calculating how long it would take them to break camp. It was then that she noticed Peyton was gone.

She looked at David. He was grinning like a boy, his face catching light from the sky.

"Did Peyton go to the bathroom?" Beth asked.

David checked the blanket. His smile faded and he sat up straighter in his chair. "Piper," he said. "Where's your sister?"

Asking this was pointless. Piper couldn't hear David over the noise of the fireworks. No one could hear him but Beth. Piper was so absorbed with tasting the inside of Garrett's mouth that anyone could see the whereabouts of her younger sister was the furthest thing from her mind. David concluded as much after a few seconds, and he picked his way across the blanket, over the cooler and between thermoses, to ask Piper again. Piper sat up and looked around. Shrugged. David asked something of Winnie and Marcus, who mimicked Piper's actions. *We don't know.*

Beth stood up. She felt sorry for David—a missing child was a parent's worst nightmare. Even when the child was thirteen. Even in a place as safe as Nantucket.

"They don't know where she went?" Beth asked.

"No," David said. He scanned the patchwork of blankets around them. "How long has she been gone? And how did she leave without my noticing?"

"You went to talk to some people," Beth said. "Maybe she met up with friends."

"Maybe," David said. "Or maybe she just went to the bathroom."

"That's probably it," Beth said. She, too, wondered how long Peyton had been gone. Beth remembered handing her two oatmeal cookies and then offering to refill her lemonade, but that was before the fireworks started. Beth tried to remember if she'd seen Peyton with a sparkler. The sparklers were a long time ago, certainly allowing enough time to go to the bathroom and come back. Unless there was a horrendous line.

As if reading her mind, David said, "I'm going to check the bathrooms. Will you stay here?"

"Of course," Beth said. "She'll probably make it back before you do."

Beth's optimism flagged once the fireworks ended, because at that point, chaos broke out. Children started to whine and everyone and his brother tried to jam their way through the narrow passageway between the dunes that led to the parking lot. People poured past them, like a stream moving around a rock. Beth stood on her chair and waved her arms so that Peyton might be able to locate them. Marcus followed suit, standing on the cooler, waving the flashlight that Beth had packed. Winnie folded the blankets and the unused chairs while Garrett and Piper clung to one another—Piper suddenly so concerned about her sister that she needed constant petting from Garrett. Beth almost snapped at them to separate and help, but what kind of help was needed? They simply had to stay put until Peyton materialized out of the crowd, and Garrett and Piper were doing just that—staying put with their hands all over each other.

David returned, his eyes darting everywhere. The key, he said, was not to panic because Peyton had a good head on her shoulders and she could find her way to the police station once she got to the road.

"It's not like she's a tourist," he said. "This island is her home."

They waited until the last stragglers left the beach. At this point, Beth was tired and had to go to the bathroom herself. She walked through the cold sand toward the now-abandoned portable toilets. Because she was from New York, she couldn't help thinking of how the fingers of evil could touch anyone, even here. Beth eyed the dark ocean. With a missing child on the brain, it looked sinister.

On the way back she was more hopeful. But from a hundred yards away she could see David standing on the cooler; as she neared, she heard him calling out Peyton's name. Beth joined Winnie and Marcus who were huddled nearby. They told her that Garrett and Piper had gone to the lost child tent, or whatever it was, that the police had set up.

Beth helped David down from the cooler. Even touching his hand made her feel conflicted.

"She'll turn up," Beth said.

"Oh, I know," he said. "I'm not worried."

"Of course you're worried," Beth said. "She's your baby girl.

You don't have to play tough guy with me, not under these circumstances. Maybe she went home."

"There's no way she would have gone home without telling me. It's too far to walk. It's four miles in the dark."

Garrett and Piper approached, Piper's face looked ready to crumble. "The police haven't seen her," she said. "Your friend was there, Dad, Lieutenant Egan, and he said he'd send his guys out to scan the area. He said if she doesn't turn up in the next twenty minutes, you should go talk to him."

"Twenty minutes, my ass," David said. "I'm going to talk to him now." David charged through the sand toward the parking lot, calling Peyton's name along the way. Beth stayed with the other kids.

"None of you saw her leave?" Beth asked. "Who spoke to her last?"

"I told her I liked her shoes," Winnie said. "But that was during dinner."

Piper nuzzled Garrett's neck and ran a hand inside the collar of his polo shirt. Something about Piper touching Garrett made Beth uncomfortable. She wondered if this were a typical mother-son-girlfriend dynamic at work, or if there was actually something about Piper that was unlikable, which only Beth discerned.

"This isn't like my sister," Piper said. "Peyton is such a goody-goody. It's not like she ran off to smoke and drink with her friends. She never does anything on her own unless she asks Dad, like, six times if it's okay. So I don't know what to think. Maybe she was abducted?"

"She wasn't abducted," Beth said. "But she may be lost."

Piper sniffed. "We used to play on this beach when we were kids. If she got lost, she'd wait for us in the parking lot. Plus, the police tent is in the parking lot and she wasn't there." Piper's tone was condescending—it was the tone of voice she normally reserved for David, and Beth was about to let her know that it wasn't an okay tone to use with her boyfriend's mother when David jogged toward them through the sand.

"They're going to start a real search," he said. "I'll stay here. Beth, you take the kids home. To my house. Keep your eyes peeled for her on the way. The police seem to think she got bored, or angry, and decided to walk home. They said they see it every year. Also, check the machine, Piper, when you get in. Maybe she left a message. I'll call you later to see if she's turned up."

❧

Beth and the kids trudged back to the car, everyone so loaded down with stuff that there was no opportunity for kissing or hand-holding. It was a silent march out to North Beach Street and then up the Cobblestone Hill. They piled into the Range Rover and drove to David's house, slowing to check the identity of each person walking on the side of the road along the way. No Peyton. The house was dark except for the onion lamp by the front door.

"She's not home," Piper said. "God, I hope she left a message."

The kids trooped into the house while Beth stood at the back of the car and separated out David's belongings from her own— his chairs, his thermos, his blanket. She knew there wouldn't be a message. No one had spoken to the girl, no one noticed her missing until she was long gone. Peyton had been ignored, so she ran away. It didn't take a brain surgeon to figure it out, only a mother.

When Beth walked into the kitchen, the kids were sitting on barstools around the island.

"No message?" she said.

Garrett shook his head. Piper started to cry quietly. Beth put a hand on her back.

"And you checked the whole house?"

Piper nodded, then moved into Garrett's arms where she collapsed.

"Maybe she went to our house," Winnie said. "It's closer. Maybe she got tired and decided to wait for us there. She knows we don't lock it."

"Okay, we'll check," Beth said. "Piper, you stay here and wait for your father's phone call. Tell him our plans."

Piper clung to Garrett with a ferocity Beth had only previously seen in two year olds. "Can Garrett stay with me? Please? I'm freaked out to be here by myself."

Beth hesitated. Garrett staying here meant only one thing: sex. In a bed, probably, which would have irresistible appeal. Beth fought off images of the cottage on Bear Street with David. All summer long, sex on a bed, sex every which way.

"I don't think that's a good idea," Beth said. "Because how will he get home?"

"I'll have Dad run him home when he gets back."

"David shouldn't have to do that," Beth said. "It's late. Garrett will see you tomorrow."

Garrett threw Beth a dirty look. "I'm not ten years old, Mom. I'll stay here with Piper and if David won't take me home then I'll walk."

"In the dark?"

"Yes," Garrett said.

Beth heard the challenge in his voice and decided she wasn't up for it. "Well, if Peyton's at our house, we'll come back. Obviously. And if she's not there, I guess we'll come back anyway and wait to hear what David says. Or I will. Marcus and Winnie may want to go to sleep." Beth closed her eyes. Teenagers were going to be alone in a house full of beds no matter what she decided, that much was clear. "So I'll be back in a short while, then. A couple of minutes."

Beth drove to Horizon saying a prayer to God and Arch and anyone else who would listen. *Please bring the girl home safely.* Horizon, too, was dark, except for the porch light.

"She's not here," Marcus said. "Man, this is getting weird."

The three of them went in, Beth and Marcus each carrying a load of picnic stuff.

Winnie said, "Mom doesn't care who's dead or missing as long as the dishes get done."

"Winnie, that's not fair."

Winnie acknowledged as much with a pat to Beth's head. "Sorry, Mom."

Beth turned on some lights and checked all the rooms on the first floor. She checked the deck then went upstairs and poked her head into the bedrooms, hoping to find Peyton asleep, like Goldilocks. No such luck. Beth returned to the kitchen. "Listen, you two stay here. I'm going back to the Ronans' house in case another vehicle or another set of hands is needed. You guys get some sleep." She wanted to get back to Garrett and Piper as soon as possible.

"We'll clean up," Marcus said.

"If you want," Beth said, so grateful for this offer that she wondered if Winnie's statement weren't right on the money. "Garrett and I will be home shortly."

"Okay, Mom, good luck," Winnie said, and Beth could tell

Winnie was anxious for her to leave. *Are you watching this?* she asked Arch on her way out to the car. *Everyone wants me to leave so they can fool around!* Somehow the prospect of Winnie and Marcus didn't worry her nearly as much as Garrett and Piper, and so she hurried back to David's house.

The house was as she left it, with the front light on and a light in the kitchen. Beth slammed the car door to warn of her impending arrival. But no one was in the kitchen. Beth called out, "Hey, I'm back!" and was met with silence. She listened to the hum of the refrigerator and the drip of the sink, her heart racing. She twisted the spigots of the sink and the dripping stopped.

"I'm back!" Beth shouted.

Silence.

"Garrett!" she hollered. "Garrett Newton, get down here this instant!" She marveled at how much like a typical mother she could sound.

Still nothing. Either the house was remarkably well built or they, too, had disappeared. Beth was faced with having to go upstairs and check on them. She was starting to boil inside. How dare they put her through this! She stormed up the stairs, only partially cowed by the fact that she'd been up these stairs two weeks earlier when she was snooping around. She heard noises coming from the bathroom. Beth moved toward the door. She heard a groan, her own son's distinctly sexual groan. Okay, that was it. Beth couldn't stand to hear anything more. She pounded on the door.

"Meet me downstairs, Garrett," Beth said. "We're going home."

There was silence, then some shuffling, then an, "Okay, Mom, give me a minute?" As though she was supposed to believe he was in there alone.

Beth returned to the kitchen, furious. She started rehearsing a lecture for the drive back to their house—God, what was she going to say? She should have stayed at home in blissful ignorance. They were upstairs in the bathroom. Unbelievable. No parent would tolerate this! Beth studied the pictures on the refrigerator, but only for a second. The pictures of David, whom she had kissed! The pictures of Piper who was having sex with her son upstairs! Suddenly, Beth was distracted by flashing lights. A police car pulled into the driveway. Beth went to the door. David and Peyton stepped out of the car.

"Oh, thank God," Beth said. The girl looked defiant—arms welded across her chest—but fine, otherwise. David chatted with the officer at the wheel for a second, clapping him on the arm, and then the police car drove off. Beth opened the door for them.

"What happened?" she said.

Peyton glared at Beth, a look so hateful that it startled her.

"I'm going to bed," she spat.

When she disappeared, Beth looked to David. "Where was she?"

"One of the cops found her sitting by herself on Steamship Wharf," David said. "She was waiting for the early boat so she could sail to Hyannis to see her mother."

"Why?" Beth said, though of course, she knew why. "What's wrong?"

"She thinks everyone is paired up but her. The other kids, and you and me. She felt left out, so she ran away."

"Ouch," Beth said.

"I reminded her that she was my date tonight," he said.

"You didn't treat her like your date," Beth said. "You kept trying to get rid of her so you could talk to me."

"Ouch," David said.

"It's true," Beth said. "And I hate to open your eyes to other unpleasant realities, but when I got here a few minutes ago I found Garrett and Piper locked in the upstairs bathroom together. One doesn't have to be a Rhodes scholar to figure out what was going on in there."

David's face fell. "I guess not."

"We have to keep our families separated. Maybe the girls *should* go visit their mother." Beth put a hand up to stop his objections. "I'm not telling you what to do with Piper—"

"Yes, you are."

"I just want you to know that the Newtons will be keeping a low profile at Horizon for a while."

Garrett appeared then, eyes cast to the floor.

"We're going," Beth said. Garrett was already headed toward the door, which David held open for them.

"At least everyone's safe," David said. "Happy Fourth of July."

"And *don't* drive by my house tonight," Beth said.

"I wouldn't dream of it, Bethie," he said.

chapter 5

Just like that, Piper was getting shipped off to her mother's house—not for a long weekend, not for a week, but for ten whole days. Garrett was grounded from the car to boot, because his mother had caught him and Piper in the bathroom together.

"What were you two doing up there?" Beth had asked him as they drove home from the Ronans' house.

He couldn't believe she was embarrassing him like this. He'd held out hope that she would be cooler, that she would just let the issue drop. "It's none of your business what we were doing," he said. This, he suspected, was the answer Piper would give, and she was a master at handling her father. "If you want details of somebody's sex life, get your own."

Beth slammed the brakes of the car and they both pitched forward. "Out," she said. "You're walking home."

"What?"

"I do not want you in this car. Get out."

Garrett opened his door and the light came on. Beth's face was a block of ice. "I'm going back to Piper's," he said.

"You can try," Beth said. "But David won't let you set foot in that house."

Garrett stepped out onto the gravel road and slammed the door. "Bitch," he muttered. The Rover took off sending a spray of stones and dust from its tires. "We were having sex!" Garrett called out after the car. He stood where he was, waiting to see if his mother would stop, but she didn't. She kept on going, leaving him there.

"Well," he said, to nobody except his father, he supposed. "What do you think of that?"

He headed home because he suspected his mother was right about David. It had been Piper's idea to fool around upstairs, to hurry up and do it before his mother returned. Garrett was nervous and it took him a while to relax and concentrate on her body. Then, when his mother knocked, he was so startled that he pushed Piper away and made a mess of the condom and everything. Piper laughed at his nervousness, then she got angry. "God, Garrett, calm down. We're practically adults. Anyway, this is *my house*. Your mother is trespassing." Garrett felt ashamed at himself for acting so flustered. Piper was right. His mother *was* trespassing, trespassing on his life.

As he walked, Garrett thought back to the previous autumn when Arch had taken him and Winnie to Central Park to give them the "sex talk." Arch warned them in advance that this was going to be the topic of discussion and so they should think up all the questions they had and Arch would do his best to answer them. Winnie was nervous about it—she did everything in her power to get out of going along—but it ended up being the best conversation Garrett could have dreamed of. Arch was funny and honest and realistic. *You two will probably have sex in the next few years. Enjoy it. Use condoms. Be considerate. And, most importantly, don't mistake sex for love. They are two different things that feel the same in the heat of the moment.*

Reviewing this advice, Garrett felt a little better. He'd followed it to a "T." He wasn't sure what his mother's problem was. He'd done nothing wrong.

❧

He wasn't surprised, though, when all hell broke loose the next day. Marcus went to the beach early to swim in the waves, and as soon as he left, Beth began to lecture Garrett and Winnie about sexual responsibility.

"It's a private thing, an *intimate* thing between two people," she said. "It's not something you flaunt in front of your mother or anyone else."

"I hear you, Mom," Garrett said. "But you walked into Piper's house. You were, technically, trespassing."

This sent Beth into a flurry of expletives, at the end of which she grounded him from the car. Two weeks.

"Good," Winnie said. "Because I want to go for my license and I can't practice with Garrett hogging the car."

"What about Winnie?" Garrett challenged. "Not flaunting sex in front of Mom's face means Winnie can't have sex with Marcus."

"We're not having sex," Winnie said. "Why don't you figure out what you're talking about before you open your big mouth, lover boy."

"This is bullshit," Garrett said. He walked out the front door and considered taking the car—but that was a line even he wouldn't cross—so he hopped on a bike and pedaled to Piper's. Garrett rode as hard as he could, over the dirt road, hitting all the bumps on purpose. He hadn't ridden a bike since the year before, and it felt good to get the exercise. He'd have to be in shape for soccer in September. He should start jogging, like his mother. But Garrett didn't want to think about his mother or September, when he would be separated from Piper. Nor did he want to think about the sex in the bathroom, although his mind kept returning to the subject, as he tried to gauge how much of an ass he'd made of himself. Pushing Piper away, disengaging, fumbling with the condom, trying to hide the evidence as he heard his mother pounding on the door. At the time he hadn't thought of Beth as trespassing; he'd thought of his *mother* catching him having sex with his girlfriend. That was enough to make anyone act like a moron.

He reached Piper's house in less than ten minutes, but when he arrived, he was chagrined to see that both David's pickup and the painting van were in the driveway. Meaning, David was home.

And not only home, but right there in the kitchen, sitting at the island with Piper and Peyton, the three of them drinking coffee. Garrett knocked on the frame of the screen door, although he had an urge to eavesdrop on the conversation. It looked serious—it was serious, definitely, if David stayed home from work.

All three of the Ronans looked up at the knock. Garrett expected Piper to run to the door, but seeing him seemed to cause her physical pain. She winced.

David was the first to speak. "Come on in here for a second, Garrett."

Garrett sensed that his timing was bad. "I'm interrupting?"

"Not at all," David said. "Because we have something to tell you. Both girls are leaving this morning to see their mom in Wellfleet. They'll be gone until the fifteenth."

"The fifteenth?" Garrett repeated. He tried to locate himself in the month. Yesterday was the fourth, today the fifth. The fifteenth was ten days away—ten precious summer days that he would not be spending with Piper. He gazed at her, asking her with his eyes if this was anything she had control over, but her face was deep in her coffee cup. So he guessed not. This was more parenting gone haywire.

"You and Piper may talk for five minutes in the driveway, alone," David said. "And then she's going upstairs to pack and I'm taking her and Peyton to the airport." He checked his watch and carried his coffee cup to the sink. "Understood?"

Garrett, speechless, was already outside. He kicked at the pebbles of the driveway and waited for Piper to follow him out. Instinctively, they walked to the very end of the driveway, which was shielded from the house by a Spanish olive tree. Garrett took her in his arms and noticed for the first time that she'd taken the diamond stud out of her nose, revealing a sore-looking divot.

"What happened?" he said.

"I have to go. He's seriously pissed this time. Because you and I were upstairs, but also because of Peyton. He thinks you and I, whatever, our *behavior* was one of the reasons Peyton ran away last night. He called Mom and they talked for, like, two hours. They both think this is the best thing."

"You don't think it's the best thing, do you?"

She dropped her chin to her chest. "I don't know, Garrett."

"What do you mean you don't know?" he said. "Do you *want* to be separated for ten days?"

"Not really."

Not really? Garrett felt like his heart was going to explode. He wondered if she thought less of him because he acted like such a buffoon in the bathroom.

"I love you," he said, and his father's words popped into his mind: *Don't mistake sex for love.* But Garrett wasn't mistaken here. He did love Piper. Just the thought of not seeing her for ten days made him want to do something drastic.

She didn't respond to his declaration. He'd always been good at reading other people's thoughts, but here he was drawing a blank.

"You love me, too, don't you?" he asked.

She touched her nose. "Yes."

Garrett let out a long stream of highly relieved air. Then, he felt buoyant. They were in love!

"Five minutes is up!" David yelled from the house, though clearly it had only been three or four minutes. "Inside, Piper. Pronto!"

Piper kissed Garrett on the mouth, but chastely. "I'll see you when I get back," she said.

"Wait," he said. "Give me your mom's phone number. I'll call you from town. I'll call every day."

She took a few steps backward, shaking her head. "I don't think you should," she said. "I'll see you when I get back." She waved, but in a way that looked like shooing.

Garrett watched her retreat to the house. His lungs ached; he felt like a scuba diver descending deeper and deeper where the pressure of the water was unbearable and there wasn't enough oxygen to survive. Ten days! He waited until Piper reached the door, hoping she would turn and wave, but she didn't. She stepped into the house—or was pulled in, Garrett couldn't tell—and the door closed very tightly behind her, leaving him with nothing to do but climb on his bike and pedal morosely away.

※

Under certain circumstances, ten days could seem like a very long time. For example, Garrett imagined that ten days in prison would seem like a long time. Ten days of hard manual labor would seem like a long time. The first ten days after Garrett's father died had seemed like an eternity. But even that didn't drag on quite as long as ten days without Piper. Especially when Garrett's favorite pastime became reviewing those minutes with her in the driveway in his mind.

On the bright side, Piper had told him she loved him. On the dark side was her response of *not really*, when asked if she wanted to be separated for ten days, and the fact that she didn't want him to call her, and the more awful fact that when she left she didn't kiss him with any kind of passion. The conclusion Garrett drew—the only conclusion he could live with for ten days—was that David had said or done something to scare Piper right out of her normal personality. She was sheepish, she was *timid*. Without the diamond in her nose she hadn't even looked like herself; she was Wonder Woman without her magic bracelets. The only part of the conversation Garrett could really take to heart was the part when Piper said she loved him—because that one word, "yes," had sounded completely sincere.

Garrett called up a favorite saying of his father's: *It's fruitless to speculate.* Garrett would simply have to wait until the fifteenth. There would still be plenty of summer left. In the meantime, he tried to make it through the hours. The mornings dragged, even

when he managed to sleep until nine, which wasn't often now
that he was falling asleep shortly after nine at night. The sun
rose at five and a stripe of light fell across his face around six-
thirty, and that usually woke him. He figured he might actually
knock a couple of books off his summer reading list. He finished
Franny and Zooey, which he liked, even if he didn't fully understand it, but then he got bogged down in *A River Runs Through
It*. Talk about a boring book! Ten days would seem like a very
long time if you were standing knee-deep in cold water trying
to catch a fish without any bait.

The worst punishment for Garrett was having to spend time
with Winnie and Marcus. They were so happy, so obviously a
couple now, that it turned Garrett's stomach. Winnie practiced
driving the Rover with Beth in the passenger seat and Marcus in
the back; he went along for moral support, Winnie said. Garrett
thought meanly that Marcus would probably never get his
driver's license; he would never own a car, and could probably
count on one hand the number of times he'd taken a cab. Still,
Marcus joined the driving lessons, leaving Garrett alone in the
house to contemplate the injustices in his life.

On the fourth day without Piper, Beth asked where she was.
Garrett was shocked by the question. Although he hadn't told
anyone about Piper being banished to Cape Cod, he counted on
Beth, at least, to intuit it. Why else would he be moping around
the house?

"She went to see Rosie," Garrett said. "She'll be back next
week."

His mother raised her eyebrows. "She went to see Rosie," she
repeated. "How about that."

On the seventh day, it rained. Winnie and Marcus started a
Monopoly marathon at the kitchen table. The wind was out of

the southwest and the house shook. Garrett helped Beth close all of the shutters and the storm windows, while Marcus and Winnie rolled the dice. Garrett watched them, stupidly wishing that he could play, but resenting them too much to ask. Beth, probably taking pity on him, asked him to build a fire while she went to work making a vat of clam chowder. Garrett got the fire roaring, then helped his mother by peeling potatoes and dicing onions. Once the soup was simmering, he crashed in the recliner in front of the fire and vowed not to get up until he'd finished *A River Runs Through It.*

He was eighteen pages from the end when the electricity went out. He heard a cry from the kitchen—"Oh, no! Our game!"—and he knew Beth would be rummaging through the utility drawer for candles and matches. Garrett put down his book and leaned back in the recliner.

You love me, too, don't you?

Yes.

A few minutes later, Beth brought him a candle. "How're you doing?" she asked.

"Fine."

Garrett was surprisingly grateful when she sat down next to him.

"I don't like being angry at one another," she said. "This thing with you and Piper . . ."

"I love her," he said. It felt brilliant to admit it. "I'm in love with her."

His mother searched his face. "Okay."

"You think we're getting too serious too fast," he said. "I know you think it. But you're not me and you're not Piper."

"That's true," she said. "Do twenty-five years of experience count for anything?"

"You don't remember what it feels like to be young," he said. "You don't know what I feel like. She's only gone for ten days, right? But it feels like *forever.*"

"I do remember what it feels like," Beth said. "I was in love at your age."

Garrett felt a split second of connection with his mother, until he realized what she was referring to. "With David?" he sneered.

"Yes, with David. I was in love with him. We were having sex."

"I don't want to hear about it," Garrett said.

Beth faced the fire. *I know what I'm talking about!* she wanted to shout. *Please believe me!* Instead, she said, "You're so young, Garrett. Piper is just one in a long line of girls."

Garrett held his book up so that it blocked Beth's face. "See, you don't know what I feel like. Because if you knew, you wouldn't say that."

"Summer does something to the brain," Beth said. "It's intoxicating. Everything shimmers. And when you fall in love in the summer, it's the best love you can possibly imagine. Especially here. Because there are sunsets and walks on the beach and fireworks. But summer loves aren't meant to last. They burn very hot and bright, and then they go out. Eventually, Garrett, they always go out."

"You're not making me feel any better," Garrett said. "You're making me feel worse."

"If I never split with David, honey, I wouldn't have married your father."

He felt a different kind of sadness then, a sadness because the ease with which he used to talk to his mother was gone. Now, every conversation was unpleasant for him. "Please don't say anything else," he said.

Garrett waited for Beth to leave the room, but she remained next to him in the candlelight, lost in thought. After a minute of listening to the howling wind and the *rat-tat-tat* of rain against the shutters, Garrett returned to his book. He wasn't really reading, he was skimming, because damn it, he wanted to finish. And more important, he wanted Beth to understand that his relationship with Piper was *his*; it wasn't some reincarnation of her and David. She couldn't predict the ending based on something that happened a generation ago.

Garrett finished the book and set it victoriously on the side table. Beth was asleep, thank God, and since there was nothing else to do, Garrett blew out the candle, eased back in the recliner and closed his eyes. *You love me, too, don't you? Yes.*

❦

That night, a gust of wind pushed open Garrett's bedroom door. Garrett was tired, and he contemplated leaving the door open, but he felt oddly exposed, so he got up. Then he saw something move in the hallway. Somebody: Marcus slipping into Winnie's room.

Garrett's first instinct was to sound an alarm. *Hey! Stop! You can't go in there! This isn't allowed!* If Marcus were sneaking around in the middle of the night then he must be having sex with Winnie. So Winnie had lied to Garrett and Beth, lied right to their faces. Garrett was suddenly wide awake. He crept down the hallway toward Winnie's room.

He stood outside Winnie's door and suspended his breathing, thinking of his mother banging on the bathroom door while he was inside with Piper. Winnie's door didn't close properly, and when Garrett pressed his forehead against the door frame and squinted, he could see in. He was a despicable person after all, a Peeping Tom, a pervert. *If you want details of someone's sex life, get your own.* He was a hypocrite! But he was propelled forward by his desire for justice. It was bad enough that Marcus was here for the summer, but having sex with Winnie! Garrett would turn them in; Beth would be forced to send Marcus home, and she would have to admit she never should have invited the kid here in the first place.

When Garrett peered in, what he saw was this: Marcus and Winnie lying in bed, fully clothed. Winnie was wearing her sweatshirt and Marcus had on a T-shirt and shorts. Marcus was holding Winnie from behind, spooning her, his chin resting on top of her head. They appeared to be sleeping. Garrett stood there for several minutes, waiting for more to happen, but nothing did. They slept. Like an old, married couple. Garrett stepped into the room and yanked Marcus out of bed. Marcus hit the floor, ass first. Winnie sat up, confused. She nearly screamed because she saw *Garrett* in her room. Garrett stood over Marcus with his fists in the air. He'd never fought anybody in his life, but he was going to fight Marcus now.

"Get up," Garrett growled. "Get *up*, motherfucker."

Marcus blinked, rubbing his backside. He squinted at Garrett. Here it was, his biggest fear realized, but Marcus found he wasn't scared. He was merely annoyed. "What are you doing here, man?"

"Garrett, *get out*," Winnie hissed. She climbed out of bed, pulling the bottom of her sweatshirt down over her rear end.

"No," Garrett said, in a loud voice that he hoped would wake Beth. "I'm not getting out until Marcus tells me what the hell he's doing in your bedroom."

Marcus held his palms up. "We were sleeping, man."

And though he knew this was the truth, Garrett kicked Marcus in the chest as hard as he would have kicked a soccer ball if he had an open shot on goal. His adrenaline surged. He *hated* the guy.

Marcus took the blow with a sharp release of air, and fell over his knees, guarding his chest with crossed arms. His breath was gone and he flashed back to a time, years earlier—before he became a master at holding his breath underwater—when a cousin had dunked him in the municipal pool and Marcus thought he was going to die. *Where was the air?* Marcus's vision turned red, and when it cleared, he saw Garrett dancing in place, waving his fists. "First your mother causes our father's death," Garrett said. "And now you're trying to screw my sister."

Garrett's leg shot out again, and Marcus felt like a dog being kicked by a cruel child. It felt like every mean word and deed of the past nine months was contained in that second blow, which caught Marcus in the windpipe. He fell over backward. Thinking of the hour and a half he'd sat, all alone and completely naked, in the swim team locker room as he waited for Arch; the way his father sprayed the baseboards of their room at the Sunday Sermon Motel with Raid to get rid of the roaches; how not one of their neighbors had spoken to them since the murders, and Vanessa Lydecker wouldn't even open the door to her apartment when she saw it was Marcus through the peephole.

All Marcus could do was wheeze. It occurred to Garrett that Marcus was really hurt, possibly even dying. Winnie picked up the lamp by her bed. She wanted to bash Garrett over the head, but she was afraid of showering Marcus with broken glass.

"You asshole! You jerk!" she screamed. "How dare you! You kicked him! You hurt him!"

"It's not fair!" Garrett said. "He doesn't belong here, Winnie. He doesn't belong in this house and he doesn't belong in your bed."

With slow deliberation, Marcus sat up, then got to his feet. His chest and throat throbbed with a red, glowing pain, and from that pain came a power, monstrous and terrifying, a sudden knowledge that he was capable of really bad things. Marcus's lungs felt like they were bleeding and he couldn't swallow, but that hardly mattered. He grabbed the front of Garrett's T-shirt and threw Garrett onto the bed. He had four inches and thirty pounds on the kid, and Marcus marveled that Garrett had had the guts to come after him in the first place. But it incensed him, too. Garrett thought he was superior because he was *white*, because he was *rich*. Marcus punched Garrett right across his pretty face and instantly there was blood everywhere. Marcus backed away. He coughed a loogie up into his hand. The room spun. Winnie shrieked and dropped the lamp onto the floor, where it shattered. She was screaming now, screaming for Beth.

Marcus cut his foot on a shard of glass from the lamp. Now his foot was bleeding and maybe his lungs, and certainly Garrett's face. There was blood everywhere and Winnie was going hoarse in her upper registers trying to wake Beth. Marcus stumbled forward and looked at Garrett who had his arms up now, shielding his face. Marcus wanted to call him a baby, a sissy, a *pussy*, but what he said was, "I'm not going after your sister, not like that anyway. We're friends."

Garrett tried to spit at Marcus, but he only managed to dribble some bloody saliva.

"Do you want me to hit you again?" Marcus asked. Wondering if fighting back all along would have been this easy, this gratifying to the dark side of his psyche.

"No!" Winnie said. "Look at him, Marcus! God, he's *covered* with blood."

The bedroom door swung open and the light came on. Beth entered the room in her seersucker bathrobe.

"What," she said, her voice hoarse and murderous, "is going on?" She saw the blood and gasped. "Garrett!" she said. "What *happened?*" She spun on her heels and pinned Marcus with her eyes. "What have you *done?*"

It was the blood that was the problem, Marcus realized. Garrett was covered with blood and Marcus wasn't. His mind skipped beyond explaining the course of events, beyond being sent home, beyond being found guilty of assault, and sent to a juvenile detention center until his eighteenth birthday. It skipped to this: *They all think I'm just like her.*

"Marcus," Beth said. "What have you done?"

"I punched him," Marcus said.

"Mom, you don't know what happened . . ." Winnie said.

Beth didn't seem to hear. She helped Garrett up and led him to the bathroom where she dabbed at his face with a wet towel. So much blood, but thankfully not much actual damage—a swollen nose, maybe, and by the morning, a black eye. Winnie crowded into the bathroom with Beth and Garrett, crying now, because this was all her fault.

"We were just *sleeping*," Winnie said. "And Garrett barged into my room and started beating Marcus up."

"Garrett beat *Marcus* up?" Beth said. "Looks to me like it was the other way around. Just look at your brother! Look at his *face.*"

Back in Winnie's room, Marcus sat on a clean part of Winnie's bed holding a wad of Kleenex to the gash on his foot. *They all think I'm just like her.*

"Garrett started it," Winnie said. "He kicked Marcus in the

chest, twice, really hard. He came into my room, he pulled Marcus onto the floor and then he kicked him!"

There were splotches of blood now on Beth's bathrobe. "Garrett?"

Garrett inspected his face in the mirror. It looked like someone else's face.

"Garrett attacked Marcus in his sleep, like a *coward*," Winnie said. "So Marcus hit him back. Marcus only hit him once." Winnie had seen in Marcus's eyes, though, the possibility of more, and it frightened her. She ripped off a long piece of toilet paper and blew her nose. This was all her fault.

Garrett touched his eyelid. He had a sharp headache.

"Garrett should mind his own fucking business!" Winnie said. She wasn't sure yet if her mother realized she had broken a lamp. Every piece of furniture in Horizon had, like, seventy-five years of history behind it, and so her mother would blame that on her, too.

Garrett raised his eyes to meet Beth's gaze. He had no words.

"I don't know what to do," Beth said. "I don't know how to fix this." She wasn't crying but her voice was so defeated that it was worse than crying.

Marcus stood in the doorway of the bathroom. His voice was gravelly. "You've been wanting to kick me like that since the first day here," he said to Garrett. "And I've been wanting to punch you for wanting to kick me. Because I, myself, have done nothing wrong. I am not a criminal. All I did was show up. Because your father invited me. *Arch Newton* invited me."

Everyone was quiet. Beth opened the medicine cabinet and hunted for bandages. God, how she wished she could just keep the kids separated—locked in their own rooms like jail cells, like cages at the zoo. *This is too much!* she wanted to shout, loud enough so that Arch could hear her. *This is too much for me to deal with alone!*

"It doesn't matter what happened," she said. "I want you kids to get along. For my sake. This is the hardest summer any of us will ever have. The name-calling has to stop. The fighting is unacceptable. If Arch were here . . . frankly, I can't imagine what he would think."

"If Dad were here," Garrett said, "none of this would be happening."

"Well, he's *not* here," Beth said. "He's not here and so we have to deal as best we can without him. We *have to deal.*"

Winnie glared at Garrett. "Why can't you just leave us alone? God, I could kill you!"

"Winnie!" Beth said.

"I'm sorry," Garrett said. He was suddenly exhausted, and his longing for Piper was worse than ever. He wouldn't be surprised if she never wanted to see him again. He was a mean, evil person and his head hurt. And his foot hurt from where he'd kicked Marcus, like maybe he'd broken a toe against Marcus's chest.

"I'm sorry, too," Marcus said. He snatched a bandage for his foot. *They all think I'm just like her.* He limped back to his room, thinking what he was really sorry about was that he would never get to touch Winnie again, never get to hold her while she slept.

Winnie went back to her room to sweep up the pieces of the lamp. Sniffling, because this was her fault.

Beth put ointment and a small bandage on the cut under Garrett's eye. "Oh, Garrett," she said. When she first walked into Winnie's bedroom and saw Garrett bleeding and Marcus looming over him, she thought . . . well, she thought Marcus had attacked him, and her instincts were to protect her son. But now, she faced a feeling ten times worse: her son was the bully. Her own child was bringing this pain down on his own head.

Garrett missed his girlfriend. Then he missed his father. Then he missed himself—the happy, good-natured person he used to be. He couldn't even thank his mother for nursing his wounds. He hobbled back to his bedroom; outside, the wind groaned. He deserved to die in his sleep.

❦

Garrett spent the next few days hiding in his room, emerging only for meals. His right eye was swollen shut and mottled purple and green, and his mother, taking pity on him, bought him a bottle of extra-strength Tylenol for the pain. Marcus had a lump on his windpipe and a bruise the size of an egg on his chest. Winnie had broken an antique lamp—the only valuable thing in the whole house if you believed what Beth said. Horizon took on a cautious hush, like a hospital where everyone suffered from hurt feelings.

By the time Garrett's face resumed its normal shape and color, it was the fifteenth. He woke up on that morning in a panic. He didn't know when or how Piper was arriving on-island, and he certainly couldn't ask David. He considered staking out the house on his bike, but that was psycho, and since he was finished with psycho behavior, he decided his only alternative was to sit home and wait.

Which was pure torture, a hell unimaginable—far, far worse than waiting for Piper when she was off-island was waiting for Piper when she was on-island, or might be. The key was to keep busy, and so Garrett joined Marcus and Winnie at the beach.

They looked surprised to see him, but they didn't get up and leave, though he wouldn't have blamed them if they did. He swam for the first time all summer and the water felt great. He bodysurfed in the waves until his nose stung and his lungs ached and then he headed up to the house and made sandwiches for everyone, including Marcus, who said it was delicious after the first bite.

After lunch, Garrett started to read the third book on his summer reading list, *Animal Dreams*, by Barbara Kingsolver. A *chick* book, he realized after twenty pages, something added to the list to appease all of the neo-feminist girls in Garrett's class. He put the book down, incredulous that the reading list should be so ill-suited to his tastes, and he checked the clock for the very first time that day. Two-thirty. Garrett went to the front door and looked down the long stretch of dirt road that led to their house. No Piper. He tried to be rational. She would either ride her bike or have David drop her off as soon as she got home. And it was Sunday, so David wouldn't be working. Garrett stood at the door for a long time, long enough to feel desperation seeping into his skin. Garrett hopped on his bike and rode to Piper's house, just as he promised himself he wouldn't.

He cruised by the house, checking for clues. The yard was empty, thank God, since the worst thing, which Garrett hadn't considered until he sailed past, would have been David out mowing the lawn. But no, the house looked quiet; both of David's vehicles were in the driveway. Which meant what? Either Piper was already home or not home yet.

It's fruitless to speculate.

Garrett rode out to Cisco Beach, then back home. It was 3:30. When she still hadn't appeared at seven o'clock, he began to feel sick. Sick like he had stomach cancer and was dying. He told Beth he wanted to skip dinner—they were going out for dinner, she said, to Bluefin for sushi, didn't Garrett remember? No, he answered, he didn't recall hearing anything about it, and besides sushi would make him hurl. His mother and Winnie and Marcus left without him, which was just as well. He wanted to die in peace.

At eight o'clock, he stood on the small deck of his room and prayed: *Please let her still love me. Please.*

At nine o'clock, there was a noise downstairs and Garrett, who was lying in bed listlessly reading his chick book, jumped to his feet. But it was his mom and Winnie and Marcus, back from dinner.

"We brought you some food!" Beth called out.

Despite his deep agitation, he was hungry, and solitude had proved to be more excruciating than company, so he decided to go down and eat. It was fruitless to speculate, he told himself. Maybe Piper had been forced into staying another day, maybe she missed her flight or lost her ticket and was stranded in Hyannis. Maybe she decided she didn't love him after all.

When he reached the bottom of the stairs, his mother was standing there, and then the front door opened and Piper stepped in. For a second, Garrett didn't know what to do or think. He was transported to a state of elation and relief that was beyond anything he'd ever felt. Tears blurred his eyes.

"Mrs. Newton?" Piper said. "I know it's late, but is it okay if Garrett and I go for a walk on the beach?"

Garrett wondered why Piper was calling his mother "Mrs. Newton," when before she'd always just called her Beth. Beth may have been asking herself the same thing, but she just said, "Sure. Of course."

Piper walked down the hallway, through the kitchen, and out onto the deck without acknowledging Garrett in any way. Garrett spied the plastic container of jewel-colored sushi on the kitchen table, but his hunger had vanished. All he wanted was to be at the beach, alone, with Piper.

Piper descended the stairs to the beach in a hurry. She was practically running, and because it was so dark, Garrett worried she might trip. But he understood her instincts—to get to the beach as quickly as possible, where they could be alone.

When they reached the beach, Piper jogged to the left. Garrett ran after her.

"Hey, where are you going?"

Finally, she looked at him. Her nose ring was back in place, and Garrett took this as a positive sign. "I want to get away from the house," she said. "Far away."

She wanted to make love, then, on the beach. Garrett allowed himself a joyful yelp as he raced after her. And then she stopped, and he was able to gather her up in his arms.

"I love you," he said.

She raised her eyes to him. Her long hair spilled over the shoulders of her jean jacket.

"Let's sit down, Garrett." Her breath smelled like cigarettes; she'd gone back to smoking, then, while she was away. But Garrett decided not to say anything about it. *You love me, too, right?* he wanted to ask.

"I missed you so much," he said. "It damn near killed me to be without you for so long."

She sighed. "I have something to tell you," she said. "Something big and you're not going to like it." She plopped down in the sand and pulled him down next to her.

She was going to break up with him. She went away and

decided that she didn't love him after all. Here, then, was his punishment for attacking Marcus, for being a person so unlike his father that it was hard to believe they were related. Garrett took her hand. "What's going on?"

Piper fell back onto her elbows as if the weight of her news was too much to bear sitting up. "My mother and I had a long talk while I was over there. A lot of long talks. I told her all about you. I told her your name."

"Yeah?" Garrett said. "That's good, right?"

"She knows you're Beth Newton's son, Beth Eyler's son."

"That pisses her off?"

Piper squeezed his hand so hard he thought she might break his fingers. "There was a reason why my dad didn't want me to tell my mom your name."

"What reason is that?" Garrett asked.

"They were married."

"Who?"

"Our parents."

Garrett was confused. Piper sounded so grave, and well, so horrified.

"Of course our parents were married," he said. "They're our parents."

"No, Garrett," she said. "My father, David Ronan, was married to your mother, Beth Eyler. In 1979. They were married for two weeks before your mother filed for divorce. They were *married*, Garrett. This is a huge secret they've been keeping from us our whole lives."

Garrett wanted to tell Piper she was nuts, off her rocker. There was no way that what she said was true. "Did you . . . ask . . . your dad?"

She nodded. "Affirmative."

"Did he have an explanation?"

"An explanation that took three hours and kept us from eating dinner. Do you want to hear it?"

"No," Garrett said. Could it be true? he thought. His own mother married to David.

"Not only did they keep it from us," Piper said. "But my dad said, he *said*, Beth told him that your father didn't even know."

"My father didn't know?"

"That's what Dad said."

Garrett felt heavy and cold, like a piece of petrified wood. His mother had been married before, married to David, and nobody knew. Arch had been kept in the dark with Garrett and Winnie, dragged along to Nantucket each and every summer, oblivious to what had happened in their mother's youth.

"What are you going to do?" Piper said.

"I don't know. What are you going to do?"

"Aside from never trust my father again, you mean?"

"Yeah, aside from that."

"I don't know," she admitted.

"Maybe we should run away and get married ourselves," Garrett said. "They couldn't stop us."

"No," Piper said. "They couldn't."

※

In the middle of the night, there was a knock on Winnie's bedroom door, and she assumed it was Marcus, although he swore that after the scene with Garrett, he'd never, ever come to her room in the middle of the night again.

"Come in?" she whispered.

The door opened. Winnie was crushed and indignant when she saw that the person staring at her through the darkness was not Marcus, but her twin brother, who these days ranked right up there with the biggest jerks she'd ever met.

"What do you want?" she demanded. "He's not here, as you can see, though it wouldn't be any of your damn business if he were."

Garrett sat at the foot of the bed. Winnie rolled away to give him room, though she didn't summon the energy to sit up.

"I have some really bad news," he said.

Winnie doubted this was true. One of the consequences of her father's death was that *really bad news* no longer existed. For Winnie, the really bad news was that her father had been killed in a plane crash—all other news was only bad news, or usually, not-so-bad news.

"You broke up with Piper?" she guessed.

"No!" Garrett hopped to his feet and lunged like he was going to sock her for even suggesting such a thing.

"Calm down," Winnie said. She liked saying this. So often it was she who was hysterical and Garrett who was the cool customer. Recently, the tables had turned. Her brother was a nut case. He thought he was so much older than Winnie—getting his license, having sex—but what he didn't realize was that Winnie was maturing this summer, too. Her friendship with Marcus was helping her to deal with her grief and move on. He was helping her to grow on the inside, as a person.

"Don't you want to know what the news is?" Garrett asked.

"If you want to tell me," Winnie said.

Garrett eased back down onto the bed. Winnie yawned, looked at the clock. 1:30. Her heart cried out. The usual time for Marcus.

"I found out something about Mom," Garrett said. "Something big."

He was baiting her. He wanted her to jump up and down, begging, "Oh, please, Garrett, please tell me!" But first Winnie considered the possibilities. Something big about Mom. The words had the unmistakable scent of gossip about them. And gossip meant sex, right? So Beth was having sex with David. Winnie had to admit she didn't love the idea. She wanted her mother to be happy, true, but she wished that happiness would be found in a place that did not involve any man other than Winnie's father. However, this was childish, and since Winnie now eschewed all childish thoughts and emotions, like the ones Garrett so grossly displayed the other night, she figured she would have to be happy for her mother. She would have to celebrate this relationship with David.

"God, Garrett, grow up," Winnie said. "Mom is an adult. She can do whatever she wants."

"She lied to us," Garrett said.

"Didn't you listen to what she told us a few weeks ago?" Winnie asked. "That sex is a private thing?"

"Sex?" Garrett said. "You don't even know what I'm talking about. I'm talking about a lot more than just sex."

"Okay, fine, tell me. What is it then?"

Garrett paused. Of course, now that she'd asked, he was going to make her wait.

"Mom was married to David," he said. "The summer between her junior and senior year in college, 1979. They got married at the Town Building here on Nantucket." He leaned forward and whispered viciously. "They were *married*, Winnie, and she never told us. And worse than that, she never told Dad."

Winnie felt the bottom of her stomach swoop out. This *was*

really bad news because this news altered the way the whole world appeared. Everything shifted, reconfigured. Winnie recognized the reaction in her gut. Her father dead? Of course not. Her mother married before? Impossible.

"Where," Winnie said, "did you hear this?"

"From Piper."

"Oh, please," Winnie said. "Piper is *lying*. Or she has bad information. Like, if David told her that, he's the one who's lying. He probably *wishes* he was married to Mom."

"I thought the same thing," Garrett said. "Except Piper heard this from her mom, Rosie."

"So Rosie's lying."

"It's a matter of public record," Garrett said. "It's registered at the town clerk's office. David told Piper this. Anyone can go check."

"So tomorrow," Winnie said. "We'll check."

"I don't need to check," Garrett said. "I know it's true."

"I'm going to check," Winnie said, "in the morning." She paused. "And Dad didn't know?"

"That's right. Mom told David that Dad didn't know."

"He died without knowing," Winnie said.

Garrett stood up. "I can't believe her! I can't believe she'd keep a secret like that from her own family! I want to wake her up right now and make her admit it to our faces."

Winnie thought about this idea. She wasn't ready for another big, messy middle-of-the night scene. Besides, Winnie didn't want to hear her mother admit it. It would be too heartbreaking for everybody. Winnie felt betrayed—of course she felt betrayed!—but she also felt deeply ashamed for her mother. Who kept a huge secret like that? Lots of people, probably, all over the world, every day. But Winnie didn't like lumping her mother into a category with other secret-keepers and cover-uppers: the Bill Clintons, the Richard Nixons. It made her mother seem too fallible, too human.

"How long were they married for?" she asked.

"Two weeks."

"Only two weeks?" Winnie tried to decide if this made things any better. She decided not; getting married was an unalterable fact, like having a baby. You were either married or you weren't; duration didn't matter. Beth had been married before. "Unfucking-believable." Garrett probably thought she was cursing to show off, but truly, that was the only phrase that came to mind. Beth had been married before, to David Ronan. For two weeks. She never told Winnie and Garrett, and, even worse, she never told Arch. This was like a brick wall Winnie had to scale without a rope; she had no idea where to find a fingerhold of understanding. Her own mother. Among other emotions was a raw hurt, because Winnie and Beth were friends. They were the female half of the family, comrades, confidantes, or so Winnie thought. Aside from Marcus, Winnie considered Beth to be her closest friend. And not only a friend, of course, but her *mother*. The first and last person she went to with everything. Her safe place, her absolute, final refuge. And yet what Garrett just told her changed all this. Beth was now someone Winnie barely knew, a woman capable of hiding a huge secret.

Winnie stared at Garrett's shadowy figure at the foot of the bed. He was waiting patiently while she processed the news. Reality settled over Winnie: there was no one left in her family that she could trust.

"What should we do?" she asked.

"I have an idea," he said.

Garrett's plan of action was drastic and mean, the kind of get-even scheme that only the mind of a teenager could conjure. But Winnie immediately recognized that in this instance he was right. The twins would exercise the only power they had left, and they would do it secretly, the following night. The plan was so awful and so irrevocable that Winnie insisted they be positive of their mother's guilt before going through with it. She would check in town the next day.

The morning was as bright and beautiful as any morning on Nantucket had been so far that summer, and yet for Winnie it was the start of a day of subterfuge, and that cast a gloomy pall on her spirit. She climbed out of bed as soon as she heard the water for Marcus's shower, pulled on her jean shorts, which she wore almost as frequently as her poor sweatshirt, and padded downstairs. She stopped and stared at herself in the hallway mirror. Her face was tan, her hair practically white. Although she and Garrett were twins, it was much commented that Garrett resembled Arch, and Winnie was a dead-ringer for Beth. This had always made Winnie pleased and proud to hear. Her mother was no super model but she had a kind of clean beauty that made people think of good diet and good breeding and lots of time spent in the fresh air. Now, Winnie was appalled at the features she shared with her mother. Would she do something awful like Beth had done?

No.

Winnie sat out on the deck with a bowl of Cheerios, gazing at the water. This news about Beth had at least restored Winnie's appetite; she hadn't voluntarily fixed herself breakfast in four months. Winnie heard noises in the kitchen and dread clutched her heart. She could *not* face Beth this morning, and maybe not ever again. She wished fervently that she and Garrett were leaving for college in the fall. But unfortunately there was still an entire year of living at home with their mother before their escape into adulthood.

Winnie listened to the rustlings in the kitchen until she was certain it was Marcus, and then she relaxed somewhat. When she finished her cereal, she propped her legs on a second chair and lay back, basking in the early morning sun. It was far too warm for the sweatshirt, but she wouldn't take it off, especially not now. Not unless she replaced it with a T-shirt that said MY MOTHER IS A LIAR.

Marcus joined her at the table with his breakfast: two peanut butter and beach plum jam sandwiches on raisin bread, a hard-boiled egg, a nectarine, and a giant glass of Gatorade.

"Hi," he said. "You're up early. Did you *eat?*"

Winnie didn't answer except to move her hand indicating, *Hi, so what, of course.*

Marcus took a huge bite out of one of his sandwiches.

"I'm going into town this morning," Winnie said.

Marcus swallowed and took a long pull of his Gatorade. "Really? Why?"

One of the things that made today so painful was that Winnie and Garrett had agreed to keep this a secret, at least until their plan was executed. This meant no telling Marcus, even though Marcus would understand. He was angry at his own mother; he practically hated her.

"I have to buy some books for school," she said.

Marcus nodded, unimpressed. The best kind of lie, Winnie realized, was a boring one.

⚘

The worst kind of lie was the kind that Winnie uncovered at the town clerk's office less than an hour later. Winnie was nervous as she entered the Town Building—it was air-conditioned and hushed with polished concrete floors. It had long corridors like a high school. The building felt different from the rest of Nantucket—this was an office building, where people *worked*. Winnie stood for a minute outside of the town clerk's office. A brunette woman wearing a melon-colored dress and stockings and heels sat typing at a desk. When she looked up, Winnie walked away, the soles of her running shoes squeaking against the polished floor. Now she felt like an idiot, but she didn't know what to say. What if the woman asked her for ID? She didn't even have a driver's license! She should have insisted Garrett come with her; he was better at dealing with adults than she was, but Garrett hadn't wanted to come. He was certain of their mother's guilt; he didn't need proof.

Winnie decided to walk around for a few minutes. She climbed the stairs and the first office she came to was the DMV. How ironic it would be if she took her driving test now and returned home with her license. Even that would be enough to hurt her mother's feelings. Beth was excited about waiting in the awful DMV room while Winnie took her test. She wanted to be the first passenger that Winnie drove legally on her own. Winnie hesitated; maybe she *should* take the test. That would be enough punishment for Beth, and then she and Garrett could forget about their horrible plan for tonight. Winnie closed her eyes and tried to picture herself parallel parking, but when she did, she saw herself hitting the granite curb and popping a tire. Winnie moved on: past the court rooms, past the passport office, all the way to the stairs at the opposite end of the building. Then, without options other than leaving or finding out the truth, she marched back to the town clerk's office. The woman in the melon-colored dress looked up and smiled in such a friendly way that Winnie decided it was okay to speak.

"I want to check and see if my mother was married in 1979," Winnie said. "Is that something you can help me with?"

Melon stood up and walked over to a large gray filing cabinet. "Name?"

Deep breath. "Winnie Newton."

"We're looking in 1979," Melon said. "What month?"

"Summer?" Winnie said. "July, August?"

"And you said the last name is Newton?"

"That's my last name," Winnie said.

Melon smiled at her as though Winnie were telling a joke and she was waiting for the punch line. "Is that the last name I'm looking for?"

"No," Winnie said. *Oh, God, Garrett!* "I'm sorry. My mother's last name at that time was Eyler. Elizabeth Eyler. E-Y-L-E-R."

Melon nodded definitively as if this made much more sense. She started flipping through the cards in the filing cabinet. "Nope, nope, nope," she whispered. "Nope, nope, nope."

Winnie didn't know what to do with her hands. Putting them in the back pockets of her jean shorts seemed too casual, too teenagerly. She decided it would be more reverent to clasp them in front of her.

"Nope, nope, nope."

A very small part of Winnie held out hope that this was all
a hoax, a mistake, even a lie concocted by the Ronan family.
How Winnie would relish telling Garrett he was wrong. If there
were no record of the marriage here, then she would never believe it was true.

"Here it is!" Melon said brightly. "Eyler and Ronan. Oh." Her
forehead crinkled. "David Ronan? Your mother was married to
David Ronan?" She put a hand up. "Don't answer that. It is *none*
of my business." She handed the card to Winnie. "It's fifty cents
for a Xerox copy, and a certified copy costs five dollars and takes
three business days."

Winnie pulled a dollar out of her pocket. Thank God she
thought to bring money! "Just one copy, please."

"My pleasure." Melon took the dollar bill from Winnie, and
removed fifty cents from her desk drawer. Five seconds at the
copier and a bright flash of light later, Melon handed Winnie
the change and the proof of her mother's betrayal. Melon smiled
again, in an intimate way, and Winnie felt her face turn red.
Melon obviously knew David Ronan, and now the news of his
secret first marriage would leak out. But, really, what did Winnie
care?

When she gazed down at the marriage certificate, the first
thing she noticed was the word "Divorced," stamped in large
black letters across the top. Winnie scanned the paper, line by
line. Bride's name: *Elizabeth Celia Eyler*; Bride's D.O.B.: *May 2, 1958*;
Groom's name: *David Arthur Ronan*; Groom's D.O.B: *September 18,
1957*; Date of marriage: *August 16, 1979*; Officiant: *Judge Leon Macy*;
Witnesses: *Kenneth Edwards, James Seamus, Kelly Wilcox*. The marriage certificate was all signed, sealed, and official-looking. It was
real. Winnie felt like she might vomit up her Cheerios right into
Melon's typewriter. She pressed the paper to her chest, whispered, "Thank you," and ran from the building.

She sat outside on a park bench with her head between her knees. Okay, this was really bad. This was—not the worst—but the second-to-worst. Her mother and David all signed, sealed, and official on a card in the Town Building where anyone could look, where anybody could get a copy for only fifty cents! Well, she and Garrett had been betrayed, that was all there was to it. Winnie tried to imagine what her father would do if he were still alive and he'd found out this sickening news. She tried to imagine him getting angry, except he didn't get angry at Beth. He would probably say he was disappointed—not because Beth had been married before, but because she chose to conceal it. Deeper down, he might be sad and maybe even a little jealous. Arch, though, had a way of understanding and then forgiving other people's flaws—Constance Tyler's, for example. Arch might even say it wasn't any of their business—but that thought evaporated immediately. Beth was his wife, their mother! This was their business!

Winnie climbed on her bike. She would go home and lay low until nightfall, when she and Garrett would inflict their revenge. What they planned to do would break their mother's heart, but Winnie no longer cared. She had a copy of the marriage certificate in her pocket, made official by a younger version of her mother's signature. Now it was Beth's turn to learn what it felt like to be shut out, to be excluded from life's most important knowledge.

※

Beth was out for a run when Winnie got home. Winnie wrote a note and left it on the kitchen table. "Don't feel well! Please do not disturb!!!—W." But of course Beth knocked on her door as soon as she got home. Winnie had anticipated this very situation and moved her small dresser in front of the door as a blockade.

"Winnie," Beth said gently. "Honey, what's wrong?"

"Period!" Winnie spat out. How she loathed even the sound of her mother's voice!

"Did you take any Midol?" Beth asked. "Can I make you some chamomile tea?"

"Go away!" This in the most venomous voice Winnie could muster.

"You're not acting like yourself," Beth said. "Are you sure there's nothing else wrong?"

"*I* am a self-respecting woman," Winnie said. Her point being that the woman on the other side of the door could not be described as such. The bigger point being that her own mother, who heretofore had been a paragon of virtue, was now someone else entirely.

Beth tried the door and found herself stymied by the dresser. Winnie couldn't help smiling with self-satisfaction. There was something about a house with no locking doors—everyone felt justified to barge in on everyone else. But not this time.

"Winnie, what have you done?"

"I said, 'go away!' "

Silence. Then, "Fine, fine, fine. If that's the way you want it. I'll be out on the deck eating lunch. Let me know if you need anything."

When her mother was safely down the stairs, Winnie whispered, "Liar."

⁂

Later, there was a distinctive knock on the door. A Marcus knock.

"Hey," he said. "Open up."

For him—yes. But only him. Winnie didn't even want to see Garrett until later. Winnie shoved the dresser aside and it scraped some green paint off the floor. *Oh, well!* Winnie didn't care; it was her mother's house. She'd finally stopped feeling guilty about breaking the valuable lamp. She couldn't be bothered anymore about her mother's heirlooms.

She opened the door to find Marcus holding out a plate: a BLT on toasted Portuguese bread with a handful of Cape Cod chips. Winnie's stomach reared up. She hadn't realized she was hungry.

"Your mother told me to tell you that these are Bartlett tomatoes," he said. "Also, she didn't put on too much mayonnaise."

"Mom made the sandwich?" Winnie asked dejectedly. She'd entertained a brief fantasy that Marcus made it.

"Yep."

"I'm not eating it."

Marcus walked past Winnie into the room and sat on the bed. Winnie closed the door behind him and slid the dresser against it.

"Well, then, I'm going to eat it," Marcus said. He took a huge bite out of the corner and tomato seeds slipped down his chin.

"I'll have half," Winnie conceded. She was hungry and had no intention of going down for dinner. She and Marcus sat side-by-side on the bed eating the sandwich and all of the chips, using a couple of Kleenex as napkins.

When they finished, Marcus said, "You've been up here all day."

"Yeah."

"Girl stuff?"

Winnie sighed and lay back against her pillows. "Let me ask you something," she said. "What if one of your parents did something really bad—"

"Like commit murder, you mean?"

Okay, she deserved that. She thought about how to start over.

"What if one of your parents kept a secret from you your whole life. Like, oh, I don't know . . . like they flunked out of college or had a child out of wedlock. Would you be pissed?"

Marcus shifted on the bed and glanced up at the ceiling. Winnie followed his eyes—there was a light water stain and a tiny black spider. Without a word, Marcus stood up, collected the spider in a tissue, and let it go out the window. Winnie marveled. Any other guy would have squished the thing to death. When Marcus sat down again, his eyelids drooped. After two months together, Winnie knew what this meant: he was shutting her out!

"Wake up!" she said impatiently.

"What's going on, Winnie?"

Winnie chewed her thumbnail. Garrett had sworn her to secrecy, but that wasn't fair. After all, *Piper* knew about Beth and David. Winnie motioned for Marcus to come closer. He rolled his eyes—she was being silly—but he leaned in.

"What is it, Winnie?"

"Mom was married before," Winnie said. "She was married to David."

Marcus straightened. *Married* to David. Well.

Winnie studied Marcus's face; she was interested to know how someone else would react. He seemed nonplussed, like he didn't get it.

"When was this?"

"When she was twenty-one years old," Winnie said. "They were married for two weeks. And she never told us."

"How'd you find out?"

"Piper's mother, Rosie, told her and Piper told Garrett. I checked it out this morning when I was in town. I made a copy of the marriage certificate." She pulled it out of her pocket, unfolded it and presented it to him. "Here. This is it."

That explained why she'd acted so strangely at breakfast. Marcus *knew* she wasn't going into town for books. He looked over the marriage certificate. "Did you talk to your mom?" he asked.

"Hell, no. I'm never talking to her again."

Marcus guffawed. "What, over *this*?"

"Yes, over this. She lied to us, Marcus."

"Maybe she had her reasons. Maybe she was embarrassed."

"That's no excuse."

"Why? You can't tell me you've never kept a secret from your mother."

Winnie thought for a minute. She couldn't think of a single thing she had ever kept from anyone. "I don't keep secrets."

"Some people do," Marcus said, thinking uneasily of the still-blank legal pad in his room. "It's called privacy."

"Privacy isn't okay under these circumstances," Winnie said. "Besides, there's worse news."

"What's that?"

"She never told my dad," Winnie whispered. In her mind, this was such a horrible fact that it couldn't even be spoken aloud. Her dear, departed father deceived by the woman he loved.

Marcus set the marriage certificate down on the bed. Here was Beth's secret, then—the one she kept from her whole family but almost told *him* on the Fourth of July.

"You need to talk to your mom, Winnie," he said. "You need to work this out."

"No way," Winnie said. "Mom is going to pay."

"Pay? What do you mean, *pay*? You're being ridiculous."

Winnie bristled at this. "Shut up! You don't talk to your mother. I don't see you 'working things out' with her! She's sent you at least three letters that I know of, and you haven't opened one of them."

"First of all, my letters are none of your business," Marcus said. "Secondly, *my* mother did something really bad. She *killed* a woman and a nine-year-old girl. She killed them inside our home with a knife from our kitchen. I have a reason to be angry."

"I have a reason to be angry, too," Winnie said. "This changes my whole life. I've been deceived, my brother has been deceived, and worst of all, my father! I feel like my whole life is a sham. Anyway, Garrett and I have planned some revenge."

"*Revenge?*" Marcus said. Winnie kicked herself mentally—she shouldn't have said anything about the revenge. "You want revenge because your mother was married to David for two weeks twenty years ago? That's the stupidest thing I've ever heard." Marcus felt a wave of exhaustion roll over him. He closed his eyes and lay back on the bed.

"Don't pretend like you're falling asleep!" Winnie said. "You do that all the time when you don't want to deal with reality."

"Oh, do I?" Marcus asked, his eyes still closed.

"Yes, you do. Anyway, why are you taking Mom's side? You're my friend. You have to take my side. My side is the *right* side."

Marcus stood up and studied the dresser in front of the door. "You're crazy, you know that?" He moved the dresser with enormous ease and stepped out into the hallway. "You need to put your shit into perspective. You wouldn't know a problem if one bit you in the ass." He sounded truly pissed and Winnie groped for words to reel him back in, but then she told herself she didn't care what he thought. Marcus was the person who was supposed to *understand*. Okay, maybe Beth wasn't a murderer but that didn't mean Winnie's feelings weren't hurt.

"You know what you are?" Winnie said. "You're self-absorbed."

"*I'm* self-absorbed?" Marcus said. "Sister, look in the mirror."

"Fuck you," Winnie flung out. "I wish I hadn't told you."

"I wish you hadn't told me either," Marcus said. "Because I used to respect you. I used to think you had a decent heart."

"I do have a decent heart," she said. "And this *is* a real problem."

"Don't get me going," Marcus said. "If you want to hear about real problems, I'll tell you sometime. But what I'm hearing now is you judging something you don't understand. You need to talk to your mother."

"I told you, I'm never talking to her again," Winnie said.

"Well, then," Marcus said. "It sounds like you've made up your mind."

"I can't believe you're being such a *hypocrite*," she hissed. "You don't talk to Constance."

"This isn't about me," Marcus said.

Winnie was so furious—here was Marcus making *her* feel like the bad guy!—that she slammed the door, but it bounced back in her face. Marcus walked down the hall to his room without another word. Winnie closed the door as best she could and moved the dresser in front of it. Then she flopped face-first on her bed. She *didn't* understand. That much was true. She didn't understand anything anymore.

The plan was scheduled for one in the morning, to be completed by three. Garrett had read that these were the hours that the average person—one who went to sleep at ten-thirty and woke at seven—slept most soundly. Before one A.M. a person was in light REM sleep, and after three the average person woke at least once to use the bathroom. Garrett sounded convincing on this point and Winnie conceded. After all, she didn't want to get caught. She found it impossible to fall asleep, and thus lay awake in a state of fearful agitation, replaying her conversation with Marcus. After she skipped dinner, she thought he might realize that she was depressed and come up to check on her, but he didn't. On top of everything else she had to deal with, now she and Marcus were fighting.

At exactly one o'clock there was the lightest of taps on her door. Winnie stood up. Her body felt tingly and numb; she was shaking. She pulled on a pair of jeans and picked up her flip-flops; they would be too noisy to wear down the stairs. When she opened the door, she found Garrett standing there with a strange, peaceful expression on his face. He, too, was wearing jeans, and his Danforth wind breaker. He held the urn in both his hands.

They slipped downstairs. The house made noises, but these didn't phase Winnie. She was used to being awake in the middle of the night because of Marcus, and had learned that the house creaked, as though complaining about growing older. There was a little bit of light cast through the living room windows by the stars and a crescent moon. Garrett eased open the front door.

Winnie said, "I think I'm going to eat something."

Garrett whipped around. "What?"

"I'm hungry."

"Tough."

"Tough for you." Winnie went into the kitchen and opened the refrigerator. There were always leftovers when Beth cooked, the remnants of dinner, all wrapped up: BBQ ribs, Beth's macaroni salad, and three buttermilk biscuits. Winnie had smelled the biscuits baking earlier.

"I'm taking the biscuits," she said.

Garrett narrowed his eyes. "You went three months without eating and now you can't wait two hours for biscuits?"

"No," she said. "I can't. And they have to be warm."

"What?"

"Or the butter won't melt." She put the plate of biscuits in the microwave and set it for one minute. Every time she pressed a button there was a loud, electronic beep. Garrett lowered himself gingerly into a kitchen chair, the urn in his lap.

"I can't believe you," he said. "Do you *want* to get caught?"

Winnie didn't answer. She watched her biscuits, bathed in light, as they circled around inside the microwave. She took the butter dish from the fridge. Maybe she did want to get caught. Maybe she did want her mother to come down and find them both there, with the urn.

The microwave beeped five loud times to let her know the biscuits were finished. Garrett said, "I'll wait for you in the driveway." Winnie got a knife from the drawer, sliced open the hot biscuits, and put a pat of butter inside each one. Then she wrapped them in plastic; she could eat them on the way. But she needed a drink. She opened the fridge again and took out a Coke. Popped it open right there in the kitchen; it sounded like a cap gun. Winnie waited, willing her mother out of sleep. *If you wake up, you can say good-bye!* But there were no stirrings from upstairs. Whatever Garrett read about human sleep patterns must have been correct.

She walked out to the driveway carrying her snack. She took a swill of her Coke, then followed Garrett to the car.

The hardest part had been deciding where. Winnie wanted to scatter the ashes right off the deck—that way their father's remains would become one with their property, one with Horizon. Garrett disagreed; he wanted to really hurt their mother by scattering the ashes somewhere she would never think of. After they'd bandied about several possibilities—the cornfields of Bartlett Farm, the marshes around Miacomet Pond, the Easy Street boat basin—Garrett claimed he had the perfect place in mind. But they needed the car. Winnie was going to drive because technically Garrett was still grounded from the car. Winnie was nervous about driving in the dark but Garrett said he'd be right there in the passenger seat, helping. It would be easier, he said, without so many cars on the road.

They climbed in the Rover, just barely clicking their doors shut. Winnie held the keys. They felt foreign in her hand and Winnie was reminded of the only time she ever smoked a cigarette and she wasn't sure how to hold it. She wiggled the key into the ignition and took a breath. This was the biggest risk: that Beth would hear the car. But, as Garrett pointed out, even if she did hear it, it would be too late. They'd be gone and she would have no way to follow them.

Winnie backed out of the driveway. Garrett peered through the windshield at the house and Winnie nervously glanced at her mother's bedroom window. Nothing. Winnie pulled onto the dirt road, and when she was a safe distance from the house, she switched on the headlights.

Garrett leaned back in his seat, the urn in his lap. "Home free," he said.

"Now will you please tell me where we're going?" Winnie said. She resented the fact that Garrett got to choose their father's final resting place. Winnie had also suggested scattering the ashes into the ocean—maybe because she was a swimmer, and felt more at home in the water than she did on dry land. But Garrett protested. *No way,* he'd said. *Not the water.* He'd referred to the map on his bedroom wall. *Dad will end up in Portugal. Or the Canary Islands.*

"We're going to Quidnet," Garrett said.

"*Quid*-net?" This was a part of the island Winnie had heard of but she couldn't remember ever going there, and she certainly wouldn't be able to find it on her own. "Why Quidnet?"

"Dad and I went there once, a few years ago. A secret road. A meadow surrounded by trees on one side and water on the other. It was a cool place, and I don't know, it was like the two of us discovered it."

"Where was I?" Winnie wanted to know.

"At home," Garrett said. "With Mom."

At home with Mom, the liar, while Garrett and Arch explored the island together. Winnie liked the sound of this less and less. Garrett was commandeering the mission.

"You know, Garrett," Winnie said. "It's not like it's *Daddy* in that urn. It's just the remains of the body that belonged to Daddy."

"I know," Garrett said defensively, but Winnie saw him clench the urn. Of all of them, Garrett was the most protective of the

ashes—after all, they'd sat in his room all summer. To be perfectly honest, Winnie didn't like to think about the ashes. Her
father's burned remains. She wanted to scatter them so they'd be
gone. So she could be left with the memories of her father that
lived in her mind. Dr. Schau, however, had reminded them in
the final therapy session before they left for Nantucket, that scattering the ashes was an important symbolic act. It was one tangible way to say good-bye. Winnie felt a pang in her chest at
the thought of Dr. Schau. After they did this, how would they
ever be able to face Dr. Schau again? She would think they were
evil children—stealing a coping mechanism, an avenue of healing
away from their mother. And then there was Marcus: *You wouldn't
know a problem if one bit you in the ass.* It wasn't as if Beth had
committed a crime. She hadn't hurt anyone physically, and she
hadn't broken any laws except for one that Winnie and Garrett
held in their heart: *We should know everything about our mother.*

"I'm having second thoughts," Winnie said. She clenched the
wheel as they rumbled over the ruts in the dirt road, and yearned
for her biscuits. She wanted one, now. She pulled over to the
side of the road, located the biscuits in the console, and stuffed
one in her mouth over Garrett's protests. She drank some of her
Coke. "Remember how Dad always said, if you have a choice
between the right thing to do and the easy thing to do, choose
the right thing?"

"Well, what about Mom?" Garrett said. "She chose the easy
thing by lying to us for seventeen years."

"It probably wasn't easy," Winnie said. "It's never easy to lie
because you're always so afraid someone will find out."

"Trust me, Winnie," Garrett said. "We're doing the right thing.
She lied to Dad, too, don't forget."

"I guess," Winnie said. Garrett was older than her by four minutes, and he had put himself in charge. But, in a brilliant twist of fate, *she* was driving the car. She could turn around and go back to the house; she could foil this plan. Winnie ate the second biscuit. The butter greased her lips. "I don't know, Garrett."

"Come on," he said. "You're the one with the marriage certificate."

True, true. The marriage certificate was in the back pocket of her jeans. Winnie thought of Melon smiling at her with such compassion, as if to say, *You poor girl. Your mother and David Ronan.*

"You're right," Winnie said. She finished the second biscuit, drank some more Coke, and signaled left, even though there wasn't another car for miles. "Let's go."

❧

Nantucket was bigger than Winnie realized. She'd been coming here every summer since she was born and yet her experience of Nantucket consisted of the south shore from Cisco Beach to Surfside, and the roads that led into town. Once or twice a summer they drove out Milestone Road to get ice cream from the 'Sconset Market, and two or three times they'd done the Milestone–Polpis bike path as a family. But driving through the moonlight with Garrett and her father's ashes, Winnie saw whole sections of Nantucket she never even knew existed. The winding dirt roads between Monomoy and Shimmo, for example. There were whole neighborhoods—lots of people lived here. How did Garrett find these roads? He went exploring with Piper, he said. He directed Winnie back to the Polpis Road and they cruised past Quaise, Shawkemo Hills, and Wauwinet.

Winnie put her window down and the night air rushed in. They had the radio on, the oldies station, hoping they would hear a song that reminded them of their father, and as it turned out, every song that played reminded them of Arch. "Here Comes the Sun," by the Beatles, "Red Rubber Ball," by Cyrkle, even "Puff, the Magic Dragon," which he used to sing to them as kids. Winnie started to feel like they were doing the right thing. It was a perfect night, the island was as beautiful as she'd ever seen it, and their father's spirit was filling the car.

Garrett gave her plenty of warning before her left hand turn on to Quidnet Road; she put on her blinker.

"You're doing a good job driving," he said.

This pleased her. "Thanks."

He told her to take another left onto a dirt road. The road was bordered on both sides by tall trees that arched above them. A tunnel of trees, and every so often through a break in the leaves and branches, Winnie spied the crescent moon.

"We're almost there," Garrett said.

After a while, the trees on the left hand side opened up to a meadow, and beyond the meadow was the flat, calm water of Nantucket Sound. Winnie caught her breath. "This is it?" she said.

"Yeah," Garrett said. "It's cool, isn't it?"

"You came here with Daddy?"

"That one time he and I went surf casting out at Great Point?" Garrett said. "We explored on our way home and found this place. He said he wanted to bring you and Mom here for a picnic."

"Really?" Winnie said. "Where should we stop?"

"Up here," Garrett said.

Winnie pulled onto the shoulder. The radio was playing Linda Ronstadt singing "Long, Long Time." Garrett opened his door and they both blinked at the dome light. "Let's do it," he said.

Winnie's heart pounded in her ears. She was unable to move. "Garrett?" she said.

He came to the driver's side and helped her out of the car. He kept his arm around her as he steered her into the meadow. There were Queen Anne's lace, black-eyed Susans, and a thicket of low blueberry bushes.

Garrett opened the urn. He put the top of the urn by his feet, and when he straightened, he reached into the urn, but then he withdrew his hand.

"You first," he said. "You throw first."

"Why?"

"Because you were his little girl," Garrett said. "He loved you best."

Immediately Winnie's eyes were blurred by tears. She sniffled. "Oh, Garrett, you know he loved us exactly the same."

"He loved us a lot," Garrett said. He was crying, too, and this made Winnie cry harder. She knew she would never forget this moment as long as she lived. Her twin brother, this hidden meadow, and the water beyond it, the music in her head, her mother's secret in her heart. Winnie slipped her hand into the urn. The ash was fine and silky with a few chunks. The remains of her beloved father, the man she loved first, the man she would always love beyond any other man, even Marcus. Winnie called up the memories she had left: her father across the table from her at EJ's Luncheonette eating his red flannel hash; her father in the balcony of Danforth's indoor pool, whooping like a rodeo cowboy as a signal to her to give the last lap of the race all she had, her father on any one of five thousand nights coming in to kiss her good night on the forehead, never shutting the door without saying, "I love you, Winnie. You're my only little girl." He had been a great lawyer—that was why his obituary ran in all of the New York papers, including the *Times*—but he'd been an even greater father. This, she realized, was the highest compliment anyone could give a man.

With a wide, circling motion of her arm, Winnie scattered him, set him free, let him go.

chapter 6

Just like that, Marcus's summer was falling apart. He wished he'd never heard the secret news about Beth and David—it was family business and he'd been dragged in, first by Beth, then by Winnie. Marcus had promised Beth he would support Winnie, but her reaction to the news was so overblown, so immature, that Marcus could feel nothing but disappointment in her. Their relationship, whatever it was—boyfriend/girlfriend or just friends—was turning to rags faster than Winnie's sweatshirt.

Marcus couldn't figure out what the twins' so-called revenge was, but there was a definite change in their behavior. They spoke very little to Beth, and when they did speak, it was in a cool, formal tone, the way you would talk to a stranger at a bus stop. One-word sentences, short, tired phrases, crisp and distant. Beth tolerated it for about a day and a half, then she confronted them at dinner. "All right, kids. What's going on?" Garrett and Winnie didn't blink, didn't crack a smile; they simply looked at each other meaningfully and retreated into themselves, like a set of twins Marcus read about once in a magazine article who had their own spooky form of communication.

Winnie had also stopped talking to Marcus. When they occupied the same space—the kitchen, for example, while making breakfast or lunch—Winnie smiled at him benignly, like Marcus was someone she'd met once before but whose name she couldn't recall. He wanted to shake her—*this is not how you treat people when you're angry!* But Marcus didn't want to give Winnie the satisfaction of knowing how much her behavior bugged him. After all, he had his own life. He had, he reminded himself with increasing guilt each day, a *book* to write.

He couldn't stop himself from thinking of her, though, from listening to every word that came out of her mouth (mostly words directed to Garrett, or to Piper, if she was around). He couldn't help himself from listening for her in the middle of the night; he knew her footsteps, and when they were in the house together, he kept track of her. One afternoon, as he hung out in his room, he heard her march up the stairs and stop just outside his door. He tried to steady his breathing as he waited for her to knock. Marcus was ready to forgive her—even to apologize.

Strangely, no knock came. Instead, there was a whooshing sound as an envelope skated across the wood floor. Marcus shook his head. It was just like a woman to write a note.

When he bent over to retrieve the envelope, however, he saw that it wasn't a note and it wasn't from Winnie. It was a Western Union telegram and that, he realized with a surge of fear, meant only one thing: Zachary Celtic. Zachary had bugged Marcus for a phone number, a fax number, an e-mail address—he wanted a way to contact Marcus to check on the progress of the book.

When Marcus reported that there was no computer at the house where he was staying, no fax machine, *not even a phone,*—*That's right,* Marcus had said, *I guess these people I'm staying with are old-fashioned or something*—Zachary Celtic had grudgingly written down the address, saying he would send telegrams.

So here was a telegram, delivered by a person so angry with him that she couldn't even knock on the door and hand it to him. Marcus slit the envelope with his pinky nail.

21 July

Dear Marcus,

    How is the book coming along? No pressure, man, just checking in. September will be here before you know it! Call if you need guidance—that's what editors are for! (And to rip the shit out of your first three drafts, of course—only kidding, man!)

Best regards,
Z

Marcus winced. Zachary Celtic wasn't used to writing to black people if he thought the only name they related to was "man."

The telegram reignited the panic that lay in the bottom of his stomach like cold kindling. With trembling hands, Marcus took the legal pad from his bureau drawer. *My mother is a murderer.* Even that was more than Marcus wanted to say. He tossed the legal pad onto his bed and opened the louvered folding door of his closet. His beautiful white shirt was the only thing hanging. Marcus's black leather duffel lay across the closet floor, as hideous as a body bag. The only thing that made Marcus feel worse than the duffel was the pair of dock shoes, the left shoe stuffed with Constance's unread letters. Those three things—the shirt, the duffel, and the shoes—were physical proof of the five hundred dollars he would never be able to pay back and thirty thousand dollars he would never see unless he could figure out how he wanted to tell his story.

Marcus lay back on his white bed. *The dead bodies in your own apartment . . . your mother, pretty woman, too, strapped to the gurney, facing the long needle . . . the blood-splattered sheet . . . You get to tell the story in your own words, kid. I'll bet that's something you've been itching to do . . . Your mother as, like, an educated woman, a teacher and everything, and one day she just . . . snaps.*

Yes, Marcus thought, she just snapped.

He didn't know why his mother had killed Angela and Candy; he didn't *have* an explanation and it wasn't fair—to his readers or to his mother—to make one up.

❧

Winnie and Marcus didn't sit together at the beach anymore. Instead, Winnie sat on the deck with Garrett and sometimes Piper, and Marcus went to the beach alone. He swam the butterfly, some of his strongest swimming, because he knew Winnie was watching. He thought about how he could have won first place in every meet last season. He'd held himself back on purpose. Now *that* took skill, because nobody suspected he was throwing his races. Or maybe his coach did suspect and decided to keep quiet because he didn't want Marcus to win. He didn't want to face the headlines any more than Marcus did. MURDERER'S SON WINS ALL-QUEENS INVITATIONAL.

Marcus grew lonely, especially in the hours after dinner when he and Winnie normally played games. Now he stayed in his room, listening to his portable CD player, reading about spies, thinking about his mother.

For the first time all summer, he missed TV. And with utter dismay, Marcus realized that he wouldn't be able to write a word while he was so agitated about Winnie.

He considered going home. It was nearly the end of July; he'd had six good weeks. The atmosphere in his white room wasn't conducive to writing, that was a big problem, so the best thing was to get home—away from so much whiteness. Away from the Newtons.

He called home on a Tuesday night, enjoying the unconcealed intrigue on Winnie's face when he stood up from the dinner table and announced that he was riding one of the mountain bikes into town. She didn't say anything, but her eyebrows moved a fraction of an inch, belying her thoughts: *What is he doing in town at night?* It was likely she also had questions about the telegram—Marcus had checked the envelope and was relieved to discover there was no return address to give him away. Let her wonder. Let her wonder, too, when he disappeared for good.

It cost two dollars and fifty cents in quarters to get a line to Queens on the pay phone, and at first the answering machine picked up. Marcus listened for a few seconds to his father's melancholy intonation, "We're not in at the moment, please—"

Then, the voice was cut off, replaced by the breathless alto of Marcus's sister, LaTisha. "Yeah? What?"

"Or 'hello,' " Marcus said, thinking despite himself that even if the Newtons had a phone they would never answer by saying "Yeah? What?" "You could say hello."

"*Marcus?*" LaTisha said, her voice interested, if not apologetic. "Is this Marcus?"

"Yes."

"How are you?" LaTisha asked. "How's Nantucket? Is it incredible? Dad says you never describe it."

Marcus looked out at the darkened street. The shops were lit up and people strolled by eating ice cream cones. A Lincoln Navigator rumbled down the cobblestones and stopped in front of Twenty-one Federal. Two women climbed out wearing brightly colored sundresses, followed by a man wearing a navy blazer over what Marcus guessed was a Paul Stuart shirt. The man escorted both women up the steps of the restaurant while the driver of the Navigator—whom Marcus could only identify as a madras-clad elbow—called out, "Order my drink while I park this beast! Mount Gay and tonic!" How to describe such a place to his father or LaTisha? All Marcus could think was that *this* was the life Constance had visualized for herself—a life of glamour and privilege and ease.

"It's fine," he said.

"*Fine?*" LaTisha repeated. "That doesn't help me any. What's the beach like? And the house. Is it really, really huge? Is it a mansion?"

"It's not a mansion," Marcus said. "It's just a house."

"On the beach, right?"

"On a bluff overlooking the beach."

"A *bluff?* That sounds cool. And the family—is the family okay, or are they, you know, snotty?"

"Snotty" was the wrong word, though Marcus understood why it was the word that came to LaTisha's mind. Because that was what Marcus had feared, too, before he got here—that the Newtons would be snotty, snobby, that they would look down on him. That was the reason for buying the props—the shirt, the deck shoes, the leather bag. He had thought, before he spent any time with these people, that it would be about money. But it was ten times as complicated as that. The Newtons were just so very sad—as sad as Marcus was—and they kept getting sadder. Marcus cleared his throat and shook his head. He didn't want to start feeling sorry for them now.

"The family is fine," Marcus said. A blatant lie. "Listen, is Dad there?"

"It's Tuesday," LaTisha said. "He's at support group until nine-thirty."

"Oh," Marcus said. He'd forgotten about the support group. The details of his life in Queens had all but vanished from his mind. "What are you doing?"

"Nothing," LaTisha said. "Watching TV with Ernestine."

Ernestine was a girl with learning disabilities from down the hall who had remained LaTisha's steadfast friend through everything. Marcus suspected Ernestine lacked a full understanding of what had happened with their mother, but he was glad LaTisha had her for company, even if all they ever did together was watch TV.

"The house here doesn't have a TV," Marcus said.

"*What?*" LaTisha said. "You're kidding, right? They don't have TV? God, Marcus, what do you do all day? And at night?"

"I swim during the day, and you know, sit on the beach. I read. Listen to music. Hang out . . ." He almost said, *Hang out with Winnie,* but he caught himself. "I relax."

Suddenly, LaTisha's voice grew suspicious. "You're calling Dad because you want to come home, right? Geez, Marcus, I don't blame you. You must be bored to death. Well, I'll be happy if you come home. I miss you. This place *sucks* when you're not here. Pop is practically never home and I have this ridiculous curfew. Eight o'clock. It's not even dark at eight o'clock. And if he's not here he has Mrs. Demetrios check on me. I'm almost thirteen, for God's sake!" She paused to catch her breath and Marcus pictured her young face and her skimpy braids. When Constance first went to jail, LaTisha cried all the time because Mama wasn't there to do her hair. "I thought I might make a little money this summer, but nobody calls me to baby-sit anymore. They probably think . . . well, who knows what they think."

"They probably think you're going to kill their children," Marcus said.

"Yeah," LaTisha said, as though this were something she had realized and accepted long ago. "Anyway, things would be better if you came home."

"I'm not coming home," Marcus said. As bad as shit was, at least he wasn't frying on the griddle of hot city blocks, or worse, trapped inside, supervising his sister, watching reruns of *Three's Company* and begging the air conditioner to do a better job. He felt sad about this—*home* should be a place you wanted to run to no matter what. It should be a refuge. "I just wanted to check in is all."

"Well, as much as I told you I was glad to get rid of your ass this summer, I'm really not. It feels like everyone is dropping out of this family."

"I'm not dropping out," Marcus said.

"I know," LaTisha said. "It just feels that way."

"You should . . . read more," Marcus said. "Go to the library."

"*Library?*" LaTisha said. "Now you sound like Mama." Before Marcus could assert his obvious difference from their mother, LaTisha added, "I'll tell Pop you called. You'll call back—when?"

"Soon," Marcus promised. "I'll talk to you later, sis. Okay? Tell Ernestine I said hello."

He hung up the phone then looked out at the charming Nantucket street. He was a person who belonged nowhere.

※

A few days later, there was a knock on Marcus's bedroom door. Marcus had his legal pad out and was jotting down notes, if not actual sentences. It hardly mattered to Marcus—he was so relieved to have words on the page, even if those words had no more meaning than entries in a dictionary: "Princeton University," "smack," "petty theft," "child prostitution," "anger," "social services," "intent to kill???" Now that the ball was rolling, or if not rolling than at least moving, *of course* there would be an interruption. Marcus tucked the legal pad under his white pillows and grumbled, "Come in."

It was Beth, a fact that both relieved and disappointed him. She looked awful—thin and desiccated like a plant that needed watering. She gave him a smile, though, and held out an envelope. Marcus's first thought was, *Another telegram. Leave me alone, man.*

"From Constance," she said.

Even worse! A fourth letter from Mama.

"Okay," he said. "Thanks." He took the envelope from Beth and dropped it on the bed in front of him as though he planned to read it once Beth left. Beth, however, remained in the doorway smiling at him. Then her friendly smile turned into a worried smile and she said, "Can I talk to you for a minute?"

This was the last thing he wanted, though he was surprised it had taken her so long to confront him. Garrett and Winnie had joined forces and so it only made sense that Beth and Marcus would do the same. Except neither of them wanted to. Marcus was used to being cast out on his own—that, after all, was what he'd expected from the summer: the twins wrapped up in their own exclusive cocoon, Beth lost hopelessly in the outer space of her grief. As for Beth, well, she believed she understood her kids well enough to know that whatever was bugging them would pass. But now their bizarre aloofness had lasted more than a week and showed no signs of abating. She needed help.

Beth closed the door to Marcus's bedroom and sat on his bed. The letter from Constance lay between them, a boundary.

"I was just wondering," she said, "if maybe you knew what was going on. In this house, I mean. With the kids. Winnie and Garrett. Their behavior. This isn't like them."

Marcus lowered his eyelids, an involuntary sign for her to stop. Obviously he knew what she was talking about; he wasn't an idiot. The question was whether Marcus was going to tell her the bad news. He considered the consequences. If he told Beth the truth—that her secret was out—Winnie would *never* forgive him. Furthermore, the workings of this family were none of his business. He felt badly for Beth—yes, he did—but he couldn't speak.

He shrugged.

Beth hooked his gaze, trying to pry him open with her eyes. "Winnie hasn't *said* anything to you?"

"Winnie hasn't said anything to me," he repeated. "In about ten days."

"They're pushing us away," Beth said. "It's not like they're openly hostile, but I'm beginning to feel like their butler. Know what I mean? I've been thinking of inviting our therapist to come for the weekend. Kara Schau—you'd like her."

The therapist. Marcus supposed that's what rich people did

when they had family troubles—invited the therapist for the weekend. He shook his head, then eyed the letter.

"I'd like to be alone now," Marcus said. "I don't mean to kick you out of a room of your own house, but I really do want to be alone."

What could Beth do but respect his wishes? She stood up to go.

"You'll let me know if you learn anything?" she said.

The woman was just begging him to lie to her. Sometimes, he supposed, that was what people needed.

"Sure," he said.

※

That night, Winnie went to the movies with Garrett and Piper. They didn't invite Marcus along, and it took Beth to ask, "Isn't Marcus going with you?"

They didn't answer her, and Marcus quickly stated that he wanted to stay home. He went upstairs to his bedroom, listening through his open window to Winnie's voice, her laughter, the sound of the car doors slamming. He felt so angry with her, and yet their separation didn't seem to bother her at all. As the Rover drove off, Marcus pulled Constance's most recent letter from the inside of his dock shoe and opened it. He decided he would read it, then throw it in the trash.

July 24

Dear Marcus,

Through everything I have never stopped loving you. I will wait as long as it takes.

Mama

Marcus crumpled the letter and threw it at the mirror. "It's bullshit!" he said, louder than he meant to. "Bullshit!"

The fury in his voice bounced back at him from the white walls of his room. Beth was somewhere in the house but she didn't call up to him. He opened the other letters; they all said basically the same thing: *I love you, child . . . I think of you every day . . . I pray to hear the sound of your voice . . .*

"It's bullshit!" Marcus shouted. God, it felt good to yell. It felt good to let go for once. At home, his father and sister would have been frightened, not to mention baffled, by his anger. He ripped the letters in half, though he yearned to destroy them more permanently—with fire or water. He stuffed the pieces of paper back into his dock shoe then threw the shoe at the door of his room, a fast ball. He pulled his notebook out of the drawer, tore out the single page that constituted the sum of his work this summer and started a fresh page.

Dear Mama, he wrote. *If you loved me, you wouldn't have done it.*

꙰

Later, there was a thunderstorm. Marcus woke up to a loud crashing, loud enough to make him think lightning had hit the chimney. The house shuddered. Marcus lay in bed, listening to the deep rolls and sharp cracks of thunder. He'd never heard a storm like this before. He looked out his window—the sky flashed with light, bolts of lightning hit the pond in the distance, and rain poured down in sheets. Out in the driveway, he noticed the windows of the Rover were down. Winnie and Garrett had forgotten to roll them up when they got back from the movies. They deserved to have a ruined car—they were spoiled brats, both of them. But then Beth entered his mind. He'd already disappointed her once that day and so Marcus threw on a T-shirt and ran downstairs and out the front door. The rain pummeled his back. He dashed for the car. They always left the keys in the ignition, even when they parked in town. *Any idea how fast this car would be gone in Queens?* Marcus asked once. He turned the key in the ignition and put up the windows. Then he leaned back in the driver's seat, straightening his arms to the steering wheel. He thought of driving away. But there was no escaping this island in the middle of the night. Marcus relaxed against the leather seat until it sounded like the rain was abating a little. But three seconds outside—from the car to the front door—left him soaked. He peeled his shirt off as he climbed the stairs, cursing himself for being such a slave. When he got into his room, he tossed the wet shirt onto his chair, missing Winnie by a few inches. She was standing there, in his room.

"What the hell?" he said.

She looked different. He switched on the night-light that Beth gave him the first day of their vacation so he could find his way to the bathroom. It was a scallop shell night-light and it glowed pink; this was the only time he'd ever used it. It gave off just enough light for him to study Winnie. She was staring at him. It occurred to Marcus that maybe she was sleepwalking. Then he pinpointed what was different—she wasn't wearing the sweatshirt. She was wearing a short pink nightgown. Marcus felt his body temperature rise. He dug through his dresser drawer for a dry shirt.

"If your brother catches you in here, I'm dead meat."

"He doesn't care anymore, Marcus."

"Yeah, right."

"No, really, we talked about it."

"I'm sure you did," Marcus said. He imagined some elaborate trap—sending Winnie in here to give Garrett a reason to attack him again. "Where's your sweatshirt?"

"I'm finished wearing it," she said.

"How come?"

She moved closer to him. "I can't explain it, really. I just don't feel the need to wear it anymore. I might wear it once in a while, if I get cold."

"Oh," he said. Along with everything else, he felt betrayed that the shedding of the sweatshirt took place without his knowledge. Because Marcus knew that meant something bigger had happened, a change in Winnie's brain or heart. He thought the retiring of the sweatshirt deserved some kind of ceremony, the sweatshirt that Marcus had worn once himself. He still hadn't told Winnie about that, and now he figured he never would. "Well, congratulations." Although he meant it, his voice was laced with sarcasm.

"Thanks," she said. "It's a good thing."

The pink nightgown was sheer and through it, Marcus could see the outline of Winnie's white panties. He was afraid to go near his bed, but there wasn't anywhere else to sit, aside from the chair where his soggy shirt lay in a puddle. "Do you mind telling me what you're doing here?"

"I came to apologize."

"Did you?"

She lowered herself onto the bed next to him, and Marcus glared at the floor, allowing only the side of Winnie's foot in his view. "I acted badly. I said mean things."

"Yeah, and there was a lot you didn't say."

"I know."

"You haven't said shit to me in over a week, Winnie. You cut me out."

"I'm sorry—"

"You can't treat people like that. You've been horrible to your mother."

"She was horrible to us."

"She *wasn't* horrible," Marcus said. "She just kept a part of her past private."

"An *important* part."

"Fine, an important part. There's no law saying that parents have to explain themselves to their children, Winnie." He raised his head and looked at the brown smudge on the door where his shoe had hit. "My mother hasn't explained herself. I don't know why she killed those people and I probably never will. Everyone has their secrets."

"I don't," Winnie said.

"Well, I do," Marcus said. "I have a big secret that nobody knows about, but if I told you, you'd probably be mad at me for keeping it, even though it's mine to keep."

"I won't be mad at you," Winnie said. "What is it?"

"Why should I tell you?" he said. The nightgown left her shoulders bare—bare shoulders, bare arms, bare legs to midthigh. And her neck. For ten days there had been no Winnie, and now there was all this. "When you and I first became friends, I thought I wanted to be a part of this family. Now I don't want to. You know the other night, when I went into town? It was to call my pop and tell him I wanted to come home early. Do you know how bad things must be for me to want to go back to *Queens?*"

Winnie touched his leg, and Marcus jumped up. This was a terrible room for confrontation because there was practically nothing in it. He crossed the room in three steps and sat on top of the wobbly dresser. His shirt was dripping, making a puddle on the floor under the chair.

"Please don't go home," Winnie said. "I didn't mean to hurt you."

"What about the last ten days? What about not one kind word in ten days?"

"I was confused. And angry. And I thought you were angry at me. And Garrett—"

"Don't even mention his name," Marcus said, rocking the dresser back and forth. "I should have beat him blind when I had the chance."

"Garrett and I have to confront my mother," Winnie said. "We have to get this out in the open."

"I told you that before."

"I wasn't *ready* before. I had a lot to think about."

"Whatever," he said.

"I'm sorry I slammed the door in your face," she said.

"I'm used to people treating me that way," he said. "I'm used to being shunned. That's all I get at home. But here everything was different. Everything was better."

"I was feeling better, too," Winnie said. "Until."

"Until."

"My mother," Winnie said.

"Your mother? What about my mother?" Marcus said. "Can't you tell the difference between a misdemeanor and a felony?"

"No," said Winnie. She rubbed her arms as if she were cold. "Anyway, I'm sorry I didn't sit on the beach with you. That was mean."

"I managed."

"You looked good swimming."

"Thanks."

"Did you miss me?" she asked.

He shook his head. "I had other things to worry about."

"I want you to forgive me."

"What do you care if I forgive you or not?"

"I came here tonight because I want you to know how I feel."
She stood up and held her arms out like she was handing him
something very heavy. "I feel like I'm in love with you. I'm in
love with you, Marcus."

It wasn't until that moment that Marcus noticed the thunder
was growing fainter, and so Winnie's words seemed very loud to
Marcus, so loud he felt the entire world could hear. His throat
ached in the same place where Garrett had kicked him, and he
realized he might cry.

"You're in love with me?"

"Yes," Winnie said.

"I don't see why I should believe you," he said.

"I guess you should believe me because it's true," Winnie said,
nodding at the bed. "I want to be with you. Really *with* you.
We've been waiting all summer for this. You know it as well as
I do."

Did he know it? He was too aware of Winnie in her pink
nightie to answer. What would happen if he got his ass off this
fragile heirloom dresser and went to her? Winnie pulled him
across the room and pushed him into the bed, her skinny arms
surprisingly strong from so much swim practice. He wondered
again if this were some kind of trap, the big trap, the one that
would get him sent away. Winnie ran her hand up the inside of
his T-shirt and suddenly Marcus didn't care who came barging

in. He felt vulnerable, but the swirling tornado of anger inside of him was stilled, just from having her in his arms. He had missed her, this blond girl from Manhattan with all her quirks and flaws and rays of light.

"All right," he said, thinking that the best life would be one where they could exist in an alternate universe, without their families.

She kissed him very softly on the lips, and slid out of her nightgown. Marcus remembered again of all those swim meets where he'd held himself back. Now, Winnie had given him the green light; she was waving him on toward the finish. Tonight, he was going to win.

Beth couldn't believe she'd been so dumb, so blind, so naive. For nearly two weeks the twins' behavior had been so inexplicable that she'd called Kara Schau's office twice, only to learn that Kara was on vacation in the Hamptons. It was by chance that Beth went to the liquor cabinet for vermouth for a recipe and found the nearly empty bottle of Malibu rum. She knew for certain that neither she nor Arch had touched the rum in years, and so the culprits had to be the kids. They were drinking! Beth was chagrined that she hadn't guessed the problem sooner and yet relieved that the answer might be so simple. They were raiding the liquor cabinet. She decided not to say anything about the Malibu until she figured out exactly what was going on. She wanted to check the twins' rooms, which she did under the auspices of dusting one incredibly hot and muggy August morning. If they were going to be sneaky, well, then, so was she.

Winnie's room was an organized mess. She'd started wearing clothes again, instead of just the Princeton sweatshirt. Beth wondered at this development but didn't dare question it. She found the sweatshirt folded neatly on a chair in Winnie's room. There were other clothes on the floor, some books, a journal. A glass of brown liquid on the night table. Beth sniffed it, then took a sip: warm, flat Coke. Okay. She made a few cursory swipes over the dresser and mirror, over the bedposts, and over the windowsill with her soft yellow cloth. Her spirit balked at the thought that in three short weeks, she'd be dusting this room for real—the final clean before closing the house for the winter. Although it had been a difficult summer, Beth hated the idea of leaving. The only way she'd made it through the spring was by thinking of Nantucket. New York was beautiful in autumn, and crackling with excitement—new theater, new restaurants, getting the kids back to school, the leaves changing in Central Park—but this year none of it held any appeal. New York was funereal, depressing, the site of tragedy. Beth understood that after the kids graduated from Danforth, she may have to sell their apartment and move somewhere less painful.

She walked down the hallway to Garrett's room, wiping the frames of the watercolors that hung on the walls. Garrett was out with Piper, and Marcus and Winnie were at the beach. Beth was relieved to see that Marcus and Winnie had worked things out, although neither of the twins had spoken to Beth in a normal way in almost two weeks. She confronted them several times, but this only made things worse, and so Beth forced herself to let it go—it was just some awful, weird phase—but now there was the alcohol to explain it, and possibly worse things: marijuana, ecstasy, LSD.

Beth poked around Garrett's room until she found a box of Trojans in his nightstand drawer. This stopped her cold, and she sat on his bed with the box—a huge box—in her lap. Well, it wasn't exactly shocking, and she supposed she should be relieved he was using protection, but it made her sick-hearted to be holding physical evidence of her son's sexual life. She returned the box to the drawer and checked in the closet and under the bed. There she found the trunk of her uncle Burton's traveling artifacts. No six-packs, no baggies of weed.

Beth dusted the bedposts and the top of Garrett's dresser. The urn of Arch's ashes was sitting on the dresser and Beth spoke to him in her mind. *I'm in way over my head here, babe. Sex, alcohol— God knows what else. You're supposed to be here to help me. This is the heavy lifting. I can't do it on my own.* It didn't help that it was now August, the part of the summer when Beth would begin to anticipate Arch's two-week vacation. He didn't love Nantucket the way she did, but she adored having him on the island for those two weeks, even if he did spend too much time at the dining room table working.

Last year, on the night he'd arrived, he was the most relaxed she had ever seen him. He'd come off the plane wearing his Nantucket red shorts and his Yankees cap backward, his white polo shirt untucked. He convinced Beth to take a walk on the beach with him after the kids went to bed. There was a half-moon hanging low and phosphorescence in the water. They held hands and caught up on what had happened the previous week— this time last year Arch was defending a major magazine conglomerate against charges of lifestyle discrimination, a case he eventually won. They talked about what they wanted to do with the kids over the next two weeks—picnics and outings and lobster night. Amid all this happy chatter, Arch stopped and presented her with a velvet box—but shyly, nervously, like he was about to propose. Beth took the box, knowing that whatever was inside of it was way too expensive and absolutely unnecessary, but marveling, too, at the butterflies in her stomach—even after twenty years. Romance!

The diamond ring. The "We Made It" ring. Because it was a moonlit August night on the beach below their Nantucket cottage. Because Garrett and Winnie were healthy, bright, well-adjusted kids. Because Arch had a successful career. Because after twenty years they were still in love.

"We made it," Arch said as he slipped the ring on her finger. "It's easy sailing from here."

Beth wondered if she was remembering wrong. She didn't think so. Everything had been that perfect, momentarily. It would be two months later that Arch took Connie's case. It would be seven months later that his plane crashed.

Tears blurred Beth's eyes as she lifted the urn off the dresser. It was lighter than she remembered; it was light enough to make her pry off the top and check inside.

The ashes were gone, and in their place was a piece of paper. Beth set the urn down on Garrett's dresser and unfolded the paper. It took her a minute to realize what she was looking at, but then the names and dates, typed in their little boxes, came together. It was a marriage certificate. Hers and David's.

The room was very hot and close and Beth felt like she was going to faint. She flung open the door to Garrett's small balcony and stepped outside, sucking in the fresh air and the sight of the ocean. Beth considered hurling the urn off the balcony onto the deck below. But instead she clung to the empty urn, the urn that once contained the remains of her husband, and she carried it downstairs. A glass vase of zinnias sat on the kitchen table, and Beth removed the flowers and carried the vase outside to the deck. It wasn't a particularly good vase, but it had been in the house for as long as Beth could remember. It was a vase that Beth's grandmother used for her favorite New Dawn roses, which had climbed up the north side of Horizon until Gran died and the roses withered from lack of care. It was a vase that Beth's mother used for the flowers Beth's father always brought on weekends from their garden in New Jersey. Beth lifted the vase over her head and flung it against the deck. It was satisfying, the honest sound of breaking glass.

Let them cut their feet to ribbons, she thought. She then filled the urn with water and arranged the zinnias inside, placed the urn on the kitchen table, where they couldn't miss it. She thought about ripping the marriage certificate to shreds and leaving that on the table, too, but instead she just crumpled it up and threw it in the kitchen trash with the coffee grounds and eggshells.

They knew about David and they had scattered the ashes without her.

❧

Her instincts told her to get out of the house. She couldn't see the twins; she would kill them. Strike them, at the very least. Garrett had the Rover, and so Beth changed quickly into running clothes, tucked two bottles of water into her fanny pack, and took off down the dirt road.

It was hot, and before Beth even reached the end of Miacomet Pond, she stopped to drink. How dare they—that was all she could think. How dare they delve into her past, how dare they unearth her secret, and how dare they punish her for it. They never thought what it might be like for her. They never considered how difficult each day was, each night alone.

She had visualized scattering the ashes at sunrise on the morning of their last day—out in front of Horizon, into the sand and the dune grass. She had planned to say something meaningful; she had wanted to write a prayer. Well, it hardly mattered now. The twins had stolen Arch from her.

Beth reached a section of dense woods on Hummock Pond Road. She wanted to disappear among the cool trees. Let the kids raise themselves since they thought living was so easy. Let them get from age seventeen to middle age without making any mistakes. Then Beth heard Arch's voice in her head: *Your mistake isn't the problem, honey. It's that you concealed it.* She had hidden the truth from him, too, her own husband, dead now. On the ride home from the Ronans' cocktail party six years ago, she had almost told him. Her joints were loose from too much wine, and just the fact that they'd spent three hours in the same house with David made Beth want to confess.

There's something I want to tell you about David, Beth had said to Arch, as they sped through the night toward home. *Something you should know.*

Arch chuckled. *I liked the guy well enough. You'd better not say anything or you might change my mind.*

Even though she was drunk, those words registered. There was no reason for Beth to bring up the unfortunate, unchangeable past. There was no reason to upset Arch or herself. For years, she had felt her brief marriage to David Ronan was too private to share, and that was how it would stay. Her private history.

꽃

When she got home she was dismayed to find the Rover in the driveway. She had downed both bottles of water, she was slick with sweat and her vision was blotchy. She needed to eat, she needed rest. She couldn't bring herself to face her children. What would she say? Where could she possibly start?

When she walked inside, the house was quiet and Beth removed her socks and shoes on the bottom step of the stairs. She might be able to forego lunch and just pull her shades and climb into bed. She was so overwhelmingly tired that she knew she could sleep until morning. But then she heard whispering and she forced herself to tiptoe down the hallway and poke her head into the kitchen.

Garrett and Winnie were sitting alone at the kitchen table staring at the urn now filled with flowers. The broom and dustpan were out, and beyond the twins, Beth could see the deck had been swept clean. When the kids looked up and saw her, Beth had a hundred simultaneous memories of their faces. She remembered seeing them for the very first time, when they were an hour old, sleeping in their incubators in the hospital nursery. She pictured them on their second birthday, their mouths smeared with chocolate icing. She saw them at age ten, the first time they ever took the subway alone—the six line down to Union Square where Arch was going to meet them. She visualized them in the future, walking down the aisle at Winnie's wedding—Garrett in a tuxedo and Winnie in a pearl-colored slip dress, arm-in-arm, Garrett giving Winnie away. More times than Beth could count in the last five months, she had thought, It should have been me who died. But now, gazing at her children and the urn of flowers, that sense of guilt, guilt at *surviving*, vanished. She was their mother. They needed her more than they needed anyone else. Including Arch.

Beth poured herself a Gatorade. The only sounds in the kitchen were the cracking of ice, and the distant pound and rush of the waves outside. Beth drank the entire glass of liquid, then poured herself another. The silence was helpful. This was going to be the most important conversation she ever had with her children and she wanted to pick her words carefully. She couldn't help herself from asking, "You scattered the ashes without me?"

Winnie traced a scar in the table. Garrett said, "Yes."

Beth sat down; her legs felt weak. "Why?"

"We were angry," he said.

Beth imagined Kara Schau as an invisible fourth party at the table. She would praise Garrett for identifying his emotions. Beth wasn't as pleased. What she thought was: When you're angry you break a vase, you yell, you resort to sarcasm. You do not deceive your mother in the cruelest possible way.

"Angry about what?" she asked.

"You were married," Winnie whispered. "And you never told us."

"That's right," Beth said. "I was married and I never told you."

"And you never told Dad," Winnie said.

"And I never told Dad."

"You lied to all three of us," Garrett said. "Your family."

"I did not lie."

"You lied by omission," Garrett said. This was a legal premise that he'd learned from his father. What you didn't say could be just as damaging as what you did.

"It happened a long time ago," Beth said. "Before your father, before you. It has no bearing on your lives." She swallowed some more Gatorade. "It is none of your business."

"Except you're our mother," Winnie said. "We thought we knew you."

"You do know me."

"It doesn't feel like it," Garrett said.

"We want to know the whole story," Winnie said. "We want to know what happened."

"Oh," Beth said. This she wasn't ready for. She had devoted so much energy to not thinking about the details of August 1979 that to conjure them up would be like calling a voice or spirit back from the dead. "I'd like you to respect that it's my private past. It's not something I want to share—with you or anyone else."

"Piper knows the whole story," Garrett said. "But I wouldn't let her tell me about it. I wanted to hear it from you."

"Piper heard the story from David?"

"From Rosie, actually," Garrett said, knowing that this detail, beyond all others, would prod his mother to speak. "So I wasn't sure how accurate it'd be."

"It wouldn't be accurate at all," Beth said. She was livid at the thought of *Rosie* giving away her secret. Rosie!

"Just tell us, Mom," Winnie said.

Beth leaned back in the chair; it whined. "Where did you put Daddy's ashes?"

They were both quiet and Beth watched them exchange a quick look. She wanted to tread carefully here because she wanted the truth.

"In Quidnet," Garrett said. "We'll show you where. Later."

Later, meaning after Beth explained herself. It was blackmail, but what did she expect? These were teenagers.

"Where's Marcus?" Beth asked.

"He's in town," Winnie said. When Winnie saw the broken glass on the deck and then the urn right there on the *kitchen table*, she'd warned Marcus that there was going to be a confrontation, and without hesitation, Marcus said he would make himself scarce.

"Go ahead, Mom," Garrett said. "Tell us."

✤

It was nearly impossible to explain the romance of that sixth and final summer of Beth and David. But maybe not—because here were her twins, each experiencing love for the first time. Still, Beth feared she wouldn't be able to convey the heat and light, the depth and weight of her love for David. It was their sixth summer together; they were each twenty-one. When they rejoined in late May they realized that they had grown into adults, or almost. David had moved out of his parents' house and he rented the cottage on Bear Street. Beth was given full use of her grandfather's Volkswagen bug, which still ran, though barely. It was the perfect summer. David worked as a painter six days a week from seven until three; Beth didn't work at all. While David painted, Beth ran errands for her mother, helped out around the house, and sat on the beach in front of Horizon. Then at three o'clock, she disappeared. Beth's mother was preoccupied with Scott and Danny, who, at fourteen and sixteen, were turning her hair white. Beth's father flew in from the city every other weekend. And so Beth was free—she met David at his cottage at 3:15 and for her, the day began. They swam, they sailed, they went to the nude beach, and they raked for clams that they cooked up later with pasta for dinner. They went to bonfires and drank too much beer and fell into bed in the wee hours giddy and spinning. They made love.

David asked Beth to marry him in August. It was his day off, a Wednesday. Beth heard David rise early, before the sun was up, and when she opened her eyes, he was sitting on the edge of the bed holding a tray. A blue hydrangea in a drinking glass, a slice of cantaloupe, a bowl of strawberries. A bottle of Taittinger champagne.

"Whoa," she said, sitting up. "What's this?"

"Will you marry me?"

Beth laughed. She remembered wanting to open the champagne. She remembered David wrapping his hand around the back of her neck.

"I'm serious. I want to marry you."

"I want to marry you, too."

"Today."

"What?"

"We'll get dressed, we'll go to the Town Building."

"You're a nut."

"Next week, then. Next Wednesday. Will you marry me next Wednesday?"

"You're serious?"

"Yes," David said. "Bethie, I love you."

Beth never actually said yes, but she never said no either. She got swept along by David's enthusiasm and by her own desire to have the summer last forever. They were going to get married.

But Beth couldn't bring herself to inform her parents. She didn't dare breathe the word "marriage" under Horizon's roof.

Beth and David went to the hospital to have their blood tested. Beth bought a white sundress in town. She savored the tingly, secret excitement, the outlandish daring of it—she was getting married! They bought rings, inexpensive ones, plain gold bands, a hundred dollars for both.

The morning they were to be married, David rose early again. He returned with a huge handful of purple cosmos.

"Your bouquet," he said.

Only when Beth saw the flowers did she have her first pang of regret for what had yet to happen. This was her bridal bouquet. The white crinkled cotton sundress hanging in the closet was her wedding dress. She and David were going to climb into the bug, bounce down the cobblestone street to the Nantucket Town Building and get married. David was absolutely *glowing*—he looked the way she always thought she would look on her wedding day. But it was a different wedding day that she'd dreamed of: six bridesmaids in pink linen dresses and six grooms-men in navy blazers. Her father walking her down the aisle. She hesitated. The trappings of a wedding didn't matter. Who cared about a cocktail hour, a nine-piece band, chicken Kiev, and chocolate wedding cake? She took the flowers from David.

"They're perfect," she said.

※

Winnie and Garrett stared at her. Not in many years had she held them in this kind of rapt attention.

"Are you saying you knew you were about to make a mistake?" Winnie said.

"I had mixed feelings," Beth said. "But you hear about cold feet all the time—a bride and groom are *supposed* to have cold feet. And I loved David. I was twenty-one years old. If I'd wanted to back out, I would have."

⚘

When she emerged from the tiny bathroom in her white dress and rope sandals with the cork heels, David fell back on the sofa with his hand over his heart. "You look so beautiful you scare me," he said. "God, Beth . . ." His eyes filled and Beth felt a swell of pride. This was exactly the kind of reaction she wanted from her husband on her wedding day. She wanted to bowl David over; she wanted to bring him to tears. Beth was pleased with how she looked—young and blond and very tan. The dress, while not a wedding dress, was perfect for a girl like her on a summer day. Her spirits lifted.

David drove into town but had trouble finding a parking space. It was overcast, and the town was filled with people lunching and shopping. Beth remembered being terrified that her mother would see her, or a friend of her mother's. She squeezed the purple cosmos; they left gold dust all over her hands, and she had to wash up in the public restroom of the Town Building before the ceremony.

The wedding itself was unremarkable. A judge wearing Bermuda shorts married them in a room without windows. The room was empty except for a conference table and three folding chairs. The judge stood on the far side of the table, looking not so much like a judge as one of Beth's father's golf partners. Two male law students who were working in the probate court for the summer were brought in to witness, along with a secretary from the selectmen's office. Those three strangers sat next to Beth and David in the folding chairs. The law students were just kids not much older than Beth and David, and they looked put upon for being asked to watch for ten minutes in the name of legality. The secretary was older, with kids of her own probably. She dabbed her eyes with a tissue as Beth and David said their vows. Before Beth knew it, it was over. She signed the marriage certificate, the judge in the Bermuda shorts kissed her cheek and said, "Congratulations, Mrs. Ronan." He left shortly thereafter to meet his wife at the Yacht Club.

David and Beth went for lunch at the Mad Hatter, a place they went when David got a cash bonus for a painting job or when Beth's father slipped her extra spending money before returning to New Jersey.

Their table, Beth noticed right away, had a centerpiece of purple cosmos, and there was a bottle of Taittinger chilling on ice. For reasons beyond her understanding, these details, arranged by David ahead of time, made her heart sink. He was trying so hard and yet it didn't seem like enough. That was what Beth thought as she sat down. The two of them, alone for their wedding reception, didn't seem like enough.

Beth drank nearly the whole bottle of champagne herself. Throughout lunch, David talked nonstop about plans: getting her things moved into the cottage, her finding a job, the fall and winter on Nantucket, a vacation in March—a belated honeymoon—to Hawaii or Palm Beach. Kids. (Kids! At the mention of kids, Beth laughed. She was a kid herself.) Beth ate a plate of fried calamari, then a lobster roll, then a hot fudge sundae since the restaurant didn't have cake. A glob of hot fudge sauce hit the front of her white dress and she blotted it with a wet napkin, but to no avail. There was a spot, she was sullied. She reached for the champagne bottle, and finding it empty, waved their waiter over and ordered a gin and tonic. She felt David watching her. When she met his eyes, she saw so much love there it frightened her. She urged him to get the bill while she bolted her drink. When it was time to go, she had to grab onto the table in order to stand up. The ring irritated her finger. David led her out to the car, and when they got home they made love. Beth fell asleep before the sun even set.

In the morning, David left for work. It was lying in bed, alone and dreadfully hungover, that Beth confronted the gravity of what she had done. She had eloped with David. She went into the bathroom and looked in the mirror, which was still foggy from David's shower, and she held her hand up alongside her face. The ring told the truth: she was a married woman. She took three aspirin then went to the kitchen for coffee and found the bouquet of purple cosmos limp and wilting on the counter. It was enough to bring tears to her eyes, but she didn't cry. She was too scared to cry—scared because she was going to have to tell her parents.

She got dressed in the same shorts and T-shirt she had left the house in two days earlier and drove home. Never had Horizon seemed so imposing. Beth understood as she walked into the house that her parents might be angry enough to disown her and ban her from both Horizon and their home in New Jersey forever.

Beth found her mother sitting at the kitchen table—the very same table where Beth sat with Garrett and Winnie now—smoking a cigarette and drinking coffee, sick with worry because Beth had spent two nights away from home.

"You've been with David, haven't you?" her mother said.

Beth nodded and then held out her hand to show her mother her wedding ring and her mother dropped her cigarette on the floor and cried out, "You've gone and done it! Oh, dear child, I have to call your father!" Beth's mother flew out the front door in her housecoat, and drove their woody wagon to town where she could use the telephone. Beth picked the cigarette up off the floor—it left a burn mark, which she pointed out now to Garrett and Winnie—then went upstairs and packed her things and left the house, in her mind, for the final time.

A few days later, Beth had a job as a teller at Pacific National Bank, a bank where her parents, pointedly, did not have an account. Her hours were similar to David's and they resumed the rhythm of their summer. Swimming, sailing, dancing at the Chicken Box. David called her "Mrs. Ronan." Beth scanned the streets for her parents before she stepped outside. She expected her father to show up on their doorstep any second, but he never came. This made Beth feel even worse. Her father was finished with her. She began to worry that she would never see either of her parents again.

What Beth remembered most about the two weeks that she and David were married was that David was so happy. Seeing him so happy made Beth realize that she wasn't as happy as he was. In fact, she was miserable. As she took deposits and cashed checks at the bank, she thought longingly of returning to Sarah Lawrence. She'd already registered for courses—courses she knew David would find elitist and useless: Discourses on Gender and Ethnicity, History of the American Musical Theater, The

Literature of the Lost Generation, Etruscan Art. Beth wanted to finish college and then move to Manhattan and get a real job in publishing or advertising. She didn't want to be a bank teller living in a rented cottage on Bear Street, estranged from her parents who had provided her with every possible advantage in life. One evening at dinner, which Beth now felt a wifely responsibility to prepare, she broached the topic of returning to Sarah Lawrence.

"I won't live apart for another winter," David said.

She took his hand; his wedding ring was already flecked with paint. "You can come with me," she said.

"To *New York?*" As if she had suggested Mongolia, or the moon.

"You'll like it."

He withdrew his hand. "There's no way I'm leaving the island. I have a job here. I want to save money for our future."

"I want to finish college," Beth said.

"We wouldn't be able to afford a year of your college," he said. "Plus a place to live, plus food. Your daddy's not taking care of you anymore, okay? It's me." His voice softened. "I love you, Mrs. Ronan."

"Stop calling me that."

"What?"

" 'Mrs. Ronan.' It makes it sound like you own me. You don't own me." She started to cry.

"Hey, hey," he said. "I know you want to finish your degree. I'll help you make some calls. There's a community college in Harwich. You could take the boat over a couple days a week, maybe."

Beth pushed her plate away. They had been married thirteen days.

⚜

That night, she lay awake watching him sleep. She remembered back to the evening she met him, six years earlier. David had just inherited a dirt bike from an older cousin and he was giving it a whirl up and down West Miacomet Road. Beth was sitting on Horizon's front stoop, shucking corn with a paper bag between her legs. She watched this boy zip past then back again. He was shirtless and barefoot; his hair glinted gold in the last of the day's sunlight. Eventually Beth became so entranced that she stood up and watched him unabashedly. He stopped at the end of the driveway.

"Want to go for a ride?"

Up close, the bike looked hardly sturdy enough to support him, much less the two of them. But Beth nodded—she abandoned the pot of corn and the bag of husks and silks and climbed onto the back of this strange boy's dirt bike. By necessity, she linked her arms around his bare torso and with a sensation like a rocket launching, they took off. Beth was sixteen years old, flying over the bumpy roads at a speed she'd never imagined. The wind tossed her hair. It was the first time she'd tasted freedom.

In the morning, after David left for work, Beth packed her things. She left her wedding ring on top of a white piece of paper on the kitchen table, where he would be sure to see it.

⚜

Winnie's eyes were wide. "Then what happened?"

"I drove home," Beth said. "My parents were sitting right here at this table eating breakfast with Danny and Scott. Grandpa was eating shredded wheat, Gramma was having a cigarette and coffee, and the boys had scrambled eggs with ketchup."

"You can remember that?" Garrett asked.

"Like it happened this morning," Beth said.

⁂

The house had grown silent as soon as the front screen door clapped shut behind her. By the time Beth made it to the kitchen, all eyes were on her.

"I'm back," she said brightly, as though she'd just returned from a semester abroad.

Her mother shooed the boys out of the kitchen. Her father methodically finished his shredded wheat—it was well known that even a fire couldn't keep Garrett Eyler from his shredded wheat—and then he approached Beth, kissed her on the forehead, and grasping her upper arm said, "You did the right thing."

At these words, Beth broke down. Her mother took over— leading Beth upstairs to her bed, which was freshly made, lowering the shades and saying, "You stay right here until the worst has passed." As though they were expecting a storm.

What her mother was referring to, of course, was David, who screeched into the driveway in his painting truck at half past three. He pounded on the front door. Beth sat up in bed, petrified. She heard him yelling, "Let me see her! I love her! Let me talk to her!" And then Beth heard the low, calm tones of her father. "I've contacted my lawyer. It will all be taken care of." The conversation continued—David's voice growing so hysterical that Beth had to peek out the window. She saw her father and David standing just outside the door. David's expression was so anguished, his voice so desperate that Beth collapsed and pulled her two feather pillows over her head. She didn't listen to another word; she didn't even hear him drive away.

❧

"And that's it?" Garrett said.

"That's it," Beth said. "That's the whole story. My father's attorney took care of the divorce. I didn't see David again for several years, and by that point, we were both married to other people. And I made the conscious decision never to think or speak of it again. To anyone, including your father. I'm sorry if you feel betrayed, and I'm even sorrier if you feel I betrayed your father. But that was my decision. It was an event from my past. *Mine.* Do you understand?"

The twins nodded mechanically, like marionettes.

Beth felt drained. There were other things she wanted to discuss with the kids—the Malibu rum, the whereabouts of the ashes—but those things hardly mattered to her at this moment. The only thing that mattered now was that she had told the one story she'd tried with all her might to forget. The reason she'd tried to forget was because of the expression on David's face that final morning. It was the look of a man whose dream had been crushed without warning. It was the look of a man who *would* have loved her forever, who would have taken her for a ride on the back of his dirt bike into infinity.

Beth stood up. She made herself a piece of toast at the counter, ate it in four bites, then went upstairs to her room. Her business with the twins was finished for the time being; they would have to process all they'd heard. What Beth realized before she took a Valium and fell into bed for a nap was that there was one more person she needed to talk to about all of this before she put it to rest for good, and that person was David.

⁂

Beth thought of biking or driving out to David's house that evening before dinner (it grew dark at seven o'clock now, a sign that August had arrived), but Beth didn't want to talk with David in front of his girls. She let a few days pass. Her relationship with the twins returned to almost normal, however they seemed to bestow upon her a new kind of respect—maybe because she had finally owned up to the truth, or maybe because they had never before imagined her as a person capable of getting married on a whim by a judge wearing Bermuda shorts. When Beth saw Piper, she, too, treated Beth differently, more formally, always calling her "Mrs. Newton." One night, Beth screwed up the courage to ask Piper where David was working.

"This week, Cliff Road," Piper said. And then, as if she knew what Beth was planning, she added, "One of the new houses on the left just before you reach Madaket Road."

Beth decided to go see him the following morning, climbing into the Rover at the ungodly hour of seven o'clock. She wanted to catch him early, say her piece, and leave. Unfortunately, there was a blanket of fog so thick that Beth couldn't see any of the houses from the road and she worried that she wouldn't be able to find the right one. But then she spied two huge homes with fresh yellow cedar shingles on the left, and she took a chance and chose the first of the two driveways. There were a number of vans and trucks—one of them David's.

Beth parked in a spot well out of everyone's way and climbed out of the car. She began to feel nervous about this plan—after all, David was working. He had a business to run, contracts to fulfill; he didn't need his old girlfriend showing up to rehash something that happened back in the Ice Age. Beth glanced at her car and considered leaving, but what if he saw her? That would only make things worse.

The house was so new that there was no front door, only an extra-wide arched opening. The floors were plywood, but all of the drywall was hung, and a boy of about eighteen knelt in the hall sticking a screwdriver into an outlet, which seemed to Beth a perilous undertaking. When the boy saw her, he stared for a second—clearly there weren't many women on these work sites—and Beth was able to ask for David.

"They're painting on the third floor," the boy said, finally blinking. Beth wondered if something was wrong with the way she looked—she'd taken extreme care in appearing casual. Khaki shorts, white T-shirt, flip-flops, her hair in a clip. Beth thanked the boy and proceeded up the stairs, two flights, to the third floor, which was comprised of a long hallway with many doors—bedrooms, bathrooms, a big closet. Beth found each one being painted a tasteful color—buttercream, pearl gray, periwinkle—but she did not see David. The kids painting were all teenagers, too. Beth asked one of them if he knew where David was.

"On the deck at the end of the hall, drinking his java," the young man said. This kid was very pale and had black hair to his shoulders. "You his wife?"

Beth walked away without answering.

At the end of the hall were French doors, one of which was propped open with a gallon can of primer. The doors led to a huge deck that overlooked Maxcy's Pond, which through the fog, had a dull silver glint, like a pewter plate. David sat in a teak chair, drinking his coffee, reading the newspaper. Beth watched him for a second, his right ankle was propped on his left knee and the paper rested on his legs. His sipped his coffee, turned the page, whistled a few bars from the music inside. Beth realized how enraged she was. At him, at Rosie—God, Rosie—and at herself.

"This is quite a view," she said.

He swung around so quickly he spilled his coffee. When he stood up, the paper slid off his lap onto the deck.

"Beth," he said. "What are you doing here?"

"I had a sneaking suspicion you didn't actually work," Beth said. "And I see now that I was correct."

David wiped the coffee off his arm with a napkin, then he folded the paper up, but seemed at a loss for what to do with it, so he tucked it between the rails of the deck. It slipped through the rails and fluttered to the ground, three stories below. Beth took the chair next to his.

David gazed glumly at the newspaper below. "I've been here since five-thirty getting my guys set up," he said. "I was taking my coffee break."

"Not a bad life," Beth said.

"Why are you here?" David asked. "You certainly didn't come to praise my choice of career."

"You know why I came."

He looked at her in that old, intense way that made the bottom of Beth's stomach swoop out. "I had nothing to do with it," David said. "Rosie told them."

"Oh, I know," Beth said. "That only makes it worse."

"She's been wanting to tell the girls for years," David said. "She was just waiting for the opportunity to present itself." David sank into his seat. "Finding out that Piper was dating your son was irresistible."

"It's none of her business," Beth said in a tight voice. She felt herself losing control and she reached for her mental reins. She breathed in through her nose; her ears were ringing with the injustice of it. Rosie kept the secret for twenty-five years only to let it splash at the worst possible time. "It's nobody's business but ours. Yours and mine."

"We were *married*, Beth." David looked at her, as if for confirmation, and she nodded. "It's a part of your past you have to face."

"But that's what I mean," Beth said. "Why shouldn't I be able to face it when I want, or not at all? It belongs to me. But no one else thinks that way. You don't believe I have a right to my own past, and neither do my kids. So I was forced to tell them the story about you and me and that summer, the cottage, the blood tests, the cosmos, the judge. I told them everything. Okay? I hope you're happy."

David was quiet for a moment. "How did you explain the part where you left me?"

"I explained it like it happened."

"And how, exactly, *did* it happen?" David asked. He raised his palms and showed them to her, then he placed them on the sides of her face. She pulled back—this was already too much contact—but his hands held her steady. In her mind, she saw a struggle, she sailed over the deck's railing to the ground where the newspaper lay in the mud.

"Let go of me," she said, as calmly as she could.

"I loved you," he said. "And you left me."

"Yes," she said.

He dropped his hands from her face and stuffed them into the pockets of his gray canvas shorts. Beth gazed at his tan legs fleeced with golden hairs, his crooked toes. His person was so familiar to her and yet he had changed. They were both different people now from the characters in the story she had told the twins. She noticed for the first time some gray hairs around his ears.

"I've thought about it so much this summer," David said. "I haven't seen you in what—three weeks? four?—and yet I've thought about you every day. I thought about kissing you."

"David."

"I thought about making love to you."

"David!"

"And I asked myself over and over, *What do you really want from this woman?* She just lost her husband. What do you really expect?" He grabbed onto the rail and leaned forward as though he were the one contemplating a headlong dive. "Do you know what I decided?"

"What?"

"I want to know why you left me."

Beth bounced on her toes. She felt the bike path calling her. She didn't want to explain herself; she wanted to run away, just as she had twenty-five years ago.

"There were a lot of reasons," Beth said. "Mostly, I wanted to finish college."

"You could have finished on the Cape."

"I wanted to finish at Sarah Lawrence."

"You have no idea how snotty you sound," he said.

"Maybe that is snotty, or maybe I just like to finish what I start."

"Except in the case of our marriage," David said.

Beth stared at the pond, which was a shade darker now. It was going to rain. "I couldn't stand to disappoint my parents."

"Now we're getting somewhere."

"I wanted to live my life the right way, David. Graduate, get a job, get married in a church with my parents' blessing."

"You were a coward," David said. "You weren't brave enough to follow your heart. When you actually agreed to marry me, I thought I had changed you into the kind of person who took risks. But when you left I saw that you were the same scared little girl you were at sixteen. Afraid of doing anything wrong, afraid of being your own person."

He was trying to hurt her and she couldn't blame him. At the time, Beth felt she had a choice between pleasing her parents and pleasing David, and, in the end, she chose her parents. But deep down, Beth also knew she was doing what was *right*. Thinking about that lunch at the Mad Hatter made her cringe inside, even now. She wouldn't have lasted eighteen years as David's wife. She would have taken off long before Rosie had. This, however, wasn't a sentiment that ever needed to be spoken out loud, even if David was prodding her to admit it.

"I acted as my own person," she declared. "I left of my own free will, because I knew it would be better for both of us."

"Well, it wasn't better for me."

Beth stood up. "What is it you want me to say? That I'm sorry? Of course I'm sorry! Of course I remember what happened. When I was telling the story to the kids, I remembered every single detail down to what Danny and Scott were eating for *breakfast* the morning I went back home." She glanced at David and was dismayed to see that there were tears in his eyes. Why was he ripping the scab off this old wound? *Leave it alone!* she pleaded silently. *We're old now. We have gray hair.* "I was wrong for the way I left you. I was wrong not to tell you to your face, but I simply couldn't. I was afraid. I knew I was going to hurt you and I didn't have the courage to sit and watch. I loved you, David, in that blind way that teenagers love each other. But I was smart enough to realize that it wasn't love for the long haul. When I left, I did us both a favor. That doesn't make it right. I'm sorry. Even now, I'm sorry."

"You didn't do me a favor by leaving," David said. He lay across the chair like he'd been shot. His neck was exposed, and his Adam's apple; she could see his pulse. Beth imagined her young self climbing onto the back of his dirt bike, and holding on to him for dear life. Kicking up dust into the sunset. That was how this all started, and this was how it was going to end, here on the deck of a complete stranger's house.

"I *am* sorry, David."

"So am I."

They remained silent until the first raindrops fell, and then Beth announced that she should let him get back to work.

"I'll see you out," he said.

They walked down the hall, past the rooms with their heavy smells of paint and blaring music and the teenage boys who would ask one another on their lunch break if Beth was David's estranged wife. A few of the kids would say yes, a few would say no, and nobody, Beth realized, would be completely wrong.

chapter 7

Garrett's days with Piper were dwindling. The Newtons were scheduled to leave the day after Labor Day, and when Garrett checked the calendar, he found himself staring at the fourteenth of August. They had less than three weeks left.

That night, Garrett and Piper went to the Gaslight Theater to see a heist movie. Piper knew a guy who worked there and so they were able to buy beers at the bar and take the beers into the theater with them. Piper took one sip of her beer and excused herself for the bathroom. She was gone a long time—she missed all of the trailers. When she returned, she took Garrett's hand and squeezed it so hard that Garrett winced and looked over, even though as a rule, he disliked it when people talked in movies.

"I threw up," she whispered.

Garrett moved his arm around her shoulders. "Do you want me to take you home?" he asked.

She shook her head and slumped in her seat toward him.

Garrett hoped she wasn't getting sick; the thought of even a day without Piper disheartened him. He drank his beer and the rest of Piper's as well.

After the movie, Garrett drove to the beach. No matter what they did at night, they always parked at the beach on the way home. But when Garrett pulled up to the water, shut off the engine and made a move to kiss Piper, she raised her hands to shield her face.

"Hey," Garrett said. "What's wrong?"

"I don't feel well," Piper said.

"Still?"

"Still."

Garrett rested his hands on the steering wheel and looked helplessly out the window. Even though they had more than two weeks left, everything had started to take on a sheen of nostalgia. The ocean at night, for example. Garrett soaked in the sight so that when he went back to New York he might remember what it was like—the waves, the reflection of the moon on the water, the way it felt to have Piper next to him.

"Do you want me to take you home?" he asked.

Piper didn't respond. A few seconds later when Garrett looked at her, he saw she was crying again. Piper had cried three nights in the past week because she was so upset about his leaving. That was probably why she threw up earlier. Garrett knew from his experiences with Winnie that girls threw up when they got upset. He didn't like the fact that he was causing Piper to cry and vomit, although he was glad she was going to miss him.

"It's only a year," Garrett said. "Not even a year. Nine months—September to June."

"That's not it," Piper said.

"I'm *not* going to find another girlfriend," Garrett reassured her. "I already told you, there isn't a girl in New York City as pretty as you."

"Garrett."

"We'll talk on Sundays when the rates are low, and we'll e-mail every day. God," he said. "I wonder what people did before they had e-mail?"

"I'm late for my period," Piper said.

This took Garrett so by surprise that at first he couldn't decipher what she meant. "What?"

"But I'm, like, super erratic. My cycle can be twenty-eight days for six months and then I'll skip a cycle all together. It's happened before. A bunch of times. At least twice."

"Are you telling me you might be pregnant?" Garrett asked. He couldn't believe this. They had used condoms every single time they had sex. He'd made sure of that. He'd been so, so careful—well, except for the time his mother caught them, when he hurried, when he fumbled while disengaging. But that was so long ago, the Fourth of July. He leaned his head back. *Oh, please, God, no.*

"Might," Piper said.

"How late are you?"

"Pretty late." She burst into a fresh round of tears.

"Okay, okay," Garrett said. He had to keep her from getting hysterical. What was it his father had always said? *It's fruitless to speculate.* There was no need to jump ahead and consider how neither of them was prepared to become a parent at seventeen. Not with a year of high school and four of college and three of law school for Garrett. No need to jump ahead to where Piper might get an abortion—it certainly couldn't be done on Nantucket—or how to pay for it or what their parents would say.

"You need to take a test," he said.

"Where am I going to get a test?"

Garrett wrinkled his brow. "At the store? I don't know. The pharmacy?"

"I *live* here, Garrett," Piper said. "I know at least three people who work at the Stop & Shop and my father is friends with the couple who own the pharmacy. He paints it every year. I can't go buy a pregnancy test. Everyone knows me."

Garrett felt like Piper had thrown a huge blanket over his head and he was having a hard time shaking it off. "So what are you going to do?" he asked.

"*Me?*" she said. "It's not *my* problem, Garrett. It's *our* problem. If I am pregnant, it's half your fault."

"I know," Garrett said defensively.

"*You* should buy the pregnancy test," Piper said. "Nobody knows you."

She had a point; he knew practically no one on the island other than his family. Still, the idea of buying a pregnancy test was humiliating. Buying a box of condoms had been bad enough. The condoms—Garrett couldn't even think about the condoms without shrinking inside.

"Okay," he said. "I'll do it."

Piper seemed to relax a little at this promise. She fell across the front seat and lay her head in his lap. A few seconds later, she fiddled with the zipper of his jeans, but Garrett took her hand and held it tightly. His body was filled with nervous tension that would be impossible to battle. He held Piper close and after several minutes he felt her body melt into his. She was falling asleep.

"Piper," he said. "I'm taking you home."

When they pulled into the Ronans' driveway, Piper roused herself enough to undo her seatbelt. "So you'll get it?" she asked. "Tomorrow?"

"Yeah," he said. He pulled Piper toward him and kissed her. "Do you think you are?"

Her eyes were only half open. She was, as Garrett's mother would say, falling asleep in her soup.

"No," she said dreamily. "Probably not."

Garrett felt a rush of relief. It was, after all, her body.

"Okay," he said. "I'll see you tomorrow. I love you."

"I love you, too, Garrett."

*

The next morning, Garrett rose early and drove to the Stop & Shop. He bought a pint of raspberries for his mother, who loved them, a bag of Doritos, a package of bacon, a jar of olives, a six-pack of root beer, and the pregnancy test. He dashed for the checkout line. The cashier, an older Jamaican woman, rang up the groceries without even glancing at him. Garrett paid with cash, refused his receipt, and hurried from the store.

Once in the car, he transferred the pregnancy test from the shopping bag into the backpack that he normally used for school—he'd brought it to Nantucket filled with the books on his summer reading list, but now it was going to serve as the place where he would hide the pregnancy test until that evening when Piper would take it. They were going to meet early, while it was still light out, and head someplace private.

At home, his mother was the only one awake. Garrett sauntered into the kitchen holding the bag of groceries—the backpack was already tucked into the dark recesses of the front hall closet. Beth stared at him as he put the shopping bag on the table and began emptying its contents.

"I bought you some raspberries," he said.

"You went to the store?" she asked. "What on earth for? Was there something special you wanted? You should have just told me, honey."

"And olives," Garrett said, holding up the jar. "You do like olives, don't you?"

At six o'clock, Garrett and Piper picked up sandwiches from Henry's and drove out to Smith's Point to catch the sunset. This was one of the things Garrett wanted to do before he left the island for the summer. In previous years, Garrett's father had arrived for the last two weeks of August and they did stuff as a family every night, including a sandwich picnic at Smith's Point. As Garrett drove over the rickety wooden bridge at Madaket Harbor, he noted how vastly different this year was from last year. This year he was the one driving the car with his girlfriend in the seat beside him, his girlfriend who thought she might be pregnant. His father was dead; his mother had been married before. Garrett reeled at the enormity of it. He glanced at Piper. She looked pale, and nervous. He took her hand.

Garrett lowered the air in his tires at the gatehouse, and then he and Piper drove over the huge, bumpy dune to the beach. Piper groaned and clenched her abdomen. Garrett's heart sank.

"Are you *okay?*" he asked.

"Just get there," she said.

They drove out the beach to the westernmost tip of the island. Across the water, Garrett could see the next island over, Tuckernuck. Piping plovers scuttled along the shoreline; the air smelled of fish, and in fact, the only other people on the beach were a couple of surf casters in the distance. Garrett spread out a blanket and unloaded the bag of sandwiches and the shopping bag that contained the Doritos and the root beer. It was a clear night; the sun was a pinkish-orange ball dropping toward the blue horizon. Piper sat resolutely in the Rover.

"Aren't you getting out?" he asked.

She moved in slow motion, like she was running out of batteries.

"Do you want to take the test before or after we eat?" he asked.

She shrugged. "Before, I guess. While it's still light. I have to pee anyway."

"Okay," he said. He double-checked their surroundings; they were shielded from the fishermen's view. He took the test out of his backpack and studied the instructions. "You pee in this cup, and then you put the stick in. If a second line shows up, it's positive. If not, it's negative." He handed Piper the cup and with the lethargic movements of an amoeba, she disappeared into the nearby dunes.

Garrett tapped the plastic stick against his palm. *Dad?* he beckoned. But this moment was too monumental and too scary to share with his father. Garrett tried to clear his mind. He could smell his meatball sub and his stomach growled. He'd been too nervous to eat anything all day, and now he was starving.

After an eternity, Piper popped out of the dunes, holding the cup discreetly at her side, blocked from Garrett's view. "Give me the stick," she said.

He handed it to her and she opened the back door of the car and moved inside. Garrett's pulse was screaming along like a race car. He was too nervous to pray.

"How long does it say to wait?" she asked.

Garrett didn't have to check the instructions; he had them memorized. "Three minutes, but no longer than ten."

Piper checked her watch. Garrett lost all control. He tore open the bag of Doritos and stuffed a handful into his face. He felt like an ogre, a glutton, but he couldn't help himself. Piper didn't even seem to notice. Nearly half the bag was gone when Piper stepped from the car. Garrett paused in his eating; his lips burned with spicy salt. Piper emptied the contents of the cup behind the Rover's back tire.

She smiled at him. The diamond stud in her nose caught the last rays of the setting sun. She waved the stick over him like it was a magic wand, changing his life forever.

"It's positive," she said.

The summer was fading fast. It got dark earlier, and there was a chill in the air at night. Garrett read the last two books on his summer reading list; he started running three miles each morning to get ready for soccer. Anything to lend normality to the very abnormal set of circumstances that bore down on him as surely as the impending autumn. Piper wanted to have the baby.

"But why?"

This was the question Garrett had asked over and again for the past three days. Garrett realized he should stop asking, because every time he asked, Piper came up with a more convincing answer. She valued the life inside her, she believed in a woman's right to choose and her choice was to have the baby, she couldn't bring herself to destroy a life that had been formed out of her love for Garrett.

Garrett countered with the predictable arguments—they had high school to finish, college to attend, years and years of life experience to acquire before either of them would be remotely capable of raising a child.

"Who said anything about raising a child?" Piper asked.

She wanted to have the child and put it up for adoption. There were thousands of good people in the world who were aching for a baby, she said.

"What about your senior year?" Garrett asked.

"What about it?" she said. "The baby isn't due until April. I can accelerate my course work, take my exams early and graduate."

"Yeah," Garrett said. "But you'll be pregnant."

Piper stared at him like he was the stupidest person on earth. "That's right," she said.

Being pregnant empowered Piper. From the second she saw the positive result at Smith's Point, she had transformed before Garrett's eyes. She stopped being his girlfriend and became someone's mother. She scared Garrett now, the way religious fanatics scared him. Only Piper's religion was her body. Her body was changing, producing a hundred thousand new cells every hour, she said. She was desperate to see a doctor, to have an ultrasound and blood tests—but to do this, she needed access to her father's insurance.

They had to tell their parents, she said and soon. There were only two weeks before Garrett returned to New York.

Garrett read and ran and moped, avoiding Beth and Winnie and Marcus. He moaned internally over his bad luck. He threw the remnants of his box of condoms into the trash. They were doubly useless—Piper didn't want to have sex anymore. She didn't want anything to harm the baby. She quit smoking for good, she said, and she began eating a lot of red meat and vegetables, although she was having a hard time keeping food down. Piper was going to have the baby and that was that. Garrett couldn't believe he had no say in the matter. For the rest of his life, Garrett would have to live with the fact that his child was walking the earth.

Piper insisted on presenting a unified front. She wanted to tell their families together, in one large group. She stopped by one day at lunch, and Garrett entered the kitchen to find her and Beth sitting at the table planning an end-of-the-summer barbecue. Beth seemed energized by the idea. His mother was so predictable—she wanted to keep the last bits of summer alive by filling the house with people.

"You don't mind that David is coming?" Garrett asked his mother later.

"I cleared the air with David," Beth said. "I think he should come. He's been an integral part of the summer."

There was an understatement. Garrett felt just as he had at the beginning of the summer when his mother announced that she had invited the Ronans for dinner. He didn't want them to come! If Beth hadn't invited them in the first place, Garrett wouldn't be in this gut-wrenching position. They might have had a peaceful summer.

Over the next few days, Garrett watched Beth pull out all the stops. She ordered clams and lobster tails from East Coast Fish, and beer from Cisco Brewery; she bought New York strip steaks; she bought French cheese and summer sausage and baguettes, and a jar of mustard that cost sixteen dollars; she made potato salad and coleslaw and corn pudding. She bought red and yellow tomatoes and made her own pesto. She made peach pie and homemade ice cream. She baked a chocolate cake. She decorated the house with zinnias and gladiolas and huge black-eyed Susans.

"I wish it could always be summer," Beth said wistfully.

Garrett wondered what Beth would say when she heard the news. He was surprised to find he didn't care what she thought—there was no way that she could be more distraught about Piper's pregnancy than he was. He couldn't wait to get back to New York. In less than a week, his feelings for Piper had changed. His love for her had evaporated, and in its place was fear of her and her plans.

On the evening of the barbecue, the Ronans arrived at six o'clock, the three of them unpiling from the front seat of David's truck. Winnie and Marcus were already out on the deck drinking Coke and holding hands. Winnie was trying to convince Marcus to eat a clam. Garrett eyed them enviously. They hadn't been stupid enough to let themselves get pregnant; they had made it through the summer intact. It wasn't fair—except that Garrett knew they would both be supportive when they heard the news, far more supportive than Garrett would have been under the reverse circumstances. First Garrett shuddered at the idea of Winnie bearing Marcus's child, then he shuddered at his own flawed character. He deserved a life of nasty surprises, he decided, and he steeled himself for what was to come.

The dinner went smoothly. David and Beth shared a big bottle of Whale's Tale Ale, Winnie talked to Peyton about what it was like to start high school. Piper held on to Garrett's hand and beamed benignly at everyone, in a fantastic imitation of the Virgin Mary. She said very little and ate even less—just a tomato and a tiny piece of steak. Beth noticed right away. Garrett wasn't surprised; his mother always noticed when someone wasn't eating.

"Are you okay, Piper?" Beth asked, as she began to clear the table. "You barely ate a thing and you've been so quiet. This isn't like you."

Piper squeezed Garrett's hand under the table. Here it comes, he thought. All hell is about to break loose. He wished for a final time that God would step in and save him.

"Thank you for noticing, Mrs. Newton," Piper said, in a loud, attention-seeking voice. "I didn't eat very much because I feel sick."

"I didn't realize you were sick," Beth said. "That's too bad."

"No, it's good," Piper said. "I feel sick because I'm pregnant."

Winnie let out a shriek. Everyone else was silent. Garrett stared at his plate—a mixed pool of juices from the steak and tomatoes, a few kernels of corn, a smudge of pesto. After what he considered to be a reasonable amount of time for this bombshell to detonate in each diner's mind, he glanced up. Someone was going to have to say something. One of the adults? Beth had retaken her seat without so much as a creak or a whisper, and now she sat with a stack of dirty plates in front of her, a totally blank look on her face, the way she must look, Garrett thought, when she first wakes up in the morning and she can't quite place where she is or where she's been. David was inspecting his glass of wine as though an insect or a small piece of cork were floating on the surface. He was so intent on this task that Garrett thought he hadn't heard; however, a few seconds later, he was the first to speak. When he did, it wasn't to Piper at all, but to Beth, across the table.

"How about that?" he said, raising his glass. "We're going to be grandparents."

"*What?*" Beth said. "Are you kidding me? Surely she's not keeping this baby?"

Garrett turned to watch Piper. Her face was unwavering in its calm repose. "That depends on what you mean by 'keep,' Mrs. Newton."

"You'll have an abortion," Beth said. "You're still just a child."

"I will not have an abortion," Piper said. "I've given it a lot of thought and I've decided that I want to have the baby and put it up for adoption."

"*Adoption?*" Beth said.

"Adoption," Piper said.

"What you want may not matter," Beth said. "You have to do what's best for everybody involved."

"I'm the mother," Piper said. "I have to do what's right for me and for the baby. Maybe you're not aware of the law. It's the mother's right to choose."

"That's a very self-centered attitude," Beth said.

"I think what's *self-centered* is wanting me to get an abortion so the matter is taken care of and you don't have to worry about it."

"She's got a point," David said.

Piper glanced at her father, and as if strengthened by this confirmation, continued. "I don't want to terminate the pregnancy. I want to give the baby life, then share that life with another family. That's the choice I've made. It's one I can live with."

David stood up and moved to Piper's chair. He knelt in front of her and she fell into his arms in a way that made her seem like a very young girl to Garrett. He got a lump in his throat.

Peyton started to cry. "You always do things like this," she said to her sister. "You do it for attention. But you never think of anyone else. Me, for example. Everyone at school is going to make fun of me."

Winnie rubbed Peyton's arm. "No one will make fun of you."

"They'll say my sister is a slut."

"They'll think Piper is brave for sticking to her principles," Winnie said. "I think you're brave, Piper."

Piper couldn't respond. Her face was hidden in David's shoulder.

Garrett looked around the table. He was both relieved and offended that no one was paying attention to him. Everyone was focused on Piper. This moment was all about her.

"I think you should take some time before you make a final decision," Beth said. "Even if you don't plan on keeping the baby, simply giving birth can be traumatic, physically and emotionally. And then there's your schoolwork, applying to colleges—"

"Don't try to talk her out of it, Mom," Winnie said. "After all, we're talking about a human being here. A human being who is related to everyone at this table—well, except for Marcus."

Marcus held up his palms as if relinquishing all claims of being related to the baby.

"We're talking about a cluster of cells," Beth said. "A microscopic organism. Not a human being, not yet."

"It's a human being," Winnie insisted.

Piper separated from David. "I'm having the baby. You should take as much time as you need to absorb that fact. I'm going to see a doctor and I'm going to research adoption agencies so that I'm sure the baby ends up in the best possible home. They've made it so that you can practically handpick the family that takes your child."

Peyton shook her head. "You are such an alien," she said. "I can't believe you're my sister."

David returned to his seat, only now he gripped the table and lowered himself gingerly into the chair, as if he were an old man. "Honey, we need to show your sister support. We have to rally around her."

"What about me?"

These words came from Garrett. He waited a beat to see if anyone had heard—yes, everyone at the table turned to him.

"I guess the question for you, young man, is why weren't you more careful?" David said.

"I was careful," Garrett said. He'd used condoms every time, and it was just the one time when his mother startled him when he wasn't paying full attention. But he couldn't explain that. "We had some bad luck."

"Good luck," Piper said, rubbing her still-flat stomach. "I consider this good luck."

"You consider this good luck," Garrett said to Piper. "So I guess what I think doesn't matter. And this is my child, too."

"I care what you think," Beth said.

"So do I," said Winnie.

"So do I," said Marcus. "What do you think?"

Garrett's eyes blurred with tears. What he thought was that if he had to sustain any more growing pains, any more major changes in life or death, he would explode. What he thought was, *thank you* to his mother and his twin sister and yes, even Marcus, for caring about him despite the fact that he possessed a despicable character. What he thought was, *I am sorry, I am so, so sorry* to the child that Piper carried within her. *I want to do better by you, but right now, I just can't.*

When Garrett spoke, his voice was thick with confusion. His normal voice had abandoned him.

"Let's just do what Piper wants," he said. "She's the mother. It's her decision."

Beth sighed. David clapped Garrett's shoulder. Winnie said, "Well, congratulations, then!" Marcus saluted Garrett. Peyton went over and touched the top of her sister's hair, as if checking for a halo. Garrett fell back in his chair, he was exhausted.

"Is there dessert?" he asked. He was grateful when Beth said, "Of course! Yes!" and bounded into the kitchen to serve it. Anything predictable, to Garrett, was now unspeakably precious.

Winnie couldn't believe it, but she was jealous. For years she had heard of girls her own age having babies—once even a girl at Danforth—and it was always spoken of with distaste. It was called "getting in trouble." But why? As Winnie lay in bed with Marcus that night, she longed to be filled with another human life, a life that could miraculously be created out of thin air and passion.

"It would be romantic, wouldn't it?" Winnie asked. "To have a baby?"

"Don't talk that way," Marcus said. "It won't be romantic for Garrett and Piper. Those two didn't even kiss good-bye tonight."

Winnie had noticed. The relationship between Garrett and Piper was different now, and not in a good way. Garrett kept talking about going back to New York like there was nothing he'd rather do. Meanwhile, Winnie wanted to stay on Nantucket forever. Once she got back to New York, everything would change. She would go back to living on Park Avenue, Marcus would go back to Queens. They could still see each other; it was thirty-five minutes on the subway. But it wouldn't be the same. They wouldn't be living together; they wouldn't spend every afternoon on the beach swimming; they wouldn't eat breakfast, lunch, and dinner together on the deck. Instead, Winnie imagined herself stepping off the train in an unfamiliar neighborhood where all the other girls her age were black or Hispanic and *tough.* Smoking cigarettes, chewing gum, dishing out attitude when they saw Winnie and Marcus walking down the street holding hands. Winnie had been to Marcus's apartment once before with her father and Garrett—the building was shabby, and although Marcus's apartment was nice on the inside, it looked like an apartment where the mother was absent. There had been dishes in the sink—lots of them—and there were two TVs blaring in different rooms. Marcus's sister, LaTisha, he said, came home from school and plunked herself in front of the set until bedtime. She did her homework in front of *Oprah* and ate her dinner in front of *Jeopardy!* Winnie didn't want to place herself in that apartment or on the street in Queens, but she was afraid the trip to Manhattan would intimidate Marcus just as much, and that he wouldn't come. New York, Winnie was certain, would stink. They wouldn't be safe from the rest of the world like they were here.

A few days later, the Western Union truck pulled up in front of the house. Winnie was the only one around. Garrett and Beth had gone running together and Marcus had fallen asleep down on the beach. Winnie was in the kitchen making sandwiches when she heard the crunch of tires on the shell driveway and she reached the front door in time to meet the driver and sign for an envelope. Winnie became sore with the memories of previous summers—the FedEx truck came nearly every day with documents for her father.

The Western Union man tipped his hat at Winnie in an old-fashioned way that made her smile. She looked at the envelope and saw it was addressed to Marcus. It was a telegram, she realized, another telegram for Marcus. There had been one a few weeks earlier, back when they were angry at one another, and she had forgotten to ask him about it. From one of his parents, his father probably, telling him it was time to come home. She wanted to throw the envelope away, or else she wanted it to contain happy news, like Marcus had been offered a college scholarship. Like his father had found a great new job and they were moving to Manhattan.

Winnie took the envelope down to the beach along with their lunch. Marcus was still asleep, face down, on his beach towel. He was so tall and solid; at night, when he held her, she wanted to melt into him and disappear.

She nudged the bottom of his foot with her big toe. "Turkey sandwiches," she said. The days of Malibu and Coke were over, but she'd brought a thermos of icy lemonade. She laid out lunch as Marcus rubbed his eyes and sat up.

"I'm really going to miss this," he said. "You know?"

Winnie squinted at the ocean. A seagull stopped at the edge of their blanket and squawked for some of their lunch. Winnie threw a piece of bread crust. Finally she understood the heartache her mother felt every year when she left this island. It was falling in love here that did it, Winnie guessed. It was falling in love here that made you never want to leave.

"A telegram came for you," Winnie said. She pulled the envelope out of her jean shorts. "Just now. Western Union."

Marcus looked at the envelope but didn't reach for it right away. Winnie's heart dropped. It was bad news. She remembered the morning of March sixteenth, her mother coming into her bedroom while Winnie was getting dressed for school. Her mother didn't have to say a single word; Winnie knew in her gut that her father was dead.

"Is everything okay?" Winnie whispered.

The seagull returned, begging for more. Throw the telegram to the seagull, Winnie thought. Throw it into the ocean. It seemed plausible on such a gorgeous day that bad news could simply be tossed away.

Marcus opened the envelope, shaking his head all the while. Maybe it was from Constance. Could a person send telegrams from prison?

"What does it say?" Winnie asked.

He fell back onto his towel. "There's something I have to tell you. Remember back a couple of weeks ago when I got that other telegram? I know you were the one who slid it under my door."

Winnie nodded. It was awful of her to slide the telegram under the door like Marcus was some kind of leper, but at the time she'd been too indignant to knock.

"And remember when I told you that I had a secret?"

Of course she remembered! She felt like shaking him. Didn't he understand that his every word printed indelibly on her brain?

"Yes," she said. "But you don't have to tell me what it is if you don't want to."

"I want to," Marcus said. "These telegrams? Are you ready?"

Winnie was pretty sure she wasn't ready, but she nodded.

"They're from my editor."

Winnie smiled at him. She thought he'd said "editor."

"I don't understand," she said.

"I have an editor," Marcus said. "At Dome Books in New York. His name is Zachary Celtic."

Winnie felt like the butt of some kind of joke, though she

wasn't sure yet if she was supposed to be angry or laugh along.

"I still don't understand."

Marcus squinted at the ocean. The sun seemed to have gotten brighter in the past few minutes. So Winnie was skeptical. She believed in him, but not that much.

"I have a book deal with Dome," Marcus said. "This guy, this editor, Zachary Celtic, offered me thirty thousand dollars to write a book about what happened with my mother."

"You're kidding," Winnie said. "Thirty *thousand* dollars?"

Those three words had power, Marcus realized, even over someone with plenty of money like Winnie. They'd held so much power over him that he'd agreed to write a book he didn't want to write. There, he'd admitted it.

He didn't want to write the book.

"They gave me five hundred dollars already," Marcus said. It sounded like such a paltry sum when compared to thirty thousand, but since Marcus now knew he had to pay it back, it seemed like a lot. "But I spent it. And what this telegram says is that the first fifty pages and a complete synopsis are due next week, September first. 'Per our agreement.'"

"You've written fifty pages?" Winnie said.

"No," Marcus said. "I've only written one page. I had writer's block this summer."

"Maybe they'll give you more time," Winnie said. "Like an extension on a term paper?"

"More time won't help," Marcus said. "I'm not going to write it at all."

"Really?" Winnie said. Now she was having a hard time processing what he was telling her. He had a book deal for thirty thousand dollars but he was giving it up? Turning it down?

She felt compelled to push him toward greatness. Marcus could be a writer, a real writer, before he even turned eighteen. "Why not?"

"I don't have it in my heart," Marcus said. "I'm furious with my mother and I know better than anyone else that what she did was wrong, but that's not stuff I want to explain to the rest of the world. I want to work it out privately."

"But you don't talk to your mother," Winnie said.

"Yeah, I know," Marcus said. He felt like crumpling up the telegram and tossing it into the water, but it had the phone number of Dome Books on it and now he had to call. "Don't get me wrong. I want to be a writer. And I will be someday. But I'm not writing this story. I kept thinking of your dad, too. He wouldn't have wanted me to write this book."

"Yeah," Winnie said. "He wasn't into exploiting his cases."

That word, "exploiting," was the one that made Marcus squirm. Along with the horrible things Zachary Celtic had said at lunch, and the way the five hundred dollars was handed to him—cash in an envelope—so seedy, so underhanded. They were buying Marcus's betrayal. "Anyway, that's my secret. I have a book deal with this big publishing house for all this money but I'm not going through with it."

"Well, okay, then," Winnie said. She poured two cups of lemonade and handed one to Marcus. They clicked cups in a toast, though they had different ideas about what they were drinking to. Winnie thought they were drinking to Marcus's future career as a writer, if not with this book then with another. Marcus thought they were drinking to his freedom.

※

Winnie was thrilled to accompany Marcus on even the smallest errand; standing in line at the post office to get stamps with him was a delight. But this—going with him in the morning to call his editor and turn down the book deal—was monumental. Marcus was so nervous about the prospect of contacting this man, Zachary Celtic, that he said he wouldn't come to Winnie's room at all that night, even though she begged him to as they sat on the deck looking at the stars. She reminded him that their nights together were dwindling in number.

"I can't," he said. "My guts are bound up about this call tomorrow. I just want tomorrow to come so I can do it."

"What are you going to say?" Winnie asked.

"I'll just tell him I'm not writing it. I'll tell him I'll return the five hundred bucks."

Even though Marcus and Winnie were in love, there were certain things she was afraid to ask. Like where he was going to get that kind of money.

"And what about your mother?" Winnie said.

"What about her?"

"Will you go see her when you get home?"

He squeezed her hand so tightly she nearly cried out in pain. "I don't know what to do about my mother," he said.

꽃

In the morning, they rode their bikes into town and called Zachary Celtic from a phone booth. Marcus had brought the telegram along with him. He dialed the number, then pumped the payphone full of quarters; his pockets were heavy with them. Winnie stood at Marcus's back, outside of the booth. She was afraid she wouldn't be able to hear the conversation, and for a moment she wondered why he'd invited her along when clearly this was something he wanted to do by himself. She looked up and down the street at the people walking their dogs, drinking coffee, waiting for the shops to open. A man on a bench nearby read the *Wall Street Journal* and talked on his cell phone about the upcoming football season. Marcus had two fingers plugged in his ear and his head bent forward. Winnie heard him say, "Zachary Celtic, please. True crime. It's Marcus Tyler calling." His voice was strange. Winnie wanted to touch him in some reassuring way, but she was scared to. The man on the bench blabbed into his cell phone, bragging now about the dinner reservations he'd managed to "score" at the Pearl and American Seasons. Winnie nearly shushed him. Marcus pumped more change into the phone. He turned around and smiled weakly at her, saying, "They're seeing if he's available."

"Do you have enough money?" Winnie asked.

He patted his pockets for confirmation, then he yanked Winnie into the booth with him. She was relieved. The two of them wedged themselves on either side of the telephone, and Marcus managed to squeeze the door shut. He held the receiver in one hand and Winnie's wrist with the other. Then he swallowed, and when he spoke, his voice sounded like that of a nine-year-old boy.

"Mr. Celtic? Yeah, this is Marcus Tyler? Yes, I got it yesterday. Listen, I have some bad news."

Winnie squeezed his fingers.

"No, more time isn't going to help. When you first asked this spring, I thought I could write it. I definitely wanted the money, and I understand it was, like, a huge leap of faith to offer that kind of cash to a kid. But I tried all summer, and I can't seem to get any decent sentences on paper. At first I thought it was writer's block, but then, I don't know . . ." Marcus took a huge breath, sucking all of the remaining oxygen out of the phone booth, then said in his normal voice, "I don't want to write it."

There was silence, then the frantic, faraway voice of Zachary Celtic talking. Marcus listened with his eyes squeezed shut, like he was enduring some awful pain. He took a breath to speak, but was shut out. Winnie hated to see him like this—trying to say his piece, but failing. She felt as badly as she would have at a racial slur—standing with Marcus on Second Avenue, say, while cab after cab passed by Marcus's outstretched hand.

"Mr. Celtic?" Marcus finally said. It sounded like he was interrupting. "I'll pay you back the five hundred dollars. No, really, I want to. And I'll pay you back whatever it cost you to take me to lunch that day. Just please don't say anything bad about me to Ms. Marchese because I need her to write me a college recommendation, you know?" He paused for a minute then dove back in. "Except, see, I don't think I'm going to change my mind. What's done is done. Angela and Candy are dead, my mother is in prison for the rest of her life, my uncle only has half a brain, and I don't have any explanations for that. I've made up excuses on my mother's behalf, I've tried to justify her actions, I've tried to understand every possible reason why she killed two people but I don't have the answers. I'm not even sure my mother has the answers. But it doesn't matter. *I'm not going to write this book.*" Marcus hung up the phone on Zachary Celtic, saying, "I'll send you that money, sir."

The receiver hit the cradle so hard there was a residual

metallic ring. Marcus stared at himself in the front of the phone.

"Well," he said.

"You did a good job. You said all the right things."

"Think so?" Marcus asked. He touched the receiver as though he wanted to call back and start over. "He said in true crime hot topics go cold real quick, but that he thought my mother's story would always have appeal, in case I ever changed my mind." Marcus wiped sweat off his forehead. "I'm not going to change my mind."

"I know you won't," Winnie said.

"I'm determined to pay the guy back, even though he said I should hold on to the five hundred bucks. He said that was money he was willing to gamble with. But I don't take money for nothing."

"Do you feel better?" Winnie asked. "Now that it's over?"

Now that its over. Marcus feared that this thing with his mother would never be over; it would be a part of him for the rest of his life. However, the dread about the phone call was gone, leaving Marcus feeling empty, in a clean way, like a vessel that had been washed out. "Yes," he said. "I guess I do." He took Winnie in his arms and hugged her, and then they opened the door and stepped out into the fresh air.

❧

Piper scheduled her first ultrasound appointment before Garrett left because she wanted him to come with her.

"I don't think that's a good idea," he said.

They were sitting side by side on Horizon's deck in upright chairs like an elderly couple—not sunbathing, not reading—just staring at the ocean and thinking. They still hung out together in the afternoons, though evening dates were over; Piper was too tired and Garrett had no desire to pursue her. He figured his reluctance to go to the appointment would just be one more thing that pissed her off, but instead she took both his hands and looked him dead in the eye. "I know there's a person inside you who wants to do the right thing."

But how, he wondered, was going to the ultrasound appointment the right thing? It wasn't a baby he was ever going to know.

"Right now this baby is in our care," Piper said. "It's our responsibility to make sure it enters the world healthy."

The appointment was the following day at two. Garrett drove Piper to the hospital. They sat in the waiting room watching the action in the adjoining ER—a man had fallen off his moped and done something unnatural to his arm, followed minutes later by a little girl who had been stung by a jellyfish—until Piper's name was called.

A nurse led them down the white hallway to the X-ray room. Garrett's heart was thudding like a bowling ball hitting the gutter. He thought of that first walk on the beach with Piper, then the bonfire where he met her awful friend Kyle, then buying the box of condoms, the first time they made love, then the Fourth of July, the long stretch of days while she was at Rosie's, the summer evenings they spent parked at the beach. It all seemed like it happened eons ago, with another person.

Garrett had expected a doctor, but the woman who entered the room to do the ultrasound was young, with a ponytail and thick Boston accent. She patted the exam table, indicating that Piper should sit down on it.

"My name's Marie," she said.

Then she asked Piper questions: *Bladder full? Date of birth? Date of last menstrual period?* If Marie was surprised that Piper was only seventeen, she didn't let on.

"Go ahead and lift your shirt, hon," she said.

Piper did so—the days of halter tops were over—and Marie squirted a clear jelly onto Piper's abdomen. Garrett was embarrassed; he stared at his feet in his Sambas and wished he were running across the soccer field in Van Cortland Park right now. Only four days left until their ferry.

Marie switched on a monitor and a blank computer screen lit up. Then she moved a thick wand over Piper's belly. The screen came alive with blobs and swirls.

"Where's our baby?" Piper asked. She propped herself up on her elbows and studied the screen.

"Patient, hon," Marie said. "We're looking for something the size of a pea." Garrett noted that Marie had yet to acknowledge his presence in the room, although he was growing used to being ignored where Piper's pregnancy was concerned.

"Here we go," Marie said. A white peanut appeared on the screen. Marie zoomed in. "There's your baby."

Garrett gazed at the screen with interest. The peanut, he could see, was moving. The peanut had tiny arms and legs.

"See this dark spot?" Marie said. "This is the baby's heart. Here, wait a sec."

Marie fiddled with a knob on the computer. Suddenly, a rhythmic whooshing sound filled the air.

"What's that?" Garrett croaked.

"What's *that?*" Marie said, as if she couldn't believe anyone would be brave or stupid enough to ask. "Why, that's your baby's heartbeat."

The baby, Marie said, was due March twenty-seventh. "But frequently first pregnancies are late."

"Good," Garrett said. "Maybe the baby won't be born until April. March is a terrible month."

Piper glared at him. "What do you care?"

"My father died in March," Garrett explained to Marie.

"Sorry to hear it," Marie said. "Well, look at it this way, if your baby is born in March, it will become a good month."

Garrett rolled his eyes. The woman didn't know what the hell she was talking about.

"I'm going to take a few pictures for your doctor," Marie said. "And for you, if you want one."

"Of course I want one!" Piper said. "Can you tell if it's a boy or a girl?"

"Nawp, not yet," Marie said. "Another eight weeks or so and you'll come back for a second round of this. They can tell you then."

"I feel in my heart that it's a girl," Piper said.

Garrett shut his eyes. He needed to sit down. A girl, a boy— the baby would be one or the other. God, it was all too much. He managed to stay on his feet while Marie took pictures of the white peanut from different angles.

"I just need to develop these," she said. She handed Piper a couple of tissues for her belly. "You clean up. I'll be back in a sec."

Once Marie left the room, there was an awkward silence. Piper swabbed the gunk off her skin, then handed the tissues to Garrett.

"What am I supposed to do with these?" he asked.

"Throw them away." She nodded to a trash can near his feet.

He slammed the wad into the can with all his strength.

"You're angry," she said.

"What?"

"You're furious with me. You think this is my fault."

"I don't think that."

"Of course you do." Piper stood up from the table and tucked in her shirt. "You think it's my fault I'm pregnant. But I have news for you, Garrett. You have to accept fifty percent responsibility."

"Fifty percent responsibility but not fifty percent say in what happens."

"You saw the baby floating around on that screen," Piper said. "Do you honestly want to kill it?"

"I don't know what I want."

"I'll tell you what you want. You want to be back in New York where you can pretend none of this ever happened. Where you can pretend I don't exist."

"That's not true."

"It *is* true. But you know what's funny? I don't care. I don't care that you knocked me up and now you don't love me anymore. It doesn't bother me! All I care about is doing the responsible thing here, the adult thing, and I'm doing it! I'm taking responsibility for this child without compromising my future. You never would have made this decision because it's too hard and you're not strong enough. This doesn't fit into the life plan you concocted for yourself. Well, guess what, Garrett? Part of being an adult is learning that sometimes in life, pieces don't fit."

"We're not adults, though," Garrett said. "We're kids. We're kids having kids."

"You're a real summer person," Piper said. "I realized that when this whole thing started."

"What's that supposed to mean?"

"You show up here for three months of the year when the weather is nice and the water is warm and you use the island. You use it up. Then in September you go back to wherever you came from and forget all about this place. Because you don't really care about Nantucket or the people who live here." Piper's voice was high and shrill; her face was flushed. "You probably won't even come back here for the birth."

Garrett stared at her. "Of course I'm coming back for the birth."

"You are?"

"Yes." He actually hadn't given it a moment of consideration, but he would not stand here and have this girl call him a coward and be right. If his child was going to be born here, he would be here. And his mother and Winnie, too. They would all get a chance to see the baby, to hold him or her, then say good-bye.

"Well, fine, then," Piper said. "But you're not going to be my labor coach. Peyton has already offered."

"You're going to have a thirteen-year-old labor coach?" Garrett said.

"By March, she'll be fourteen," Piper said.

The door swung open and Marie stepped in, holding an envelope. She looked between them. "Everything okay in here?" she asked.

"Sure," Piper said.

"Here are the pictures. I got two for you—" She handed two to Piper. "And one for you." She handed one to Garrett.

Garrett scrutinized his picture, grateful that he had gotten a good shot, where the arms and legs were visible and he could see the dark spot where the baby's heart was.

He looked at Marie. "This is my baby," he said.

She clapped him on the shoulder. "You're a lucky man."

✤

At home, Garrett found Beth in the kitchen packing up the place mats and napkins, the coffee grinder, the food processor. She had saved the Zabar's shopping bags and was filling them with the things they couldn't get in New York: loaves of Something Natural herb bread, containers of smoked bluefish pâté and clam chowder, huge beefsteak tomatoes from Bartlett's.

She smiled indulgently as he walked into the kitchen. "How'd the appointment go?"

He shrugged. "Okay." The picture was in his shirt pocket— he'd pulled it out twice after dropping Piper off to look at it. "Here, want to see?" He handed the photo to his mother.

Beth held it up to the light.

"These are the arms and legs," Garrett said. "And this dark spot? That's the heart."

His mother turned the picture and squinted. Despite her most fervent wishes, a few tears leaked from her eyes.

"I know you're disappointed in me," he said.

She wiped her tears away quickly. "I wasn't thinking that at all. I was just thinking of all of the things your father is going to miss."

"Can we come back for the birth?" Garrett asked. "The baby is due March twenty-seventh."

"This house doesn't have heat," Beth said. "And it's going to be tricky with school. I don't even know when your spring break is."

"Please?" Garrett said.

Beth handed him back the picture. "I guess we'll figure something out," she said.

※

With only two days before they were to leave, Beth became very busy. First, there was packing—and when Beth looked around the house, she saw things everywhere that had to be put into boxes. It overwhelmed her. She got up before dawn and made herself a pot of coffee. When Arch had come at the end of August, they used to awaken early all the time and watch the sun rise, brightening the water. It was Arch's favorite time of day, the time when Nantucket, to him, seemed its most at ease.

Beth poured a cup of coffee and sat down at the kitchen table. She heard a groan, followed by the splintering noise she'd been fearing all summer, but before she could steady herself, the chair she was sitting on crashed to the ground. Beth hit the floor with a tremendous wallop—her whole body vibrated and there was a sharp pain in her right wrist. The surprise and the pain of it was enough to make her cry, but all Beth could think was that the ancient chair finally breaking was some kind of message from Arch. Things can fall out right from under you and you will survive. Beth picked herself up. Brilliantly, her coffee remained intact on the kitchen table. She took a long sip, then rotated her wrist a few times. It still worked.

She inspected the chair, wondering if it could be salvaged, but decided, in the end, it should go into the trash. Furniture was one of those things that could be replaced.

※

She left the house for a run before any of the kids got up, inhaling the air like she might never breathe again. She ingested the sight of the land—the flat blue pond, the green dunes, the gold sand, the ocean.

She didn't want to leave.

Of course, she felt this way every August—but in previous Augusts, Arch had been around to help, and he was very matter-of-fact about packing up. He washed and vacuumed the car—three months of accumulated sand and grime from driving on these dirt roads—then he brought the empty boxes up from the basement and he packed while Beth cleaned. It took them twenty-four hours. Arch double-checked their reservation at the Steamship. They gave all of their perishables to Mrs. Colchester three houses down who stayed until Columbus Day; they ate their final dinner at the Brotherhood, locked the house, tucked the key under the mat, and left. Beth had been sad to leave since she was five years old, old enough to realize that the island had a soul that she loved as much as she loved a real, living person.

Why were they going back to New York? What waited for them there? The kids had another year of school, the most critical year. Beth had the apartment, her position on Danforth's advisory board, a few friends who would allow her to be a third or fifth wheel at dinner parties. She had Kara Schau. She had her gym, her hairdresser, the best Chinese food in the world at the Jade Palace, the museums, which she rarely visited anymore, though she felt encouraged by their stately presence in her neighborhood. There was Arch's mother, Vivian, on Fifty-ninth and Sutton Place, whom they would see once a month for a lunch of roast beef and watercress sandwiches. It was a bleak picture.

And then there was the matter of the baby. Beth marveled that she and David hadn't ended up in the same pickle so many years ago—thinking back, she couldn't remember what they had used for birth control. Beth felt sorry for Garrett and disappointed in both him and Piper, although she had to admit, Piper's decision was mature and responsible. David and Rosie had raised her right, and Beth was mortified to discover that she herself felt much like Garrett—hoping for an abortion, hoping that the whole mess could just be swept under the rug. But no—there was to be a baby in March. Now that it was an undeniable fact, now that Beth had seen the ultrasound photo, her feelings changed. That baby was her grandchild. The mere word made her gasp with disbelief—she was far too young!—but it was true. The baby belonged to all of them. It whispered in Beth's ear, begging her to stay.

❧

She packed the kitchen and the dining room, leaving only breakfast things. They got sandwiches from Something Natural for lunch and ate strange combinations of leftovers for dinner. The kids were good about helping—they gave Beth their clothes for one final wash and she did all of the beach towels except for two, since Winnie and Marcus wanted to swim right up until the final morning. Beth packed up her room and started cleaning. She dusted every surface in the house with a rag, then bleach and water. She vacuumed all the floors and had Winnie beat the rugs. As long as there were tasks still ahead of her, she had time left. And so she took out all of the screens and sprayed them down with the hose; she rinsed all of the deck furniture. She went into town and bought an approximate match of the kitchen chair she had broken. She delivered a big bag of perishables to Mrs. Colchester, and because the woman wasn't home, Beth left the bag on the front porch with a note that said, "Another summer ending!"

Then, with less than a day left—they were leaving on the 9:30 boat the next morning—Beth decided to broach the topic with the twins that gnawed at her insides. She couldn't leave the island without doing so.

She found Garrett in his room neatly folding shirts and shorts and putting them in his suitcase, but Winnie had to be called up from the beach. Beth promised Marcus, "I'll only borrow her for a few minutes." Once she had the twins in the same place, the upstairs hallway, as it happened, she took a deep breath.

"I need you to show me the place where you put Daddy's ashes," she said.

They nodded, as though this request were long overdue. Garrett abandoned his packing and Winnie yelled from the edge of the deck to Marcus. "I have this thing to do. I'll be back in a little while."

The three of them walked silently out to the Rover, where Beth climbed into the backseat. It was late afternoon, sunny, a gorgeous day in early September. Garrett sailed up the Polpis Road, a section of Nantucket Beth had always found beautiful, with handsome homes along the road, and winding dirt roads that led to either the harbor or the moors. She studied the backs of the twins' heads. There was something odd about sitting in the backseat while they drove. It was the role reversal—years and years had passed with Arch and Beth up front and the kids in the back. Beth supposed she should be sad, but what she felt was freedom. She didn't have to be responsible; she could let them lead the way.

With them facing forward, it was also easier for her to bring up the crazy idea that had been festering in her head the past few days.

"What if we stayed?" she said.

Garrett reached for the volume knob of the radio and turned it down. "Did you say something, Mom?"

Beth cleared her throat. "I did. I asked you, What if we stayed?"

Winnie turned her head, though not far enough to meet Beth's eyes. "Stayed where?"

"Stayed on Nantucket. This year. What would you think?"

"No way," Garrett said.

"You could go to Nantucket High School," Beth said. "We could get heat for the house. A furnace! And we'll put in a phone. When the baby is born, I could take care of him or her. Piper wouldn't have to put the baby up for adoption. I mean, you guys will be going to college next year, anyway, and I could, you know, live on Nantucket and raise the baby." Her voice gained strength and conviction, like the plan was a dream she was remembering more vividly as she kept talking. Raise the baby herself, of course! With occasional help from David. Piper and Garrett could visit all the time, whenever they wanted, but their baby would be like a much younger sibling instead of their child. It would be a real Nantucket baby, who would grow up in Horizon, the fifth generation of Beth's family to sleep under its roof. The idea of the baby, the bassinet, the stroller Beth would push while jogging, the outfits she still had from when Winnie and Garrett were young, the wooden toys, the silver spoon that would deliver pureed pears and sweet potatoes into the tiny pink mouth—it all sounded so superior to returning to New York that Beth was crushed when Winnie snapped her fingers and said, "Mom! Earth to Mom! Return to reality!"

"The baby is going to be put up for adoption," Garrett said.

"And we're going back to New York," Winnie said. "That's where we live."

"But your father—"

"Dad would want us to go back to New York," Garrett said. "And finish at Danforth."

"Is *here*," Beth said. "Your father is here."

As if on cue, Garrett hit the turn signal and directed the car down the road to Quidnet. Beth sealed her mouth. She was losing her mind. Stay on Nantucket? Keep the baby? She was talking nonsense. She was trying to make these minutes in the car be about something other than what they were really about. They were really about going to see the place where Arch's ashes were scattered. Thinking about the ashes meant thinking about the decision to cremate, those wretched days in the apartment with all the people drinking coffee and preparing Beth sandwiches that she couldn't possibly eat. It meant thinking about the day the doorman called up to say she'd received a package and opening the box that contained the urn, sent to her via UPS like it was something she'd ordered from a catalog.

Garrett drove through a thicket of trees and then Beth saw a meadow and on the far side of the meadow, the harbor. The water shimmered in the late afternoon sun. Garrett pulled over. He opened the door and helped Beth out like she was an invalid.

"This is it," Garrett said.

She couldn't have wished for a more beautiful spot. It was flat and calm and quiet. It was everything a final resting place should be.

"All these years on Nantucket," she said. "And I've never been here."

"Dad and I discovered it," Garrett said proudly.

Winnie and Garrett each took one of Beth's hands and the three of them stepped out into the meadow. Beth bowed her head. *Thank you*, she said—to God or to Arch, she wasn't sure—

thank you for this, the most awful summer of our lives. As crazy and gut-wrenching as it was, we made it. We are stronger. We are closer. We are still standing here, together, a family.

To her children, she said, "When I die, will you bring my remains here? Will you put me here with Daddy?"

Winnie rested her head on Beth's shoulder. "We don't want you to die."

"But when I do . . ."

"We'll bring you here," Garrett promised.

⁂

The next morning, Beth woke at six and went downstairs to tend to the last details of leaving: a note for Carl Drake, the caretaker, breakfast for the kids, all of the trash taken out. Beth looked at the ocean as often as she could. Impossible to believe that to-morrow it would be Park Avenue. But that, really, was the story of her life.

Marcus was the first one to come down.

"Is there anything I can do to help?" he whispered. He was wearing the same white oxford cloth shirt he'd worn the day they arrived—Beth didn't recall seeing it at any other time this summer. She closed her eyes and remembered opening the door to their apartment in New York and finding Marcus there, wear-ing this shirt, carrying his black leather duffel bag, which now was packed and waiting at the bottom of the stairs. The son of Constance Bennett Tyler, convicted murderer. But he was more than that, as Arch had promised. This was a fine young man—smart, considerate, good in a way that so few people were good anymore. When Beth opened her eyes, she realized how much she would miss him. He had become like a third child to her.

"Is there anything *I* can do to help?" Beth asked. She wasn't quite sure what she meant by that—all she knew was that she wanted to make the rest of Marcus's life easier for him, as easy as his days on the beach here had been.

Marcus wondered if Winnie had said anything to Beth about the five hundred dollars, because her words sounded like an offer of money. But he'd already made up his mind to get a job as soon as he returned to Queens. He sat down at the kitchen table and let Beth pour milk on his cereal. "There's no way I can thank you for this summer," he said. "This summer saved me."

"Oh, Marcus."

"It gave me peace. And it gave me love."

"Well, you gave us things, too, you know," Beth said. "You gave us yourself."

"That doesn't seem like much in comparison," he said.

Except it was. At that moment, Beth understood that Arch hadn't invited Marcus to Nantucket for only Marcus's sake. Arch had invited Marcus to Nantucket for all their sakes—Beth's, Garrett's, Winnie's—so they could learn from him about character. About how to rise above.

"You have to promise to come see us," Beth said. "You have to promise to let us know how you're doing."

"I will." He dug into his cereal with gusto. All summer, Beth had loved to watch him eat because he was so enthusiastic about the food she put in front of him. She remembered with an ache in her throat the way he'd tied the bib around his neck before eating his first lobster. It was going to be a huge loss to have him leave their midst. She would wonder about him all the time; she would worry.

"We're coming back here in March or April, when the baby

is born," she said. "Just for a week or so. Will you come back with us then?"

"I don't know if Garrett wants me here," Marcus said. "He might just want family."

"Marcus," Beth said. "You are family."

Marcus smiled, gracing the room with his dimples. Beth could tell he felt as she did—that as long as there was a bright spot on the horizon, they might make it successfully through today.

"Sure," he said.

※

And so they went: out to the car, which was packed to the top, once again. Garrett sat up front and Winnie and Marcus climbed in the back. Beth stood in the front door—first looking at the car and then turning and looking at the empty house.

"See you in the spring," she said.

She locked the door and tucked the key under the mat.

The scene at Steamship Wharf was as chaotic as one would expect for Labor Day weekend. The standby line was twenty cars deep. Beth was grateful for her reservation. She pulled into a spot for ticketed cars and let the engine idle. They still had a few minutes before boarding.

"Do any of you want to use the bathroom before we get on the boat?" she asked.

No response. In her rearview mirror, she saw Winnie asleep on Marcus's shoulder. Garrett was in outer space somewhere, and who could blame him?

A few minutes later, the car in front of theirs inched forward in anticipation. Beth herself was exhausted—she wanted to get the car onto the boat, then pull a pillow out of the back and

sleep for an hour. The drive home was always so draining, followed by the torturous business of delivering Marcus to Queens,
then unloading all of the stuff from the back of the car and
hauling it onto the freight elevator of their building. How would
she ever make it through the day?

Finally it was her turn to go. A steamship worker with a griz-
zled beard motioned her forward. Just before Beth drove up the
ramp onto the boat, she saw David's van and then David himself
sitting on the bumper. Wearing khaki shorts, a green polo shirt,
the flip-flops, sunglasses. Grinning at her, he lifted his coffee cup
in her direction—a toast.

There was no point in analyzing why she felt so happy to
see him or how touched she was that he found time in his day
to see them off, or how safe she suddenly knew she was—there
was someone in the world who cared for her, who probably even
loved her, and who would be here on island, waiting, the next
time she returned. For now, David was what she needed most:
he was her friend.

She decided not to wave; she didn't want the kids to notice
him. He wasn't there for the kids, anyway; he was there for her.
Beth did put down her window and turn her face in his direction.
She wanted to give him something to hold on to while she was
gone—the memory of her smile, warmed by the summer sun.

chapter 8

The most amazing aspect of life, Beth thought, was the way that time passed—the days, the months, one following the next without slowing down or stopping for tragedy or triumph.

They returned to New York and—how else could she say it?—resumed their lives. It took two weeks for Beth to readjust to New York, but then one day she woke up and realized everything was back to normal. The laundry was done, the apartment had been cleaned, the last of the Nantucket bread and tomatoes had been consumed—now the kids were devouring bags of apples and gallons of cider, almost faster than Beth could buy them. Winnie had her first physics quiz and she rattled off formulas in a cheerleader's chant. Garrett had his first soccer game at the end of the week, plus his application for Princeton was due soon, if he wanted to qualify for early admission. One night, Beth found him in Arch's study on the phone—odd, because he normally took calls on the cordless in the kitchen. He was sitting at Arch's desk doodling on a legal pad, and with his head bent, he looked so much like Arch that Beth caught her breath, inadvertently announcing her presence—she had planned to slip out of the room unnoticed. But Garrett looked up and saw her and she asked, "Who are you on the phone with, honey?" The typical response whenever she asked either of the kids this was, "None of your business," but this time Garrett moved his mouth away from the receiver and whispered, "Piper."

Beth stood in the doorway for a beat. She wanted to ask, *How's she feeling? How's the baby? What does the doctor say?* She wanted to talk to David. The phone line led directly to Nantucket, and although she was now back in New York, Beth yearned to transmit herself there. Instead, she nodded and closed the door.

❦

Winnie started her senior year at Danforth a changed woman. She was no longer the naïve goody-goody spoiled brat child of privilege whose life had been torn apart by the untimely death of her father, she was no longer a girl who thought it was okay to wear her father's Princeton sweatshirt as though it were a mourning band or torture her body by denying it food. And she was no longer a virgin, physically or emotionally.

While it was true that her relationship with Marcus changed—there was no way to keep up the intensity of their friendship when they lived apart—it ended up being okay for both of them. Winnie's time was occupied by school. She nurtured the friendships that she'd all but ignored as of March sixteenth, and she tried to foster friendships with one or two of the African American kids at her school, although she soon realized that just because these people were black did not mean they had an excellent character like Marcus. Winnie did her best to eat as much as she could and three afternoons a week she worked out in Danforth's weight room as she prepared for the upcoming swim season. She was going to surprise everyone on her team by trying the butterfly this year.

Marcus's life got incrementally better. During the summer his father had cleared the apartment of most of Constance's things, which helped. Marcus had school which he took seriously; he studied hard. He, too, went to the gym three afternoons a week, and he got a job working two evenings plus Saturdays at a pizza shop in the student union at Queens College. It was a job that could easily have gone to a work-study student, but Marcus's old boss at the grounds department put in a good word for him, even though he knew about Marcus's mother. Marcus didn't actually make pizza—no tossing or spinning of dough, no painting of sauce or collage of toppings—but he did become proficient with the pizza peel, the pizza cutter, and the cash register. He made $6.75 an hour and by mid-October had saved almost two hundred dollars toward his debt to Dome Books.

On Sundays, Marcus took the seven line into Manhattan to watch the Giants game at Winnie's apartment. Those afternoons on the leather sofa were a quiet fantasy. They snuggled under a fleece blanket, and although there was no opportunity for sex— Beth was always around—they reveled in the warmth of each other's body, just as they had on those nights in Horizon when they'd done nothing but sleep. Beth served them Cokes from a silver tray and made delicious pub food—potato skins, chicken fingers, mushrooms stuffed with sausage and Parmesan cheese. Sundays that autumn made Marcus glad to be alive.

Thanks to Beth, he'd met four times with Kara Schau, who

actually traveled to Benjamin N. Cardozo High School to speak with him during his study hall. Mostly, he talked and she listened, but she left him with a few helpful sentences: *You can be related to someone who's done a bad thing and not be a bad person. You can love someone who's done a bad thing and not be a bad person. You can even be someone who's done a bad thing and not be a bad person.* It helped Marcus to think this way, and he cut a deal with his father— sometime before the holidays he would go up to Bedford Hills to see Constance. He refused to partake in the weekly phone calls with Bo and LaTisha. When he was ready to talk to Mama, he told himself, he would do so face to face.

The first Saturday in November he rescheduled his work shift and he and Winnie went to the prison together, on the train. They were as solemn as they would have been at a funeral, holding hands and gazing out the window as the last of the fall leaves in Westchester County passed them by. Since Marcus had never been to the prison before, Bo told him what stop to get off at and how to catch the free bus to the prison grounds.

"It's not a pretty place," Bo said. "You know that, right?"

Marcus knew it intellectually, but that was different from actually *seeing* the Bedford Hills Correctional Institute—the barbed wire, the armed guards, the stench of lost hope, the absolute concrete and metal desolation of the place. It was hell on earth. When Marcus and Winnie stepped down from the bus, they were herded into a huge waiting room filled with other visitors. Marcus gripped Winnie's arm and led her to a space on a vinyl couch. There were glass-topped coffee tables with torn magazines and coloring books and broken crayons—because the waiting room was filled with little kids. It could have been a pediatrician's office except for the edgy way the adults acted, sneaking glances, both shameful and interested, at one another. Everyone in the room loved someone who had done a bad thing.

During the wait, Marcus nearly fell asleep. He felt his body wanting to check out, shut down. Because it was too much to handle—the prospect of seeing his mother. Winnie was reading her English assignment, *Macbeth*, and Marcus wished he'd brought something to read, though he doubted anything would distract him. Finally, over the buzz of the room, Marcus heard his name. He helped Winnie up and walked toward the heavy black woman who was waiting for him. He tried to clear his mind as he would before a swim meet.

Constance, when he saw her, was behind glass, but Marcus marveled at how familiar she was. His *mother*. Mama. He'd expected her to look sad or tired; he'd expected her to look older. But, in fact, she looked much the way she had his entire life— with smooth brown skin, wide brown eyes, and the hair she always claimed she could do nothing with. At home, she wore silk scarves over her head, but here she made do with a navy blue bandana.

In those initial moments of studying her face—and yes, she looked as terrified and unmoored as he did—he waited for his anger to surface. This was what he was worried about—his anger. But instead he felt a profound sadness—his mother had ruined her life. Marcus's life—as the summer had taught him and as his father had promised—would move on past the murders. But for Constance this prison was the last stop.

Constance sat and Marcus sat and they both picked up the phone.

Her voice was the same soft-and-scratchy tone, forever irritated by constantly explaining the basic tenets of the English language to kids who didn't want to learn.

"Hello, child," she said. "I'm glad you came."

When she spoke, Marcus remembered one of the words Kara Schau had given him: "acceptance." He didn't have to forgive, he didn't have to understand. All he had to do was show up. And here he was.

"Hello, Mama," he said.

Winnie was standing a foot or so behind Marcus, a mere observer to the proceedings, but she teared up as she watched Marcus and Constance. She wondered what it would be like to see her father again for fifteen minutes. She would be tempted to give him news—about falling in love with Marcus, or about Beth being married before, or about Garrett becoming a father himself—but then she realized that she would do what Marcus was now doing: telling his mother he loved her.

Winnie couldn't hear Constance's voice, but she read her lips: *I know, child, I know.* Just the way Arch knew, wherever he was, that Winnie loved him and would keep him alive every way that she could.

It might have been the sound of Winnie crying that brought Marcus back to himself. He pulled Winnie forward, closer to the glass.

"Mama," he said. "This is Winnie Newton, Arch's daughter."

Winnie had imagined this introduction twenty times the night before as she tried to fall asleep. She imagined Constance falling to her knees in gratitude, waxing on and on about what a great man Arch was. But now, in the actual moment, when Marcus handed Winnie the phone so that Constance could speak to her, what Constance said was, "I would have known you anywhere. You look just like your father."

And this, of course, endeared Constance Tyler to Winnie forever.

✼

By holiday time, Piper was six months pregnant. As Garrett moved through the days of his life—classes, the end of soccer, the beginning of intramural floor hockey, weekends with friends at the movies, even the occasional date (which he kept secret from his mother and sister)—it was easy enough to forget that the first girl Garrett had ever loved and might still love a little was suffering physically and emotionally as Garrett's child grew inside her on an island thirty miles out to sea. At times—when Garrett took Brooke Casserhill out to dinner at a Peruvian chicken place, for example, where they were able to smuggle in a bottle of wine lifted from Brooke's father's wine *cave*—Piper seemed far away and less than real. She seemed like folklore. But at other times, mostly in the dark hours when Garrett should have been sleeping, Piper and her plight took on a gravity that nailed Garrett to his bed.

He tried to figure out what she expected from him. She accused him of being a kid. Well, yeah—he was seventeen years old, a senior in high school, just like she was. Had she wanted him to marry her? Raise the child? If that was the adult thing, and maybe it was, then Garrett conceded: it was out of his reach. He couldn't do it.

He called her every month after her doctor's appointment, and their conversations consisted almost entirely of the clinical: how much weight had she gained? (Fifteen pounds.) What was she measuring? (Twenty-four centimeters.) Did the AFP screen come back normal? (Yes.) Did she test positive for gestational diabetes? (No.) When would she sign up for Lamaze classes? (After the first of the year.) The baby kicked all the time now, Piper said, and the girlfriends who'd shunned her when they found out she'd let that *summer kid* impregnate her were now the ones who were most eager to lay their hands on the firm sphere of Piper's belly and feel the baby drum from the inside.

Garrett had had no idea that a single baby could consume so much mental energy; always, in these conversations with Piper, it seemed like there were a hundred small points of discussion all revolving around the baby. In history class, Mr. Rapinski spoke of women in Third World countries who excused themselves from the assembly line of whatever factory they worked at, gave birth in the restroom and handed the infant off to a family member to care for at home. But it was nowhere close to that easy for a couple of white American upper-middle-class teenagers.

Garrett didn't tell anyone in New York about Piper or the baby, and he forbade Beth and Winnie to mention it to anyone but Kara Schau. His mother understood. "Every man, woman, and child is entitled to one secret," she said. "I had mine, now you have yours." Garrett hated putting himself in a similar situation to his mother, and he wondered if the adult thing to do was to come clean, confessing to everyone he knew that he had impregnated his summer girlfriend and then left her to deal with it by herself. Then he could accept blame; he could wear the scarlet letter. *You want to be back in New York where you can pretend none of this ever happened,* Piper had said. She was right! Garrett didn't want to be whispered about; he didn't want the information fermenting his teachers' opinion of him as they wrote his college recommendations. He didn't want to lose any friends. He couldn't wait until March when Piper would birth the baby, then give it away, and the ordeal would be ended.

⁂

The holidays came, and because they were the first holidays without Arch, they could only be described as bearable. In January, Beth took the twins to Hunter Mountain to ski, and for the break in February, the three of them flew to Palm Beach and stayed at the Breakers. Garrett praised his mother for these trips, these *distractions*, and helped out as much as he could—carrying luggage, arranging the limo to and from the airport, and being as amiable as possible.

While they traveled, he found himself thinking about the baby more often. He'd never realized how many children inhabited the world. Babies in car seats and strollers clogged the train station and airline terminals. Garrett heard their cries during takeoff and landing. He noticed, in every public bathroom he used now, the beige Koala changing station bolted to the wall. These had been there all along—they hadn't been installed to torment him—and yet he never remembered seeing one before. At Hunter Mountain, Garrett, Beth, and Winnie ate dinner at a Mexican restaurant and Garrett became so preoccupied with a blond two-year-old boy at the next table who did a fire engine puzzle over and over, shrieking with delight each time he completed it, that Garrett barely touched his fajitas. At the Breakers, he separated from his mother and sister and lay on a lounge by the baby pool where he watched the little ones cavorting in their water wings. A baby, an actual baby, lived inside of Piper and this time next year that baby would be crawling or walking or swimming. His child. His little boy or girl. It hurt him in a way he couldn't name. It was worse than heartbreak. It was worse, in a way, than losing his father.

⚘

Beth thought that March would never arrive, but then, of course, it did. They marked the one-year anniversary of Arch's death quietly—dinner in the apartment with Arch's mother. Trent Trammelman called Beth in the morning to say that the law firm was donating money in Arch's name to establish a scholarship fund at Danforth. Arch's secretary, now the secretary for a new attorney, sent flowers, and a bunch of thoughtful souls sent cards. Beth hated the idea of a death day as an anniversary, and yet once it was past, she felt relieved. A milestone survived. Since Christmas, friends had been inviting Beth over to meet men—single, divorced, widowed—and once Beth caught on, she always begged off, saying, "Please, it hasn't even been a year." Now that the anniversary had come and gone, her excuse vanished. And yet, Beth couldn't bring herself to think about dating. All she could think about was their impending trip to Nantucket.

Beth spoke to the headmaster at Danforth: this was a very important family trip (she did not call it a vacation), and for reasons she couldn't specify, she didn't know how long they'd be gone.

Everyone at Danforth accommodated them. Winnie and Garrett both had excellent grades and they'd both been accepted to college. Garrett got into Princeton on early admission, and Winnie had been accepted at NYU, though she was still waiting to hear from Columbia, Williams, and Brown.

They were free to stay on Nantucket as long as they cared to.

❧

Marcus was coming along for the week of his spring break. He, too, had been accepted to college—Queens College, a short bus ride from his apartment, and Colgate University, upstate. Colgate was a white person's school, but his English teacher, Ms. Marchese, encouraged him to apply. He wrote an essay about his mother. The admissions committee was so impressed by the essay that they offered him a full ride for all four years, giving Marcus an opportunity worth much more than thirty thousand dollars. Marcus spoke to the swim coach and the head of the black student union, both of whom encouraged him to come. But the deciding factor was the enthusiastic call from one of the English professors who'd read his essay. *You have a way of turning words on a page into pure emotion,* the professor had said. *You have the makings of a fine, fine writer.*

❧

Beth had never been to Nantucket in March, and as soon as she stepped out of the Rover onto Horizon's shell driveway, she understood why. The wind was brutal, whipping across Miacomet Pond in cold, wet sheets. The sky was low and gray and the ocean was a roiling black. The town had been practically deserted—less than half of the businesses showed any signs of life. In New York, trees had already started to bud; crocuses were up. But not here.

This time, Beth had brought her cell phone, and as soon as she sent the kids to the Stop & Shop for firewood and groceries, she called David. He'd sent a Christmas card—no picture, no note—just the three names signed in his handwriting at the bottom. She was nervous dialing his number and not because of Piper. A couple of times over the winter she caught herself repeating his words of the previous summer. *I thought about kissing you. I thought about making love to you.* When she got very lonely—weekend nights at home when the kids were out and she could hear New York frolicking outside without her—she entertained the possibility of her and David together. Not married again, but together. As companions—that's what she wanted as she grew older—someone to spend time with once the twins left. Would it be so crazy if that person was David? She went so far as to wonder if he would ever visit her in the city. He'd never been there to her knowledge. She could show him the city the way everyone should experience it.

When David answered the phone, she said, "Hi, it's me."

"Me?"

"Bethie," she said. Flirting with him already. "How's Piper?"

"Two centimeters dilated, ninety percent effaced," David said, sounding like a doctor himself. "She's as big as a house. I mean, huge. I can't believe this is my little girl. I just can't believe it."

"Yeah," Beth said. They were silent a minute, listening to the static of the cell phone. "You'll call us as soon as . . ."

"As soon as," David said. "The doctor said any time now. How long are you staying?"

"We're staying until Piper has the baby," Beth said. "That's why we came, after all."

"Right," David said.

"Has she . . . changed her mind about adoption?" Beth asked.

"No."

"So, how will it work, then? Will they come get the baby? Take the baby away?"

"There's a procedure, yes. The people from the agency are professionals, Beth. They've met with Piper and gone over the range of emotions she can expect. They give her twenty-four hours with the baby, then she signs a document and the baby goes. Piper made it clear that she and Garrett want to name the baby, and that's allowed."

"She and Garrett want to *name* the baby?" Beth asked.

"Yes."

Beth took a deep breath of the shockingly cold air inside Horizon. The house felt stingy without any heat. They were all going to spend the night on air mattresses and sleeping bags in front of the fire. Roast hot dogs, that kind of thing. It would be fun for about three hours.

"I don't know if I'm going to be able to handle this, David. Watching some stranger carry away my grandchild. How about you?"

He sighed. "Oh, Beth. I've lived with this decision every day for the last nine months. I've had to deal with people coming up to me on the street, telling me how irresponsible I am as a parent and Piper is as a person. She lost two of her closest friends, she says the kids at school stare at her all the time, and her teachers treat her differently, too. They treat her like she's stupid. But she's not, of course. She got into BU and BC, and was wait-listed at Harvard. Her grades are the best they've ever been and she's going to college, just like she said she was going to. But it's been hard. I guess you haven't had to give it much thought while you were in New York."

There he was, using the same old refrain—*I had to live with the pain while you were away.* God, this was a bitter man. But no, that wasn't quite right. He had a point; she was lucky. She had always been able to lead a double life; she had always been able to escape.

"I gave it a lot of thought," she said. "I thought of it every day."

"Did you," David said. "Well, I bet Garrett didn't tell his buddies. And I'll bet you didn't report it to his teachers. In fact, I'll bet no one in New York knows why you're mysteriously off to Nantucket this week."

Where was all this anger *coming* from? "Not true," Beth countered. "My therapist knows."

"Your therapist," David said. He breathed forcefully into the phone, then chuckled. "God, I need a therapist. We'll see you at the hospital then, Bethie?"

She was grateful that he used the nickname. "Okay."

She hung up the phone and stared at it for a moment, wishing that the conversation had gone better, that there had been some kind of connection between the two of them. This was the man she fantasized taking to brunch in Soho?

It was true that none of the kids had acknowledged the real reason they were here. On the ride up, Marcus and Winnie perused the Colgate catalog and admission packet line by line, trying to figure out what Marcus's freshman year might be like. ("It sounds cool," Winnie concluded. "It sounds cold," Marcus corrected her.) Garrett drove the entire way and didn't take his eyes off the road except to collect money for tolls. Now, all three kids stampeded into the house with bags of groceries—a pile of Duraflame logs and every kind of junk food imaginable. This was a camping trip for them. Winnie and Marcus braved the icy staircase to the beach because they wanted to check out the ocean, and Beth sent Garrett to the basement to switch on the water heater. When he came back upstairs, she said, "I just spoke with David on the phone. He said any day now. He said he's going to call us." God, even she couldn't say it: Piper *is due* any day now. He's going to call us *when the baby is born.*

Garrett's face was wooden, expressionless. "Okay, thanks."

Beth touched his shoulder. He pulled away. He was so foreign to her. In six months, he would leave for Princeton and she would never know him again, not really. Such was the sadness of sons.

That night in Horizon was unlike any Beth had spent there. Because of the cold, she supposed—the cold changed things. For a few years, when Beth was in college, she had arrived in early May, when the house was chilly and damp. She kept the fireplace lit and walked around in her grandfather's Irish fisherman's sweater and jeans and thick socks. But those days didn't come close to this kind of cold—a cold that required the Newtons to sleep in fleece jackets inside their flannel-lined sleeping bags in front of the fire. Winnie and Garrett brought the same gear they wore to Hunter Mountain—Bodnar ski jackets and Patagonia microfiber pants. Marcus had to make do with layers—T-shirt, long-sleeved T-shirt, sweatshirt, a fleece that he borrowed from Beth when the leather jacket he brought grew stiff and almost cracked.

They got a fire blazing, and when the sun went down they roasted hotdogs, made popcorn in an old-fashioned popcorn maker, and Beth got the stovetop working where she warmed up cider. They all took showers—Beth was the last one in and her hot water conked halfway through. She dried off as quickly as she ever had in her life and jumped back into her clothes.

They arranged their sleeping bags lengthwise so that everyone's head faced the fire. Winnie and Marcus were in the middle, Beth and Garrett on either side. The kids talked about school mostly, and college. Beth drifted in and out of the conversation; her mind was consumed with her conversation with David and with her own discomfort. She interrupted them.

"Tomorrow," she said, "we're checking into the Jared Coffin."

Before they could protest or cheer (Garrett and Marcus were all for it; Winnie liked things just as they were, cozy like this), the phone rang.

Piper was in labor.

"Her water broke right in the middle of *The West Wing*, and now her contractions are a minute and a half apart," David said. "We just got to the hospital a few minutes ago. You can either come now—it might mean a long time waiting—or I can call you when the baby is born."

Beth looked at the kids. Even Marcus's expression was that of the keenest interest. They would never sleep, that much was clear.

"We'll come now," she said.

Compared to Horizon, the hospital was positively tropical. Beth shed a layer of clothing before they reached the admitting desk.

"Which way is labor and delivery?" she asked.

A nurse directed them upstairs. Standing in the elevator, Beth squeezed Garrett's hand. He squeezed back.

"It's going to be okay, honey," she said. "Babies are born all the time, every day, all over the world."

"I know, Mom," he said.

The elevator opened on the second floor and they followed signs. Beth was hurrying, though she, who had been in labor for eighteen hours with the twins, knew how long it could take. They came upon a pastel-colored waiting room filled with over-stuffed sofas and chairs. The kids flung themselves all over the furniture—yes, it was more appealing than sleeping on the floor of that icebox. There was a woman on one of the couches read-ing a copy of *Martha Stewart Living*, and she looked up, alarmed at the invasion. She was very attractive, with honey-colored hair tied back in a braid. The woman looked them over, no doubt wondering what they were doing there—this was a maternity ward, not the common space of a college dorm. The woman opened her mouth to speak.

"Beth?" she said.

Beth smiled, politely at first, flipping through her mental Ro-lodex. Who was this? Then a quiet panic infiltrated and she fought to keep her smile steady. She really *had* been out of touch in New York. Because although she had given the impending birth of this baby hours and hours of thought, *never once* had it occurred to her that she would have to see Rosie. But here she was—of course—Rosie Ronan, Piper's mother. The other grandmother.

"Oh, God, Rosie," Beth said. In her mind, Beth realized, she had filed Rosie away as "absent." Like Arch. Not there. Beth went to the woman and took both her hands, even went so far as to kiss her on the corner of the mouth. This was *so* awkward. More awkward than the cocktail party so many years ago when Rosie introduced Beth to a friend as "David's old flame," right in front of Arch. At the time, Beth had swilled deeply off her glass of Chardonnay, and Rosie laughed and said, "Well, we're all adults, right? What's passed is past!" Now here she was—hadn't aged a day in six years—if anything, she was prettier than ever. Beth turned Rosie toward the kids who were halfway to sleep—who could blame them? it was eleven o'clock and the day had been long—and said, "Winnie, Marcus, *Garrett*, this is Rosie Ronan, Piper and Peyton's mother."

Her kids, always polite with other adults, took a few seconds to process what Beth was telling them. Garrett groaned under his breath; he knew he should be the first one to his feet, knew it by the way his mother hit his name the hardest—this woman was, after all, sort of like his mother-in-law. Before Garrett could summon energy to stand, Marcus jumped up. Garrett was grateful for this; it gave him a few seconds to think.

"Marcus Tyler," he said. "Congratulations on your impending good news."

"Thank you," Rosie said, with such a sense of entitlement that one might have thought it was *Rosie* who was having this baby. Beth wondered what she was doing out here in the waiting room, but before she could ask, she watched Garrett rise from the love seat. With a gallantry Beth rarely saw in him anymore, he introduced himself and then he introduced Winnie. "Garrett Newton, Mrs. Ronan, and this is my twin sister, Winnifred Newton."

"It's nice to finally meet you," Rosie said. "Piper and Peyton and David are down the hall in a labor room. I've been banished for making too many suggestions." She smiled sheepishly at Beth, and Beth, against her will, sympathized with her. It *was* always the mother who took the brunt of a teenager's anger.

"Is Piper making any progress?" Beth asked. Just standing so close to the maternity ward brought it all back to her—how delivering a baby was a fight for ground, a struggle for centimeters, one painful contraction at a time.

"Some," Rosie said. "She wants to wait for as long as she can before she takes the epidural. She read somewhere that it slows labor. She was moaning pretty loudly in there and she lost her dinner. The nurses here are outstanding. There's a nurse back there with Piper now who was here when I had both Piper and Peyton. Of course, it wasn't that long ago."

"Only seventeen years," Beth said, then felt like she had stated the unstatable. She removed her layers until she wore only a turtleneck and jeans. The hospital's heating system blew hot, dry air out of a vent directly under Beth's feet. "So I guess we'll just wait then."

"Is it okay if we drift off, Mom?" Winnie asked. She was curled up in a large armchair and Garrett and Marcus were each spread out on a love seat. That left a space on the sofa next to Rosie, who had returned to her magazine—perhaps hearing the blunt declaration of her daughter's age upset her. Beth sat down, then said, "Garrett, do you want to at least tell Piper you're here? In case she wants to see you?"

Garrett opened his eyes and stared at the acoustic tiles of the ceiling. He was so tired, this all seemed like a dream. He looked to Rosie Ronan, and she nodded at him. "That might be a good idea," she said.

Garrett rose.

"You can ask one of the nurses where she is," Beth suggested.

"I'll find it," Garrett said, walking away.

Beth removed her boots and propped her stocking feet on the glass coffee table. She fell asleep before Garrett returned.

❧

When she woke, the waiting area was dark, though the lights in the adjoining hallway were on. All three kids snored shamelessly, and when Beth glanced next to her, she saw Rosie Ronan sitting right there, legs crossed at the ankle, eyes closed. Then, suddenly, Rosie's eyes opened and the two women gazed at each other.

"Beth," Rosie whispered, as though she were seeing Beth for the first time. "Beth Eyler."

"Beth Newton," Beth said. "I haven't been Beth Eyler for twenty years."

"In our house," Rosie said, "you're always called Beth Eyler."

Beth didn't like anything about that statement, and she sensed she wasn't supposed to.

"Any news about Piper?"

"They gave her the shot," Rosie said. "She's sleeping."

Beth nodded slowly, then tried to close her eyes, as though drifting off to sleep. Rosie allowed it for a few seconds before she spoke again.

"I was very sorry to hear about your husband."

Beth opened her eyes. "Thank you."

"David told me what a difficult time you had this summer."

Beth resented this even more: the thought of the bereaved Newton family as a topic of conversation between the Ronans.

"We're doing okay now, thanks."

Rosie uttered what sounded like a soft laugh, egging Beth to look her way. "I was just thinking about the circumstances that led the two of us to be sitting here together," Rosie said. "It's extraordinary."

"I guess it is."

"To think your son impregnated our daughter."

Beth thought about telling Rosie that Piper was hardly an innocent in all this. Those halter tops, the way she clung to Garrett—but she had no desire to fight. Instead, she stood up and turned toward the lighted hallway, thinking she would grab a cup of tea if she could find a vending machine—anything to get away!

"You're leaving?" Rosie asked. A challenge.

"I'd like something to drink," Beth said, and then to be gracious, "Would you like anything?"

Rosie rested her head against the back of the sofa, her eyes at half mast. "I'm all set," she said. "But you might ask my poor husband if he wants a Coke or some coffee. We've been here since nine-thirty."

Beth blinked; the heat was drying out her eyes. "Your poor husband?" she said. "You mean, David?"

Rosie answered with her eyes closed. "I mean David."

It wasn't the woman's words, but her tone of voice that informed Beth. It was the slight smile of victory on her closed lips. David and Rosie were back together. Beth was shocked, incredulous, and crushed, a part of her. It wasn't fair, was it? For them to reunite just as Beth was beginning to glimpse the possibility of moving on, and the desire, if only nascent, to want to move on with David. She brought her hand to her mouth and bit down on the diamond of her "We Made It" ring. It wasn't fair because Beth was, once again, left alone.

A hand touched her shoulder. Beth turned to see a nurse. Gray-haired, big-bosomed, with the kind of weary and wise face that seemed to answer Beth's thoughts by saying, *You're right. It's not fair. But you'll manage. Everyone does.*

What the nurse actually said was, "She's pushing. We're very close. Would you ladies like to come watch the birth of your grandchild?"

Rosie followed the nurse down the hall.

The thought of being in the same room with Rosie and David addled Beth, but that baby was the reason she was here. She walked alongside Rosie, love for this new child rising to heat her skin like a fever. Halfway down the hall, she remembered Garrett and she hurried back to the waiting room to wake her son. Her son who, due to the miracle of life, was about to become a father.

Epilogue

One *person dying* is like a single drop rejoining the ocean. If Arch could tell his wife and children—and the grandchild who is about to emerge into the world—anything, it would be this: *It's all going to be okay, even in death, especially in death.* But he lacks the power to communicate; he isn't a ghost, only energy crackling in the air.

At a quarter to three on the morning of March twenty-fourth, he is in a delivery room of Nantucket Cottage Hospital. Piper Ronan is in the birthing chair, Peyton Ronan is moving a wooden rolling pin over Piper's lower back, David Ronan is sitting in a straight-backed chair borrowed from the cafeteria with his hands covering his eyes because Piper has forbidden him from watching. Carla Hughes, labor and delivery nurse, has been on this ward for twenty-one years and has helped to deliver twelve hundred babies, though this is her first second-generation child. She helped deliver Piper nearly eighteen years ago. Carla isn't one to pass judgment on the mess kids get themselves into. She has three teenaged sons herself—one of whom makes honor roll every report card, one of whom was arrested for taking a baseball bat to their neighbor's mailbox, and one of whom has yet to distinguish himself as saint or sinner. Carla will say that this particular seventeen-year-old girl is a model patient. She doesn't complain, and doesn't make demands, although she did send her mother out of the room, but this is to be expected from even the most seasoned patient. So far the delivery is going smoothly. Carla imagines it has something to do with the youth of Piper's body—the muscles are loose and flexible. A teenager's tolerance for pain is high; just look, for example, at her pierced nose.

The doctor monitors Piper's progress.

"Three more pushes," he says to everyone in the room.

Outside the door wait Beth, Rosie Ronan and a barely conscious Garrett. Arch focuses on his son. If he had a body, he would give Garrett a hug. The birth of this baby is confusing him; he doesn't know how to cope with it. Despite all of his conflicting emotions, Garrett is looking forward to holding his child, if only for a few minutes. Arch remembers holding his own children for the first time. What he remembers most vividly is how grateful he was that God gave him two arms: one for a baby boy, one for a baby girl.

Beth and Rosie Ronan are doing everything in their power to suppress their eagerness. Both are afraid to even poke their heads in. They can hear through the crack in the door the sounds of Piper struggling: the breathing, the moaning. Rosie is ashamed that she has been banished from the room, but that, she figures, is the price she pays for leaving the girls to their father. It will take a while for either of the girls to trust her again, to trust her and David together.

Beth is afraid to enter the room because David waits on the other side. Arch understands the complexity of her feelings. Another thing he would like to tell her is this: *Every man, woman and child is entitled to one secret.* Arch's secret is that he knew about Beth's first marriage from the beginning. During their engagement, Arch clerked for a judge and one day during a lull he checked to see if his future wife had ever appeared on public record. In death, all is forgiven, but in this case, Arch forgave Beth long ago. He hopes that someday she will forgive herself.

Piper bears down, remembering the first time she laid eyes on Garrett Newton, when she went to his house last June for a cookout. He'd looked so sad. Handsome and sad—an irresistible combination. Now she's the one who's sad, because twenty-four hours after the birth, this child will be handed into the waiting arms of a couple from South Hadley, Massachusetts, a philosophy professor and her husband. Her own baby whom she's felt kick and squirm inside of her every hour for months, who stepped on her bladder last week, causing her to leak in her maternity overalls during calculus class. Her baby—for nobody knows this baby yet but Piper—will be carried out the front door of this hospital, leaving Piper alone with an aching body and bleeding psyche. She imagines meeting the child again someday and being asked to explain: *Why did you give me up?*

I am so very young, Piper thinks.

Another contraction on the horizon, like a Mack truck, and Piper knows it's headed right for her.

Peyton is proud of the job she's doing as birthing coach. She's the only family member who hasn't made Piper cross. But Peyton is tired. It's nearly three o'clock in the morning and she's starving. Her parents promised her a huge Downyflake breakfast as soon as Piper and the baby went into recovery, and so that's what Peyton thinks about: blueberry pancakes with blueberry syrup, a plate of crisp bacon, a glass of fresh OJ.

"Here comes the head," the doctor says. "Give me one more big push."

Piper grits her teeth. The epidural has all but worn off. Nothing in the world prepared her for how this feels.

"One more," the doctor says.

"I can't!" she screams.

"I have the baby's head," the doctor says. "I need one more big push."

Arch sends her a surge of energy. This is, after all, his grandchild.

Piper takes a deep breath and thinks, though she's not sure why, of Nantucket as a baby, floating in an amniotic ocean. Then, even stranger, of Nantucket as her mother.

She hears her baby cry. Feels a hot, wet weight on her belly.

Piper grasps for the child and it is brought up to her, close, where she can smell the tang of blood and fluids from her own body.

"It's a boy," the doctor says.

A boy, Arch thinks.

A boy? Piper is confused. She'd been so sure . . .

"A boy!" David cries. He kisses Piper's forehead and hugs Peyton. He has never been so proud of his daughters. Then he's out the door and nearly knocks over Beth and Rosie and Garrett. "It's a boy!" he proclaims, so elated by the news that he doesn't have time to wonder if Beth knows that he and Rosie are back together and that he has finally let what's passed be the past. He kisses both women.

There is laughter and crying. Beth hurries down the hall to wake Winnie and Marcus. Garrett slides down the wall until his ass hits the floor. *A boy.* A son of his own, just like he always thought he wanted.

They name the baby Archer Newton. The adoptive parents will add their own last name—they may even change his first and middle names—but for the next twenty-four hours when the baby is in the arms of the people around him, the people who loved him first, he will be Archer Newton.

No one is surprised by the name except, perhaps, Arch himself. The way that life continues, the way that human beings persevere, regenerate, *keep going,* summer after summer, season after season, generation after generation, amazes him. Even now.

Acknowledgments

Thank you—

To the professionals: Michael Carlisle, Jennifer Weis, Jennifer Reeve, Sally Richardson, George Witte.

To Becca Evans, Lauren and Mara Rosenwald, Julia Chumak, Amanda Congdon, Margie Holahan and Sally Hilderbrand, lifesavers all.

To Clarissa!

To Congdon & Coleman Insurance, Wendy Hudson at Bookworks, Roberta White at Mitchell's Book Corner—and Wendy Rouillard of *Barnaby* fame, because everyone should have a friend in the business.

To my inner, inner circle—Eric, Randy, Heather, and Doug—and to Judith Hilderbrand Thurman, for keeping the spirit of our shared childhood with Dad alive.

Finally, a big hug and kiss to my steadfast cheering section, my source of endless sunshine and encouragement and love, my very own "boys' club": my husband, Chip Cunningham, and our sons, Max and Dawson.

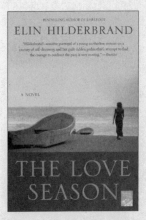